IN THE NAME OF ISHMAEL

GIUSEPPE GENNA was born in Milan in 1969. He has worked in Italian television and was the editor-in-chief of *Poesia,* a literary journal. *In the Name of Ishmael* is his first UK publication.

'*In the Name of Ishmael* is a masterpiece of unease, which transcends a plot that reads like a cross between Dennis Wheatley and *La Dolce Vita*... Swift pacing, choppy sentences, sexual and narcotic urgency, staccato summaries and an Ellroyesque liking for dossiers combine to make the reader greedy for more.'
Guardian

'The Milanese writer has created an elaborate, compelling thriller from the premise that the US operates a network of spies and assassins in Europe... As the conspiracy unravels, it embraces a vast range of mysterious crimes, including the deaths of Roberto Calvi and Olaf Palme and the shooting of the Pope in 1981. Montorsi and Lopez finally confront each other – one of them has been "turned" and is now working for the brotherhood. At the climax, the conspiracy rounds on its own members. When a group of double-agents makes an unsuccessful attempt on Kissinger, we are told that "the shot had missed and the bullet had lodged in the base of a sculpture by Miró". It's a neat, lyrical detail typical of this sophisticated thriller. It's no surprise that Genna is also the editor of a poetry magazine.'
Daily Telegraph

'Giuseppe Genna's edgy and ingenious thriller leads the reader up a frantic series of blind alleys, through a satisfying mire of corruption, prostitution and sadomasochism… Genna handles his parallel narratives with skill. In the incorporation of real characters such as Mattei and Kissinger, his influences include Pynchon and Ellroy. The latter's presence is also felt in the tough, lyrical prose, superbly rendered by Ann Goldstein.'
Independent

'The narrative has a good dose of torque and thrust. Events rattle past the reader and each chapter is headed by the scene's time, date and location. This contemporary, speed-injected feel is well translated from the Italian by Ann Goldstein. But it is the Stygian atmosphere Genna generates that is most successful… His writing has life force that keeps the pages turning.'
TLS

'Like Le Carré, Genna has a flair for plotting of labyrinthine complexity… The novel is hugely atmospheric… and contains several passages of real descriptive brilliance. Genna is a laureate of mental and physical exhaustion, a precise anatomiser of the phenomenology of anxiety, insomnia and boredom – a poet of the procedural.'
Time Out

'You can't accuse Giuseppe Genna of lacking ambition. He weaves fact, supposition and fiction into a fantastical conspiracy theory… There are echoes of *The Usual Suspects* and *The Day of the Jackal* here.'
Ireland on Sunday

'One of the year's best books.' *Herald*

In the Name of Ishmael

Giuseppe Genna

Translated from the Italian by Ann Goldstein

Atlantic Books
London

The story narrated in this book is 100 per cent fictional. In the novel certain 'real' personalities or events appear, but as purely narrative devices. The names of certain companies, institutions, media organizations and political figures are used only to represent the imagery and substance of the collective dreams that have sprung up around them. The actions taken or not taken, the plots surrounding them, the conversations or thoughts attributed to them are entirely products of the author's imagination, created for the sake of this entirely fictitious novel's atmosphere and plot.

First published in paperback in 2001 by Arnoldo Mondadori Editore S.p.A.

First published in trade paperback in Great Britain in 2004
by Atlantic Books, an imprint of Grove Atlantic Ltd.

This paperback edition published by Atlantic Books in 2005.

1 3 5 7 9 8 6 4 2

A CIP catalogue record for this book is available from the British Library.

1 84354 267 6

Printed and bound in Great Britain by Bookmarque Ltd, Croydon

Atlantic Books
An imprint of Grove Atlantic Ltd
Ormond House
26–27 Boswell Street
London WC1N 3JZ

1

THE BEGINNING

Milan
October 27, 1962
02:40

The man in black braked to a stop, opened the car door, went around to the back, lifted the lid of the trunk, and, groping in the dark, took out the plastic shopping bag. He stopped to look around. The street was empty, a dead end without lights. He waited for his eyes to get used to the dark. He began to distinguish the outlines of things. He saw the entrance gate. He threw the shopping bag, bulging and heavy, over the bars. Then he climbed up, over. He advanced a few yards toward the perimeter wall. It was low enough. He threw the bag over, listened to the thud on the other side. He searched with his hands for cracks so he could pull himself up. He missed, he struggled. Giving a heave, he reached the top of the wall, straddled it, and looked down, astonished.

The stadium lights had been left on over the deserted playing field. The rugby game had taken place in the late afternoon, hours before, but it got dark early now. Perhaps the lights had been forgotten. They emitted an opaque glow. On the field, a mist was exhaled by the earth that had been torn up and then leveled again after the game. The goalposts were tall, pure white lances pointed at the low black sky. A spectral land.

At the foot of the wall, he saw the bag, with its sharp, irregular bulges. One small arm was sticking out of it, a bluish, milky color, reaching toward the sky. He jumped.

He landed. He stopped to listen. A sudden rustling, to the left, close by. Maybe footsteps. Maybe the custodian. Panic seized him and he drew his gun, pointing the barrel at the bushes. The rustling was moving in his direction. In the phosphorescent darkness he could distinguish every leaf. He was ready. The bushes parted. He was about to pull the trigger. Then he saw the fat, thick shape of an enormous stray cat. It was heading indifferently toward him; it approached the bag, began to sniff it. The man kicked the cat, and it hissed but retreated.

He picked up the bag. He looked for the plaque and saw it, a luminous stone slab behind the goalposts, near the little playground, all according to the instructions he had been given. He stayed close to the wall. The mud made it hard to walk. He was breathing heavily. The small stiff arm sticking out of the bag seemed to wave with each step.

On the plaque he could make out the names of the partisans who had been killed in '45, fighting against Mussolini and the German army. He bent over the stone slab set in the ground below the plaque. Large dark-red letters offered the city's homage to the partisans.

It took him some minutes to lift the slab. Then, with his bare hands, he dug. The earth was wet and soft and seemed to breathe. He scooped out a hollow roughly the right size and placed the bag in it, trying to fix the pale arm underneath. With his hands he shoveled the rest of the dirt aside. He struggled to lay the stone exactly as he wanted it. The arm wasn't visible, but the stone was awry, the earth mounded, and part of the plastic bag was showing. They would see it, the next morning. That was good.

He inhaled the sharp odor of an upended clump of grass, its roots thin white threads, like worms.

The man retraced his steps. He climbed over the wall, then the gate. He got in the car. He took a deep breath, dried off the sweat, then started the car up quickly. He accelerated. The street was deserted, and not a lamp was lighted. In the rearview mirror he saw the iridescent manmade halo of Giuriati Field fading. Again he pressed the accelerator, and the car entered the labyrinth of the dark body of Milan.

Ishmael had begun his work. This was the first sign. The body of the child had been put in place.

Milan
March 23, 2001
03:40

The Old Man was smoking a Gitane. Entranced, he was observing the grain of the cigarette paper.

The American was watching him from behind the window, but the Old Man couldn't see him.

The cigarette didn't have the same yellowish paper anymore, the *papier de mais* that he had been used to. And now there was a filter too. The smoke rose in fluid blue spirals, astonishingly clear, and as he watched it the Old Man was still more entranced. Sometimes it looked like chalk, that kind of discrete and complicated flow, or some equation taking shape, or spirit, pure spirit, the Old Man thought. Then he roused himself. It was cold. The building he was watching was dark. The fluorescent light over the entrance was broken; it flickered, and at intervals went out. To the Old Man it seemed that he could hear the clicking of the circuit that ignited the gas; it seemed to him that he was right there, under the defective fluorescent light, at the door, its dull, gilded aluminum faded by the years, the rough stone stair worn by footsteps. He could even see in to the carpet, which had once been red and now was darkened and smooth, threadbare in the middle. Farther on, perhaps near the elevator, was an ornamental plant. Maybe it wasn't true about the plant. Or it might be one of those plastic ones that sit motionless, gathering dust.

By nightfall he had seen a lot of people going in and out of that doorway. He had not seen the American, however. Everything hinged on knowing for certain whether the American was already in there when the Old Man arrived. He just had to be patient, hunching a little in his overcoat, breaking the wetness with Gitanes; the American would have to go out, sooner or later. It was another story, though, if the American was not in the apartment. Nor was there any guarantee that he would return to this place. The information was new and reliable, but the American moved quickly. He was always alert. A week before, when he had arrived in Italy, they had tried to capture him in the rest rooms at the Malpensa airport. Two of them had gone in, the way they usually did, and they had done it well. He, the Old Man, hadn't been there. He had restricted himself to coordinating the operation. His men had waited until no one was in the men's room except the American, and then had gone in. They checked under the doors of every stall. Nothing. They waited; maybe he had lifted up his feet. But they had made an enormous blunder. One of them should have stayed in the men's room, while the other went to look in the ladies' room. They hadn't in fact been certain that, at the moment he turned the corner, the American had actually gone to the men's room. They had been unable to check—they didn't want to be noticed or arouse the man's suspicions. Then they had realized their error. Meanwhile the American had vanished, slipping out through the ladies' room.

After they lost the American, the Old Man had decided to participate personally in the operations. They had given him the photograph taken as a precautionary measure when the American rounded the corner toward the rest rooms of the Malpensa airport. Son of a bitch. The typical American face, the face of someone who chews gum. The typical gaze, the gaze of all Americans: empty, cowlike, with two satisfied eyes, expressing nothing but a vague sense of possessing an advantage over everyone else. Reddish-blond hair fell untidily over the hairless neck. The American was wearing a loose green rain jacket. He carried a black briefcase of a synthetic material. It was impossible to tell if he realized that they had taken his picture. They hadn't killed him, but at least they had photographed him. Which was like murdering him by half.

He must be in Milan, that much was obvious. He had at least two operations to carry out. The information on these was quite confusing. It was enough to know that he had to do with Ishmael. He was under Ishmael's orders, this was certain. He had to be found and eliminated. The Americans would send someone else, because meanwhile, as far as they knew, the main event, the reason that the American had come to Milan, was approaching. Ishmael intended to strike—in Milan and immediately. The sources had been unable to get any information—not a single bit—on what the American was doing, because no one knew where he was. Once he was found, there were two choices: to kill him right away, wait for someone else to arrive, and get rid of him, too, and so on, until the date fixed by Ishmael had passed; or to follow the American, see what he did, gain a clearer sense of the operation, and only then kill him.

The Old Man had worked practically without stopping to try to discover any sign of the American's presence. He had mobilized his personal sources, unofficial and less efficient than those of the Service, but scattered, randomly, everywhere, a net so wide that some fish might be caught in it. He had allowed himself, in six days, exactly twenty-two hours of sleep. "After a while you get used to it," the Old Man had said to the boy the Service had sent to keep an eye on him. "It's like being a stone. You think a stone isn't conscious? To you it seems lifeless, or maybe inanimate, but that's not true. Even a stone has feelings. And it feels more than we do, more acutely. It's attentive, because it doesn't move. It's inevitable that just when you least expect it, you're going to stumble on that stone." The kid got on his nerves. He knew a lot just because he was present; he was supposed to watch both the American and the Old Man himself. It was always this way when Ishmael was involved. Why didn't the Service, for once, trust him? If he had been a mercenary . . . The Old Man smiled: a mercenary at his age . . . He had worked for the Service for years—why not trust him? The boy was inexperienced, too young. It didn't matter now. He was dead.

It was the boy who had found the American. He had taken the phone call while the Old Man was allowing himself a couple of hours of sleep. The man at the American Library had said, simply, "He's here." The Old Man was well aware that agents from the U.S.A. often used the American Library as a place for sorting messages. The boy hadn't thought twice. He hadn't woken the Old Man but had left a note and gone himself to tail the American. Fucking son of a bitch, who knew what that kid wanted to accomplish? Be noticed, maybe. Typical. Thirty-year-olds . . . When the Old Man woke up, he read the message and rushed to the library. The American was just then coming out of the toilets, and he looked around. Luckily the Old Man was practically invisible, an ordinary person. And, above all, an old man. What's to be afraid of in an old man? The pale flesh, the weary gaze, the glasses with their light-colored frames, the sparse beard, the black overcoat were banality personified. He had wandered cautiously among the tables that held the computers. The American was leaving. The Old Man waited until he was out of sight, until the American wouldn't be able to see the entrance to the toilets. The boy's head had been blown open; he was sitting, collapsed, on the bowl in the second stall. The Old Man left the bathroom calmly. With unhurried steps he made for the inner glass door at the entrance, and stood on the threshold, looking out to Via Dante. He looked to the left, to see if there was any sign of the American, then slowly to the right. Which was exactly where the American was, looking at him.

The Old Man immediately went left; pausing for scarcely an instant on the steps, he felt the American's cold gaze on his back. He turned, took out his cell phone, and called the two agents assigned to him; they were leaning on the railing at the Cordusio Metro station. The American would appear there. They were not to let him become suspicious. Follow him, yes, but barely. One, two minutes' lead. Wait for him to meet someone. If he met someone, they were to follow that person and interrogate him, make him say where the American was. Anyway, it was preferable to lose the American, let him go, since by now the damage had been done. They had to hope that he hadn't changed apartments. To kill him on the street was unthinkable; he had to be shot in the head, and no one would ever get close enough to shoot him in the head.

On the steps of the underpass between the Duomo and Via Torino, the American met a Pakistani, or an Indian, maybe a Sinhalese. Big, but soft. He handed the American a folder. He also spoke to him for a few seconds. Then the American headed to the subway station. The Pakistani, however, went back toward Via Torino. The two agents didn't want to pay attention to the Old Man's orders; they wanted to keep following the American, let the contact go. The Old Man practically shouted into his cell phone. He insisted that they follow the Pakistani. He told them to stop when it was clear that the Pakistani was heading toward Piazza Missori. They didn't want to give up. The Old Man said he would break both their heads. He himself was positioned at the Ecumenical Bookstore, looking out on Missori. He had immediately spotted the imbecile Pakistani as he turned back, trying to see if anyone had tailed him after he met the American. Now the Old Man was on him. And the Pakistani, unimaginably inexperienced for an American contact, turned into Via Zebedia, a nearly deserted alley. Never do that. The Old Man followed him, came up on him as he was talking in a loud voice into his cell phone, in Italian; the Old Man calculated that he would catch the Pakistani just at the point where there was an open entranceway. Then, suddenly, he shoved the Pakistani inside, down into the shadows. There are no concierges on that street, just darkness in the doorways. He drew his gun. The Pakistani must have known what was happening; he tried to get up on all fours. Big, but soft. The Old Man shot suddenly, deliberately; he crushed the man's knee. Then he stuck the barrel of the gun in the man's mouth and said in English, "On three, the address of the American. *One. Two.*"

The Pakistani mumbled. The Old Man removed the gun barrel. The Pakistani said, "Via Padova."

"The number," the Old Man said.

The Pakistani took his time. The Old Man began to count again. On "three" he would shoot. Via Padova was enough. But the Pakistani—really, where had the Americans found him? Incredible. Incredible that Ishmael would use such an imbecile. And Pakistani, worse. He said, "Fifty-three." And the Old Man fired.

The body of the boy at the American Library had been retrieved by replacing the cleaning people with agents of the Service. The Old Man had hurried to 53 Via Padova, not knowing if the American had already returned or if he had abandoned the place. What would he, the Old Man, do if he were in the situation of that American shit? He would go back. Not to go back would mean the trouble of making a hotel reservation. The brothels were registered; anyone who spent a night in a brothel could be traced in a flash. Normal hotels were all registered online. Hotels with more than four stars were in one system. In an hour of cross-referenced research you could trace anyone you had to trace. The American was not a moron. The Pakistani, yes, he was a moron; the American, no. Better for him to go back to exactly where he had been. To wait. In order to make sure that no one had followed him. Yes, he, the Old Man, would go himself to 53 Via Padova.

He was getting close to seventy; instinct had become reason, and he had to have faith in himself.

Behind a window, hidden in the darkness, the American watched the Old Man and, from time to time, turned to look at the man who, *identical* to him, was sitting, tied up, on the bed. The American's double trembled in the darkness.

The Old Man had been waiting for eight hours. It was four in the morning. There was a strange glow in the sky, a uniform tint that pervaded even the dim orange light of the lamps suspended over the street, ten feet above the asphalt. Four-ten.

Four-twenty.

A yawn. It was cold; his breath condensed.

Quarter to five.

Ten to.

Five to.

The American came out of the doorway.

The Old Man shifted in the shadows. He was twenty meters away, on the other side of the street. He aimed at the head. The American carried over his shoulder the same black bag that was in the photograph, and wore the same green jacket. He looked around, deathly pale. He must be frightened, tense, because that afternoon, at the library, he had not been so pale.

The Old Man fired.

The American crumpled, a sack of shit. The Old Man hurried over. The American was dead, face down, his head smashed against the sidewalk. The Old Man shot again, at close range, in the neck. Then he looked around. No one. With the tip of his foot, feeling the cheekbone through his shoe, he turned the American's face up. It had an expression of terror. Strange. The face was contorted. He almost didn't recognize it; the man seemed to be someone else. But it was the mask you wore when you left everything; it was the extreme, the final form. The Old Man smiled to himself and tranquilly walked away.

Seven minutes after the shooting, the American came out of the doorway. First he looked around, swiftly and precisely, then leaned out, quickly. Nothing. The Old Man had gone. He went over to the double Ishmael had found for him and peered down. The man was dead, his face devastated by a grimace of terror. Once again Ishmael had been perfect. The American stood up and hurried away from the corpse, in the opposite direction from the one he had seen the Old Man take.

2

ISHMAEL

Milan
October 27, 1962
04:30

He stretched his arms and opened his mouth to yawn, a mute shout in the silence. Seen from behind, in the white kitchen, his arms spread against the dark glow of the window, Inspector David Montorsi was an apparition, a household Christ silhouetted in the shadowy light, hidden at home in the middle of Milan. It was four-thirty in the morning, the impossible time, the time of insomnia. David Montorsi rubbed his jaws, stretched his arms as wide as he could, and then contracted and sank into the chair, cursing insomnia, leaning his elbows on the Formica table. The coffee wasn't yet boiling. His wife was still sleeping, in the other room.

For a couple of years, insomnia had been crushing him. During the day, he was like a ghost. Insomnia had become an obsession. He had a single thought and he kept repeating it to himself: "What a goddam pain. . . ." He didn't even wonder why he wasn't sleeping, why every night he had to face that bottomless pit. He wasn't completely awake, but he wasn't sleeping. At six, overcome, he would fall into a warm, weary sleep. Until eight. Meanwhile the coffee was slow to boil. David leaned in toward the bedroom and observed his wife—so white between the white sheets—who was sleeping, aware of nothing. He envied her; he envied her sleep. The light rustling breath in the still darkness of the bedroom, a slight *crackle* . . . *crackle* . . . He almost hated her.

The coffee boiled. He heaved a sigh full of accusation (against whom he could not say, for who was to blame for those two years of sleeplessness?), rose—he was big: six feet, two hundred pounds—poured the coffee into the cup, and sank down again at the table. His eyes were dark, almost expressionless (at the examination for the Detective Squad they had made a note: the eyes of a psychotic). He smiled in the darkness. The pale smooth skin was another problem—if you have the face of a boy, who's going to take you seriously?

He stirred sugar into the cup. The gray foam of the coffee took on dreamlike shapes. Was the world about to end? David watched the foam swirl. Kennedy and Khrushchev seemed to be ready for the ultimate war. The newspapers these days were like bulletins of an imminent end. The missiles in Cuba had incited a disastrous game. Were they on the threshold of that final war? David turned his gaze to the milky sky outside the window. Would they set off atomic bombs? He saw the sky in flames, growing red, blue, black. People spoke of nothing else. David smiled. He took a sip of coffee. Terrible. Fuck Khrushchev, fuck Kennedy.

He thought of Maura, his wife. "If you ask me, it's chemistry," she had said once. "It's chemistry that makes us love each other. We're attracted to each other like magnets." They used to say that to each other over and over again. When had they stopped? Something had changed. Maura was pregnant; she had wanted a child so badly. Now she seemed silent, depressed, distant. Was it because of the child? He chased away the thought.

Everyone was sleeping, except him.

He thought, *Fuck*.

He went back to the bedroom. Maura was still sleeping. David thought about the illness that periodically prostrated her. At first he had thought it was epilepsy. The episodes were violent, devastating breakdowns that lasted for several hours. She wept and wept and wept. An unhappiness pressed her from within, so deeply and violently that the first time he had seen Maura in crisis David had been overwhelmed and taken a tranquilizer himself. It was difficult to talk about it with her. She was terrified—*literally*—at the idea of being mad.

He was filled with tenderness. He leaned over her, watching her sleep. Since she had been pregnant, she had not suffered any attacks. She seemed to radiate a pale light.

He deciphered the position of the hands on the alarm clock. Six. He sniffed the warm air, steeped in sleep, like the distant scent of fever, or rosewood in the dark air. He lifted Maura's delicate arm. He covered himself with it, sighed again. He fell into a dreamless sleep.

The telephone rang loudly at six-thirty. It was Headquarters. The body of a child had been found at Giuriati Field.

Milan
March 23, 2001
05:30

The American walked slowly. The trick of the double had worked. Ishmael was great. They had used the double everywhere. In Panama, when "Pineapple Face" Noriega had to be protected, and they had to make the world believe that they wanted him dead. In Honduras, when the Armenian Latchinian tried to overthrow Roberto Suazo Córdoba and they tracked down a double in a sharecropper's allotment in the north of the country. The year Kissinger turned to Israel to get help from Tel Aviv for Pretoria, and a double was needed for the South African prime minister, the ex-Nazi John Vorster, who went to lay a wreath at Yad Vashem to commemorate the victims of the Holocaust, a man who had mowed them down by the dozens. The double died, in every case. He, the American, had always been there. From before the attack, until the last shot was fired, a tension similar to an electric charge tightened his belly and almost brought tears to his eyes. He never got used to it. Once when a double had been shot but not killed by two Palestinians, he himself had had to finish the man off, while pretending to help him. This time, returning to Italy for Ishmael, to help make Ishmael even greater, he had needed a double himself, and Ishmael had provided one.

How many times already had he carried out operations in Italy? Dozens. He could no longer remember how many. Italy . . . He spoke a fluent Italian with no accent, because at headquarters, at least until the early nineties, Italy had been considered an important field of action and agents were trained to speak the language perfectly. Then Italy had been definitively subjugated. Left to himself, always evasive, Ishmael was the Pontifex Maximus, he was the New Pope, the Guide, He who stops time and speeds it up at His own pleasure. Now Ishmael needed him, and the American had immediately gone to Milan, where Ishmael was preparing a new operation. As he walked, the American was almost muttering the words that were to be repeated when you were far from Ishmael: thanks be to Ishmael, because without Him we would be nothing.

He is the Creator, the Destroyer.

The American had noticed the Old Man at the American Library, in Via Dante. The Old Man had appeared behind him in the lobby. Enemies had intercepted the American, they were closing in on him, and he had to act on impulse and eliminate the boy who had suddenly showed up in the library. And he had had to do it immediately, without thinking. Ishmael demonstrated that impulse is programming; following your instinct is a swift means of obtaining justification from reason. He had fired, using the silencer. As he closed the door of the toilet behind him, he had listened to the gurgle of blood from the boy's mouth, small dense bursting bubbles. He couldn't even tell if the kid was Italian. No papers. Between twenty-five and thirty. Even with the subjugation of Italy, the enemies of Ishmael were multiplying, and it became harder every time to save him. The Old Man's gaze was searching for him; the American had realized that as soon as he came out of the bathroom. They hadn't looked at each other, but it was as if the corners of their eyes had met. Probably the Old Man, not seeing the boy, had immediately understood; he was a professional.

A few minutes later, the American was to meet with another agent of Ishmael in Piazza Cordusio. He couldn't miss the appointment; that might mean missing Ishmael. He had left the toilet quickly, deliberately ignoring the Old Man. He had hoped that the Old Man would follow him; it would be easier to get rid of him outside, in the streets perpendicular to Via Dante. He knew the area. But the Old Man had not bitten; he was a true professional. The American had made contact with Ishmael's agent, a Pakistani, or a Sinhalese, maybe an Indian. The man had communicated to him in code the place where he was to go to speak directly to Ishmael. The American had been uncertain up until the end—was he supposed to kill the Pakistani? Was he supposed to destroy every trace? Then he had realized that the Pakistani couldn't know anything about him, couldn't know anything about the code and so couldn't even know the address where the American was supposed to contact Ishmael.

It was the American who had made the mistake. He should have got rid of the Pakistani. Evidently the Old Man had intercepted him, and obviously the Pakistani had known something. Maybe the Old Man killed him after extracting the information. The enemies of Ishmael were proliferating like mad beasts. The Pakistani had talked. And so the Old Man had arrived at Via Padova.

Ishmael had had enough time to provide the double for him. The Old Man had fallen for it. They all fell for it. Always.

Milan
March 22, 2001
22:40

Lopez had got home at ten. He didn't feel like making anything to eat. The only thing in the fridge was frozen dinners. *Turn 4 times in the pan.* Disgusting. What had he bought this time? Chicken. Yes, chicken with vegetables. Cubes of frozen fat with threads of hard white flesh, bits of pepper and eggplant solid as moon rocks. He didn't feel like cooking, not even a frozen dinner. He went to the McDonald's next door.

The neighborhood stank of McDonald's. It was the cloying smell of a cookie that was too sugary and had baked too long, with a conspicuous hint of pork, like uncured salami, and something resembling the stink of old pee in a public toilet. The store was the only bright area of the street, along with the blue and yellow lights of Blockbuster. Inside there were only kids. And blacks. The kids chewed big mouthfuls, their lips greasy with yellow sauce, while with one hand they pushed the buttons of their cell phones, their eyes dull, glued to the telephone screens. Or they tried out different irritating cell-phone sounds. The blacks, on the other hand, were sitting in groups, speaking in low voices. They all watched Lopez when he came in, and stopped talking. He ordered fries and a Coke. The Coke was too watery and full of ice, and he put it aside after one swallow, disgusted; it tasted of detergent. The fries were cold, cooked only on the outside, and inside mealy and white. On the paper placemat, Lopez read instructions for winning a trip to Cuba. The Ronald McDonald character had his back to him; he had a big yellow ass. The security guard hadn't noticed Lopez, and he wasn't even watching the blacks; he was staring at the kids' frantic fingers manipulating the buttons on their cell phones. A tired Filipino moved a damp rag mop over the pale floor. Outside people were smoking. Lopez threw away the fries too, walked outside, and, huddled in his waterproof jacket, headed for the Blockbuster.

The Blockbuster was sickening.

The new tapes: Almodóvar, Bruce Willis, Edward Norton, Nicolas Cage. Every time the front door opened, an unbearable warmth poured out, along with the annoying voice of a blonde coming out of the three TV sets hanging from the ceiling. Forget the movie.

The Chinese restaurant downstairs from his house was closed. He heard the sound of the street-cleaning truck at the end of the street, probably sitting around the corner. He stuck his hands in his pockets, fished for the keys, and opened the door. Then he changed his mind.

He walked to the Provveditorato Viaduct, in Via Ripamonti, an immense empty bridge over the railroad tracks. He turned to the right, into a dark alley rank with pee and garbage. In front of the Magazzini Generali, a crowd of people were shouting. They were all very young, but Lopez didn't stop to look. He jumped the line, arriving directly in front of the first bouncer (a stocky fellow with a beard and a mixed-race face, wearing a soft red beret). All the bouncers knew Lopez well and were aware he was a cop, and *important*, and they let him in. The Magazzini Generali was one of the most popular clubs in the city. Concerts were held there, parties, openings, pulling in three million lire a night. He sat on the edge of the space where the inanimate bodies of youths and former youths, pallid in the dimmed lights, were dancing, right next to the bar with its white lamps, where people from advertising, marketing, the Internet, and p.r. crowded in, talking frenetically. Lopez observed them without seeing them. He sat still on a stool, tall and thin, with a glass in his hand, a sort of Cuba libre on ice, sometimes staring at the ice itself, deafened by the music, which echoed in the bass and struck the breastbone from within. He sat there for a couple of hours. He almost never picked up a woman, partly because there were more girls than women and the women almost all worked in advertising or p.r., and Lopez didn't like women who worked in advertising or p.r.

Other times, he took drugs.

To get high on mushrooms, here's what you do. Get the mushrooms, the ones that contain psilocybin; they don't waste you, they don't mess you up, they cost real money, and it's not easy to find them. They guarantee a trip that lasts just long enough and they don't damage your brain. In fact, the whole body absorbs the substance, uniformly, the bones as well as the pancreas and the brain. You have intoxicated bones if you eat those mushrooms. The mushrooms act, and then they evaporate. Dry them first. Put them in a gas oven for six to ten hours, at a low temperature (140 degrees F. is sufficient). When you take them out of the oven, they should seem to you like crackers, no longer soft or spongy. It's better to store them in plastic bags, half full, never more than five grams at a time. Put the bags in a watertight container. Then freeze them. Don't freeze fresh mushrooms without drying them; the cold reduces them to a sticky black pulp. At least put them in the vegetable drawer of the refrigerator, but not for more than ten days. Eat them. Wait. After half an hour, the mushrooms take effect. It's you, no one else.

You can go home.

Lopez had the mushrooms in his right jacket pocket. He ordered another Cuba libre. He asked for less ice; they poured him rum and Coke on a dozen little cubes. There were four boys and three girls, dazzled by the white light, working behind the bar. They waved their arms, rotated their torsos, moved their wrists in a continuous rhythm: accelerating at the end of every cocktail. Out of the corner of his eye Lopez looked at the girls' breasts; they didn't dance, they were still, they didn't follow the movements of the bodies that poured and shook. They all wore false smiles. They all nodded. Lopez took his cocktail to a dark corner of the space.

He ate the mushrooms; they were like brown crackers. In a stupor he watched the bloodless people for more than three hours. Then he roused himself and left. He walked home, in a daze. There were no whores.

At two-thirty he was in bed, trying to fall asleep.

At six in the morning the goddam telephone rang, jangling. A man had been murdered in Via Padova.

Milan
October 27, 1962
07:00

The Giuriati rugby field, in the freezing muck of morning in Milan: a basin of mud and opalescent fog.

His feet sank into it; the mud was like glue. In some places, a crust of dark ice clung to the ground beneath the grass and crackled under Montorsi's weight. Progress was difficult. Everywhere, steam rose from the earth. After all, it was seven in the morning. After all, it was Milan.

In front of Montorsi a sergeant was clumsily making his way (could he be fifty?), cursing at every step, in danger of slipping, the mud coming up over the soles of his shoes, caking the leather. It looked like shit. Both men were panting, one behind the other. Montorsi, while watching out for the tufts of frost-whitened grass and the slick footprints left by the sergeant two steps ahead, tried to find the goalposts with his eyes. They emerged from the mist like tall white arrows, slightly curved. The circular track around the playing field was beaten earth, burned brown.

They arrived sweating at the little knot of people: four policemen; a dark, slovenly-looking woman in a bathrobe and greenish boots; a short sturdy man in a worn blue windbreaker; two grizzled doctors in gray overcoats and felt hats; and two men in white coveralls with dirt-spattered sleeves. The sergeant in front of Montorsi planted his feet more energetically, breathless. Everyone turned toward them. As Montorsi stared at all those eyes, their gaze shifted toward the wall. On the ground was a white sheet, absurdly clean and bright in all that mud. Under the sheet, the lifeless body seemed to move, with an electric jolt or tremor.

It was the wind. It ruffled the sheet, letting you guess at the dimensions of a squarish shape, loosely wrapped in the material. A fair-haired cop, his face so white with cold that you could see he'd done a patchy job of shaving, stepped forward. Montorsi observed the fresh mud stuck to his shoes. At first he barely listened to him. He was staring intently at the shape of the thing under the bluish, luminous sheet.

". . . around six. The custodians at the Giuriati do it every morning."

"Do what?" Montorsi roused himself.

"An inspection, sir . . . I told you. They're the custodians, and every morning at six they check the track, the field itself, and the area behind the goalposts, here where we are now. It's the routine."

"And today?"

"As I was saying, Inspector, today at around six the man . . . what's your name?" he asked the stocky man in the dirty windbreaker.

"Redi. Nelo Redi," the man answered. "This is my wife, Franca. She came right away too, to see."

"So, Inspector, not to confuse things: Here at the wall, exactly at the corner of the perimeter wall, the northwest corner, thirteen partisans were shot in 1945 by the Germans. At the end of the war a memorial plaque was dedicated to them. There it is." The plaque was a vertical, rough slab of veined marble, its letters faded and dirty. "Here you can see the names. But it's not the plaque that's of interest. It's the fact that, in addition to the plaque, they placed this marble stone flat in the ground. It's the memorial from the citizens of Milan to the partisans. The caretaker says there's nothing underneath it. The partisans aren't buried under it. Nothing—there should be dirt, just dirt. Well, it's here . . ."

"Here what?"

"Exactly. I'm telling you . . . it's here, under the horizontal stone, that they found the body."

Montorsi looked at the hole, which wasn't very deep. The earth that had been removed made curls of solid mud, a little heap. A few feet away, on an angle, uprooted, sat the marble slab. A few inches from the hole, the sheet flapped in the wind, which had grown strong, tense. Montorsi glanced behind him at the field. The mist had been swept away, and the grass was gray, the sky broken by low clouds shaped like hazy purple fists. It's going to rain, he thought.

Montorsi ran a hand through his hair, his touch almost anesthetized by the cold and the wet wind. He turned to the caretaker. "Was it you who found the body?"

"Yes, yes. I make a circuit of the wall, all the way around here. It's not very high. You could climb over it if you wanted. But . . ." His right eye shifted back and forth erratically. A clear liquid dripped from his nose. A drop had stained the faded jacket. "Well, what do you want . . . there's nothing here to steal. But there's the stone, right? You never know. So I always make the circuit. It's in my contract. I have to do it."

"And today? You did it today?"

"Oh, yes, today, too. I get here, there's not much light. It's damp here at Giuriati. The fog comes up. At night, too. You can't imagine the pains I get . . . Anyway, I could see right away, from a distance, that the stone on the ground had been moved. No one has ever touched it, not since it was installed. They told me there was nothing underneath. Why do they go and disturb it, if there's nothing underneath? To damage it, to attack it in some way, I don't know. . . . These days . . ." The caretaker grew more agitated. "They were partisans. But there are no partisans here! There's only the stone!"

Montorsi smiled to himself. The caretaker was stumbling. "I get here and it really has been moved. Underneath, in one corner, here, the dirt is fresh. Here, I said to myself, someone's been digging and buried something. Guns, maybe. And then I called you. . . . This stone, they told me in the contract to pay attention to it. This is almost more important for them than the rugby field."

"What time?"

"What?"

"What time did you call us?"

"Well, it must have been six. I start at quarter of. About then."

"What time did you get here?" he asked the sergeant.

"Six-ten."

"And?"

"And we dug. You can see, Inspector. We didn't have to go very deep. We found the bag right away."

"The bag . . ."

"Plastic. The body was in a plastic bag. There, under the sheet. We put a sheet around it."

"Who opened the bag?"

"I did, Inspector . . ." the cop interrupted. The black hairs of his patchy beard did not correspond to the paleness of his damp hair, flattened under the uniform cap.

"What was it like?" said Montorsi.

"Bruised. It's a small bruised body. Male. Not even a year old, in my opinion. If you want to take a look, Inspector . . . But they've seen it, the people from Forensics. The two gentlemen here." He gestured.

They were like dead men. Two dead men standing upright, wrapped in funeral coats, black felt hats, wet, their shoes covered with mud. One took a step forward. He shook Montorsi's hand, automatically. "Pleasure, Inspector. I'm Morganti. I'm substituting for Dr. Arle, who usually works with you in the Detective Squad." Montorsi knew Arle; he was the chief of Forensics. This man he had never seen. The people from Forensics revolted him. Every time he saw one, he shuddered. Death had penetrated the pores of their skin.

"How old?" Montorsi asked.

"The child?" said the man from Forensics. "I'm waiting to do the autopsy. I imagine, though, between eight and twelve months."

"How did he die?"

"It's too soon to say. Internal hemorrhage, as a first guess."

"Has he been dead long?"

"I would say not more than a day. But we have to do the autopsy. It's too soon to say."

The wife of the caretaker was staring into the emptiness of the field. To Montorsi the grass seemed black now, rotating around her.

In a momentary pause in the wind, Montorsi watched the sheet fall, limply, over the body in the bag. He turned again toward the track, toward the field. A man—thin, almost emaciated, a pale headband around his hair, his track suit electric blue—stopped at the curve nearest them and looked. "Who's that?" Montorsi asked the caretaker.

"Arnone. His name is Arnone. A jogger. He comes here every morning."

The woman had answered, and her voice was like a mass of cotton saturated with water.

"Go on, run! There's nothing to see here!" Montorsi shouted at the man in the track suit. The man seemed to stiffen; he was incredibly thin. He started running, and every so often he turned back, looked at Montorsi and the people around him, and kept running.

Milan
March 23, 2001
06:30

A dead man in Via Padova. The last effects of the mushrooms had worn off as he slept, but Lopez felt groggy. It was dark outside; he couldn't tell if it was raining or not. He didn't eat breakfast.

It took him three-quarters of an hour to get to Via Padova. There was still a dustlike rain; the paving stones and asphalt were opaque but shiny and slippery. The car's tires didn't respond, and the steering wheel was loose, as if detached from the driving mechanism; it was like being at sea. In spite of the hour, the traffic was heavy. Looking ahead at the tie-up (an unbroken line of dented, dirty vehicles, red taillights, misted windshields, steam venting from windows cracked open), Lopez decided to take the side streets, but it was impossible to stop at the stop signs, with the grainy asphalt made slick by the fine, irritating rain. The rear window was completely fogged up; the defogger wasn't working.

After half an hour, he was jammed by construction on Piazzale Loreto. Eight traffic cops, count them, stood idle, talking to one another.

On Via Padova Lopez took the bus lane in the reverse direction, against the traffic, creating a bottleneck. Then he couldn't contain himself. Holding the emergency signal light in his hand, he stuck it out the window and forced his way through, while around him the horns went wild.

53 Via Padova. Two police cars, two unmarked cars, an ambulance, and a car from the carabinieri, the national police force. Lopez abandoned his car half on the sidewalk, half on the street. Passing cars had to zigzag to avoid its dented trunk.

* * *

The dead man lay on his back on the ground, six feet from a doorway, No. 53, in fact. His dark-green rain jacket was sopping. A black briefcase was gripped by its strap in a white hand studded with raindrops. He had been shot in the head, at close range. Twice. A grimace of disgust twisted his broad face, the slightly open mouth leaving visible two rows of small uneven yellow teeth, the eyes two horizontal black cracks, the skin hanging in folds, like a pachyderm's, around the purple swelling of the bullet hole, with its threads and fragments of flesh and bone inside.

Giorgio Calimani was leaning over the corpse. They rarely met these days, Lopez and Calimani. There were five of them under Chief Santovito in the Detective Squad, on Via Fatebenefratelli. Recruits were no longer joining the squad, and there were problems with getting a leave. Everyone knew perfectly well what the department was fated to become. In the early nineties, as the Tangentopoli scandal began to implicate politicians, judges, and police, Santovito had joined forces with the aggressive prosecutors in an attempt to make the great leap to a new job by exploiting the pressure for reform. Now that it was all over, not only Santovito but also the whole Detective Squad, like that aggressive faction of the Milan judiciary, had had its weapons blunted. Santovito was paying, the judges were paying, the whole department was paying. Calimani had been transferred to the outskirts of the city, and his assignments coincided with Lopez's less and less frequently. They ran into each other every so often on the fourth floor in Via Fatebenefratelli, said hello, had a cup of coffee.

"Hey, Giorgio."

Calimani's hair was dripping wet, his forehead divided horizontally into three equal parts by two perfectly identical wrinkles. He must have been there for a while. "Finally," he said to Lopez. "You're here."

"There was traffic."

Now it was raining hard, thick heavy drops.

"I've never seen so much rain in spring," Calimani said.

"Three thousand feet up it's snowing, freezing."

Calimani took a few moments to stand up and shake off the water. He looked at Lopez without speaking.

"So?" Lopez asked.

"Nothing."

"Who is he?"

"No identification."

Hooray. The day before the body of an immigrant had been found—a Sinhalese, a Pakistani, an Indian, they didn't know. Right in the city center, without papers. A pistol shot in the mouth. Perhaps a settling of accounts. They would close the case soon; people without papers, usually, are vagrants.

Lopez looked at the corpse. "When did it happen?"

"A little before six."

"A little how much?"

"A little. They called at quarter of. Ten minutes later we arrived."

"Who called?"

"You won't believe it." Calimani was laughing.

"Who?"

"A Moroccan. He was frightened."

"Is he legal?"

"He is."

"So he was frightened."

"Exactly . . ."

Lopez was silent. Calimani tried again to shake off the rain; he was pale with cold. Lopez, too, felt pale, and the street was freezing and dark. Via Padova was always that color—the houses were wet even when it was warm, and the blank side walls of the barrackslike projects, waiting for a building to go up next to them, had big wet stains on them, up and down, like giant splashes that allowed you to guess at a structure hidden within. "What do we do?" asked Lopez.

They did this: Calimani followed the body to the morgue—the one at the Polyclinic because there was no room at Forensics—so that he could be there when they started work on the body, and could examine the clothes, and get the autopsy report. Lopez decided to stay at the crime scene, to oversee the initial investigation and try to understand where the murdered man came from and where he was going. He watched as the body was raised to its feet—in one eye a dark pool of blood hardening but not dry—and dropped onto the stretcher. Calimani uncertainly closed the back door of the ambulance, which left with its siren silent. The police had dispersed the curious and now they were examining the area, slowly, cautiously, like moles, or like some other animals trying to decide where to make their den. Lopez decided not to resist the formality of searching the ground with its bits of metal, footprints, pigeon droppings, chewing-gum wrappers that were blackened and faded and dried and yet wet and crushed by the rain, and a plastic cork that once had been red.

He bent down, in the two square yards that had been occupied just moments earlier by the body, and began to search along with the other cops. He found nothing.

Milan
October 27, 1962
08:40

When the phone call came from Headquarters, it was starting to grow light. Maura Montorsi was used to those unexpected calls. No, she had never *really* got used to them. David had rushed out. As usual, he hadn't told her what it was. She had gone back to sleep. She had awakened at eight and made coffee.

Maura had been cheating on David for four months and he had no idea. She was pregnant and she didn't know by whom. It could be David. It could be Luca.

Luca wasn't married. She was twenty-six, Luca thirty. He worked in finance; she had never quite understood what sort of work it was. A week after she met him, she had gone to bed with him. It had seemed to her that she was making love for the first time in her life.

She and David had met when they were sixteen. They had married at twenty. David reassured her. It wasn't only his physical mass. He had entered into Maura's unhappiness, a profound sadness that periodically erupted in crises, like little breakdowns. The breakdowns devastated her. The doctor had given her tranquilizers. They made her stupid, and she avoided taking them. David had entered that unhappiness without understanding it; he had only accepted it. He had been more than Maura had hoped for. She had wanted him. He had been the only man in her life. She felt him in every fiber of her heart.

Then she had met Luca. He was a friend of a woman she worked with. She felt shivers of pleasure when she saw him. He was wild about her. After a week Maura had given in. She was terrified that David would find out. She had never deceived him before.

After two months, her period was late. Then it didn't arrive at all. The gynecologist had said she was pregnant. She had made love with Luca and also with David. The violent overflow of desire and guilt was carrying her toward a new breakdown. She could feel it. She felt little tremors, her head was whirling, and she heard what was said to her without understanding it. Anxiety. Palpitations. The breakdown would come.

She sipped the coffee, in a daze. She was amazed by David's blindness. He was a police inspector, after all. She had thought he would know about Luca *immediately*. Instead, he was too absorbed in his work. Dead people, and more dead people. He said that the dead left no traces on him, yet it was not true. Maura had measured through the years the hardening and numbness creeping over him. He was a formidable man; at not even twenty-five he had joined the Detective Squad. It was a record, or something like that. But he was also a child, innocent and inexperienced. She had realized that when she had had sex with a *man*. She lost herself completely for hours with Luca. She was unaware of time. This man peeled off her skin. She hadn't spoken to him about the child. She didn't know what to do. When she made love with David, after Luca, she realized, suddenly, that she was feeling a painful compassion for her husband. She withdrew. She couldn't wait until it was over. And it was over quickly.

She had wanted a child by David. Now she was terrified. She put the cup in the sink and saw that her hand was trembling.

She was a teacher at Parini, one of the best high schools in Milan. The work was draining. She hated the smell of sweat when she entered the classroom. She kept the windows open, even in winter, but it wasn't enough. The smell of the students' sweat clung to her.

She got ready to go.

Before she went out, she telephoned David. Then Luca. Luca's voice shook her belly. It dilated her nostrils. They would see each other in the afternoon. There was no problem. David would be at Headquarters at least until eight.

She went out. Gray sky. In the courtyard she trembled. She couldn't make out if it was anxiety or the expectation of pleasure.

Milan
October 27, 1962
09:00

The corpse of the child seemed to be shivering, its big, emptied black pupils asking for help, in the emptied mind of David Montorsi; he couldn't think of anything else as he returned to Fatebenefratelli. The child's body seemed to him a bruise, a swelling that silently expanded inside him. He arrived at Headquarters and went up to the fourth floor.

The whole office creaked around him: the shabby furniture that looked like cardboard, the moldy green curtains, and the windowpanes that rattled in the wind. Cracks threaded the office as if it were an ancient reliquary. David Montorsi seemed to fill it entirely, and not only because he was enormous. When he opened the heavy door from the corridor into his office, the old parquet floor buckled under his mass. Now he had with him the bluish image of the little body, the tiny arm that, twisted and rigid, he had seen sticking out of the rustling, dirty plastic near the stone.

He ran a hand through his hair. It was hot in the office. Outside, rainclouds were about to burst. The little body in the plastic bag was in the icy rooms of Forensics. Those men would take off their coats, put on their gloves, and cut open the chest as if it were a rabbit. The glass gave a loud shudder. Heat rose in waves from the iron radiator under the window. The telephone rang.

"Well? How'd it go?" It was Maura.

"Hello, Mau."

"So? What was the call about?"

"It was bad. Let's not talk about it. How are you?"

"All right. I'm going to the gynecologist today."

"This afternoon?"

"Yes. A checkup, nothing special."

"Shall we meet for lunch?" Every so often they had lunch together. Maura's school was in back of Headquarters.

"All right. I've got fifth period. Do you feel like waiting until two?"

"Yes. Shall I meet you in front of the school?"

"No. Let's meet at the Giamaica." In the heart of the Brera neighborhood, the Giamaica was a place frequented by painters and other artists, by writers and intellectuals. It was where they usually ate. Maura tried again. "You won't tell me? What it was this morning?"

A flash: The blue baby in the plastic bag on the ground. A new flash: The child in Maura's stomach, still intact. "Stop it, Mau, really . . ."

"How annoying you are, Montorsi. I'll see you at two."

"At two, at the Giamaica."

When he put down the telephone, he saw the vacant eyes of the child at Giuriati.

At eleven, a messenger from Forensics knocked on his door with the report from the autopsy—a rush job, as Montorsi had requested. He had to start with the report; at the moment, he had nothing else. He read it.

He was horrified. Letter by letter he reread the entire report. The thin typewritten pages exhaled the cold breath of the men from Forensics. An obscure guilt gripped him, sowing electrified images.

He reread the sentences.

The child was no more than ten months old.

He imagined the child.

Montorsi ran his hands through his hair. He was sweating, shaking.

He tried to get rid of the images in his mind—but it was turmoil. He concentrated on the most neutral part of the report.

> No fingerprints were found on the white plastic bag. Inside, the bag shows traces of soil, the same as that in the place where it was buried, in spite of the fact that it was tied in a knot at the handles. Presence of organic fluid, from the corpse, in the pre-colliquative phase.

Forensics concluded that the cause of death was homicide with a sexual component, by a maniac in a compulsive state. A psychotic.

It might be the first victim in a long series.

Montorsi tried to breathe. Volleys of violent images assaulted him.

It was eleven-twenty and beginning to rain.

INSPECTOR GUIDO LOPEZ

Milan
March 23, 2001
09:30

The Moroccan who had found the body in Via Padova was an old rag of a man, drowsy with boredom, wearing a greenish down jacket several sizes too big for him. One eye was half-open, and he was folded in two by the slippery polished wood of the bench. His arms were crossed over his chest; the yellow laces of his shoes were too long and had ended up under the soles. Lopez looked at the Moroccan dozing. He would listen to his story later. There were other things to do.

Headquarters was in an uproar. The security mobilization for the conference at Cernobbio was underway. Every year, a meeting of politicians, industrialists, and union leaders convened in Cernobbio. Not only Italians. Big shots. Europeans, Asians. Americans, obviously. All of world society would be there, at Villa d'Este, outside Milan on the edge of Lake Como, after an initial forum in Milan. This year, Kissinger was coming, along with a Nobel Prize-winning economist, an American ex-president or two, Swiss and Indian scholars, bankers, computer people. Roman high society. Cernobbio, for years, had been the crossroads of the great powers, both institutional and clandestine. Its public declarations of great ambitions, ideals, and schemes were less important than the deals made over drinks or in the recesses of remote hallways.

For Milan, for the police, the carabinieri, and the security and intelligence services, Cernobbio was the *Event*. They would be on duty 24 hours out of 24, three days out of three. The Detective Squad—Lopez's department—was the backup for the office in charge of security for the conference. There would be a frenzy of meetings between the Italian intelligence services, the foreign intelligence services, Army units, and the politicians' and industrialists' bodyguards. The Chief of Detectives, Giacomo Santovito, was very close to handing over his job and being sucked upstairs. Where was he going? To the anti-Mafia team? The security services? He kept it to himself. His next destination would be determined by his machinations around Cernobbio. He possessed no scruples about using the department to draw attention to himself and had not missed a single security meeting. Who knew what interests that whore Santovito was going to satisfy? Santovito was a master of such operations. He had kept the department right on the line between political affairs and the routine of small-time crime, in order to have at his disposal as much information as possible. "To know is to suffer, heh-heh, Guido, and we suffer," he had told Lopez a few days earlier, standing in the hallway, nervous, lean, dour, like a bureaucrat of the seventies, cigarette between middle and index fingers, his fist shut tight, which made the bluish smoke rise directly into his face, saturating his iron-gray mustache. It was clear that the promotion was assured. It remained to be seen *what* promotion.

Lopez didn't get it. To him Cernobbio was a gathering of the half dead, ex-presidents, ex-dignitaries, ex-everything. "It's the exes who make the world go around—don't you see, Guido?" Santovito had replied. "They withdraw behind the curtain and make their money and give their orders. That's how they last."

This morning, Lopez was supposed to go to the meeting about security plans for Cernobbio before he could interrogate the Moroccan. He looked at the man, dying with exhaustion, bent on the bench, left alone there to wait. *Fuck the meeting. Fuck Cernobbio and the big shots.* For an instant Lopez saw again the stiff yet limp figure of the corpse in Via Padova.

The Moroccan yawned. He looked at Lopez, thinking of nothing, until Lopez appeared before him, touched the man's shoe with his own, and the man, without asking a question, got up and followed him.

The Moroccan knew nothing and had had even less to do with it. His name was Ahmed Djabari; he had got a residence permit in '91. The following year his wife and three children had arrived. He worked, his wife worked, the children went to school. He had come out at five-thirty in the morning for a totally banal reason: He had problems sleeping, he had no more cigarettes, and he was walking, in the rain, toward Loreto, to buy a pack in the machine. He lived at 103 Via Padova. The jacket was his wife's. The shoes belonged to his older son. He had found the body barely five minutes from his house. He said that the corpse was cold. It wasn't raining, though. Bags hung under his eyes, puffy and brown with a storm of sties. He had seen the dead man. He had been afraid; he hadn't touched him. He called the police immediately—ten meters away there was a phone booth—using a phone card.

The door opened. It was Calimani, and he had news. But what was he doing at Headquarters? Why wasn't he with the dead man? He had come to see Lopez in person, Calimani said. The Moroccan made as if to go, looking at Lopez in bewilderment. Lopez nodded his head, and the Moroccan slipped between Calimani and the door.

"We have to go to the briefing, Guido," Calimani said. "Santovito's called us."

"What? There's a dead man, at the morgue. That's more important. What does Santovito want?"

"He said he doesn't give a damn about some petty crook who got himself murdered. . . . We have a briefing. On Cernobbio."

"Cernobbio . . ." Lopez sniffed. "You go to the briefing. I'm not coming. Fuck Santovito and fuck Cernobbio. There's a dead man. That's more important. Our work isn't about that shit: It's this, here. A man is dead and I'm going to see about it. Fuck Cernobbio. I'm going to the morgue. I'll take care of the crook."

Calimani smiled, shook his head, straightened his overcoat, while Lopez got up. "Guido . . ."

"What."

"He's not some petty crook. In my opinion he's not just some petty crook."

"Meaning?"

"The thing's too complicated. Go, you'll see for yourself when you get there. It's something more complicated."

Lopez didn't feel like listening to him. He didn't want to be there, didn't want to be anywhere, not even asleep, and still less did he want to see the dead man. The sky beyond his office window was the color of a thin skin that has not seen the light for days. Calimani was spectral.

"I've got an idea, Giorgio. You go to the briefing. . . ."

"And if Santovito asks for you?"

"Tell him I'm on the case of a petty crook."

About one thing Calimani was right. It wasn't a matter of some small-time criminal. Lopez had arrived at the morgue, behind the university, getting a ride in a squad car that happened to be going in that direction. He had got out at Largo Richini. It was still raining, and yet the sky was strangely luminous, in patches: Lopez thought of a wrinkled forehead emitting light. He skirted the university, crossing the strip of park that led to the hospital. The park was sheltered by trees with thick, broad leaves. Less rain filtered through them, but it was more bothersome, big drops that he could feel wetting his shirt under the jacket.

A lot of gurneys had been left standing near the morgue's entrance. It was hard to get past them. The information window was deserted. Lopez knew the way; the medical examiner's morgue at Città Studi was often full, and so the bodies were unloaded on the morgue at the Polyclinic. He opened the flexible plastic door through which the dead passed. The plastic was almost sticky with use; the lower part, which had been a dirty yellow color, was faded, and the upper part, which had once been clear, was milky. Inside, the light changed, became electric and artificial; relatives of the dead gathered in tight knots around an empty point, their coats dark, their faces white, their gazes blank. The doctors and their assistants, carefully dressed in bright green shirts, clattered through that unreal atmosphere, which smelled of formaldehyde. He slipped around the families. "Spending time with the dead you become like the dead," an old doctor in the morgue had said to Lopez, years earlier. The doctor was no longer there—he had retired or else was dead himself.

The deputy pathologist led Lopez down a hallway. The lights were opaque and the air turned sweet and heavy. They had already sutured the corpse closed, the doctor said. "The report will be drafted by tonight. Do you want it right away?"

"No, tonight is fine."

The doctor opened a heavy metal door. Inside, it was cold, freezing. Their breath condensed into a heavy, oily vapor. The fluorescent light was pale and still; it made the angles sharp and clear. The body from Via Padova was lying, stiff and white, on a table that to Lopez seemed to be made of extremely worn aluminum.

"The first shot killed him." The doctor had handed Lopez a pair of gloves and had put on a pair himself. "Two shots, the first fatal. The second was pointless, fired twenty seconds after the first. At close range, unlike the first—probably just to be sure."

"So the first shot wasn't from close up?"

"No. It was fired with millimetric precision, aimed at the left temple. He fell and hit his face on the sidewalk. He lost his incisors. We found them loose in his mouth. It was incredibly precise. Whoever did the shooting *knows* how to shoot."

"The second shot?"

"As I said, it was probably fired for insurance, a few seconds afterward. The killer approached, and this time he shot at close range, in the neck. There were no bone fragments from the cranium; the bullet pierced the left eye."

The bruised face of the corpse seemed to look into the void with its remaining eye, watery blue; the mouth was half-closed—the doctor's hands had opened it for the autopsy—and Lopez could see the broken row of teeth and a blackish rivulet that had coagulated inside the lower lip, now brown and swollen. The nostrils were dilated. There was a big black hole in place of the eye. A few hairs stuck out of the ears. The tendons of the neck were rigid. A gray sheet, a large heavy plastic plate, lay over the body. The head emerged from it twisted, pulled away from the stiff, straight body—an oblique appendage. Lopez breathed in mouthfuls of wet, frigid air. Somewhere something was dripping.

"However, it's not the shots that turned out to be interesting." The pathologist's gloves lifted the fold of thick textured gray plastic, creating an enormous bubble above the body of the dead man. He grasped two purple fingers, the fingertips turned up so that Lopez could observe them under the fluorescence. They were two big purple blisters. Lopez looked questioningly at the doctor.

"The fingerprints were erased. With lye. It corrodes, leaving the skin underneath untouched. There's no possibility of reconstructing the fingerprint."

"Usually it's the underground groups that do that."

The doctor raised his eyebrows. "Yes. But this man is not a member of the underground."

Lopez took a step back, looked again at the man's stiff, oblique face. The pathologist was right. He was not from the underground. Maybe from the north. The skin, already cracked in many areas and swollen into boils on his neck and wrists, was pale, almost gray. The hair, fine and blond and thin, was tangled and knotted in clumps on his neck. Lopez seemed to recognize some familiar features, which might have belonged to an actor—in any case a notable if unspecific resemblance to someone he had already seen.

"There's more." The doctor let go of the corpse's hand, which remained hanging in the air, like twisted rubber, the wrist rotated ninety degrees, an unnatural position that caused Lopez to watch as it slowly turned, rolling around to straighten itself, like folded plastic resettling. The doctor was lifting off the sheet.

The man was naked, his stomach distended; there was, painfully, no trace of abdominal muscles amid the sutures. Some scattered blond hairs. He was immensely white, and against the whiteness long blackish stripes stood out, along with localized bruises and agglomerations of clotted blood, and suddenly the body was a single blot, like certain fish that live on the bottom of the sea, which Lopez had seen in a documentary.

"Bruises?"

"Bruises. Lashes. Scratches. The worst is on his back." The body rolled over heavily as the doctor pushed on it. The back was purple and blotched. Four deep wounds made parallel lines in the area between the shoulder blades, which were even more bruised, the color of skin that has been sucked for a long time. "A deep scratch. On a possible scale of pain, it would be equivalent to losing a tooth. He was abused. And not only superficially."

"What?"

"We realized it at the end of the autopsy. We were examining the rectal canal. There are signs of tiny wounds in the anus, and traces of a hemorrhage deeper inside, much deeper. Caused by an object, perhaps, of narrow circumference but long."

Lopez clenched his jaws, and saw the clenched jaws of the corpse pressing on the metal of the table, the nose flattened, the hole where the bullet had entered the neck wider and clotted with dried blood. "Did you find semen?"

"No. But traces of a lubricant . . . Among the components was Vaseline. . . ."

"Maybe the homosexual circles?"

"I doubt it."

"Why?"

"Because homosexuals don't ordinarily use this type of lubricant for such activity. They use more viscous lubricants, and anesthetics, but only in the case of penetration with an arm or a fist or a large object. *Fist fucking*. Extreme dilation. I repeat: Here it's a question of an object longer than it is wide."

"How long before he died?"

"You mean after the penetration?"

Lopez nodded.

"Three, maybe four days. The traces were disappearing, the ones we found. And the wounds were closing up. The clotted blood from the hemorrhage was not very fresh. Yes, three or four days."

They shook hands that were still slippery from the powder inside the gloves. Lopez would send an agent to pick up the completed report that evening.

The mechanics of death. The mysteries of leaving the world. The final disgust. The sutures of the autopsy. Lopez bumped into the inert relatives of the dead on his way out, into the rain, under the low sky.

Milan
March 23, 2001
10:00

The American had been there that morning when the body was found in Via Padova. First, keeping his distance, he had searched carefully among pedestrians and policemen for the Old Man's unmistakable profile. He hadn't seen it. He had scanned the windows of the buildings nearby; the people looking out had nothing to do with the Old Man. The American had spent what was left of the night walking in the rain, around the neighborhood. He could not go to a hotel; they would trace him. He would contact Ishmael that evening. It would be too risky to ask for help before that. The train might be a better choice; he could spend the night on the train, between Milan and Brescia, and then return to Milan. But he had gone back to Via Padova, to the doorway from which he had sent out the double, to try to intercept the Old Man. *The best place to find the killer is the place where he killed you.* There was no one, however. In a public toilet he had changed clothes. He had destroyed the jacket, and now he was wearing a worn-out coat and a red woolen cap, like a dock worker. *Be in plain sight and you will be hidden.* Ishmael, the most secret, is right before the eyes of all and no one sees him.

Finally the police had arrived. He had figured out which of the two inspectors would work on the murder. He had to control the investigation as well and eventually throw it off track; it might disrupt him, might keep him from doing Ishmael's work. He had seen the body—*another himself!*—lifeless, pale, stiff yet slack in the limbs, loaded onto the ambulance, while the soaking-wet cop who would not be on the case got into the ambulance with the stretcher. He said they were going to the Polyclinic morgue; the one at Forensics was full. The other inspector, the one who would be on the case, had stayed with the officers who were examining the area; he didn't know that the Old Man had cleaned everything up, that they would not find a single clue. The sky was gray. Thunder rumbled outside Milan. It was cold and would get worse. Everything was getting worse; Ishmael would put a stop to that.

The policeman would have to show up at the morgue. Maybe the Old Man would reappear there, too. The American had to find out, before getting in touch with Ishmael.

From a telephone booth behind the hospital gates, on the opposite side of the street, he had been able to observe the entrance to the morgue. Groups of relatives. Hearses. A man in a green shirt was beating his clogs against the cement, having tramped through the puddle in front of the steps at the entrance.

The American had gone into the phone booth, and when the glass fogged up he left. He stood apart from the flow of hospital patients, who entered more to the right, near the emergency room or the grim, corroding old pavilions. The black branches of the trees shook dirty rain onto the wall of the university. Between the morgue and the hospital, a continuous line of cars arrived and departed, their tires and horns squealing as they stopped, then leaped forward.

For an hour, then two, no cop and no Old Man. *Better that way.*

If the Pakistani had revealed the American's address to the Old Man or to other enemies of Ishmael, perhaps someone had also learned the code. If the Old Man had intended to eliminate the Pakistani immediately after extorting the address on Via Padova from him, he would not have had enough time to communicate the code. If instead he had captured the Pakistani, Ishmael was in serious danger. The American observed the dark leaves, weighted with water, and then his gaze slid back to the entrance. An ambulance with its siren off. Empty gurneys. Ishmael had helped him and he had put Ishmael in greater danger. Ishmael had to be protected at any cost. *He* had to protect Ishmael at any cost.

Suddenly he had seen the cop in charge of the investigation in Via Padova moving slowly forward, dragging his shoes on the pavement to clean off the mud. He had come from the square behind the university. The American watched his man, noted his expressionless gaze. He went into the morgue.

He emerged in less than an hour. He wasn't carrying any

BOOKS etc Edinburgh

08/07/05 13:46 F 1 27575

1 @ 7.99	1843542676		£	7.99*
	IN THE NAME OF I			
1 @ 6.99	1740594770		£	6.99*
	LONDON BEST OF 3			
SUBTOTAL			£	14.98
SALES TAX @ 0.00%			£	0.00
TOTAL			£	14.98
TENDER Cash			£	15.00
CHANGE			£	0.02

BORDERS (UK) LTD 122 CHARING CROSS RD

VAT 650072371

papers, unless they were in his pocket. But autopsy reports come from the morgue in large envelopes. The last time he had been in Italy, seven years earlier, the American had had to go in person to the prison morgue at San Vittore, to alter the report on a politician who had been arrested for corruption, or something like that. The politician had been killed in the shower and it had to appear in the report as suicide, suffocation with a bag tied over his head. The newspapers had talked about nothing else. Ishmael had arranged it. Ishmael had been great even then. After the politician's death, Italy's internal situation had suddenly worsened. Ishmael had moved every pawn on the proper occasion, by the proper means.

The American checked the time. He had nothing else to do; he stayed for more than an hour after the inspector left. He would have to intercept some of the cop's telephone calls. Only then would he know if the police were aware of Ishmael or if they were still in the dark. Soon he would speak with whomever Ishmael had assigned him as the contact. He had deciphered the day's code the night before. The code was difficult, for it is difficult to approach Ishmael. It had taken him an hour to interpret it. An address: 45 Corso Buenos Aires. A clue: the Engineer. The time of the appointment: 16:30. It was dark. Spring going backward. *Suddenly the Old Man appeared.*

He was walking slowly among the puddles, wet, the light brown raincoat highlighting him against the smooth, leaf-shadowed wall of the university building. He looked tired, with his hat pulled low over his forehead and his hands in his pockets. He seemed to drag himself along. He looked around. The American withdrew into the phone booth. The Old Man turned his back (bent, weighed down) and entered the morgue. The American didn't move; he held his breath in order not to make the plastic windows of the booth opaque. He waited with no sensation of time passing. Then he saw the uncertain outline of the Old Man stop on the threshold of the morgue. He was checking the contents of a manila envelope.

In the space of a few seconds the American asked himself the necessary questions. *Does he have the autopsy report? Did he steal it? Have they discovered the identity of the double that Ishmael provided? Is the Old Man a cop? Is he working with the inspector in charge of the investigation? Why did he split off from the police and try to kill me? Do the police know about Ishmael? Should the Old Man be killed or should I let them believe that they have killed me?* He held his breath for several more moments. Then he left the phone booth, passing the gate in no hurry and dodging the unmoving and anxious traffic, following the Old Man as he headed for the square behind the university, his back to the American.

Largo Richini. Via Pantano, between tall opulent houses, to Torre Velasca. Behind it was the Duomo. The Old Man turned at the Tower, through the underpass, beside a gas station. Was he walking to police headquarters? He went up the little street leading to Corso di Porta Romana. The American tailed the Old Man, zigzagging from one sidewalk to the other; he had time before he had to meet Ishmael's contact. The sidewalks were shiny, the rain heavy. The Old Man sometimes seemed about to slip and fall; the American could see his shoes, suede, with smooth soles, through the gaps between the cars. The Old Man hadn't noticed him. Then he saw him sink, his feet disappearing, then his calves and knees.

He was cautiously descending the smooth marble steps of the new metro station. Seven years ago, it had just been completed. The American hurried, trying not to slip, to keep from losing the Old Man.

But he had lost him. Though he had gone down the steps with extreme care, looking right and left, and had taken one direction, as far as the ticket window, the Old Man wasn't there. The American looked around, trying not to attract attention. Then he saw, next to the shuttered newsstand, in an emerald-green garbage basket, a rolled-up wet raincoat. It was the Old Man's. Had the Old Man realized he was being followed? The pockets were empty. The American looked around, bewildered. He saw the crowd emerging from the trains, two hairy ticket inspectors with bluish skin laughing and chatting with each other on the mezzanine, a thin kid at the ticket machine. Beyond the ticket-validating machines was a dark tunnel that echoed the sealed hissing sound of the train's automatic doors on the platform beyond. He cursed. He swallowed, put the bundle back in the basket, went past the newsstand, and turned again to the darkness and the rain outside.

He couldn't see, at the end of the passageway that led to the trains, in the dense crowd coming out of the cars, the Old Man silhouetted against the light, watching him.

Milan
October 27, 1962
11:10

David Montorsi slammed the door of his office, furious, exhausted. They wouldn't give him anyone to help in the investigation of the child; everyone was busy. Something must have happened, at some high level, because agents from the intelligence services had been showing up much more frequently on the fourth floor at Fatebenefratelli. To him, they would obviously say nothing. He was the rookie. The intelligence agents went in and out of the Chief's office. In the corridor were groups of people he had never seen, all silent, keeping to themselves. Montorsi had returned to his office staggering, like a drunk. In the middle of his forehead beat the inert image of the child's small white arm.

He didn't know where to begin. The unnerving image of the lifeless arm of the child. *Who could have done such a thing?* The words sounded round and black and shiny, impenetrable, fundamental.

Drowning in impotence, he sat down, clasped his hands behind his neck, put his feet on the desk, and looked out the window. The rain fell heavily, straight down. From inside the room, with the film of heat released by the radiator, the weight of the rain appeared warm, but he knew that outside it was cold. So, he thought, there were three points of departure: the body of the infant, with the violence that had branded it before death; the place it was discovered, under the partisan memorial at Giuriati; and the fact that the department wouldn't give him any help on the investigation—and certainly none of his colleagues would lift a finger on their own. His mind broke up the thoughts, in order, out of order, as it tried to follow the sequence of images, just as the scalpel had cut open the chest of the child on the table at Forensics. He tried to calm himself. He couldn't.

The first element, then: the body of the child. Most important was the fact that it was an infant, probably not even ten months old. Then there was the violence. Blind, twisted violence, the means by which it was inflicted so far unrecognizable (he glanced at the report, shuddered, and broke out in a sweat again). Two possibilities, therefore. Either the violence was a matter of compulsion (the perversion of a psychotic, the pure obsession of a murderer). Or else there was a method behind it that could be deciphered, however difficult that might be. Both these possibilities led to a central question, some specific motive for the killing, having to do with madness channeled in a precise direction—madness and method. The report from Forensics called it *homicide with a sexual basis*. There were two hypotheses: the parents had got rid of the child; or one or more maniacs, "lovers" of children, had raped and killed it.

He had to move in two directions, doing the best he could with this small solid bit of nothing, contained in the action of whoever had killed the child. He could check all the birth records in Italy from a year to ten months before the day of the murder. How many names would there be? He had no idea. Nor did he have any idea what purpose such a list would serve. Did such an archive exist? And were the children described physically? Would it be necessary to do a further autopsy and find some distinctive natural mark that would allow the child to be identified? And if the child had not been born in Italy? His shoulders drooped; he unclasped his hands. He could try the second route, which was more concrete: look for information about sex maniacs who violated children.

The second element was the partisan memorial. Why would someone go there to hide the little body? Montorsi had examined the marble slab and the earth dug out from underneath it. Whoever had done it had approached the wall, climbed over it, and gone onto the field. It must have been very late: It was pointless to suppose that the custodian had been awake and perhaps had made a circuit of the field in the darkness. Furthermore, it was highly improbable that a passerby had seen someone climb over the wall of Giuriati. So, between one and five in the morning. And why right beneath the plaque? Why not just dig behind one of the oaks that grew along the inside of the wall, where the custodian would never find the buried bundle? Was it possible that whoever had dug under the memorial stone had intended to give *particular meaning* to that act? If there was a particular meaning, it had to do with that plaque, after all. Montorsi resolved to look into the local partisan associations.

Finally, the third element, which had nothing at all to do with the child: His superiors didn't believe in him and wouldn't give him any help. His anger and frustration swelled. Maybe they took him for a kid. Without assistance from the department, he himself would have to get in touch with agents who investigated crimes against children; find all the partisan associations and compile a list of questions, and perhaps ask for an additional autopsy. But maybe it was just a matter of a few days before they would give him someone. He felt rancor and pain, like an immense bend in a black river.

He decided to start with sex maniacs. He would ask the coordinator of the Vice Squad, at Headquarters, a man on the first floor called Boldrini. Sex maniacs who preyed on children—he realized suddenly that he was visualizing men with white faces, without eyes, who were cutting open the child. And then he thought of Maura, who was carrying his child in her womb.

He telephoned Boldrini. He went down to the first floor, to a new circle of evil.

Milan
March 23, 2001
11:20

It was still raining when he left the morgue. Lopez restrained a sigh that was more annoyance than discouragement as he looked at the gray and rust-colored hospital from the little mortuary building, on the other side of the street. *This is a city that gets dirty when the rain washes it.* On his left, through the big gate, partly blocked by a red and white pole, old people headed agitatedly toward the old pavilions of the Polyclinic. Lopez plunged into dense, cold air, under dripping black branches. He retraced the route he had come by.

The body of the man in Via Padova had made less of an impression on him than the bruises, and, most of all, the bruise he had been unable to see: the anal bruise. So this could be a murder with a homosexual component, in spite of what the doctor said. Lopez had worked on similar cases; crimes of passion or hysteria were difficult to read when they were random. There was little to do but listen to the interminable theories of relatives, friends, and lovers. Wait months, perhaps years.

One case, involving a lesbian, had taken a year and a half to solve. The woman had been found nude and strangled on the bed in her own house, but otherwise unviolated. A Catholic school teacher, she was tall, with a few white hairs and the bitter face of one to whom life has granted little or nothing, and who has granted little or nothing to others. She kept the kind of tidy house of one who is obsessed by shadows that call from within. Lopez recalled the holy pictures hanging on the walls, their metal frames perfectly polished, the glass that covered the big crude devotional images sparkling clean. He remembered the photographs of the students, one anonymous class above another, hanging on a wall as white as whitewash. Beside the bed was a worn breviary, open and turned upside down. In the nineteen-nineties, a breviary. He had listened to the woman's mother and father, grown gray and feeble with the years, poor but neat, saddened more by old age than by the death of their daughter. There were no men in the teacher's life, and Lopez had had a hard time finding out if the woman was merely a frigid old maid or an extremely retiring lesbian. She kept to set schedules, her occupations and telephone calls pared to the bone. He had listened and tried to assemble those few elements that left him uneasy; there appeared to be no hint of injustice to rectify in the life of such a barren, stripped-down person.

Lopez had forgotten about the murder for a year, until he had had to look into the report of a disappearance of a girl, a lesbian from the outskirts of the city. Within a few days they had found the body, distended and already decomposing, in a canal outside Milan. The clothed corpse, decomposing internally, had burst, stretching the clothes tight. When they cut them off, the skin had split. Her things were still in her pockets: wallet, house keys. Only a shoe was missing. Within a few hours, Lopez had reconstructed the girl's friendships, identified the woman who was her girlfriend, and picked her up in her studio apartment in the center of Milan. She had not cracked under questioning, had not admitted the crime. It was during the second search of the dead girl's apartment that Lopez himself took from the bottom of a drawer a pile of Catholic holy pictures, and then it was all suddenly clear: three lesbians, the teacher, the girl in the canal, and the one being questioned. One murder had been committed for who could say what reason, and a second murder perhaps to cover up the first. After that the girlfriend had crumbled. Lopez had had to hit her, hard. He recalled how the woman, with the blood drying on her lips and her eye swollen shut, had mumbled slowly about jealousy and other crap. That night when he got home, some hours after the interrogation, he found under his nails dried crusts of the woman's blood.

It would be better to listen to Santovito and his lucubrations on Cernobbio than to pursue the killing on Via Padova. Investigating the murder of a homosexual was too complex. It took too long. A homosexual crime reveals less of itself than a random crime. The obscure places are legion. He thought of the dark bruise and the blood coagulated inside the bluish corpse. No, I'm not going to Headquarters either, he said to himself. He had two pieces of business to take care of first. *He had to get some money. And then he had to spend it.*

He stopped at the telephone booth on Largo Richini, at the entrance to the university. The middle one—the two on the sides were missing the receivers. The plastic windows were cracked. Lopez inhaled the damp cold and coughed as he dialed the number. He spoke a few words, almost in a whisper. At the other end, someone said yes.

Behind the black piazza there were white taxis. The wind hissed along the electrical wires, swirled the intermittent rain, and swept along the ground. Lopez's body moved, the white door opened, and as he entered the darkness of the taxi he thought of the piercing object that had been inserted by force into the anus of the man in the morgue.

The story was this. The stuff costs; the whores cost; it costs even if you're not a flashy dresser. So you need money. Fatigue is an evil nursling, the cut-off arm of the one-armed, the distance that separates the cripple's leg from the ground. Lopez swam in fatigue and (even more fatiguing) knew that he was doing it. It wasn't only working in the department. It wasn't only the green walls, the dust, or the memories of a period of energy that now seemed like a dream (the power and vibrant tenderness of the moment when something *begins*). It wasn't only the fatigue of the shifts, endured with the easy gravity of a falling body. Nor was it just the empty hours he spent penetrating the thick air of Milan in the middle of the day, following Chief Santovito's orders in anesthetized inertia, measuring with chalk marks the sidewalk between an oily bloodstain and a spent cartridge. Or the colleagues who come, who go, who are forgotten.

The day had two halves, like the mind. One was white, the other was secret, because it was dark. During the white half of the day, the fatigue ate at Lopez openly. He was gnawed at by the compromises with Headquarters, the brief operations that were as far from *morality* as the infinite expanse of a universe, and the bitter tolerance of human mediocrity, in which one was immersed during an investigation. For years, Lopez had been struck by the mediocrity of what happened before his eyes: houses where vulgar knickknacks lay beside a body with its head split in two; the bodies of two children found in the trash in a deserted industrial area; the human and animal stink when fire broke out at Porta Garibaldi, in the immigrants' center, the cause of the fire camp stoves, torn greasy paper, and an empty pack of cigarettes. Mediocrity: the shape of man. *His* life was mediocre. He thought of the years, silent and saturated with compromise, after the seventies, when he had changed course and joined the police, doing a thesis on criminology. His radical friends ("companions of the Movement") had been astonished. One of their number had become a cop, lending himself to the work of social cleansing. At Headquarters they had given him responsibility for their ugliest operation: he had flushed out his old companions one by one, he had torn them, ten years after the political and often violent protests ended, from that limbo of silence where they had been crouching. He had condemned them: former terrorists arrested in the center of Milan, seized at home (the utterly grief-stricken looks of the wives), or taken at the Central Station. Lopez had destroyed their dreams, scientifically, pitilessly. Times change. And now, when even this final work of normalization was finished, what was left to Lopez of that sordid struggle against time?

There was still the dark part of the day. There was still the dirty work. The taxi carried him not only across the city but into the dark half of his day.

That was the story. Because the stuff costs, whores cost, and everything costs, Lopez had contacts who got money for him for jobs that had nothing to do with his office on Via Fatebenefratelli. Dirty work to do, muddy work. Shit to shovel. Whores to search out and return to their pimps. Transvestites to be found. Drugs to transport from one point to another of the city, without risk. Pills that had to be unloaded in the outskirts in complete tranquillity. They called Lopez; and Lopez was there for them, always. There never were actual crimes. He was to facilitate, to help, to silence, to obtain payments, to make the seen unseen.

Once a boy from the projects on Via Mosè Bianchi had found, in a hole in a wall in a dark corner of the courtyard, a bag containing a ball of tinfoil. Inside were pills worth a couple of million lire (ecstasy but also downers). The kid had found the bag soon after it was left there and a little before it was supposed to be picked up. It had disappeared. Lopez didn't have to discover that the boy had taken it. They had understood on their own. They had simply called Lopez, told him about the boy, and asked him to recover the bag. It had taken a couple of hours. The boy had a fiancée; the fiancée had a brother; the brother lived in Baggio and hadn't been around for a couple of days. Lopez had gone to the apartment of the fiancée's brother, breaking down the thin wooden door with a sharp blow from a crowbar, and found the two boys unconscious in the first room, the tinfoil package open and the table covered with red and white pills and tablets, and also on the table notes and phone numbers for selling the stuff; the two morons wanted to make some money themselves. He had repacked the ball of tinfoil, stuck a dozen pills in his pocket, and put everything back in the bag, while the boys awoke to whine at him and be sick, the younger one still with dried strips of mucus on his cheek, like an addict. After which he had broken the boy's leg, the right one, with a sharp blow, because bone, too, is a weak and fragile wood, like a door. He had left while the two were howling (the other one, whom he hadn't touched, was howling too). He had stopped, in the car, outside Baggio; he thought it over, reopened the package, and took out another fifty pills. Then he had delivered the bag. They had given him half a million lire. Out of two million recovered, half a million for three hours of work.

Shit work. It was all shit work. Swimming in shit is much more tiring than swimming in water.

Now, however, the story was this. Sonia Hoxha was an Albanian prostitute, who worked in Porta Vittoria, near the abandoned station where the Romanians had built an encampment out of nothing, and which had been demolished to make way for a university campus. Sonia Hoxha worked all week, except Mondays. She lived in a tiny two-room apartment above the Rolling Stone. It was there that she brought her clients for full services. The apartment was owned by a seventy-year-old Albanian who was the chief of two or three clans in the area south of Milan. Sonia, too, belonged to the old man: She had been his property for five years. It would take seventy million to ransom her, if anyone wanted to. She had tried to get away from him once. Thanks to a client who was in love, she had found a job at Rinascente, at a million eight a month. The Albanians went and got her. They had told her that if she didn't return to the street they would go to

Valona and seize her little sister. Sonia had come back, but afterward the little sister had developed a tumor and died. Since she had no other relatives, Sonia could no longer be blackmailed; barely a month later she had disappeared. The Calabrians had told the Albanian about Lopez. He wanted Sonia back. He spoke of her as a thing. He was impressive, an old Albanian who talks about buying and selling and smiles with brown and yellow teeth. If she was still in Italy, the Albanian wanted her back. It would be worth two million to Lopez.

The previous night, only days after she ran away, Lopez had found Sonia. The man who had taken her home was an imbecile from a gym, a gray-haired instructor with a fake tan and clothes bought at Boggi (which meant that he was fond of dressing well but didn't want to spend the money). Lopez had found out about him by coincidence, although he no longer truly believed in coincidences. At the Matricola, an Irish pub on the ring road, in Porta Romana, a guy had turned up talking about a friend of his. He said his friend's in love with a prostitute—"You should see her, boobs like so, blue eyes . . ." The prostitute, he said, is Albanian. His friend has money, the guy said; he's a partner in three gyms. He picks her up off the street, has her staying at his house. He was supposed to get married, this guy, but since he's fallen in love with the whore he's not getting married anymore. He keeps her at home, because the pimps aren't supposed to know where she is.

The friend had smiled, and Lopez had listened. They stayed in the bar until nine, an hour after closing, laughing and drinking Negronis. Then they left. Lopez was waiting in the car. The man who had been talking got into a shiny black BMW. They had started out, Lopez behind the BMW. The man had parked a short distance away, in a narrow street off the Corso di Porta Romana. Lopez had got out, leaving the car on the sidewalk, while the man fumbled in his pockets for his keys and walked, heedless and slow, down the middle of the street. Lopez grabbed him by the lapel, threw him off balance, and dragged him behind the row of cars onto the sidewalk. He was white, terrified. Lopez had his gun out, and he aimed it between the man's eyes as he asked him for the address. The man didn't understand—it was clear that he couldn't believe what was happening—while Lopez kept on asking for the address. When the man understood *what* address, he stammered out the words. Lopez put the gun back in his pocket, and the man went on muttering. Lopez said that if he even tried to telephone the Albanian whore's man, he, Lopez, would be back. The man was still on the ground, his eyes wide open, crying. He said no in a whisper of a voice.

Lopez had driven to the gym instructor's building on Piazza Piola. He had rung the bell beside the name Rudella. A man's voice answered. Lopez moved away from the entrance. From the doorway an old couple emerged. Then a man came out; Lopez asked for a cigarette, the man said he didn't smoke, and Lopez recognized the voice from the intercom; it was Rudella. Lopez had seen him at the Matricola. He waited a little longer near Rudella's house and went through the street door when it opened for a woman in her fifties; he climbed the stairs, looking at the nameplates. On the third floor, he saw "Rudella, A." on a fake brass nameplate. He listened. Silence. He went down, got back in the car, and parked behind his house because of the street cleaning. It was ten o'clock. Lopez didn't feel like a frozen dinner. He had gone to McDonald's and the fries were disgusting, and then he had gone to the Magazzini Generali and taken his drugs. Then the body had been found in Via Padova.

From the phone booth behind the university, Lopez called the Albanian. He told him that he had found the girl, Sonia, and that he would bring her there in an hour. He asked for the money, if he had the money with him. The Albanian had said yes.

It was still raining. It had been raining for days. He asked the taxi driver to wait. It would take him a few minutes.

There was no one in the porter's booth. He got on the elevator, stopped at the third floor.

Rudella's voice answered from behind the door, asking who it was. He opened immediately when Lopez said it was the police, that he was issuing a summons. Lopez gave the man a shove and closed the door behind him. By the time Rudella reacted, Lopez already had the gun on him.

"Where is she?"

"Where is who?" Rudella was trembling with rage. Lopez raised his hand and hit him in the face with the gun. Rudella fell like an empty sack, bleeding from his mouth. He didn't cry out.

The door at the end of the hallway opened. It was Sonia Hoxha. Lopez didn't point the gun at her. She understood. Lopez waited. The woman went back into the bedroom and didn't close the door. Rudella was on the floor; he wasn't bleeding much. His face grew white and he was curled up like a fetus, his hands over his injured mouth, and he was weeping. A thread of dark red flesh hung from his chin.

The woman came out of the bedroom, dressed, with a bag over her shoulder.

They said nothing. Lopez opened the door for her, letting her go first, and as she left she turned to Rudella and whispered, "I'm sorry." He cried harder, because of the pain, not the woman.

They got in the taxi.

They said nothing all the way to the Rolling Stone.

The old Albanian opened the door for them, smoking, a glass of wine behind him on the Formica table in the kitchen beyond the room where Sonia brought her clients to fuck. The whole place was saturated with smoke. When the old man saw Sonia, he raised his gnarled hand, palm open, for the ritual slap, and at that moment Lopez said, "The money." The Albanian lowered his hand, nodding, annoyed, and dragged himself into the kitchen. He pulled the money out of a plastic bag. The old man watched as Lopez counted the bills, twenty hundred-thousand-lire notes. Sonia sat down on the bed in the first room. She was holding her head, which hung like a dead weight in her pale hands; during the taxi ride Lopez had noticed that her hands were covered with little wrinkles. She was like a bag of dirty laundry, slumped on the bed, sitting with her ass falling over the edge because the mattress was so hard, and she growled "Thanks" at Lopez as he left, watching her inhale the stale, rusty air of the room, and the old man stood in the doorway, between the kitchen and the bedroom, his hands at his sides.

Lopez was going slowly down the damp stone stairway, which stank of cat piss, when he heard the old man shout and the whore cry out in pain.

Milan
October 27, 1962
11:10

Headquarters was in an uproar, and not only on the fourth floor, where the Detective Squad was. David Montorsi dodged a silent group of men in dark suits, as he went down the stairs, to the first floor, to see Boldrini, at Vice, and try to find a contact with sources in the circles of sex maniacs (if there were such sources, and if there was a circle of "lovers of children"). The men who were laboriously climbing up, hands on the banister, supporting bodies made fragile by the years, puffing out their cheeks, were important people; Montorsi felt an embarrassed contempt as he examined them.

On the first floor it was even worse, because coming out of every office, it seemed, were people who were closely connected with Headquarters but didn't belong to Headquarters. Someone was running with an envelope in his hand. At one point when Montorsi passed by an office, he looked in at two men talking on the phone (one was talking, one was listening), in black suits, until the door was shut in his face. Without knocking, he went through the last door on the left, before the corridor ended in a gray-green wall, identical to the one three floors above.

"What's all that mess out there?" Montorsi said as he entered.

"Something's up. They asked for offices, and they're getting them." Boldrini was flabby, with watery red eyes, greasy hair dirty at the roots, and a shirt that seemed to be perspiring old sweat, like the room itself.

Montorsi closed the door. "But who are they? Is it the intelligence services?"

"Looks that way. Do you think they would tell us at Vice? We are the lowest rung on the ladder."

"You're wrong, Boldrini. *I'm* the lowest rung on the ladder."

The rain outside intensified the acrid smell of the room. Montorsi watched the rain, his back to his colleague. Maybe it was sleet.

Boldrini sneered. "The young Montorsi complains. Welcome to the club. David Montorsi, what can we do for you?"

"Yes, sorry, Bold. I have a report I ought to hand over to you, at Vice, but before I do there are still a couple of things I want to check. The body of a child was found . . ."

"Yes, today, at Giuriati."

"You know about it already."

"Not much. Is it a sex crime?"

"Well . . . in my view, yes. Also according to Forensics."

"So, hand it over to us. What do you care about a sex crime? With all that the Detective Squad has to do in Milan . . ."

"Yes, I know. It's a shit case, look. They gave it to me . . ."

"So you give it to us . . ."

"But it's not so simple, Bold. It's that—"

"With everything you people on the fourth floor have to do . . ."

"Be quiet. Look—"

"That's what I'm saying. You work too much, up on the fourth floor. Then you got the new directives, the new strategies, and you work on political crimes too. . . . Detectives seems to have been transformed into the Political Squad under the Fascists. The strategies are decided high up. We simply go and get ourselves screwed carrying out *their* strategies. They never ask our opinion, in the planning stage—"

"But come on, Bold. . . . You think there's a strategy behind the forces of order. . . ." Montorsi smiled.

"No, no. It's all deliberate. Here either the machine works the way we know it should work or else goodbye."

"You have faith in efficiency? Aren't we Italians?"

"Listen, Montorsi. Okay, we're Italians. But when there's a sex crime, the police in half of Europe telephone me—me. No one else has the system I've set up here. Not even Paris."

"They say you asked for money for a computer, that machine with the perforated cards. . . ."

"That's right. But they'll never give it to us. Imbeciles. What do they think we're going to do in ten years? That we'll work without computers?" Boldrini was *truly* furious. "I tell you, Montorsi, we are doomed to end up like America. Unless we all end up *in* America, under the missiles. For four Cuban peasants, look what a mess." He pointed to the front page of the *Corriere*, where two giant photographs were set side by side, Kennedy versus Khrushchev. "But if war doesn't break out, I'll tell you what happens. What happens is we become like America. You think that in ten years there won't be a common archive, like the Americans have? Including states, I'm telling you, different states. Like Texas and Georgia. In ten years, Europe is the United States of Europe. You think it's not going to happen?"

"We're cops, Bold, not the intelligence services—"

"So you say! But in your opinion, excuse me, how do you think it will work in ten years? I'm telling you, in ten years the police will be intelligence. Believe me—"

"Listen, Boldrini, about your archive."

"Tell me."

"For this business of the child . . ."

"You want to check it yourself?"

"Yes, if it's not a bother. It's just that it doesn't seem to me purely a sex crime."

"But why?"

"There's something odd about it. Whoever it was put the body where it was easy to find, first of all. It seems as if that was done on purpose. It wasn't buried. They were pretending to bury it. They wanted the body of the child to be found."

Boldrini nodded. "Here's what happens, Montorsi. Let's say you're in a hurry, you don't want to be seen . . ."

"Yes, but you don't go and hide it there, at Giuriati, under the partisans' memorial. You see?"

Boldrini stopped nodding. His look became serious. His eyes became a dark veil. "Under the stone?"

"Yes, they put it under the stone in memory of the partisans. At Giuriati."

"Under the memorial to the partisans. Maybe you're right, then, it's something for the Detective Squad. A political matter. And if it is something political, what does the baby have to do with it? Are there obvious traces of a sex crime?"

"It's more the violence of the murder."

Boldrini stared at him, perplexed, interrogating him without words. His stare had no content. Then he shook his head. "Listen, do what you like. The archive is at your disposal."

Montorsi nodded. "Thanks, Bold. Another thing . . ."

"Tell me."

"I also need some information. I want to know how it works in practice. If you've infiltrated the ring . . ."

"What ring?"

"A pedophile ring. Assuming it exists."

Boldrini lowered his head, exhaling noisily. A smoker's lung. "Look, Montorsi, you're touching on something that we haven't been able to establish here yet. You ask me certain questions, you embarrass me. I don't have the money. They won't give it to me. It's difficult to verify certain hypotheses."

"What sort of hypotheses?"

"The ring. The pedophile ring, to be exact."

"You're working on it?"

"Yes. When a child is found, usually, we intervene. But only *after* it's been found."

"But you have a theory about a ring? You think that an organized plan of investigation would be useful?"

"A preventive investigation. But try and tell them upstairs. Try and ask for money, for investigations into a ring of pedophiles."

"And what theory did you come up with?"

"What theory do you think I've come up with? Either there's no money, or else . . ."

"Or else?"

"Montorsi, come on. Go look through the records. Go ahead."

"Or else it has adherents in high places?"

"Hey, you're beginning to get it. If they don't give me the money to investigate something like that, there are two hypotheses: Either there's no money or they don't want to investigate something like that."

"But you are investigating, right?"

"Shit, Montorsi."

"I need someone who knows something about the ring."

Boldrini went pale and silent. "Go ahead," he said finally.

"If the business of the child isn't political, then it might have something to do with a pedophile ring. It would be random violence and have nothing to do with Detectives. Maybe it was put under the memorial as a distraction, no?"

Boldrini sighed, his hands crossed under his nose, his elbows resting on the desk. Montorsi noted that his shirt was worn at the elbows. "Come by tonight, Montorsi. Let's see if I have something for you."

"Tonight."

"Let's see what I can do."

Montorsi was leaving the sweat-soaked room, almost revived by the black coolness of the suits of those men he saw out in the corridor, when he heard Boldrini call to him: "I ask you, Montorsi—"

"Discretion, Bold. Discretion."

"Right."

Already he saw the black suits of the men at the end of the corridor rustling, toward the light, toward the door.

11:40. Crossing the little courtyard leading to Via Fatebenefratelli, David Montorsi watched from below as the sky broke up. Sudden sunshine distorted the light on the walls of the building. The air was clear, the colors rekindled. Men and women rapidly trod the shiny pavement. He ran a hand through his hair, which felt saturated with fog, before putting on his hat. He turned back, and glanced at his window, the last on the left on the fourth floor.

He saw the light go on.

Someone had entered his office.

He straightened his hat, pretending not to notice anything. He breathed in order to observe his breath condense, as he glanced to the right and to the left, to see if anyone was watching him, and then he went out to the street.

Outside of Headquarters, in Via Fatebenefratelli, not a single car passed as he pretended to go into the café opposite the entrance, which was guarded by two rookies. Then he swerved past the café, turned left toward Piazza Cavour, and suddenly stopped. He lowered his hat as he checked again to see if anyone was following him or watching where he went. Breathless, he saw a messenger in blue emerge from Headquarters (they came in swarms, from Cordusio, the central post office). Then he saw three men bent in the dazzling light cleaned by the rain, walking toward Headquarters. He recognized the identical overcoats and felt hats of the two men on the sides; they were the ones from Forensics he had seen at Giuriati. He strained to make out the features of the man in the middle, who was older than the other two. He was wrapped in a dark, soaking-wet greatcoat, and limped slightly. It was Dr. Arle, the head of Forensics.

Montorsi veered to the right, breathing hard, into Via dei Giardini. Sunlight and the shade of the trees reflecting off the wet asphalt. Via Borgonuovo. Wild rays of sun pierced the cloister of trees that ran parallel to the street. The green newsstand on the right was a sparkle of emerald. The public fountains, also green, radiated fresh light. He went into the bar on the corner. Solid spirals of smoke filtered from tired lungs, evolutions of breath stale with alcohol. He asked for a coffee while the machine blew out a weary, formless damp steam. There was a pay phone near the toilet. He picked up the heavy black receiver, resting his left hand on the telephone box on the wall. He thought of the dark suits of the group of old men who were climbing the stairs to the fourth floor at Headquarters. He thought of Arle and his assistants. He thought of Boldrini. He thought of the pedophile ring.

A risk, he thought. It was worth the trouble of trying.

Then he dialed the number.

One ring.

Two rings.

Buzz. Three rings.

"Boldrini. Vice." Interruptions and disturbance, strange frequencies.

Montorsi tried to disguise his voice. "It's Forensics. A message for Dr. Arle."

The response was at first uncertain, as if from that room on the first floor consumed by sweat. Boldrini said, "Just a second. I'll give him to you."

David Montorsi put down the heavy receiver. He took a step back and turned. His coffee was ready, scalding hot. A short man, with burst capillaries on the surface of his barklike skin, laughed, opening his mouth wide and crushing his thick iron-gray mustache into his cheeks.

Arle was with Boldrini, together with the two men from Forensics who had examined the little corpse at Giuriati and performed the autopsy. What did they want with Boldrini? How could Boldrini have known about the discovery of the body? Montorsi stood there in a stupor, as the warm steam from the coffee condensed in little drops on his cheeks.

Who had gone into his office when he left the building?

Milan
March 23, 2001
12:30

The business of the whore had gone well: *two million*. To return to his office, in Fatebenefratelli, Lopez decided to take the tram. The rain dripping from wet bodies that had an odor of mold, the immigrants with their gamy stink, the crowd, the jolts and jerks of the driver—he got off after a couple of stops. He decided to walk through the center of the city confounded by water.

He was soaking when he arrived. It was one o'clock. He hadn't eaten. Before he even got to his office, Santovito stepped out into the corridor, saw him, signaled to him to come in, and returned to his office. Lopez felt disgust, pure disgust. Fuck him.

Santovito was smoking, as usual. "Where the hell have you been, Guido?"

"At the morgue. The body of the guy on Via Padova."

Santovito was furious. "And then?"

"I went around to ask a few questions."

"Crap. You were taking care of your own affairs." He was shaking as he lighted another cigarette with the stub of the one he was finishing, narrowing his eyes as the flame caught. "All you do is take care of your own business, Guido."

"As do you, if I may say."

"Go fuck yourself, Guido. Do you get it or not that there's important stuff to do here, like Cernobbio?"

"To me what's important is the guy on Via Padova."

"Not to me."

"I didn't know."

Santovito breathed deeply, shook off the ash, and sniffed. "Listen, Guido. I don't give a damn about your affairs. Do what you want. Provided, however, that first you do what I want. Do we understand each other?"

Lopez's silence implied a fuck-you. "What would you like me to do, before taking care of my own supposed business?" he asked.

"Now stop it, Guido, because it's in your interest to bear with me a little. You can go ahead with this useless stuff on Via Padova if you support me on Cernobbio first. Otherwise, I'll get you extra shifts like you never imagined. And the same with this shit about looking for whores and transvestites to pick up some extra cash. Got it?"

He knew. He knew about all Lopez's jobs, and Calimani's, and the others'. Lopez couldn't understand how, but he knew everything. Lopez let out a sigh. He put on an expression of defeat, lowering his gaze to the floor. The bone given to the dog would be plastic, but it had the shape of a bone.

"So listen carefully," Santovito went on. "I've already spoken to Calimani. Powerful people are arriving at Cernobbio this time. Extremely powerful. Not just the usual industrialists this year. Gorbachev is coming. Bush is coming. Bush the father, I mean. Kissinger is coming, for example. This conference is very important to me. More than in other years. Got it?"

Lopez nodded silently.

Santovito rubbed his nose and crushed the cigarette in the ashtray. It didn't go out but continued its smoky lament. His gaze became thoughtful. "They're afraid," he said.

"Who's afraid?"

"The intelligence services. Ours and the Americans'."

"Have they got information?"

"Yes. There would already be enough to worry about in the normal course of things. This year it's dangerous. After Seattle, the meetings are all at risk. In Davos. Bologna. Prague. The one at Genoa will be a debacle. I'm glad it's not going to be my problem."

"But what did they pick up? It takes something to put the Americans on alert. There's something going on inside Italy?"

Santovito opened a drawer of his desk, took out a manila folder, and tossed it down in front of Lopez. "Now take this and read it. It's a report from American intelligence to the Italians. They're predicting an attack. They predict that here, at Cernobbio, they'll strike."

"Who?"

He let out another sigh, wearily. A rough, doughy sigh. "At first it seemed improbable to us. Something that we have no experience in—we would confine ourselves to taking care of security. A mechanical job. Except that before the meeting starts, at Cernobbio, we have to check for . . . it's complicated. Complicated and improbable. Apparently improbable." He clasped his bony, nicotine-yellow hands behind his thin, iron-gray head. He was like an illness that was thinking. An illness that seems ready to break out and never does.

"But you mean the anarchist groups, Giacomo?"

"That would seem likely. No. No, the Americans are not afraid of the anarchists. They eat them. . . ."

"Is it Islamic terrorists, the ones who blew up their ship and the embassies in Kenya and Tanzania?"

"No evidence of that, although I suppose that's a possibility, too. But that's for the intelligence services to worry about." The air had incorporated the metallic odor of old smoke. "It's a sect." He shook his head. He was almost smiling. "They're looking for a sect."

"A sect?"

"Eh, yes . . ."

The information Santovito possessed was detailed and precise. The scenario was complex. This was something completely new. How had the American intelligence services managed to reconstruct the thing almost in its totality? Lopez and Santovito talked for an hour, elbows on the wide, dirty fake-mahogany desk. Lopez yawned out of hunger. Santovito talked and talked, his syllables choppy, eyes yellowed by tar and nicotine. The ashtray was overflowing with gaseous ashes, still smoking. The air wasn't air. They made wild conjectures. They didn't move away from the words of the American report, which Santovito had given to Lopez and had summarized for him. Lopez would have to study it. He took it, left the office, abandoning Santovito's glassy gray voice as he talked on the telephone.

It seemed to him good and just to roll himself a joint in the bathroom.

In the uncertain light of the stall, on the toilet seat too weak to hold his weight for long, he mixed the marijuana with tobacco on the folder holding the report. He lighted the joint. He welcomed the first rasping in his throat like a vaporous messiah. A new voice, silent and well known, opened up in him, moving from the guts to inflame the head and eject the stale air between forehead and nostrils.

He opened the report, struggling to understand the order of the pages. The joint ended up falling out through the paper, through the threads of the oily tobacco. He remained for minutes in the dim, poorly lighted space.

When he came out he had reconstructed the plan.

He was going to immerse himself in danger.

Milan
October 27, 1962
11:20

Recess. She had taught the class without thinking about the children. She had called David. She was irritated by the usual reluctance with which he spoke to her about the case he was working on. She was tired of David. She was tired of the child. She had told him a lie, that she was going to the gynecologist that afternoon. The checkup was set for the following week: David wouldn't notice. She would spend the afternoon with Luca.

She felt air in her lungs. The thought of Luca let her breathe.

David stirred her weariness and *rage*. Her compassion for him was turning into anger.

Luca provoked pleasure and desire. Only to think of him meant to forget herself. To forget David. Forget the child.

She had finished her class and her head was split in two. On one side was the child. She couldn't decide. Should she talk about it with the gynecologist? The child was a knot in her throat, a fist of anxiety in her stomach. The other half of her head held Luca. Without the child, it would have been easier. Her skin spoke for her. It was torn from her, magnetized by that man.

She went out of the teachers' lounge. The children were swarming in the corridor, and Maura passed through a crisscross of voices and stupid laughter. The pay phone was in the front hall. She dialed Luca's number. When Luca answered, she dissolved.

Perfect. She would have lunch with David. She didn't feel like it. Right afterward she would go to Luca's house. Luca often worked at home. Finance, high-level banking—Maura hadn't understood much. She went back to the teachers' lounge and sat with her legs crossed, anticipating the afternoon's pleasure. Her colleagues were correcting homework, talking in low voices. Fabri

Comolli came in, the colleague who had introduced Luca. She smiled. She crossed the room directly toward Maura.

"How's it going?"

"Fine, Fabri. You?"

"All right. The kids wear me out." They both smiled. "Listen, I wanted to invite you over tonight. A little party, at my house. Some people are coming over after dinner. Can you and David come?"

Some people. Luca, too? "Who's coming?"

"A couple of friends. Some colleagues. Listen to music, sit around. Nothing special. Do you feel like it?"

Maybe Luca wasn't going. "I'll have to talk to David. You know how he is. You never know anything until the last minute . . ."

"So, come without David."

Maura smiled. She thought of going home and waiting for her husband. The tremors of her crisis rumbled in her, imminent. To stay out with other people would be good for her. "Yes, you're right. Who cares about David?" They laughed and settled things for the evening.

The bell rang. She had to go back to the classroom.

She would see David at lunch. She wouldn't tell him anything about the after-dinner gathering at the Comollis'. She would call him in the afternoon, at the last minute, to keep him from accepting. She would talk about it with Luca. She would tell him to call Fabri. She would be *without* David and *with* Luca, in the midst of others.

The idea was like oxygen. She could think again. The following week she would talk to the gynecologist. There would be problems. She would have to go to an illegal doctor. She wouldn't keep the child.

Suddenly the weight vanished. She felt the anxiety at the center of her stomach dissolve. She went into the classroom.

Milan
October 27, 1962
11:50

Arle with Boldrini, at Vice. And someone had gone into his office. Montorsi looked from the bar into the street flooded with light. The last of the rain dripped in dazzling beads from the trees. He went out of the bar, into the light.

In Piazzetta Reale, next to the Duomo, the partisan association had an archive, where, perhaps, he would find some information on the plaque at Giuriati.

The tourists were reappearing in the center of Milan. The sun shone through cracks in the sky, cutting the cold.

Why were Arle and the two creeps from Forensics in the office of Boldrini, at sex crimes?

Why had Arle not been present at Giuriati that morning?

Why had one of the two creeps from Forensics identified himself as "Dr. Arle's replacement"?

Why, in the end, had Boldrini insisted that the investigation of the child at Giuriati be handed over to him, at Vice?

Why had Boldrini confided in him his hypothesis of the pedophile ring, and the political connections of those who were part of it, if he was trying to get the Giuriati case for Vice and if he knew that, because of a suspicion that politics was involved, the case would remain with the Detective Squad?

What were all those people he had never seen before doing at Headquarters, lugubrious as the creeps from Forensics?

Why had his superiors not given him any help—*a single bit of help*—for the case of the child at Giuriati?

Why had the light in his office been turned on while he was out?

Why was it turned on just as he was crossing the courtyard?

He began to sweat, in the sun, heading toward the Duomo.

In Piazza della Scala, groups of tourists, umbrellas furled. Clothes, faces, the newsstand, magazines displayed on billboards—all blared in the light. The gray striated façade of Palazzo Marino, clothed in sunlight, was blinding. David Montorsi walked swiftly toward Palazzo Reale, beside the Duomo. There the files and documents of the historical archive of the Resistance were gathering mold.

The idea was no idea. He would check the names and the activities of the partisans executed at Giuriati, and try, groping in the dark, to find a glimmer of logic, however perverse, circumstantial, or ethereal. He felt a muffled yet acute pain: the start of a mystery when you have no idea of the plot.

Why would someone move the stone? Why stuff the child in a bag and stick it under there, under the plaque, after scaling the wall of a rugby field on the outskirts of the city?

The multicolor marble paving stones of the Galleria were still wet. He almost slipped. Outside the Galleria he saw the portal of light that was the Duomo; he felt a warmth in his chest, as if he could see the white face of Maura settle on the white façade of the cathedral. He thought of the child they would have together.

In front of the Duomo was an impressive crowd, its crazy colors in motion. The pigeons rose, in flocks, into the light. Across from the Duomo the neon signs were pale in the sun.

David Montorsi crossed through the archway of the entrance to Palazzo Reale, through shadow into the light of the first courtyard. The building was crumbling. At the second entranceway, a thin guard, drowning in his yellow-trimmed gray uniform, was leaning against the pillar, his visored cap set obliquely over his neck.

"Where are you going?"

"Historical archive of the Resistance."

"Second floor. Stairway opposite." And as Montorsi went up the two steps, looking for the entrance to the stairway, he called out, "It's closed, though."

Montorsi turned to the man and took out his police badge. As he put it back in his inside jacket pocket, he met the stupid and indifferent gaze of the custodian. "Come with me. You have the keys, right?"

The custodian laboriously climbed the stone steps with an irritating bureaucratic indolence. At a broad closed door, the custodian fumbled with the keys and opened the door.

"How long are you here?" Montorsi asked.

"Until six. But you're going in just like that, with no permission? No authorization?"

"Call Headquarters if you want," and Montorsi closed the door in the man's face.

Dark, the smell of mold, a suffocating smell oozing from the papers and the furniture. The shutters were lowered and almost no light filtered through the gaps to penetrate the dust of the vast room. Montorsi groped his way to the window, found the strap, and in a clatter of wood raised a huge shutter, almost an entire wall. A milky luminosity spread through the space, rendering the walls opaque, the desks and papers phosphorescent. There was a door in the wall next to the one where he had entered. It was closed. Two desks were perpendicular to one another. He tried the drawers of the desk opposite the window; they were locked. He tried the drawers of the second desk. Locked. A cabinet, made of pale wood, was also locked. He looked around and saw papers everywhere, a calendar on the wall opened to February, 1961, the Capa photograph of the Spanish soldier in the posture of being shot, and a dark square in the section of wall next to the window. He went closer. It was Gramsci, faded under the dusty glass. He looked for paperweights, or papercutters, on the desks. Nothing. Only paper. And pens.

He went back to the door beside the room's entrance. Maybe it led to a bathroom. He tried to peer through the lock, but the room behind it evidently had no windows; he could make out nothing. Montorsi thought of bothering the custodian again. Then he took a step back, swiveled, and charged it with a kick. The lock burst.

First there was darkness. It was so suffused with dust that he didn't even attempt to make his way in. In the pale ray of light that came from the first room, the floor was visible. Dirt-encrusted parquet, the bits of wood loose. He took one step inside, then two.

He felt on the wall for a switch. There was no wall. Or, rather, what he felt was metal, a kind of box with a plastic handle. Then, suddenly, there was light. His eyes grew accustomed to it. Montorsi saw, and started.

It wasn't a room but the beginning of a long, very narrow corridor, which he couldn't see the end of. The walls were filing cabinets, metal filing cabinets, six feet high, an endless row, extending until the corridor was swallowed in darkness. On the left wall, the one that faced the courtyard of Palazzo Reale, the files were interrupted at regular intervals, leaving a path to the windows, and a weak, milky light entered through those openings from behind heavy curtains. From the metal came the staleness of old paper. From the wood floor, which creaked in the silence, expanding and contracting, rose a warmth that smelled of wax and honey.

What is this? Montorsi wondered. He advanced slowly into the suffocating dust. At the first window, he pushed aside the coarse curtain, which left on his fingertips a grayish film he could see in the gray light pressing in from the courtyard; the sky was clouded again. He closed the curtain. Between the first and second windows, on the right-hand side, he stopped; the light was more concentrated, like a lamp in shadow. On each drawer of the filing cabinets shone a yellow label: letters and numbers. He opened one and found files of crumbling, brittle paper. Each folder listed names and dates:

Negrini, Amos, July 21, 1923; Negroli, Attilio, March 12, 1915; Negroli, Fabio, March 15, 1920; Negus, Banda del: see E38-G65-G66.

He closed it. So this was the archive. The historical archive of the Resistance.

He took a dozen steps to a corner that appeared to be a dead end but instead turned to the left, where the filing cabinets continued down a corridor that seemed as long as the first, and at the end of that was another corridor, as long as the others. It ended in a wall with a door locked by a large heavy chain and padlock. A wastebasket overflowing with rubble was leaning against the old wood.

Holding his hat in his left hand David Montorsi ran his right hand through his sweaty hair, and wheezed.

Where should he begin his search? Did the search even make sense? Why hadn't he been given any backup? He could easily spend a day here before turning up anything. And then, really, was it likely he would turn up a name or a piece of evidence that indicated even a single reason not to hand over to Vice the investigation of the child at Giuriati?

Again, he wheezed, realizing from the vitreous irritation in his nostrils that he was inhaling dust, a lot of dust.

It took him half an hour just to figure out the organization of the files on the partisans and their activities—the typewritten letters, faded ink on paper yellowed and stiffened by time, and newspapers flaking at the edges, containing articles on the Resistance. The wood floor, strangely wet in some patches near the walls, creaked in the silence. He looked at photographs of faded faces, the hair combed in a mellow, long-ago summer, the figures wearing loose, baggy clothes.

In the first corridor were the personal files of the partisans. (But could they all be partisans? There were thousands and thousands of dead and thousands of survivors.) In the second corridor was a historical reconstruction on cards, some handwritten and some typed, filed according to a numerical system that Montorsi had not yet decoded. In the third, the dried-up cartilage of newspapers (*L'Unità, Il Popolo, Il Corriere,* various local papers, *La Provincia, La Voce)* were arranged by date in files with wider drawers.

In the corner between the first and second corridors—his coat had a smell of warm dampness—Montorsi gazed, discouraged, at the hundreds of drawers of the archives, the files made mysterious by their overwhelming number. Perhaps he should come back when the people in charge were there.

He headed for the wall at the end of the third corridor, took off his wet coat, folded it over the wastebasket. He began to search.

He immediately came to the card "Giuriati, Martyrs": it referred him to two names ("see Giardino, Roberto and Campegi, Luigi") and to the history card "Martyrs of Giuriati." He tried to find this card. It wasn't there. He tried the heading "Giuriati Field," where there was a card. But the information was sparse and, at the end of the few facts, the card had been torn. Out of it he got only two dates (January 14, 1945, and February 2, 1945) and fourteen names, including Roberto Giardino and Luigi Campegi. Had they been shot? On two different dates? What had happened *before* the massacre at Giuriati? And what had happened at Giuriati?

He would have to search out, one by one, the name cards of the partisans who had been killed.

Folli, Attilio: the card, which should have been in the archives in the first corridor, wasn't there.

Giardino, Roberto: the same.

Rossi, Luciano: missing.

Botta, Enzo: missing.

Ricotti, Roberto: the same.

Serrani, Giancarlo: missing.

Bazzoni, Sergio: missing.

Not a single one of the cards for the partisans killed at Giuriati was there. He began to breathe heavily in the static dust. He shook his head at every missing card. Capecchi, Arturo; Rosato, Giuseppe. Maybe he hadn't correctly decoded the filing system for the name cards. Maybe they weren't in the first corridor. Was it possible? He tried the cards that came before and after Campegi, Luigi. They were name cards for other martyrs of the Resistance.

Campi, Mario—Rome February 23, 1920; Milan January 20, 1945—Name of battle: Campo—Brigata: Leoni (Bs)—shot in the vicinity of Lonato (Bs), following discovery of the action known as "Cuore" (attack on two convoys supplying arms directly to Brescia Center). The informer has been identified as Marella, Roberto (q.v.).

Montorsi looked under the heading "Marella, Roberto": the card was there. He had figured out the filing system correctly, but the name cards of the partisans killed at Giuriati were not in their places—were not there. He tried the last four names.

Volpones, Oliviero: no card.

Mantovani, Venerino: the same.

Resti, Vittorio: missing.

Mandelli, Franco: missing.

He had two dates. He tried the third corridor, where the newspapers that carried articles on the Resistance were filed. The order was simple: You just had to find the day.

The first date (January 14, 1945) had in some way to do with the massacre. Montorsi looked for the pages for January 15th.

There were no newspapers for January 15, 1945. He tried the second date: February 2, 1945. He didn't know if this was the exact day of the massacre at Giuriati. Had any newspapers on February 3rd carried the news of the execution of fourteen partisans at the playing field? No. *The files contained no daily papers for February 3, 1945.*

Either someone had purloined the cards or the information in the historical archive of the Resistance was incomplete, and incomplete in one subject only: the execution at Giuriati. He didn't understand. If the body of the child had been deliberately placed under the plaque, was it intended as a symbol? An insult? Was it placed there by Fascists? If someone wanted to send a signal, why would he make it impossible to read that signal? Or was it that the cards of the partisans hadn't been removed but simply didn't exist? Then what sense could he make of the cards that did exist and indicated the presence of cards that could not be found?

Montorsi sighed. His back hurt; it was weary, overworked dough. The dust, the gray light that penetrated halfway down the dark corridor, his throat burning in the midst of documents containing a history that no one now gave a damn about—he was alone, and what he had intuited—had *felt*!—was lost in the void.

He thought: "Fuck. Fuck that child . . ."

The child. He had had no presentiment of these stirrings of tenderness; it was the first time he had had anything to do with a child. He had seen dead bodies before, witnessed their enforced sojourn on metal tables, observed the immense dead-animal eye of the dead. Montorsi went to get his coat. He saw again the blue hand of the little corpse sticking out of the dirty plastic at Giuriati. I go back to Fatebenefratelli, he thought. I hand it over to Vice. Fuck, fuck the partisans, too. What did I think I was going to do here, anyway?

His coat lay on top of the wastebasket. It was floppy—like the bag with the child. Fragments of flaked paint on the wastebasket were like shreds of paper. There was no air. He picked up his coat, which now was dry. The lunar smell of ancient dust persisted. Bending over the coat, Montorsi observed the padlocked door behind the bucket. A pale glow crept from under the edge of the door. He knelt down, put his lips to the chink (a burning sensation as he inhaled: more dust). No air filtered through. The door didn't open, as he had thought, onto the stairway of Palazzo Reale.

The archive continued beyond the door.

He examined the massive padlock. It wasn't cold; there was no lowering of temperature between the corridor and the space behind the door. He placed his palms against the wood. With its cracks, thickness, and weight, it was actually like an entrance door, not an inner door. He stuck his fingertips in the furrow between the door panels; they didn't move. He took two steps back. He stopped at the first window on the right and pushed aside the curtain. The window handle was sticky. He opened the window; new air was liberated into the corridor, a bubble floating in a dead sepulcher. Light came in from the courtyard. He could make out a tall rectangular shape, the color of curdled milk, protruding over the stone courtyard. He opened his mouth, coughed. He stuck out his head and calculated, but there was nothing to calculate; the space beyond the closed door had no windows, at least not onto the courtyard. He couldn't get into the closed room by going along a ledge. There was no ledge, and there were no windows.

He drew back inside and closed the window, avoiding the dusty curtain. Then, with a running start, he raised his foot against the barred door and rammed it. With a dry, precise click, the panels parted. The big padlock dangled in the air and then clanked on the floor, broken, and what Montorsi was seeing suffocated him.

It was lying down, desiccated, brown, dried out in nodules and distensions: the mummy of a partisan enclosed in a glass display case. Montorsi went closer, his mouth drawn in like the mummy's. The head, crisscrossed by prominent, polished, dried veins, still had a few ashy gray hairs. The eyes were closed, the mouth tightened in a thin grimace, the nose almost nonexistent, sunk between two shadowy hollows. At the neck, a bright-red handkerchief had been carefully arranged; it was perfectly smooth, as if freshly ironed. A loose shirt, once white but now yellowed, highlighted the meager fibrous remains within: the thrust-forward chest, like that of an old man with emphysema, the wrists extending from bony arms in two mutilated, fingerless appendages. Blue trousers that were as if empty. White socks, much wider than the remains of the calves, the feet splayed. This stick of a man, kept awake under glass, lay on a catafalque three feet above the ground, under the emulsion of an almost mental light, which rained from the ceiling, filtered through a little pyramid of milky glass.

Montorsi approached in a stutter of steps. He leaned his face toward the glass. He saw the contracted, marbleized veins of the mummy. The eyelids, polished like shoe leather, stretched tight but not locked, unlike the mouth. The stumps of the hands rested on the coarse material that the body was lying on. An odor of shit enfolded the dried-up body. . . .

He read the card, frayed at the edges, that lay in the case.

Anonymous Partisan

The body of this fighter, who belonged to one of the brigades stationed in Valtellina, was found by Vittorio Messeri and Marcello Davanzi August 15, 1954, at the terminal serac of the Forni Glacier, above the hamlet of Santa Catarina Valfurva. The Institute of Pathological Anatomy of the University of Sondrio donated the remains of this anonymous member of the Resistance to this Archive on September 22, 1954, in the presence of the director of the Archive, Maurizio Mennella; the president of the National Partisan Association, Mario Annone; the mayor of Milan, Virgilio Ferrari; and the president of Agip, Enrico Mattei, who here commemorated the partisan, placed as a memory and a symbol of the struggle for the Resistance to the Nazi-Fascist invaders.

Below, in smaller letters:

The examination of the corpse reveals three holes where a projectile entered the abdominal region, probably after execution. The body was found intact, wearing heavy clothing and crampons on the shoes, perfectly preserved because of the temperature of the glacier. The circumstances in which the partisan lost his life are not known nor is there information concerning any skirmishes that took place at the high altitude of the area where he was found.

It was as if he were breathing. The glass was steamed up, dimmed. Maybe he really was breathing, a mineral breath.

Montorsi closed his eyes for a moment. He sighed; it was almost a sentence. He turned to go out. He felt like throwing up. He looked again at the mummy, its eyelids staring at the luminous ceiling. He regurgitated an acid retching. He took a step and felt as if he were floating, had found himself on the moon, without the force of gravity.

When he reopened his eyes, he saw on the whitewashed wall, beside the door he had broken, a picture looking directly at the mummy. In a narrow gray frame was an enormous, blurry black-and-white photograph of a child, who wasn't smiling. The child must have been about ten months old.

From the child to the mummy. The mummy. The child in the photo. The child at Giuriati. Again the mummy. Again the arm of the child at Giuriati.

He got out of the room just in time to bend over the bucket outside the door.

He retched. Again. He vomited, and it seemed to him that he was being ripped apart from within.

Milan
March 23, 2001
15:30

The American report was a hallucination.

Lopez took the last drag on the joint, watched the cloud of smoke disappear. The joint had been useless. His anxiety did not dissolve. He could hear his heart beating. Again he opened the manila folder and leafed through the report of the American intelligence services. It was mad. Absolutely mad. Chief Santovito was right. It was "improbable." And for that very reason it was fierce, searing, volatile. It was the most dangerous plan he had ever seen.

The Americans had established protocols for monitoring the Internet. Their intelligence agencies inserted a sort of receptor screen between servers and the external Net. Every e-mail message, every connection, every attempt to get onto the server or log off was fully intercepted and recorded. It was obviously impossible for the entire flow of communication to be monitored by the agents. The National Security Agency had created a search engine that automatically intercepted key words in the electronic mail traffic. The reports were issued daily. If a user of a server under surveillance wrote, in an e-mail, "Bush," or "Allah," the NSA extracted his mail from the traffic and checked it individually. The e-mails under observation amounted to thousands a day. The agency undertook detailed surveillance of the Internet activity of members of suspicious groups, associations, businesses, and individuals. It was an enormous, inanimate electronic infiltration.

The Americans were expecting signals for attacks on institutions or governmental facilities or events, especially after the demonstrations in Seattle, when the same people who were to meet in Cernobbio had participated in the World Forum of the International Monetary Fund. Analysts at the NSA had managed to reconstruct networks and channels of communication between opposition groups both violent and nonviolent, including the enormous anti-global forest responsible for the mess in Seattle. The NSA had been able to guarantee total security for the Davos summit—a forerunner of the meeting at Cernobbio, which was on a larger scale.

In the networks under surveillance they had turned up not only anti-globalists, hackers, potential Islamic terrorists, and subversive groups. The Americans had produced detailed, concrete knowledge of movements and plausible dangers concealed in factions that had not previously been under surveillance. Among the many organizations whose servers they monitored were those of certain political, social, and religious sects. They had mapped the entire United States right. The NSA had tracked all—or almost all—the e-mail traffic of the Aryan brotherhoods, including both the main groups and the minority factions.

As for communications between European servers, it was clear that the surveillance was nearly total. It was from a European computer, in fact, that the e-mail considered most dangerous had been sent. *The one that threatened the security of the Cernobbio summit.* It was the first threat. And it had nothing to do with the threats that the intelligence services had been expecting.

The mail had been sent from a German PC, which used a provider the Americans monitored. In the report Lopez read, the text of the e-mail was reproduced in full, in translation. By itself, the e-mail was incomprehensible. The final pages of the report, however, explained that in all likelihood it contained the plan that the opposition group would set in motion.

From: bob@liebernet.de
Date: January 15, 2000
To: soedebergh@lycos.com
Subject: Private

Dear Johann,

I hope you all are well at continental/church/Stockholm. Hello from me to the CO of the FC. Say hello to Linn and Rebecka. Tell them I remember fondly our sessions at the meter during the lay period.

I have news from Ishmael. A new operation is taking place. It's critical to act soon, keeping all members of the BOA separate. Communicate with them separately. Do it by e-mail, it's the most secure way. This mailbox works really well—it's anonymous and the provider is well known.

These are Ishmael's orders. We're reviving the old Paulette Rowling operation, from Science Religion days. At that time, you were with me and Robert, who is now at the continental/church/Athens and is the third person to be informed of the details. In view of the precedents, after this mail I will go underground. You should get in touch with Robert right away. Ishmael is great. He has decided on the old Paulette Rowling operation because at the time it was interpreted as an attack by Rowling. The threats against Kissinger, on the other hand, now, are to lead directly to the operation. The operation is identical to the previous one, except that there's no Rowling and the threats against Kissinger will fail. The operation will take place in Italy. Kissinger will arrive there in March. A summit meeting has been scheduled and he will be there. The place is Cernobbio, in Italy, near Milan. Get in contact with the continental/church/Milan, choose the most suitable Chief Operator, at your discretion.

Reply to Robert, at continental/Athens. Destroy this message and remember to empty the trash of the Navigator (you can't just delete the message from mail received).

Remember

we are working together for the glory of Ishmael. May you too have glory in Ishmael. Yours

Bob

P.S. Is it true that Linn went on trial? For old S.R. stuff? The name of Ishmael can't be in the records of the Swedish authorities. Anyway . . .

Without the final pages of the report, the text would have seemed to Lopez incomprehensible—insane. To the experts of the NSA, however, it was all too clear. It referred to Science Religion. It referred to Kissinger. It referred to Paulette Rowling. These three coordinates had allowed the control group at the NSA to determine—roughly—the event to which the e-mail referred.

Bob was alluding to one of the more obscure chapters in the story of the church of Science Religion, which had taken hold even in Italy and inspired both indiscriminate attacks and many new adherents. The FBI, which had never had good relations with Science Religion, had conducted a covert operation with the code name Snow White. In 1977, after raids conducted on various American Science Religion centers, the FBI had confiscated documents that led to five-year prison sentences for eleven of the sect's high-ranking members—among them Johanna Lewis, wife of the founder of the church—for infiltration, theft, and tampering with documents in U.S. government agencies and departments.

"Operation Freakout," which the documents referred to, had been the church's plan to kidnap the freelance journalist Paulette Rowling, who, according to Science Religion, was "guilty" of publishing a book (the first) exposing the activities of Lewis's church. Operation Freakout had almost succeeded, and Rowling herself had been brought to trial and nearly gone to prison. The documents contained symbols and jargon very similar to the codes used in the mail intercepted by the American intelligence services. The whole Science Religion operation revolved around death threats against Kissinger, exactly as the intercepted e-mail said. The sender, Bob, was the same person who had signed one of the documents found in 1977. The American report contained Science Religion documents from the Rowling case; in practical terms, they were instructions to church members for kidnapping the journalist. Lopez read them. He was breathless. It was an authentic intelligence operation. A perfect spy story. It was an ideal and infallible plan for entrapment.

OPERATION FREAKOUT
April 1, 1976
MAJOR TARGET

To get Paulette Rowling incarcerated in a mental institution or jail, or hit her so hard that she stops her attacks.

PRIMARY TARGETS

To remove Paulette Rowling from her position of power so that she cannot attack the church of Science Religion.

VITAL TARGETS

1) Recruit member of field staff who resembles Paulette Rowling and train her in the action.

2) Recruit member of field staff to make a telephone call. No special requirements necessary except security.

3) On this project security must be MAXIMUM. The only person who needs to know what is happening is the staff member impersonating Paulette Rowling, and she's the only one who has to know her part.

4) Enlist all members of field staff in every reciprocal interaction; coordinate these actions.

5) Find member of field staff who does T.M. (Transcendental Meditation—Paulette Rowling attended courses in Transcendental Meditation) to become friendly with Paulette Rowling to find out what sort of clothes she wears, in particular what kind of coat she usually wears, her appearance in general, how she does her hair, etc. In addition, above members of field staff will have to meet Paulette Rowling in the course of the operation. Staff member who does T.M. should if possible obtain an item of clothing belonging to Paulette Rowling.

6) Ascertain Paulette Rowling's current appearance: still skinny? hair still streaked?

7) Obtain a cheap coat similar to Paulette Rowling's and a wig that resembles her hair.

8) Find a laundry near Paulette Rowling's apartment and make sure she isn't known there.

9) The day of the operation, find out what Paulette Rowling is wearing. Find out how she's done her hair.

10) The day of the operation, have someone stake out Paulette Rowling when she leaves her apartment to check on what she's wearing when she goes out.

11) Have ready the change of clothes (secondhand) and the wig so that at the moment of the action the "Paulette Rowling" staff member can put on clothes as similar as possible in color and style.

12) Insure that the chosen laundry is open the day of the action.

13) Obtain all necessary clothes (bluejeans, etc.) possibly useful for a quick change.

14) Instruct staff member who has infiltrated the Transcendental Meditation group on what FBI or CIA is likely to ask about Paulette Rowling; to the agents' questions, our infiltrator should respond that Paulette Rowling has seen shrinks for years and has memory losses when she smokes (takes drugs) or is drunk. Work hard on this point.

OPERATING TARGETS

1) Telephone Paulette Rowling to ascertain if she is home alone. She has to be home alone.

2) After finding her alone, a second telephone call (on a work day) to an Arab consulate in New York from the phone booth closest to Paulette Rowling's apartment. Telephoner should be a girl who sounds like Paulette Rowling and must be quick, to the point, and violent. It should be a non-staff but trusted external person, and she is to say:

"I have just returned from Israel [pronounced as it would be in Israel] and I have seen what you fucking bastards are doing. At least you're not going to murder my sister. I can get away with anything. I'm going to blow you up, you bastards." Say a Hebrew curse or mutter something in Hebrew.

3) Obtain a copy of *Writer's Digest*—a writers' magazine (if it can't be found, any magazine for writers will do). The person who obtains this journal should be disguised in some way and not traceable to an organization of our church. Don't order the magazine by mail. It can be found at a newsstand or a "back issues" store.

4) Obtain the most recent T.M. (Transcendental Meditation) publication. Same security measures as above.

5) Cut out letters from both publications. Including capitals. Arrange the letters and paste them on a clean sheet of paper (not paper from our organization). If there is a blank or almost blank page in the writers' magazine, use it, crossing out anything written on it. Paste the letters to form the following message:

"You are destroying Israel. You are all the same. My sister lived there, you bastards. I was there—I saw the wonderful people. No one can touch me. I'm going to kill you bastards, I'm going to bomb you. Kissinger is a traitor. I'll blow him up, too. It makes me sick. I have to meditate. You are spying on me even in Israel. Your day will come soon. I'm going to expose you and bomb you."

Go to a library and use a typewriter to address an envelope to the consulate that is most anti-Israel (attacking it). (Don't leave prints.) Use capital letters on the envelope.

6) Place letter in the envelope, seal, and mail from the mailbox nearest Paulette Rowling's apartment.

INSURE SECURITY. NO PRINTS on letters, envelope, paper, or stamp.

INSURE no paper from our organization is used.

Entire action should be done outside of our organization.

If in doubt about "did my prints get on anything" throw everything away and start over.

ULTIMATE TARGETS

1) Field staff member telephones Paulette Rowling and makes an appointment with HER, sometime when the laundry is open. The meeting place is a bar or restaurant. One of the purposes of the action is to get Paulette Rowling drunk.

2) Staff member meets Paulette Rowling.

3) Our stakeout communicates with Case Officer and Paulette Rowling double staff member and alerts the officer regarding what Paulette Rowling has on, how her hair is done, is she wearing her usual coat, etc.

4) The "Paulette Rowling" staff member changes to the closest clothes they have that match Paulette Rowling's. If Paulette Rowling is wearing bluejeans, put on bluejeans. If Paulette Rowling is wearing her usual coat, put on the coat. Whatever Paulette Rowling is wearing (favorite sweater, etc.), a yellow dress, blue, green, etc., sneakers, a yellow scarf, etc., should be available to the Paulette Rowling staff member to change into. In other words, several different outfits should be available to the Paulette Rowling staff member so that at the moment of the action she can change immediately into the type of outfit Paulette Rowling has on.

From the moment the stakeout communicates how Rowling is dressed, our double has only 3 minutes to change and look as much as possible like Rowling. If Paulette Rowling, let's say, has her hair up, the double puts her hair up very quickly (it doesn't have to be perfect: just so it's up).

5) The Paulette Rowling double goes immediately to the laundry and (wearing sunglasses) does the following. She has to do it immediately, as if Paulette Rowling had done it on the way to meet the staff member. Paulette Rowling double goes into the laundry. She acts very confused. She says, "I'm Paulette Rowling. Did I leave some clothes here?" Obviously the laundry clerk answers no. The double demands that the clerk check. Clerk returns. Says no again. The double starts shouting: "You're crazy, my name is Paulette Rowling, check again!" When the clerk says no, or whatever, the double starts acting extremely paranoid: "You're one of them. I'll kill you. You're a dirty Arab. You fucking bastards. I'm going to bomb the President. I'm going to kill that traitor Kissinger. You're all against me."

If an item of Paulette Rowling's clothing was obtained at Transcendental Meditation the double leaves it on the counter in the laundry or drops it on the floor.

6) Paulette Rowling double leaves laundry immediately, turns the

corner, and gets into waiting car. Takes off the Paulette Rowling clothes, wig and all. Quickly changes her appearance.

7) Meanwhile, immediately after double leaves laundry, our fake observer at the laundry asks the clerk if they clean suede and also says: "Boy, was that woman crazy!" Then says casually, "I think you should call the police, with all these nuts around threatening to kill the President."

Observer should be disguised and not work on staff.

8) Observer leaves laundry and calls FBI from a phone booth about five blocks away, and says he/she doesn't want to get involved and doesn't want to leave his/her name, "but some lunatic girl just went crazy in the [say the name] laundry and threatened to bomb the place and kill the president. With all these crazies running around I thought you ought to know. The guy in the laundry also heard it." HANGS UP and gets out immediately. Observer should disguise his/her voice. All calls of this type are recorded (but don't tell the observer this, just to disguise his/her voice).

Affectionately,
Bob

A perfect plan. It had just about succeeded. The FBI's investigations had uncovered the plot just as it appeared that the journalist Paulette Rowling was going to go to jail for making violent threats.

The American report noted successive revelations that shifted the field of action from the United States to Europe, to Italy, and then to Milan, and hence Cernobbio. Bob, the sender of the e-mail, was known to have left Science Religion after the Paulette Rowling case went to trial. He had disappeared for several years from the radar of the intelligence services and reappeared in the mid-eighties. FBI agents had raided an abandoned warehouse on the outskirts of Detroit. They had surprised about forty people who were taking part in a violent ceremony. There was a child at the center. It was some sort of sadomasochistic rite. The adults had been arrested. They had confessed. They were part of a cult about which little was known, the Children of Ishmael.

Former adherents of Science Religion, people who had done time in psychiatric wards, people who had been deprogrammed, people who had lost everything or had lost nothing—Ishmael had welcomed them all, according to the report. He had made them his children. Ishmael must be the secret minister of the sect. The intelligence services had not succeeded in identifying him. Before the raid on the warehouse in Detroit, they had had no idea that they were on the trail of a sect. At the beginning of the operation, they had thought it was a ring that trafficked in children. Fresh meat for pedophiles. The child, however, had not been abused. Contained in the report were a couple of faxed photographs, but Lopez could distinguish only human forms inked in black. Bob was among the forty people who were celebrating the black mass. He had done more prison time. Then he had disappeared again. Now, twenty-three years after the Rowling–Science Religion case and ten after the Ishmael case, Bob had reappeared. In Germany. The death threats against Kissinger and the name of Ishmael had reappeared with him. The American intelligence report gave "top priority" to investigations of the threats. The mysterious Ishmael, Ishmael who "is great," was ready to eliminate Kissinger in the heart of Europe, at the Cernobbio summit. This was the conclusion of American intelligence.

The Italian intelligence services had been investigating for a month and a half. They had found no trace of Ishmael in Italy. Ishmael's "continental/church/Milan" seemed a phantom, or, if it existed, it was perfectly hidden. The carabinieri had tried to trace Ishmael's activities by checking pedophile channels: zero results. The Detective Squad had the diplomatic and delicate task of trying to get from Science Religion the names and addresses of its former members. It was almost impossible; privacy rules safeguarded the members of Science Religion, who, moreover, were aggressive, and easily provoked to sue.

Lopez wondered whether to roll himself another joint. Who the hell were they, after all, Ishmael and Kissinger? A cult figure of whom nothing was known, and a protagonist of the politics of twenty-five years ago, an old man, maybe half dead, with one foot in the grave. Fuck Kissinger. In his mind he saw the smooth, egg-like image of the body in the morgue that morning. The distended belly. The pale hair, in sticky clumps. The words of the doctor. *We realized it at the end of the autopsy. There's the problem of emptying the insides. We were examining the rectal canal. There are signs of tiny wounds in the anus, and traces of a hemorrhage deeper inside, much deeper. Caused by an object, perhaps, of a narrow circumference but long*. The internal hemorrhage. Lopez would send someone to get the autopsy report. The case of the corpse on Via Padova was much more interesting to him than Ishmael and Kissinger. Let them fuck themselves. Let Santovito go fuck himself, him and his trafficking with power. Let Kissinger fuck himself. Let Ishmael fuck himself.

The door of the bathroom opened. The neon light fibrillated. There were two men. They were speaking English. Maybe they were from the intelligence services, assigned to Santovito, given the threat of Cernobbio. They were silent. They didn't turn on the taps. They didn't pee. They remained standing. They began to whisper. From behind the closed door of his stall, Lopez could just make out the American accent. They talked for several minutes. Lopez heard mumbled syllables. Then he heard—clear, dry, precise—the syllables of the name. He opened his eyes wide, sat motionless, frozen. There was a shuffling of steps. The two men left the bathroom.

One of them had uttered—clear, dry, precise—the name of "Ishmael."

When he left the men's room, he saw them. In black suits, white shirts, and dark ties, the American agents stood outside Santovito's office, talking to each other. Lopez saw Calimani pass by the group. He looked at them, intimidated. He reached Lopez, confusion and bewilderment on his worn face. The lights were dim. Lopez returned Calimani's look with a gaze of total indifference. They barely said hello, and Calimani sidled toward the coffee machine.

Lopez went back to his office.

He called Forensics and asked for the doctor in charge of the autopsy. The doctor answered in surprise; someone had already come to get the report. Lopez said he hadn't sent anyone. The doctor told him that an inspector had showed up in Lopez's name and had taken the report. Lopez said he hadn't sent any inspector. The doctor told him to wait and checked the registration card. Yes, it was someone from the Detective Squad. His papers were in order. Inspector Aldo Vitali. Badge No. 25-T12–48.70, assigned to the Detective Squad of the Milan Police Department. He must have been about sixty, the doctor told Lopez. Tall, big, white hair. "A colleague of yours, Inspector Lopez." Lopez said he would send an agent to get a copy of the report. There was no Aldo Vitali at Detectives.

Lopez felt the familiar olfactory sensation, the enervating blind vision, the vibrating antenna. He had understood without knowing it. The man of Via Padova was not just a dead body. Someone was interested in him.

He wrote a report, rapidly, almost feverishly, about the theft of the autopsy file. He printed it out and rushed to Santovito. He had to sign it. It was serious. He would get back to the still fresh tracks of what interested him. Let Kissinger fuck himself. And Ishmael, too.

He went into Santovito's office without knocking. The American men in black were crowded around the Chief's desk and they turned to Lopez. Santovito was pale; he was smoking. "I was just talking about you," he said. "You have to go to Paris. The Americans were right. Ishmael has struck. There's been an assassination attempt in Paris. An attempt on Kissinger. It failed."

Milan
October 27, 1962
13:20

Maura put her books in her bag, looked at the clock. She had to meet David, in front of the Giamaica.

She liked the Giamaica. Writers, musicians, and theater people went there. They sat around at all hours, talked, laughed, shouted, drew others into their circle. She wanted to go there with Luca. The idea of eating with David gave her a vague sense of physical disgust. She noticed, again, that she was shaking.

Outside the school, the children hung around in small noisy groups, instead of going home. The sun was turning pale, the sky lowering again. A car horn sounded; a small truck was parked sideways, blocking the street, some men unloading boxes from it. Next to the school there was a typewriter store; perhaps they were unloading typewriters. The horn was a dark, inarticulate sound. The men moved the gray body of the truck onto the sidewalk, and the car went by, accelerating angrily.

The child. She would speak to the gynecologist. She would explain everything to him, without mentioning Luca. She had known the doctor for years; he had followed her case. He was a friend, a little advanced in age, eccentric. He lived alone; there was no need to speak to him about women. Maura smiled. The gynecologist would help her find a suitable doctor. She wasn't even at the end of her second month. There was time. David would never know. She imagined gynecological complications, a spontaneous abortion.

To Luca she would say nothing.

The sun lingered in spite of a mass of black clouds about to cover Milan. Outside the Giamaica, among crowded tables, laughing voices, squeals, a man in a beret sipped a beer, alone, and looked at her. Maura pretended not to notice. She waited a few minutes. Then she saw David's enormous figure come into view from the direction of the Brera. It startled her: She had never seen him so pale.

Maura began trembling again.

Milan
March 23, 2001
13:30

The American ate a soggy sandwich in the crowded bar in Piazza Diaz. He could make out the white profile of the Duomo; from here it resembled the remains of a glorious monument, a venerable relic at whose feet worshipers place trinkets and ex-votos. The Italians . . .

He was angry that he had lost the Old Man. He had understood immediately that the Old Man was good, a professional; he had not believed he was *that* good. Reconstructing the stages of the tail, he was unable to work out the precise moment when the Old Man had realized that he was following him. There is always a precise moment. He had succeeded in fooling the Old Man with the trick of the double; and the Old Man had fooled him by escaping into the subway, the ideal place. It was another obstacle on Ishmael's shining and glorious path. He chewed the sandwich and bit his lip. The next time—assuming that there was a next time—he would eliminate the Old Man immediately.

He went out into the thin mist. The edges of the Duomo were blurry. Exhaust fumes rose from the concrete pavement to the sky. He headed again toward the university. He had been walking for almost forty hours, without stopping.

The university was black in the fog. The light was fading noticeably. Soon he would make contact with Ishmael, at the Engineer's on Buenos Aires. He went into the vast gray entrance hall of the new wing. The students were like little statues of boredom. They took turns trying to seduce each other, wearily. They laughed with an empty laughter. He walked through air that was thick with sleep and warm breath.

The Internet links were behind the university bookstore. A girl with greasy hair and steamed-up glasses was typing at one of a dozen computers, her wide featureless face illuminated by the screen. The American chose the computer farthest away from her.

The route of the connection was via an electronic mailbox at Hotmail. An archived message, with a link to Tripod. The domains were heavily used; it was impossible to locate his presence or his passage. On Tripod was a site for skin cream. He clicked, according to his instructions, on the word "Vineland," which did not look like a link. A remote German server. Now he had to begin the ftp protocols. He downloaded two files and opened them with the navigator.

First message: The Pakistani who had given him the contact with Ishmael had been murdered a few dozen yards from where they had met. "Be alert," the American was told. It had been the Old Man. The Pakistani, therefore, in order not to die had talked; he was the one who had revealed the address on Via Padova to the Old Man. *A serious mistake.*

Second message: They had tried to kill Kissinger in Paris. This he had been expecting. The attempt had failed. This, too, he had been expecting. The American smiled.

Now it was up to him.

New York/Paris
March 22–23, 2001

How Henry Kissinger had aged! He was almost unrecognizable. His hair was completely white now, still soft and slightly curly. His eyeglasses were different: He no longer wore the thick black frames that the world had known thirty years before. His forehead was sprinkled with small coffee-colored spots. His eyebrows were still bushy, and also white. And his skin—it scarcely held up, it seemed thickened, it tried to fight the disastrous collapse of the bags under the eyes, the wrinkles that folded in on themselves in small fat rolls, a sordid design of extra flesh, vaguely pachydermic, kindly and dramatic at the same time. Only the pupils were the same. Small, of an intense blue, they cut the space as their gaze moved in small, precise, punctual increments, indicating a vigilant, unsleeping attention.

Henry Kissinger observed his own face reflected in the big window of his New York study, high up, right across from the United Nations. It was a wall of windows, more than thirty floors from the street, and the reflection of his features was faint but clear, a feeble and limpid shadow facing him. You would not have been able to tell, surprising Kissinger from behind, if he was examining the jagged outline of the semicircular band of skyscrapers or the shape of his own profile given back by the clear glass.

Suddenly he seemed to revive, as if behind the simulated attentiveness his little eyes had been lost in a spell that was leading them in some mysterious direction. He sat down heavily behind the desk (a mirrorlike mahogany surface, a big luminous telephone, a computer turned off). He was annoyed. He had on his schedule a trip to Europe. The airplane, the capitals. He had on his schedule the Beginning. The Beginning and the End.

He had raised up Ishmael. If Ishmael had become what he had

become, it was to Kissinger that he owed it. When Ishmael was nothing and no one, Kissinger had practically invented him. The divine act of an éminence grise. An éminence grise who creates another éminence grise, in the heart of Europe. He had invented him. And now? Now Ishmael was threatening him. He had become too powerful. It was a paradoxical power. The world was at a turning point. Henry Kissinger looked at the palms of his hands, at the lines that scored them, inscribing ambiguous maps, a streaked chronology of epidermis and events that had left their mark. He yawned, in irritation.

Ishmael and his mysteries. His obsessions. His obscure practices. He would put an end to it all.

When he was out of the country he did not make comments of a political nature. Often, in fact, no one even knew he was out of the country. He issued at most standard statements: the diplomacy required in Vietnam, the good old days, how fond he was of Mr. Agnelli. Everyone looked back to that bright point where he had been and had triumphed, when he was holding the reins of the world, and now did no longer. They were wrong. It worked well that way. It was the advantage of his position. It was the unspoken glory of the present, that it seemed to be overwhelmed by the splendors of the past. It was a planetary trick so subtle and refined that, when he had finally understood it, he had been amazed, dumbfounded, as when he saw the bare legs of a woman folded delicately on the sheets of his bed. Nothing is what it seems. They had all forgotten him.

He was free to do *everything*.

The morning hours are like gold. You wake up from whatever dream has tossed the night, entering a state that is neither bright nor dark, neither long-lasting nor fleeting, that has the flavor of a placid smile. You wake up in a light that filters through the perfect aluminum blinds, through uncurtained glass, in the comfort of the clean linen of pillowcases warmed by the cavity of the body. You get up, you enter the world and the golden hours.

It had been difficult waking up that morning. Henry Kissinger had struggled against a form of inertia that he knew well, struggled to rise, to put his bare feet in the cork slippers and slide the smooth soles along the polished marble floor to the bathroom, which was flooded with light reflecting from the mirrors and chrome fixtures. Confused, bleary-eyed, dazed with sleep, he felt as if he were moving in an aqueous substance, an atmosphere made of the soft middle of a loaf of bread. He saw himself reflected and distorted and tiny in the shiny steel of the faucets and in the metal pipe that led from the toilet to the tile wall. He yawned.

The mirror showed him a dim image only because his eyes were tearing and slightly reddened. He yawned again, trying to keep the lids open to see what he looked like when he yawned, but they closed. Then he checked his beard. There was a slight roughness. He would shave. It was surprising how little his beard grew. His face was still smooth. The skin was old and collapsing, but not rough.

He aimed his gaze at the mirror and stuck out his tongue, which was as usual a whitish-yellow, pasty and foul. He pulled it back in so that he could smell his breath; it was bitter, and would have been disgusting to him except for a shiver of pleasure, deep inside, that impelled him to sniff it again. He opened the medicine chest. There was a metal pillbox. Inside were small brown, almost spherical tablets, probably pastilles. He had had the pillbox for years. He read the letters on the metal: Normix. He remembered it was a diuretic he had taken long ago. He stuck out his tongue again, leaned in toward the mirror, and began to scrape it with the sharp edge of the metal box. He scraped toward the back of the tongue, intuiting the dark red form of the epiglottis. The pasty residue of that white and yellow substance that covered his tongue encrusted the box. He turned on the tap, ran the water over the metal edge. The thick residue ended up in the immaculate enamel in small grayish pieces. He began to scrape again. Now he scraped from the back to the tip. Once, twice. He checked. The paste was becoming thinner, diluted by the saliva, which was beginning to circulate. He washed the pillbox. For good measure, he scraped one last time, in the other direction, toward his throat. He broke a blood vessel. He saw the tiny rivulet of blood, brilliant, gaudy red in the by now almost colorless paste, by now reduced to almost pure saliva.

* * *

In the study, at the desk, beside the drawer his hand—cared for, smooth, almost feminine—pressed a button to turn on the intercom. Maggie answered immediately. He adored that over-eager promptness, the perceptible edge of anxiety in her voice when he pressed that button. He was not interested in big cars with darkened windows where you sank into soft leather cushions. Elaborate foods, contrived to the point of exasperation, didn't interest him, nor did the luxuriousness of the rooms where he had spent his nights, invariably sleepless, for forty years. What he cared about was that uncertain tremulousness in Maggie's voice, and the look that passed from the elevator man to the doorman in the morning when the two glass doors opened with a silent whoosh in front of him. What was power, after all? He loved to read it in those scattered pockets of humanity.

Results had never interested him as much as processes—how the plot of the old animal humanity unfolded. And the less he cared about results, the more results followed him. They seemed to stick to him, even entreated him; he was their sole representative, the advertisement for results. And so he had passed into history as a pragmatic man, the capable lord of war and peace, the shrewd puppeteer who moved the strings of the world, and it wasn't true, for he couldn't even distinguish green socks from red. Once he had secretly spent an entire day in Peking with a rip in the seat of his pants; his underwear was showing, and no one had dared to tell him, and he died of shame when he took the pants off that night, and took the underpants off and saw, disgusted, in the place made visible by the tear, but on the inside, a stain made by shit.

The intercom buzzed. It was Maggie telling him the chauffeur had arrived. Henry Kissinger picked up two light bags and crossed the tiled vestibule with a frozen smile to Maggie as she wished him *bon voyage*, walked him to the door, and closed it gently behind him.

When he went down, he liked to take the service elevator. On the ground floor there was an Italian restaurant, and every so often he looked in through the window of the kitchen, at the back, and watched the flesh of dead animals boil. "Men are like chickens; you pluck them and they don't bleed," he had said once. "Really, try it. You pluck a chicken and there's not a drop of blood. Then you eat it."

He went out, greeting the doorman of the building next to his. He had been leaving that way for years. In fact, in the beginning he had thought of it as an excellent anti-terrorist maneuver. Then it had become a habit. Precautionary measures almost always become a habit.

The chauffeur was waiting in front of his door, and, turning in his direction, saluted him by touching his cap with two joined fingers.

The flight for Paris left soon. Then he would go on to Italy, Rome, the Pope. Then to Cernobbio, for the summit. There he would be occupied with Ishmael. The limousine drove off.

As the airport came into view, he observed the new flowerbeds. The road and the grassy plazas around Kennedy had been rebuilt. The cement was almost white, the fences sparkled, and the flowers were red. They looked like plastic.

The plane to Paris. When it had climbed above the clouds and America was something indistinct, miles below, he fell asleep, sank into it; he looked like a dead man.

When he awoke, he was damp with sweat. His temples were pounding and his forehead beaded with sweat. The passengers nearby were sleeping. The lights were lowered. He touched his forehead with the back of his hand. It was wet. His shirt was soaked. He got up, took the bag from the overhead compartment, and went into the bathroom to change his shirt.

Kings do not touch doors, except those of bathrooms.

You do like this. Get up from the seat, at an altitude of thirty-five thousand feet, above the dark, freezing mass of the Atlantic, from that distance as still and dense as oil. You advance between the two rows of seats, staring at the metal door of the toilet ahead of you, like the steel-plated entrance to a vault. You move through the stale odor of the seats, of fabrics that have been rubbed by millions and millions of asses, at all hours, flung like yo-yo strings around the world, European asses to America and American asses to Europe. You think of those asses, bulimic, pumped up with vitamins, or worn out like the thin shoulder blades of Vietnamese women—asses that speak every idiom, that have sat on the resinous wood of Alpine huts in Carinthia and have slid down the aluminum slide in the playground at a nursery school in

Copenhagen. You think of them, think of the numb, uptight asses of greedy bankers who leave American investment funds to hurl themselves at European investment funds, and think of the broken-down asses of Berlin prostitutes who put their hopes in America as if in the lottery and find themselves alcoholics, them and their asses, in the jumbled, numinous industrial outskirts of Borego Springs. You think about it. Through the warm sleep of children lying curled up on the seats, through the watchful anxiety that hovers under the fragile half sleep of mothers, alongside the fingers discreetly tapping on the luminous laptops of hardworking managers who do not give in to weariness but burrow on, souls stressed by anxiety, you pass through this human kingdom suspended in a tin box at thirty-five thousand feet above a motionless dark freezing vortex called the Atlantic. You arrive at the pneumatically locked door of the toilet, and opening it you proceed inside and close it, isolating yourself, for a moment forever, from the crowd that looks ahead, into nothing, as if at a cinema without a screen, as if at a rally without a politician, at an indefinite point known as Europe.

The light is green, the water is violet. The walls are metallic and icy, the mirror slightly concave. The toilet is metal, too, but a different metal, iridescent and warm. There is paper everywhere. There is paper crumpled into the wastebasket under the sink, which is a different metal from the metal of the walls and the metal of the toilet. The wastebasket is of a metal different from the metal of the walls, the toilet, and the sink. There is an oblong roll of paper on the wall. There is a roll of paper next to the toilet and there is paper in the towel dispenser next to the sink, at the level of the concave mirror. You open the toilet and look into it. The toilet is round and wide, much rounder and wider than any toilet on which you have ever sat before. It is a perfectly dry ditch, not a drop of water in sight. If you flush, everything is powerfully sucked in and you can watch the violet water swirl slowly and noisily toward the central hole, and listen to the threatening, rapid gurgle of something that is absorbed into the unknown. Then you are curious and you stick your head in the bowl to see if, at the bottom of that hole, there is a light, if you can make out where it's all going to end, if on the other side it ends up in the sky. Kings do not stick their heads in the toilet.

Then you sit down and concentrate, and open up to the world.

God exists. Shit, God exists. Here's a man, sitting, suspended in midair thirty-five thousand feet above the ocean, and this man is shitting. He is shitting at a velocity of nine hundred parsecs. All his shit will be sucked in and absorbed into some place that has not been identified. Maybe the sky. Maybe just a reservoir that picks up whatever any of those men out there, sitting in vertical rows, lined up waiting for Europe, shit during this parabola that is drawn in midair between two points six thousand miles apart.

You shit. Pure atman. You are a spiritual being that is one with itself, a disembodied point focused in an absolute concentration that admits no interruption. You are a point that produces space. Space and shit. You are in a finite wait for the realization of an infinite desire. You are on the edge of an abyss, you are at the peak of the world, you are beyond every expectation, you have just come out of your mother's uterus. What was that story your mother used to tell you as a child? That everyone has to shit. Even kings shit, Mother. When you're frightened, you shit. The world enters you, satisfies you, at the very moment you evacuate. You evacuate the waste that you have not accepted from the world, you cleanse yourself of that intense invasion that the world practices all the time, when it enters into you and you do not go into it. There's no justice in this osmosis. In fact there's a moment when you're actually asleep, you actually seem to be asleep. You see the darkness inside you, studded with the fibrillating power of isolated whirling photemes, like hummingbirds suspended in a void. It's incredible, but at this apex hummingbirds appear. You're open to brief dreams that draw you into other spaces and other times, while the egg of shit you've been sitting on is hatched, and slowly and inexorably you are called back, to take on the world, to shake its conscience like an inexperienced recruit who nurses his resentment at the arrogance of his superior.

It's as if you'd been fucking for days. It's as if the most beautiful woman in your life had just left you, kissing you tenderly, lustfully, as if she had just now left the room after a night of fantastic sex. You sail along in the bubble of your refreshed mind.

Wash your hands. Pull up your zipper. The belt isn't in place. In front of the mirror, with cynicism and cruelty, watch yourself stick your finger up your nose, watch it dig, observe on the tip of your finger the dry, rusty secretion, and fix your pupils on your pupils in the mirror. With methodical and lashing severity, apply this absolute gaze to yourself, here, the same cold gaze with which outside of here you look at the world and dissect it.

For a moment, while you were shitting, you thought, George W. Bush is an asshole.

At 23:15 Henry Kissinger landed at Charles de Gaulle Airport, just outside Paris. At 00:10 he arrived at the Hilton. He slept badly, with bouts of insomnia. He woke at 7. He had breakfast at 8. At 9:15 he was at EuroDisney, for the inauguration of a new pavilion dedicated to dolls illustrating the history of the world. At lunch he met with two people from Lazard. At 15:30, he was to attend a meeting at the auditorium at the great Arche at La Défense. At the point where Paris ends, violently, it was cold and foggy. At 16:20, as he was walking away with his bodyguard, heading for the car at the south gate, the attempt was made. It failed.

Milan
October 27, 1962
14:00

Montorsi was shaking when he arrived at the Giamaica.

The image of the mummy. The image of the dead baby at Giuriati. His head was pounding.

Maura was waiting for him, and, as always when she was waiting for him, she was looking around, her blue eyes wide. She was small, she broke up the light, she was pale, and even from a distance he was lost in her freckles as she smiled.

"You're white as a sheet, David."

"I am?"

"You're cold, shaking. Are you ill?"

"Let's go eat, Mau. Let me get something in my stomach. Let me talk."

As they went into the restaurant with its steamed-up windows and its noisy crowd, they seemed to move disjointedly, like dolls.

She listened to him, because he couldn't hold back the images that hammered at him. The mummy. The child. The mummy. The child. Maura caressed him, but she couldn't focus on him—she was thinking of Luca.

When he had finished—in a flood of words that Maura at times pretended to listen to and yet didn't even hear—the steaming coffee was blowing in their faces, reddening them. For a moment they were silent, and David Montorsi saw that it was good to have Maura there with him, and that their child that wasn't even a child was a small warm thing that already he could feel, bewilderingly. Maura was silent. She had been speaking less and less since she had become pregnant. He thought it was because of her fear of a breakdown. He had thought the baby would cure her. It wasn't true.

He asked her forgiveness. Maura was startled. He asked her forgiveness for having told her about the dead baby, and the mummy at the archive.

Maura smiled, her gaze faraway. She caressed his head. "I'm going to the gynecologist today."

It always seemed to Montorsi that the gynecologist had a pair of panty hose over his face; he was old and his voice shook, perhaps because he had polyps in his throat. "What sort of tests are you having?"

"Um, routine, I think. I think he just wants to poke around a little. Nothing important."

"Mau . . ." He wanted to tell her about Arle, about Boldrini, about the light in his office. Better not to. He had trouble regaining control of himself.

Maura looked at him. He was upset. "Calm down, David. Forget the investigation. It's not as if they miss you, these cases. Calm down. . . ."

"There isn't even enough evidence to keep the investigation open at the Detective Squad. I'm handing it over to Vice. But something about it doesn't seem right, Mau. Why go and put a child under a stone, at night?"

"But you looked, David. There was nothing."

"The information about the partisans wasn't there. I didn't find anything, but only for now . . ."

She was annoyed. He wasn't aware of her annoyance. "Then don't drop the investigation."

He leaned his head against her arm. She reacted mechanically, accepting it. They huddled together, one beside the other, like tramps when the cold is bitter.

He went back to Headquarters. He decided to give himself a week; then he would hand the file over to Boldrini and his men at Vice, and for Detectives the case would be closed. It wasn't so much an intuition that held him. He was compelled by the mineral void of the display case and the absence of a smile on the child in the grainy photograph on the wall right in front of the dried-up mummy, a dead satellite facing an enormous planet that had once been alive. As for the cards, all those little cards inscribed in fine handwriting, thundering in the silent suffocating darkness of the metal filing cabinets, there were still a couple of dates to check, after all. At the historical archive of the Resistance, he had gleaned more questions than answers. But after all, it should be possible to get information on the massacre of the partisans at Giuriati through the newspapers. There was a journalist at the *Corriere* (he searched for the name, but it wouldn't come), a man he had consulted some time ago. When could it have been? Maybe it was the case of the dead prostitute in Comasina, when the names of two derelicts from Barona had been useful to him, men who had attempted a robbery and whose files could not be found. That was years ago. What was the name of the guy at the *Corriere*? Maybe he wasn't even a reporter.

He was tired. And when night came, he wouldn't be able to sleep, again. Waking up at four-thirty had become inevitable, and he would sit in the purple light of the kitchen, leaning against the cold ceramic tiles of the walls.

Goddam insomnia.

He had decided he would hold on to the case.

Milan/Paris
March 23, 2001
18:10

An attempt had been made on the life of Henry Kissinger. Ishmael's threats were real. The American report had been correct. The Americans Lopez had seen at Headquarters were in charge of security for the United States delegation in Cernobbio. The information on the failed assassination attempt on Kissinger was classified. It would not be made public. The Americans claimed that they had not expected an attempt in Paris. It was probable that the assassins would try again in Rome, Milan, or Villa d'Este in Cernobbio. Kissinger was already safely in Rome, scheduled to meet with the Pope. He would arrive in Milan the next morning by plane. There were the other powerful men to protect, but at this point it seemed that the probable objective was Kissinger. As the Italian in charge of security at Cernobbio, Santovito told Lopez to coordinate relations with the Americans. The would-be assassin had been killed; Lopez was to go to Paris, to find out as much as possible about the killer's identity as rapidly as he could, starting from the results provided by the French authorities and intelligence services. Lopez, however, was thinking that at seven-thirty he was supposed to meet someone for a bag of coke. He was also thinking of the body on Via Padova and the autopsy report that an old man had intercepted. He didn't give a damn about either Kissinger or Ishmael. And yet he was supposed to leave immediately. He had to rouse himself, get moving. There wasn't much time.

"Lopez . . ." Santovito gripped the corpse of a cigarette between middle and index fingers.

"Yes."

"With these Americans. Go easy, okay, Guido? It's important."

Lopez gave a little nod. It was important for Santovito's own affairs. He himself didn't give a fucking damn about Kissinger or the other powerful men or formerly powerful men who would be visiting Cernobbio. "Yes, yes."

The Americans, clean-shaven and wan, looked at him in silence. Some of them had watery eyes. They were the ones who in the toilet had spoken of Ishmael.

The flight for Paris was set to leave in an hour, from Linate. If he was quick, he might get back to Milan that night.

None of the Americans accompanied him. He would have time to roll himself a last joint and smoke it before departure, in the men's room at Linate. A young officer drove him to the airport, a rookie who couldn't have been more than twenty-five.

The sky was opening, a fruit whose luminous pulp was splitting a chalky peel. The shadow on the walls in the underpass of Viale Molise was fixed on the distorted outline of a tramp in a torn jacket who had stopped under the fluorescent lights to open his filthy plastic bag. The car reemerged at the intersection with XXII Marzo and turned, siren blaring, scattering a group of short fat women shouting and gesticulating on the sidewalk. A tram noisily rounded the corner, a new model that was being tried out in Milan, a plastic dildo slowly sinking into the body of the city, garishly lighted inside, bending on steel tracks into old familiar curves. At Viale Forlanini, the siren broke up a group of Slavs who were talking in front of a vast, high church with a dark terracotta façade, its narrow windows raised fifteen feet above the sidewalk. Lopez imagined that the priests were afraid the faithful might escape. Someone was putting up signs at the church cinema, like an oratory next to the church's grotesque body; it spread a warm light and an idea of remote comfort and peace toward the cashier at the back of the lobby, a woman in a faded maroon sweater who looked out vacantly through the windows.

The tall narrow building that overlooked the railroad seemed to sink suddenly where it met the two bridges; the structure was a giant scar that pushed its apartments into outward-tapering balconies. Tufts of dry grass growing among the stones of the overpass sparkled in the twilight. On the highway to the airport, Lopez saw the motionless line of cars entering Milan, as the police car descended from the exit ramp of the ring road, and in the triangle of white grass between the street and the entrance ramp he saw an empty plastic bag fluttering in the air, a suspended and iridescent shape that reminded him of a female face. At the barrier of billboards—a wall of paper and rigid aluminum and advertising posters, like bedsheets with writing—he saw the giant figure of a Christ appear, in the form of Giorgio Armani. He was black and white, with a hairy chest, the hairs like wires, coarse and shiny, and on his cheeks you could see the small scars of the flesh, the bristling black hairs of the beard, then the tiny nose, the folds of the lips, the almost blue hair on his head. Giorgio Armani had his arms spread wide; he was naked, with a sheet wound around his body, and on his head was a crown of thorns, and black blood dripped down his forehead and nose and lips. Giorgio Armani was white, the background was black, and you couldn't tell if he was diving into the black water behind him, or if he was crucified upright; his eyes seemed to be crying and along with the tears there was the black blood that flowed like rain and stained the white sheet covering the pubic area, and underneath, on the right, was an eagle and the name Giorgio Armani.

They had crossed the useless purple bridge before the airport and turned onto the straightaway beyond the curve—the road that leads to the little amusement part, half dismantled. They passed another tram, which rumbled despite its slow speed. They avoided the dirty white line of lighted taxis and saw, low and oblique, the formless outline of an airplane emitting a trail of heat as it slowly rose, to insert itself into the cracks in the ground-hugging clouds, and then he saw the plane accelerate, leap behind the clouds, toward the dying away of all the lights.

Alone, in the bathroom at the boarding area for the direct flight to Paris, he smoked the joint. He sat down to wait. It was hot. The faces were tired. The flight was called, and he landed in Paris an hour later.

Milan
October 27, 1962
15:00

As soon as he got back to his office, Montorsi looked for traces of whoever had been there earlier, when he was leaving Headquarters. What were they looking for? No one in the department would go into other people's offices when they weren't there. He glanced at the papers and at the closed drawers, but didn't open them, because he didn't want to make any noise; he would check later. He looked at the telephone and suspicion assailed him. Then he moved carefully. Going over to the warm ferrous exhalation from the radiator under the window, he drew the curtains. He retraced his steps, turned out the light, pulled the door to, and closed it, from the inside. He went to the telephone. From outside, anyone would think he had left his office just after going in. He lifted the receiver off the telephone, which was black and warm in the strangely golden semidarkness of the room. He could hear regular but intermittent thunder from outside the window. Carefully he lifted the receiver, placing it on one side of the cradle to keep the spring pressed down and the line silent. He pressed his thumb down on the other spring. Then he picked up the receiver completely, and placed it gently on the soft grainy leather part of the desk (not even a vibration escaped; he took *extreme care*). He looked around. There was a letter opener. The blade was light, but the handle was thin and heavy enough to hold down the two parallel switches that opened the line. He positioned it horizontally and tried it, gambling. The weight held; the letter opener was motionless on the two little spring-mounted buttons. The line was silent. It was as if the receiver had not been raised. Now he could examine it.

He attempted to unscrew the circular cap around the bottom half of the receiver. It was jammed. He tried to avoid jerks or vibrations. He laid the receiver on its side. He took a handkerchief. He felt the effort of whoever had screwed the cap on. He unscrewed it with a painful pressure on his biceps, to avoid any squeaking. He got to the last turn. He gambled again; he lifted off the round cover. It was there.

It was a bug. Someone had come into his office while he was leaving Vice and going to investigate at the archive of the Resistance and put in the bug. He sat in a drowsy stupor in the half-shadow of the office. Suddenly the telephone rang.

He began to screw the cover back on, taking the same care as before. No jolt, no vibration.

The second ring.

He stopped. He went back to screwing. He was sweating.

He stopped for another instant. *Third ring.*

Final twist.

Fourth ring.

Slowly he put the receiver back on the rough wood of the desk.

Fifth ring. He got up, opened the door, slammed it, turned on the light.

Sixth ring. He picked up the receiver. He removed the letter opener. The line was free. He waited a second. Then he spoke.

"Montorsi."

"Hello, David. It's Boldrini."

"Hey. Do you have those names for me?"

"No. . . . It's that . . ." Boldrini hesitated.

"What, Boldrini?"

"Then they haven't said anything to you. They've given me the files for the Giuriati case."

"*What*?"

"They've handed the investigation over to Vice," Boldrini said.

"Oh."

"Do you have anything new? Did you check on those things?" Boldrini asked.

An instant to think. Only an instant. "Yes."

"And so?" Boldrini asked.

Reflect. Quick. Respond. "Oh, nothing. Look, in fact it really is a matter for Vice."

"They've saved you the trouble, then."

"I guess, but I'd be glad to come and see you, Bold."

"Okay, yes, come. Sure, come."

"Listen . . ." Montorsi began.

"Yes?"

"Who brought you the stuff?"

Silence. "Omboni. Omboni brought it down."

"Oh."

"All right, come on," Boldrini said. "Besides, here you're the rookie. You're the newest arrival, David, what do you expect? You have to rise from the ranks. . . ."

Montorsi paused. "Listen, about the case. Do you need anything else?"

A moment's silence. *Bull's-eye.* "Why?" Boldrini asked. "Do you have notes that aren't in the files?"

Montorsi allowed another long moment before speaking. "No. No, no. I don't have anything that's not in the files."

Boldrini was silent again. He had fallen for it.

"Okay, Bold, if you don't need anything, I'm going to see what's going on, if there's something else for me to do."

"Good. I'll buy you a coffee one of these days."

"I accept. Call me if you need anything."

He hung up the receiver, heard the subtle *click* of the bug inside it. They were listening.

He had to organize his thoughts. He had to put some order into his suspicions. But he was a blank mind in a dark space. He tried again. Boldrini's face. The bug in the telephone. The file sent to Vice. The mummy in the archive. At the bottom of the whirlpool, the waxy arm of the child at Giuriati.

So. While he is leaving Headquarters, the light goes on in his office. Maybe they're putting the bug in the receiver of his telephone. *Maybe not.* Maybe they go in simply to get the files for the Giuriati case; they want to hand them over to Boldrini's department. A few seconds later, Dr. Arle and his assistants, the top people at Forensics, arrive at Headquarters. Montorsi would have to check on Arle—what the man does, who he is. Why wasn't he at Giuriati? Montorsi would have to be careful not to arouse suspicions. Why was he going to see Boldrini? Was it another investigation? He would think about that later. Meanwhile he had to go and see Omboni, a colleague in his own department (one who was always glaring at him; he was around forty, played the "grandfather" with him. Screw him). Omboni had brought the documents in the case to Boldrini. Montorsi had led Boldrini to think that there existed other items that were not in the file. He expected a "visit." He would have to be alert.

But all this intrigue assumed that there was something funny behind the case. What? Maybe behind the killing of the child was a well-known and powerful circle of pedophiles, which Boldrini himself had hinted at. Maybe that was the real reason that the investigation had been taken away from him. After all, his superiors had taken cases away from him before; it wasn't exactly routine, but certainly it wasn't an irregular procedure. Still, it was clear that there was something strange in the whole business. The missing cards in the archive that referred to the partisans at Giuriati. The bug. The transfer of the case. The doctors from Forensics in Via Fatebenefratelli, with Boldrini. A black wave of danger flooded him.

Paris
March 23, 2001
19:30

Lopez's plane landed in Paris at seven-thirty. There had been a delay. The inside of the plane stank of old leather. It was cold, an unnatural cold, from the mechanical breath of the air conditioner. The turbulence had been unpleasant for the whole flight.

At Charles de Gaulle, two inspectors from the Paris police hurried him into an unmarked car, where a driver in uniform was waiting. They spoke to him a little in effortful English. They entered the city through a vast cupola that was a tunnel. They came out next to the soccer stadium, whose walls were lower than he could have imagined. "It's sunken. Half the stands are below street level," one of the two inspectors told him. They both wore dark, shiny leather jackets, which reminded Lopez of cops in an Al Pacino film. They were quite young. Younger than him, anyway. For many minutes, he saw only black people and Arabs outside the windows. A local market was closing down and people were putting out small fires, sparking light flakes of ash, in iron drums red-hot around the edges. The asphalt was shiny and dark, like the jackets of the two cops. They said nothing. Lopez was thinking about the corpse on Via Padova, about the deep internal hemorrhage that had been discovered during the autopsy. He thought about Bob, the former member of Science Religion, Ishmael's man, who had sent the e-mail with the order to eliminate Kissinger. Bob had been tracked around the world, showing up in America and then in Europe and who knows where else.

Lopez didn't give a fuck about Cernobbio. He wanted to roll himself another joint, and he was pissed that he hadn't warned the guy with the coke that he couldn't meet him at 7:30. *The purple, brown, and blackish bruises on the wet distended skin of the man on Via Padova . . .* Who was the old man who had been provided with false identification that allowed him to pick up the autopsy report, at Forensics? White hair. Sixty years old. The killing wasn't a homosexual matter. It was strange to find yourself confronted by someone you knew nothing about, lying stretched out on the cold table. What was the corpse's name? What was his history? He yawned. The cold in Paris was more piercing than in Milan. He saw a woman on a street corner cover her shoulders.

They turned onto a busy avenue, hurtled toward the center of the city. The shop windows were brighter. No black people were to be seen.

They wound through narrow streets. Tall dark houses were lighting up, revealing eyes of soft light, stories woven together in tiny apartments. Tiny stories spinning connections outside of him.

They crossed a bridge. He saw the Seine as an abyss, liquid matter that absorbed light, a muddy magnet. In the background was the intermittent roar of traffic, millions of animated voices muted by the dim, eddying flow of the Seine.

They reached a dark, deserted neighborhood. Black trees shadowed the ancient walls, the gray buttresses. He saw the red-and-white cross of an emergency room entrance. A wide plastic door was open, and nurses were smoking and talking in the entrance, in the glare of the fluorescent light. Purple apartment blocks rose above the black motionless tops of slender trees.

They turned to the right, following the river. The signal lights of the cars on the opposite bank flickered like insects. They were on the Île. They turned into an empty square, more of an empty space, really, where the lights of small basement bars converged. He looked out the window and saw the street sign. Place Dauphine.

Ten meters ahead, a gate opened with a dry click. The car went through, proceeding slowly. It stopped in a courtyard, and they got out. While Lopez roused himself and looked at the old cobblestones of the courtyard, the cell phone of one of the cops rang. He spoke quickly, in a low voice, ended the call, then nodded to Lopez. They entered the building through a door on their right.

Lopez immediately recognized the weariness of the man in charge of the investigation, the slow formation of gestures and expressions. The man's name was François Serrault. He smoked lazily. He spoke an irregular Italian mixed with shreds of Spanish. He said "Bueno" continually. On the chair next to his desk lay a rumpled raincoat almost exactly like Lopez's. He had a big mole on his cheek and a wrinkle across his forehead. One eye kept closing, slightly, because of a likable tic, which suggested trust and vulnerability. He clearly didn't care about Kissinger.

The attempt on Kissinger had taken place at La Défense. Kissinger had been speaking at a conference. Serrault handed Lopez the invitation. The event, called "Human Worlds," was attended by professors, academics, financial types. Kissinger had left shortly before 16:30. The car had been waiting, with its motor running, outside the south plaza, facing toward Paris, in the vast white circular space at the foot of the Grande Arche. François Serrault ran an index finger over a small worn map. Lopez nodded. He smiled when the other said "Bueno."

Kissinger was a small man. An escort of four bodyguards had surrounded him. The first shot had missed and the bullet had lodged in the base of a sculpture by Miró, opposite the commercial center. The second shot had hit one of the bodyguards protecting the back of the former Secretary of State. The bodyguards had pushed Kissinger to the ground, and two men had thrown themselves over him. The wounded agent had fallen on the white paving stones. People ran in every direction. The three other agents had aimed at a single point and had fired in that direction, each with two guns. They had hit the assassin. He was behind a chimney, on the low roof of the FNAC center. He was alone. Sixteen bullets had penetrated his body, on the right side, the side in view behind the chimney; the bullets had been extracted during the autopsy. The report would be completed tomorrow. The man was carrying identification, a fact confirming that it was an amateur attempt. Maybe it really was an isolated incident.

His name was Georges Clemenceau. He was a former member of Science Religion. He had spent a year recovering in a psychiatric clinic in Rennes. (There was a massive hospital record available. If Lopez wished to, he could study it at his hotel. For the moment, he didn't wish to.) After being discharged from the clinic, Clemenceau had not tried very hard to find a job; he came from a prosperous family, which had in the past provided for him, and it had hired an expensive deprogrammer, one of those fellows who wrest the offspring of the wealthy from the grip of cults trying to get money out of them. His parents had paid for his stay at the Rennes clinic, which also was very expensive. Georges had gone to live near his parents, on the Boulevard Raspail. The police had already searched his three-room apartment, without result. Lopez could also go there, after he had a look at the Grande Arche. Georges Clemenceau had had encounters with other sects after his adventure with Science Religion, as his family had confirmed. The Children of God, for example. He had become friendly again with old companions from his Science Religion days, who, exiled from Lewis's movement, were engaged in violent campaigns to undermine its credibility. They called themselves the New Way. Clemenceau had followed other parareligious movements, but did not have the financial autonomy that in the past had tempted the cult gurus. His final encounter had been with a semi-satanic lodge, which, according to Serrault, was a bunch of good-for-nothings in search of easy sex. It was a sect known as the Children of Ishmael.

Lopez blinked. Serrault went on to tell him that Clemenceau had spent a night in jail, along with other bored and terrified members of the Parisian bourgeoisie, following a police raid on an event in a warehouse outside Paris. The police had actually been on the trail of a group of pedophiles. They had thought it was a matter of baby trafficking. And in fact they had found a child, at the center of a rite, nude. There had been no abuse, however. The good Paris bourgeoisie had agreed to be silent.

Lopez remained spellbound for a moment. "Ishmael," he murmured.

Serrault examined him closely. "Ishmael, yes. The Children of Ishmael, Inspector. Vous les connaissez en Italie, n'est-ce pas?"

Lopez tried to summarize, quickly, the state of the investigation in Italy. Serrault observed that it was a matter for the intelligence services; he said that the Paris police didn't know enough about it. He was surprised that the services had not kept for themselves the job of investigating an attempt on the life of "Monsieur Kisingèr," as he called him. More wrinkles, shadowy and vertical, appeared on his porous, aging skin. "It is necessary to move quickly, no?" he asked.

Lopez nodded. He had given up hope of returning to Milan that night. They reserved a room for him in a hotel in Montmartre, not far from the Moulin, and close to the great boulevard whose broad curve held in a vise the endless, diffracted center of Paris.

Then he and Serrault left, to go to La Défense, to the Grande Arche, for a direct look at the location of the assassination attempt so that Lopez could calculate the dynamics for himself. Then they would go to Boulevard Raspail. Lopez wanted to examine Clemenceau's apartment.

Milan
October 27, 1962
15:30

First, he had to sound out Omboni. It was Omboni who had handed over the documents on the investigation of the child at Giuriati to the people at Vice. Omboni was a pain in the ass.

There was not one of his colleagues with whom Montorsi got along. They treated him like a big kid. Once, walking away from a group of them, he had had an itch at the base of his neck, and when he twisted his head to scratch it, he had seen how they were laughing behind his back. His colleagues were annoyed by his youth, impatience, and the big bulk of him that wandered uncertainly through the offices. When he had solved the case of the murdered lawyer on Via Pantano, he had not received a single compliment. Three of the others had already tried to solve it (including Omboni). They had all been looking for a woman killer, because of the stockings, the high-heeled shoes, a lipstick left carelessly open on the shelf in the bathroom, and the two toothbrushes in the lawyer's apartment. Finally they had handed him the investigation, a case they considered too cold ever to heat up. Montorsi had asked that the body be exhumed for a further autopsy. This time the pathologist found lesions in the rectal canal. The lawyer (a man with an unremarkable face, a bachelor, a practicing Catholic, rich but not too rich) had been a transvestite. There were no wigs to be found in his apartment; that was why his colleagues hadn't even considered the possibility. But clerks at the wig store at the end of Via Dante, near the Castello, had with some effort recognized the man. He hadn't been alone; a boy was with him. Montorsi had managed to get a sketch made of the lawyer's companion. Sifting through the lists of lovers of transvestites, he discovered that a boy who corresponded to the sketch frequented the neighborhood of Via Monza. Montorsi had combed the area, patrolling the streets and going into the bars until he caught him. The boy had given signs of trying to escape. Montorsi had drawn his gun and pointed it. His hand trembled; he didn't fire. Later, he had thought it over; it wasn't a concealed or incumbent morality or the acumen of experience that had stopped him but, rather, a subtle, adrenaline-fueled mechanism. *He had not fired.* The stunned face of the boy as he turned around to flee, the door of the bar that was hard to close—he remembered it all. One of Montorsi's colleagues waiting in the police car parked outside had come into the bar and found Montorsi motionless, still shaking, the gun pointed straight in front of him. The colleague had grabbed the boy and handcuffed him. But Montorsi had been the one who, with a silent and intuitive stubbornness, had solved the case. They hadn't thanked him. On the contrary, they kidded him and for a while had nicknamed him Idrolitina, after the powder used to add effervescence to mineral water, to say that he was a bottle of flat water. Then it had passed. But he had never made friends with his colleagues. They would give him a case sometimes, and, when the matter seemed to be getting interesting, take it away to let an older colleague finish the job. He had got used to it. No, he hadn't got used to it. It irked him; it was a rough scratch on his pride. It was true that he was inexperienced, true that he was young, but true also that he was very good. He was *better*. That was why he irritated them.

So Omboni hated him. His dirty salt-and-pepper hair formed clumps that looked as if they had been brilliantined. He wore jackets that were too big and had a pronounced Milanese accent. He was always raising one eyebrow, a form of skepticism that David had classified among the signs of those who had accumulated too many years at Headquarters and become emaciated in character, opaque in intuition. He wondered if that would happen to him. He consoled himself by recalling something he had heard on the radio one morning, eating in silence with Maura. A psychologist had said of certain patients that their most paralyzing fear was the fear of going mad, and that as long as they continued to wonder if they would go mad it was impossible that they would. For him it was the same. He feared that inner atmosphere that made a man's gaze bovine. Time slowly corrodes, he thought. He didn't consider the violent impact of events, only the monotonous grinding of the years.

He had to drop in on Omboni. He got up and went into the corridor, and he felt that he was alone in the dirty pit of an empty swimming pool.

Omboni was sitting with his feet on the desk. He was stocky, and his calves appeared improbably bulging, as if a serum inside were ready to burst them open. He looked up at Montorsi obliquely, his glasses sitting on the tip of his nose, papers in hand, his tie hanging on the chair on the other side of the desk.

"What's up, David?" His voice, gnawed by long acquaintance with smoke, seemed to come directly out of his bronchial tubes, as if he had neither throat nor vocal cords.

"Nothing. I just wanted to ask you about the Giuriati case."

"Oh, yes. The Chief closed it. He glanced at it today, at lunch. There was a meeting—you were out. We evaluated it together. It's something for Vice. I took everything to Boldrini."

So Omboni had gone into his office long after the moment when the light went on. Had he planted the bug? "I know," Montorsi said. "I spoke to Boldrini. Is there something else for me to do? I'm free. . . ."

"The Chief said to take another look at any unsolved cases in the outskirts. There's not much to do these days. See what you can file."

"But that's office work. . . ."

"Take a vacation, then." He laughed. Omboni was making fun of him.

"What about the mess downstairs?"

"What?"

"Those people in dark suits. Wandering around the first floor."

"Oh. It's an American team. They're here to establish contacts. They're looking to set up a single structure, covering Europe. They're based here, with us, until the agreements become final."

"Who are they? FBI?"

"Something like that. CIA, something like that. They seem to be planning a single organization, an agency, I think, here in Milan. I don't really know. I think they're also connected with the military bases."

"Do we have anything to do with it?"

"They've asked for some files. That's why there was the meeting with the Chief today. You weren't here. They asked for specific cases."

"Such as?"

"Multiple homicides. Things like that. If there were elements involving other countries, in the records."

"We're becoming intelligence agents," Montorsi said, and he smiled.

"It's our fate. It's the fate of the police."

"It's the fate of Italy, that's where it's heading. . . ."

In his office again, Montorsi thought about what to do, where to go, and if his superiors had really tried to stop him and why. He had decided to persist, in spite of everything. All he needed was privacy—that no one should know what he was working on—and one investigator, himself. But that one man was no longer who Montorsi had thought he was, not since he had been assaulted by the little purple body on the field and the mummy in the archive.

The ringing telephone catapulted him out of his thoughts. The first thing he remembered was the bug. He let the phone ring again, then one more time. He picked up the receiver.

"David?"

"Mau . . ."

"So?"

They must not know that she knew. He needed silence. "Nothing. . . ."

"The kid at Giuriati?"

Shit. *Now they knew that she knew.* "Nothing, Mau. Not important. Doesn't interest us."

"It seemed important."

"Not as important as what you went to do. What did the doctor say?"

"Everything's normal."

"Should you be taking something? Did he give you any special diet?"

"No, nothing at all. Listen, I called for another reason. . . ."

"Tell me."

"There's going to be a get-together after dinner tonight with some friends from school. Will you come?"

If Montorsi was going to work on the case of the child at the same time Boldrini was on it, he needed time. "I don't know. I'm kind of snowed under with work. Where is this get-together?"

"At the Comollis'."

Fabri Comolli was a colleague of Maura's, a professor with a stupid husband interested in cars. Montorsi didn't give a damn about cars. Not that he didn't like Fabri—he had seen her observing him surreptitiously, her eyes shiny with interest. "What time?"

"Nine. Nine-thirty."

"Not to be impolite, Mau, but it's that, really, I'm overwhelmed. . . ."

Maura was silent. "I'm going, David. What time will you be home?"

"Late. Don't worry. I'll see you at home, later."

Fuck the Comolli woman. Fuck the party. He tried to concentrate on what he had to do to find out what he wanted to find out—the child, the partisans, the interceptions, the people at Forensics.

The image of the mummy rose as if from his throat. He chased it away.

He looked at the clock, its face dimmed by dust around the edges, hanging crookedly on the wall (still the slow piercing of the rain, and already his attention was wandering). Almost four.

He would go to the archive at the *Corriere della Sera*. Surely he would find at least one article on the partisans who had been executed at Giuriati.

Milan
October 27, 1962
15:10

He fucked her, and fucked her, and fucked her.

Maura couldn't breathe, didn't want to breathe. She observed herself without having time to observe herself, because he was fucking her furiously, like a stranger. The red stripe on her chest where his tongue had been, and his teeth. Her small bosom shaken. She turned, and it was *him* behind her, and she was trying to bring into focus the earthquake of her own buttocks, feeling the pressure of his broad fingers against her. She was crying. She was raging, she breathed in air like a resource to be reserved, she was lost. She clenched her teeth, gnashed them.

He fucked her and he unleashed her.

In her mind was only him, *his* smell, *his* skin. She couldn't grasp a thought, she couldn't do anything, she could only feel, endure. She lost the power of speech, the syllables overlapping, random, and she put her fingers in her mouth, she was salivating, saliva dripping on his chest, now beneath her. Incomplete, whirling, crashing words, forgotten as soon as half uttered. Stubs of words, messy nasal breaths, dripping mucus. Her rage exploded into a crashing volcanic anger that shook her small body.

They spoke through sex. She made him look at her tongue, broad, exposed; she made him look at it. Then she wanted to feel like a whore, so she tapered her tongue, flicked the velvety end of its underside. Her lips were so white they were like the skin of her face. She sniffed her own freckles.

She felt large, loose. She saw that she looked false *naturally*. She tightened her jaw, breathed out, clenched her teeth. She wanted him to enter her with his bones. She wanted to breathe him in, continuously. The idea of being a small animal annihilated her. She licked him. The hairs on his chest bothered her—she liked them because they bothered her.

The saliva dried; she was refreshed with new saliva. One of her eyelids trembled in the middle, and the other was closed, then both eyelids locked, and then her eyes opened and pretended naturally to resist a blinding light.

Great big cunt. Great big cunt. Great big cunt. I am the cunt. Come with me, cunt.

For long minutes she clung to his nipple. She wanted him to put his feet, his hands, his elbows inside her. She lay on his knee, legs apart, and tried to shove it inside her; she spread herself, wet the knee, struggled to push. It seemed to her the head of a child that she was trying to get into her belly; she was dismembered; so many gestures penetrated her.

They had begun their lovemaking as soon as Maura arrived. Luca had a beautiful house, near the Carrobbio; Maura liked the warmth of the old furniture, the carpets, the dried flowers. She liked to feel under her hands the polished, resistant wood of the headboard. She had told Luca about the party at the Comollis'. She and Luca had met on a picnic that Fabri Comolli had dragged him to. David hadn't been there, as usual. Luca had been bored by all his friends' school colleagues. Maura had been a ray of light. It had been impossible for them to resist the attraction—how could you stop something that has *already* happened? She wondered if he despised her, fundamentally; she wondered if he was afraid that she would fall in love with him. But she didn't care. He left her without strength. The pleasure exhausted her.

Maura had called her husband at his office. He would not come to the party. Maura sighed heavily, but then she felt relieved, lightened. She made Luca call Fabri Comolli and get himself invited. She and Luca would see each other that evening. Maura had smiled; he noticed the blurry edges of a shadow in her and didn't understand.

They fucked. They fucked some more, they forgot themselves.

Paris
March 23, 2001
20:40

Lopez and Serrault drove toward the Arche, where Kissinger had been shot at. A second car followed them. The sirens screamed.

On the Seine's dark eddies, a beam of light from the department stores, its reflection quivering in the dense, greenish muddy water, seemed to touch the surface from below. The Ferris wheel shone white as, slowly and regularly, it made its outrageous revolution in the Place de la Concorde, and a white plastic curtain billowed behind a group of Parisians signed up to endorse a referendum to get rid of that Disneyan obscenity in the middle of the city. Police officers stood silently, tall and unmoving, under the warm, peremptory lights of the American Embassy. Lopez bent his neck, awkwardly, to confirm that the wheel interrupted the straight line of the Champs Élysées, which, starting at the Palais Royal, pierced the multiform body of the capital as far as the Étoile and then arrowed on to La Défense in a trajectory that opened up the entire metropolis. The chatter of the radio in the squad car bounced off the bright lights of promotional vitrines. The trees flowered in clusters of opaque carbon.

The cars navigated the circle of the Étoile. The traffic grew heavier at the unmarked border of the city's dark periphery, a stretch of white houses in the opposite direction of the airport. Beyond the Champs Élysées, the exhaust fumes sank toward the earth, pressing into the smooth, shiny, clear, luminous asphalt of the city's incalculable, tumultuous spread. A manhole cover rattled suddenly. Lopez saw a car of the Metro curve, noticeably vibrating, above the complex iron arc of the elevated railroad tracks. Underneath it, some idiot was using his nails to scrape the last shreds of posters off the dirty walls. Once, a current of bad air in the Paris Metro had seemed to Lopez like ammonia, and his eyes had been red for days. Now, across from the press of orderly unaltered façades, in styles of architecture widely known and replicated, he thought of not being, or of being nothing.

"The headquarters of the Children of Ishmael," Lopez said to Serrault. "Did you search it?"

"Ishmael has no headquarters."

Ishmael has no headquarters. Ishmael is everywhere. Ishmael is great.

For years in France they had been trying to find out where Ishmael was, Serrault said. Ishmael had moved to France in the sixties. He had come from Italy. In Italy, they must know more about him. Lopez said that in Italy they didn't know anything, or at least at the Detective Squad they didn't know anything—the department was now involved in the political level of the investigation (thanks to Santovito's machinations). To Serrault, this seemed strange. Anyway, Ishmael had no headquarters. The gatherings of his Children were as transitory and ungraspable as raves, organized via cell phone, with little advance notice; until a few minutes before the rite, not even the participants knew the location. Furthermore, because of the Internet it was practically impossible to establish what channels Ishmael's followers used to communicate with each other. Ishmael had constructed a new kind of sect, nebulous as a cloud. "That's it, a cloud. A spiritual cloud," Serrault said in his rough, halting Italian. The warehouse raid, the one interrupting the rite that Clemenceau participated in, had occurred practically by accident. The operations team had been on the track of a child-trafficking business on the Internet. After the raid, the investigators had understood that the protocols of Ishmael required a child at the center of the rite.

This wasn't something new; in the late eighties, the French government had attempted to tighten the screws on secret societies and satanist groups. A pustulant boil had burst, devastating—involving, it was said, members of the political class. The authorities had been able to ban the sects but had to let their adherents go. The politicians had kept public opinion in check. Many of the occult gurus—who, according to Serrault, were entrepreneurs of deceit, getting rich at the expense of their members—had moved to Switzerland. But there was no trace of Ishmael. Despite attempts to intercept e-mail messages, investigators had lost hope. Not that Ishmael had been that important. The French authorities had been much more preoccupied with Science Religion. They were worried about the cult's databases of personal information—that with this massive index of names the goal of Science Religion was to transform Lewis's Church into a lobbying group. And—as far as they could tell and as the case of Clemenceau demonstrated—the Children of Ishmael were largely former members of Science Religion. Serrault didn't know anything else. Ishmael was a matter for the intelligence services.

"And this Clemenceau?" Lopez asked. "What was his motive? Why an attempt on Kissinger?"

Serrault thought that it was a demonstration of power. He didn't think Clemenceau was an isolated, crazy assassin. Lopez nodded. And suddenly right in front of them was the white wonder of the Arche.

He had never seen it before. From the plaza, its immense, crushing image seemed to be imprinted in the air, as if it belonged to another dimension, perhaps a spiritual one. Pale in the darkness, a square mass that confounded every vanishing point, La Défense vertically projected a new horizontal form, a form beyond the cube, spanned by the dark light of the space behind its Portal. Its smooth white body rose in a void, dwarfing the great hotels a hundred yards away, where a complex highway interchange was being constructed, bridges suspended halfway over nothing in a tangle of black metal rods.

The Arche of La Défense reconnected the line that went from the Palais to the Concorde, the Champs, the Étoile, and so on through all Paris, becoming the needle's eye for a thread into the emptiness behind itself. Infinite marble steps led to the marvelous altar of cleanly cut white stone. The Arche's black magnetism drew in the air of all Paris, sucking it into its Portal, ejecting it into the dark vacuum to which it gave access. Every magnitude disappeared before it. The three-story commercial center on the circular plaza was compressed into geologic layers, and the sculptures all around it—a finger pointing at the sky, clinking metals, a jagged agglomeration of bright-colored Lego pieces—were reabsorbed by the pavement of white stone. Astonished visitors, sealed inside elevators of glass and steel, descended pneumatically along its walls. A strong wind was blowing. It was surprising to learn that within its dark rectangular body were hundreds of offices, ascending in prestige toward the large auditorium at the top of the Arche, all invisible from the outside. It was a mechanistic celebration of an unobservable, unchecked internal bureaucracy, eating the body from within, a carcinoma without metastasis. The entire mysterious metropolis lay like a supplicant at the feet of the silent altar, which like a magnet drew everything to itself, and which, not benignly, with its mute watchful gaze, provided for whatever bowed before it.

Lopez stood dumbfounded in the cold mist of air that blew from north of the Arche. Serrault was smoking in the mist pushed to the ground by the white power of La Défense. Lopez listened to the thud of the heels of Serrault's aides getting out of the second car and asked why it was called Défense. "I don't know," said Serrault. The words were lost in the wind of the bewildering, absolute space at the foot of the Arche. Serrault took a quick, unsatisfying drag, and with index finger and thumb he flung the remains of the burned-out cigarette the way children shoot marbles.

Clemenceau had positioned himself on the roof of the commercial center, which was crushed by the scale of the Arche, and yet itself was monumental. Elsewhere it would have dominated the space for miles; here it was compacted by the Arche. Clemenceau had aimed an automatic rifle at a height twenty meters from the ground. Kissinger was moving no more than forty meters away, protected by his bodyguards. The shots, dry and quick, had lost their echo in the windswept open space. It had all happened in a few seconds. Clemenceau had not even realized that he should hide behind the little chimney that emitted a warm discharge from the air conditioning. Getting ready to fire again, he had come out from behind the column of rough spongy concrete. The three bodyguards who were standing up had aimed instantly at the precise point from which Clemenceau's shots had come. Lopez touched with his fingers the holes made by the bullets that had missed their target and perforated the fragile concrete of the chimney. He calculated: twenty shots missed, sixteen on the mark, in Clemenceau's body. The assassin had reached the roof of the commercial center by going through a service entrance, a heavy gray metal door, rusty at the edges. He had acted alone, evidently.

They headed back to the cars. The wind vibrated, a sensitive, silent shout, appropriated by the metropolis through the Portal of La Défense. Lopez didn't turn to look at it, although he was tempted, called back by the magnetic white force radiating from that giant marble goddess.

They left to go to the Boulevard Raspail, where Georges Clemenceau had spent his last year.

Milan
October 27, 1962
16:15

Before going to the *Corriere della Sera,* Montorsi had to get in touch with Arle, the man in charge at Forensics. He had to know if Arle's appearance at Vice had anything to do with the transfer of the case, and do it without raising suspicions that he was still looking into the Giuriati business. Then he would check to see if there had been any news report in the *Corriere* the day after the partisans were killed at the sports ground in '45. Then he would calm down; he would pull out the plug. He smiled at the thought that, after all, the will is a plug, driven deep into the center by some other force.

He was certain that he had got Boldrini to understand that he, Montorsi, had other notes and other material that were not in the files handed over to Vice. If they had gone into his office to plant the bug, or if they had gone in to get the files, they would go in to search for the notes. For a moment he saw himself standing reflected in the window, hands at his sides, examining the floor and the area in front of the door. He was a big man, and yet every time he unexpectedly caught his own reflection, he surprised in himself a tremulous embarrassing fragility; he was immediately uneasy. He tore a corner off a piece of paper on his desk. He calculated the arc the door made when it was opened. He opened the door just wide enough so that he could get through, and left the scrap of paper on the floor beside it, at the intersection of two parquet squares. Even if an intruder noticed it, it would be impossible to reposition it at the same point. And he went out.

He went toward the Brera again. The *Corriere della Sera* was on Via Solferino. His contact was a crime reporter named Italo Fogliese, whom he didn't know personally. Fogliese had assisted him before when he needed information, and Montorsi in turn had helped him when an editor had asked for photographs of two kids who died in an accident. He would ask him for the articles from the archive of the *Corriere*.

There was a telephone booth on the corner, near Largo Treves. A big tree, bare, bent, a vegetal scrawl of affliction, hung over the booth. It stank of pee. Dirty water pooled in the metallic cracks in the floor. Thick condensation covered the receiver. He dialed the number of Forensics.

First ring. He recalled the first time he had seen Arle's pinched, jaundiced-looking face. Arle was cutting open a chest with a scalpel. You could hear the bones crack. The smell of formaldehyde and a lingering sweetness had made Montorsi sick. Arle had given the young Montorsi a quick glance, looking him up and down, apparently not surprised to have before him someone so big; he had turned back to the chest of the cadaver, and, bringing his thumbs together, had given it a sharp blow, and the chest had split open.

Second ring. At Forensics things were always in an uproar; sometimes the secretaries had to work in the dissection rooms, and they took forever to answer. Arle had a voice fissured by the past, as if at the very moment he was speaking he had remembered something that had happened a long time before. If Montorsi had had to associate an object with that voice, he would have chosen a rock. One of those rocks in Val d'Aosta, at an elevation of about three thousand meters, gray and rough and pitted, but far from glaciers or mosses.

Third ring. Being the head of Forensics in Milan conferred power. Dr. Arle was a creature of power. It was known at Headquarters on Via Fatebenefratelli that Arle held his own with the Chief. Sometimes he himself had directed an investigation. And he knew how to protect his power: *Always be present*. It was strange that when the baby was found at Giuriati, Arle had not been there—that it had been his assistants instead, unctuous men with bodily fluids clinging to them. The wave of disgust Montorsi had felt that morning returned. The fourth ring, together with the chemical stench of pee in the phone booth, roused him. Outside, two old women were carrying pieces of unidentifiable junk in both hands.

Fifth ring.

Picked up.

A woman.

"Dr. Arle, please."

"Who's calling?"

"Inspector Montorsi."

He waited. Three stocky fellows ran by, shouting in Spanish. From the pelota court, probably, in Via Palermo.

"Arle speaking."

"Good afternoon, Doctor. It's Inspector Montorsi, I don't know if you remember—"

"The young fellow, yes, I remember. At the Detective Squad. What can I do for you, Inspector Montorsi?" His broken voice, forced into the telephone wires, ran at breakneck speed through the city.

"It's about a case. We're archiving some investigations. . . ."

"Yes . . ."

"I wanted to know, before shelving the case, if it would be appropriate to ask for an additional inquest. I'm in charge of looking over the open files. . . ."

"Yes, so you want an opinion?"

"Look, if you would be so kind . . ."

"You have the report? You want to ask for a new autopsy?"

"Yes, in effect. I was wondering if—"

"They should all do this—all your colleagues should ask for an opinion before arranging a new autopsy. You know, less work."

"Yes, I know. Just for that reason—"

"Yes. Listen. I am very busy right now. Can I make you an appointment with one of my assistants?"

"Well, it would be better if you could see it. . . ."

"I understand. Is it an old case? Did I work on it?"

"Yes."

"Let me see. The problem is, I have another job. I'm leaving, you know."

"Leaving?"

"Yes. Forensics—I'm leaving the directorship. So I'm trying to finish things up here. I'm overloaded with work."

"Do you have a private office, Doctor? If you like, I could come see you there. It's a small matter, I guarantee."

"Yes. Well, not really—"

"At the hospital? If it's more convenient for you."

"No, let's do it here. It's fine here at Forensics. Come, come. Let's say . . . tomorrow. Is tomorrow convenient for you?"

"In the morning, Doctor?"

"At ten. I'll expect you in the office. Come in as usual, ask the secretary. This time we'll meet in the office, not down in the dissection room. No corpses this time, right?"

"No, Doctor. No, only papers."

"All right, then. Until tomorrow."

"Until tomorrow, yes."

The idea was this: He would show up to discuss a case that was still open. It was practically a perfect cover. On the fourth floor of Headquarters, his supervisors had put him in charge of looking over cases that were still open, and then archiving them. There was one that gave him a hook for Arle, from August 1960. Maura had been in the mountains, in Bormio; Montorsi had been on fatigue duty. An entire family had disappeared. A bank director at the National. He had absconded with millions. Two days after the report of the disappearance, a body had been found in the San Donato canal, south of Milan. The dentures corresponded. The wife and children were nowhere to be found. The body had been buried with what seemed to Montorsi excessive haste. Other tests could have been conducted, after all. The body had been found nude, distended, the bluish veins sclerotic, just touching the taut, chalk-white skin. The irises had been eaten, probably by water rats. Montorsi himself had seen a pair of them as they rapidly surfaced, their eyes blinking mechanically, and then moved out of the light, their fur dark, shiny, and stiff. They had dived back into a deep whirlpool among the gray plants.

Now he could ask Arle to verify that the case could be closed, since in the meantime nothing had come to light about the director, the family, or the money. And with this pretext, Montorsi could see if and why Arle knew something about the dead child at Giuriati. He could find out what Arle and his two assistants had been doing at Vice two hours after the discovery of the child.

So Arle was leaving as head of Forensics. Montorsi knitted his eyebrows. For how long had Arle ruled as potentate of Forensics, his thinning hair white and slightly wavy, the thick-framed eyeglasses, the yellow skin, the glassy blue-white pupils? Montorsi had heard him talked about ever since he joined the police. He had been there forever, maybe even since the war.

Montorsi shook off the rain. He walked quickly toward the entrance of the *Corriere*.

Paris
March 23, 2001
21:30

Sirens blaring, they drove to Boulevard Raspail and the apartment of Georges Clemenceau, failed assassin of Henry Kissinger. Lopez and Serrault didn't exchange a word as the cars shot through a wide, dirty Paris. There were few lights. No one on the street. The Tower was lit up, a vertical gift package offered to the sky. The car jolted them, ascents and descents alternating at irregular intervals.

When Lopez least expected it, they stopped in front of a doorway held open by a police officer. No other police cars were in sight.

From the lighted doorway they entered an unadorned lobby. The floor—polished marble—reflected the dim lighting. They climbed the stairs, ignoring the wrought-iron elevator cage. On the first floor, the plants next to the doors seemed vivid, an intense, totally dust-free green; they looked fake. The Clemenceaus lived on the second floor. Opposite was the door of their son Georges's apartment. It was open, and an agent in a blue sweater and a black belt, his hands clasped behind his back, was stationed there. A warm halogen light filtered from the apartment out to the landing—the light of a desperate single person in search of comfort, a nest. The carpet was iron-gray, a mottled shade that clashed with the cream-colored upholstery. The apartment had no hallway; they walked right into a large room, with a table in the middle covered with papers. An overnight case open on the table displayed a stock of multicolored floppy disks. Men, in uniform and in plainclothes, went in and out, crossing the lighted threshold between two other rooms, on the left a little kitchen, neat and orderly, on the right the bedroom. Here, on the desk, something was clearly missing, perhaps the computer, removed so that the hard drive could be analyzed. A poster on the wall over the desk depicted J. Ronald Lewis, the founder of Science Religion, his face distorted by some graphic filter, with a caption in neon colors: JESUS IS DEATH. There was a small stack of books—Science Religion manuals. Two airplane tickets, used as bookmarks, faded and worn: Paris–Hamburg, round trip. Lopez reflected. The e-mail provider used by Bob, the former Science Religion member whose mail had put the American services on the alert, was German: "liebernet.de," or something like that. Lopez put the tickets in his pocket without anyone's noticing. When he got back to Milan, he would have someone find out where Bob's provider was situated. If it was Hamburg, the matter of Clemenceau's failed attempt would take on a different meaning.

Above the headboard of the unmade bed, a small white silk ribbon was attached to the wall by two nails—a Japanese custom, Lopez recalled. There was some writing on it, in tiny fanciful characters, an intense black that stood out from the silky glow of the ribbon: ISHMAEL: HE IS GREAT. Under the bed they had found the case for the gun. They had also found porn magazines. A lot of them. Sadomasochistic magazines with pages torn out. Lopez bent down and leafed through one. The women had hairstyles from the seventies and eighties. Old photographs had been republished to stimulate new impulses of pleasure.

"How many of them did you find?" he asked.

Serrault asked one of his men. "*Bueno*, about seventy," he said. Lopez was puzzled by them, and while one of the agents leafed through a copy, he examined the places where Clemenceau had torn out illustrations.

The doors of the closet were open and two agents were looking through pockets. Two photographs on a shelf, beside an ink-jet printer, were of two male faces, the one on the left gentle and dreamy-looking, perhaps partly because of the poor quality of the light; the other, on the right, was tough and lined, and resembled Harvey Keitel.

"Who are they?" Lopez asked.

"The one on the left is Clemenceau. On the right is his deprogrammer."

"Have you talked to him?"

"He's at Headquarters. He doesn't know anything about Ishmael. He had become a friend of Clemenceau's, but he didn't know anything. You can question him, too, if you like."

Lopez didn't answer. He moved on to the desk. "And the computer?"

"Tomorrow you'll have a printout of the contents of the hard drive."

Lopez looked around again for a few minutes. Then he shook his head. There was no trace of any connection with Italy. He would have to wait for information from the examination of the computer tomorrow.

He gave a grimace of impatience. Serrault nodded, an invitation to leave. They had to go to the morgue, in the basement of the Quai. They had to see Georges Clemenceau after the autopsy.

In the car, Lopez asserted that Serrault would have to summon back to Headquarters all the participants in the rite of Ishmael, from the time when Clemenceau, too, had been momentarily in the hands of the police. Serrault shook his head; the scar of a resignation that was no longer rancorous split his face cleanly—for an instant Lopez recognized it, savored it, and the Frenchman seemed to him a long-lost brother. It went up to the political level, Serrault said; Ishmael had adherents high up in Paris politics. It would take a lot of time, with secret interrogations, free passes, exchanges of information and favors, and compromises. Anyway, too much time for the needs of Lopez and the Italians. Lopez nodded, his profile standing out in the wet light of the rear window.

They reached the Quai.

The morgue was warm, clean, and modern, but it stank. Death has an olfactory formula; it is not the sweetish smell of a corpse but, rather, ether and formaldehyde. Lopez shook his head, and, hands behind his back, followed Serrault, who was preceded by two agents as they all marched behind a young but bald doctor, who was hurried and nervous.

They opened many doors of light, satiny aluminum. Lopez said to Serrault, "You people have designers for your morgues," but Serrault didn't understand; he turned around in irritation. They took a slow, dusty freight elevator. They descended to a dark level and turned onto a corridor lit by cold fluorescent lights. Then they climbed stairs to a mezzanine and went into an autopsy room. It was vast, illuminated by a lamp that, centered above the metal table, blindly struck the pale-white body of Georges Clemenceau. A pool of autopsy surgeons were talking in low voices. The bullet holes in the corpse were bluish, a hailstorm. Sixteen of them, all on target along the right side of Clemenceau's body. The clotted blood had been washed off, but in a hurry; there were traces encrusted around the purple holes. The mouth had been closed up with crude sutures. Serrault and Lopez—both now with their hands clasped behind their backs—slowly circled the metal table. Lopez observed two bruises around the big toe and two rough scratches on the soles of his feet. When he saw Clemenceau's left side, he stood still. His eyes sought Serrault.

They were the same bruises as those on the corpse of Via Padova. Lopez's jaw contracted and so did his pupils. These bruises had been caused not by a whip but perhaps a club, anyway a long thin object jabbing at the body. Bruises like leopard spots. *The exact same bruises as those on the unknown man of Via Padova.*

For a moment he felt the floor shake.

He looked at the doctors. He asked them a question, in Italian, but none of them understood what he was saying. Serrault translated. Lopez wanted to know if they had looked at the anal cavity. No, there was no reason; they hadn't explored it. They answered him with a bewildered, questioning look.

Lopez asked them to do it. The process was horrendous.

The body was turned over, with a rustling of plastic. For convenience they had to sit it up first, spreading the arms and supporting it under the armpits. The arms were stiff and by now purple around the wrists, where a lot of the blood had dripped, coagulating, and they had swelled up, like vegetables. The doctors turned it. The back and the calves were completely purple. Fluid had leaked out onto the metal table. The corpse's hair fell onto its neck. The fingers were blue. *Why was he carrying his papers?* They pulled apart the buttocks, and switched on a luminous probe that had been greased with an oily transparent ointment. Lopez could hear a wet, smacking noise. They inserted it in the anus. At the other end of the probe, a doctor was watching on a screen. Serrault was facing the blank wall, opposite the one where they had come in. They had trouble getting the probe in. It seemed that they extracted it, with jerking motions, then jabbed it in again hard, trying to overcome the resistance. The guts were loosened; the smooth muscle structure didn't hold, and the anal canal was being squeezed by the swollen interior. Lopez couldn't understand what the doctors were murmuring to one another. Suddenly they pulled out the probe, greasy with ointment and shit.

The doctor at the screen went over to Serrault and conferred with him. Serrault nodded, passing the back of his hand over his chin. Then he nodded to Lopez. He approached.

Georges Clemenceau displayed signs of repeated anal violence. Pre-existing bruises, wounds that went back days before his death. Did Lopez understand anything about it?

Yes. The man on Via Padova was a Child of Ishmael. Ishmael was preparing to strike in Milan or Cernobbio.

He telephoned the Detective Squad in Milan and got Calimani. He told him that he needed some information and a photograph from Forensics. Calimani was sighing as he took notes, but Lopez ignored that expression of weariness and boredom. He wanted them to set up an appointment with a contact for him the following day in Milan. He needed an informer, someone who had reported from the inside on Science Religion and former members of the church. Was there an infiltrator in Science Religion? Who kept track of the church's activities? Calimani didn't know anything about it. Lopez said it was urgent, that he should telephone Santovito directly if necessary. When he got back to Milan, Science Religion had to be the first appointment on his list; he had to act in a hurry. (He had to find out if the man of Via Padova had been a member of Science Religion in the past; it was the only chance of reconstructing his identity.) Lopez was speaking quickly, Calimani assenting. He needed the fax number of Lopez's hotel. Lopez spent several minutes getting it; Serrault had to ask the person who had found the room in Montmartre for Lopez. There was another photograph he needed from Forensics the next day. He asked Calimani to provide it, to talk to the people at Forensics. *He wanted a photograph of the corpse of Via Padova with its eyes open.*

Calimani was silent. Then he asked, "The tramp on Via Padova?" Lopez said he wasn't a tramp. Calimani laughed. The fax number of the hotel arrived. Lopez said he would return to Milan the next day, as early as possible.

Milan
October 27, 1962
16:35

Behind the *Corriere* building in Via Solferino, with its façade like a Fascist hospital, was the dried-up Naviglio. Tramps slept in the bed of the canal, which was overrun by purple plants. Montorsi recalled that a tramp had been found dead there not even a month ago. It seemed that a gang of kids with nothing to do had beaten him. Bruises everywhere. Montorsi had gone home disgusted. Even dead, the tramp reeked of sweat, the smell of filth released into the air by wrinkled woolen clothes worn even in August. Some dry bread had fallen out of a cellophane package he had been clutching while they beat him.

Usually, violent things didn't happen here. The newspaper building—yellow but tidy, with a luminous light of its own that endured and glowed even at night—dominated the neighborhood with a strange, prestigious magnetism. The poor had all left. Once, there had been a workers' demonstration here, and both Detectives and the Political Squad had had to intervene. Montorsi had been behind a police van as eggs and stones were thrown at the gathering mass of police. The demonstrators shouted "Fascists!" Not a single egg had broken against the walls of the *Corriere* building. At the peak of the demonstration, the Chief had ordered the police to use tear gas, and the demonstrators had taken shelter in the narrow streets perpendicular to Solferino. Even then the walls of the *Corriere* building had remained untouched, clean. The building's authority was refracted on the opposite side of the street, in the façades of the houses of the wealthy, inhabited by silent old people who wandered the halls with similarly mute, gloved helpers. More than once Montorsi had thought that at some time it would change, and they would kill journalists here, in the inert and hazy democracy of Italy. If the workers, in the hundreds, had not scratched the walls, perhaps they would begin to scratch the people.

He had never set foot in the newspaper building. The journalists had always come to him.

The lobby was vast, full of people in gray suits. On the left, behind a broad counter, were two women in outfits of a green material like that of a roulette table. In the middle, men were hurrying down a staircase at least thirty feet wide, wrestling with sheets of paper that they read as they descended. Some went up, but those were only a few. On the right was a row of wooden telephone booths with windows and doors that slammed one after another, as the same men who were coming down the stairs went in and out to make their telephone calls. The pale marble floor was decorated with tiles in a complicated Art Nouveau design that couldn't be deciphered at ground level. The lobby gave the impression of a hotel.

The woman at the reception desk was pretty and blonde. "Mr. Fogliese, please. Italo," Montorsi said.

"Editorial?"

"Crime news, I think. Local."

"Who is calling?"

"Inspector David Montorsi."

"Yes. One moment."

She worked some levers visible from in front of the counter, pressing buttons that clicked loudly, her hands moving securely in complex, automatic movements. When she got an answer, she rapidly identified Montorsi's presence to someone. Then she put down the receiver, a Bakelite instrument of a kind Montorsi had never seen before.

"Mr. Fogliese will be right down. Please, make yourself comfortable. . . ." Make yourself comfortable in the sand-colored armchairs opposite the phone booths.

The wait was less than five minutes. He was sunk in an armchair covered in a rough warm fabric when the man appeared, in shirtsleeves, thin, hair white at the temples, complexion dark, eyes intensely green, and an expression of lively intelligence. He held out his hand, introducing himself: "Italo Fogliese. Good afternoon, Inspector Montorsi."

They were a little at a loss, as Montorsi stood up, towering over the journalist by at least a foot. The receptionist, behind them, observed them as she was writing. Fogliese thanked him again for the favor of the photograph of the boys. The local news of Milan and Rome was what "drew," and photographs were important; on that occasion the *Corriere* had been the only daily to publish them. What did Montorsi need? He explained that he wanted two articles from the archive, two dates, relating to research on a partisan massacre. And if possible a later article on the dedication of the plaque at Giuriati. There was no problem, Fogliese said. Only a question of time. Half an hour, if they were lucky. Maybe an hour. Fogliese preceded him. They went up the central staircase.

"You've never been here, Inspector?"

"At the *Corriere*? Never."

Italo Fogliese was smiling. Even as he ascended the broad marble steps, Montorsi couldn't decipher the complicated design of the floor below.

On the third floor, in front of a dark wood door with an elaborate inlaid pattern, they stopped. "We're here," the journalist said. "The editorial offices, I mean." He opened the door and went in. Montorsi was behind him.

He was astonished. It was a circular space, three stories high. From the glass ceiling (panels set in a dark metal frame) a bluish light poured in. Around the walls ran a spiral ramp, like the corridor by which you entered the soccer stadium at San Siro. It was a gallery of wood, a continuum with dozens and dozens of people going up and down it, who, by turns, frenetically looked out to the floor below. Against the walls was a second wall of wood—files, evidently. At regular distances, this broad corridor, descending like a vortex, widened into suspended planes, broad platforms that functioned as open offices. Montorsi could see technicians at work, alongside people waiting with their arms folded across their chests or resting on their hips, while other men, bent over lighted desks, worked on metal pages or pulled out zinc-coated plates and examined them, holding them in the air by one corner, like iridescent copper-colored garments. Montorsi stared, astounded. He gazed at the flow of light that came from the glass-paned cupola, and followed the oblique descent of the corridor toward the ground floor, a kind of theater of wood, glass, and metal, filled with voices that were lost in the azure haze of the distance between the ground floor and the top of the cupola.

Fogliese smiled. Montorsi looked down.

At the bottom, three floors below, he saw a star-shaped structure, full of people sitting or standing, in groups or alone. The structure was distinguished by the arrangement of the desks. Crowded together in the outermost circle, far from the luminous center point, were young people hunched over telephones and typewriters. Farther in, as the circle narrowed, the desks were more spread out, until there were six that directly faced the center. There men were sitting with telephones in their hands and their feet up on the desks. At the center a kind of elevator cage emerged, coming up from the depths, around which all that activity whirled. It was a perfect arabesque, like a design in a Persian carpet, and in fact an almost oriental smoke seemed imprisoned there.

"It's making me dizzy. But what is it?"

Italo Fogliese deepened his smile. "It's where we produce the paper," he said. "These are the archives, here along the walls of the corridor. The technical areas intrude into the editorial. See, the photolithographers and the compositors, there with the pages immersed in zinc baths?" Montorsi followed the journalist's finger. "If you go down, you get closer to the editors, who are on the ground floor. It's a clock, in effect—the paper's compass. On the outside are the reporters. As you move farther in, you rise in the hierarchy. The people in charge of the pages, the chief editors, the essayists, the subeditors . . ."

"And the editor?"

"Oh, he's in his office. It's below. He comes up in the elevator."

"It looks like the Chamber of Deputies. Really. Like Montecitorio."

They went down slowly, their steps muffled on the bright red carpet along the passage that circled the walls and descended, like a gangway, toward the ground floor. "You're right, Montorsi. It's the same architect. Basile, a legend of the Risorgimento. First he designed the interior of the *Corriere,* and then they called him in to redo Montecitorio. Do you know much about architecture?"

"Well, no, only that it really looks like the hall of the Chamber—"

"Anyway, for work like ours, the architect's idea is efficient even today. You need an open space, because you have to communicate with everyone, continuously. There's a reason that the Americans invented open editorial offices, without walls or private cubicles."

"Well, if the Americans dream of an office like this . . ."

"Yes, but we're Italians. We have style." He laughed.

They reached the ground floor. Seen from below, the glass cupola and the spiral ramp along the walls seemed less impressive. Close up, even the editorial offices merely resembled a large library, with the desks arranged like spokes coming out from the center. There was a subdued roar of voices calling to voices, questions thrown into the air unanswered, answers that arrived seconds after the questions, phone calls made, clicking of typewriters. To Montorsi it did seem like a clock, a human mechanism apparently chaotic yet responding to an efficient logic. The green-shaded lamps sent a warm, intimate light over the reddish wood of the desks. He followed Fogliese toward the center to his desk, halfway along. They sat down, with Montorsi across the desk from Fogliese, his back to the center.

"All right, let's see what you need, exactly."

Italo Fogliese took notes. The two dates, the names of the partisans. He asked him to wait, and Montorsi watched Fogliese make one circuit up the spiral ramp, stopping at the first platform of offices. He spoke to someone in an iron-gray shirt, noted something, came back down.

"It's in the archive. Don't ask me how they do it, but they can find anything."

Montorsi nodded in silence, slightly overwhelmed.

Fogliese said that he had some business to take care of, and asked to be excused; he would return immediately. He went off, out of the editorial office. Montorsi remained dazed, his eyes lost in the enormous hall of the newspaper. Everywhere there was frenzy and noise.

After a quarter of an hour, Fogliese returned. Apologizing for his delay, he asked, "What are you working on, Inspector?"

"Checking some old files. I have to archive some cases."

"Oh, for the CIA?"

"I'm sorry?"

"The CIA. Don't you have the Americans over there in Fatebenefratelli?"

"Yes. But how do you—"

"Oh, it's like the archivists. Don't ask me how we do it, but we know everything." And Fogliese smiled.

Montorsi smiled, too. "All I know is that they're setting themselves up in Italy and they're starting with us."

"I understand that it's starting in Milan, but only temporarily. Then it's supposed to be Verona. The headquarters is an American military base, just outside the city."

"Yes?"

"Then, in Rome, they're supposed to be in Via Merulana, near San Giovanni. Next to the Vatican seminaries."

"You know everything, Fogliese."

Now he had brought his face closer to Montorsi, both of them warmed by the little band of the hot desk lamp, leaning on their elbows, while, underneath the desk, the journalist tensely shifted his legs. "Calm down, Montorsi. Soon they won't be bothering you anymore."

"Who? The Americans?"

"The Americans, right, the Americans." He had a friendly smile, which cheered Montorsi.

"But I mean . . . how do you know?"

"I did a little investigation, but they didn't publish it here. Of course, this being the *Corriere* . . . There are Americans behind the ownership."

"Is there any ownership that the Americans aren't behind?"

"At *Il Giorno*. They aren't there."

"*Il Giorno* belongs to ENI, doesn't it?"

"It doesn't actually belong to ENI, the company. It's Mattei's. And if Mattei is there, the Americans aren't." And Fogliese winked.

No. If Enrico Mattei was there, the Americans were not. The controversial industrialist had founded the paper in order to have a platform for a campaign on behalf of his anti-American politics. Unprecedented. In Italy in 1962, barely seventeen years after defeat, with the country in a full economic boom, this man had started an anti-American political campaign.

"What happened to your report?"

"It's at *Il Giorno*. I gave it to a colleague at *Il Giorno*."

"And will they publish it?"

"In a week, maybe two. Unless . . ." He smiled.

"Are you going to work there, Fogliese?"

"Maybe. I've had it with being a hack here. I'd rather have a separate office. The hell with this American style." He laughed. He really was a sympathetic person.

"And so the CIA organization here is only temporary?" Montorsi asked.

"Listen, Montorsi. The less I say, the better it is—for you, too. You can't imagine what's behind it." The journalist grew serious. Under the cone of light formed by the lampshade, his eyes—bright, mobile, lively—appeared to be full of tears.

"I'll take your word for it, Fogliese. Besides, a cop shouldn't have prejudices like a journalist, right?"

They laughed together. Fogliese liked the remark. "Ah, here's Lucio, with the results of the search." Lucio was the researcher. He put down a folder. He had found everything within ten minutes. Fogliese asked Montorsi if he wanted to be alone while he looked at the old issues of the *Corriere*. Montorsi appreciated this; Fogliese wouldn't understand anyway what he was looking for. The press had not been informed of the discovery at Giuriati. There had been no press conference, which meant at least three or four days of silence was guaranteed. It was the procedure, at Headquarters, with certain homicide cases. It worked better.

January 15, 1945. The first newspaper, still translucent, released a barely perceptible, slightly viscous dust. "It's the conservation medium," Fogliese said. He had stayed. "Don't worry. It's annoying, but harmless." Montorsi began to leaf through; he had the same sensation he had had at the archive. Right in the center of his mind, the image of the mummy struck him. He shuddered in disgust.

"May I be indiscreet?" Fogliese said.

"Please."

"What are you looking for, exactly?"

"Information. Information on a partisan massacre."

"Will you let me be a little out of line professionally, Montorsi?" He smiled frankly.

"It's you who are letting me be out of line professionally."

"What does a massacre of—how many years ago?"

"Seventeen."

"Seventeen years. What does it have to do with a case from today? Is it a political question? Is it neo-Fascists?"

Fogliese looked him straight in the eyes; it was as if his face had opened and rotated, one half to the left, the other to the right, and Montorsi were looking into a solid warm white space. "Fogliese, to tell you the truth, I don't know."

"Does it have to do with something that we journalists know about?" His stubborn curiosity was driving a wedge into that well-nourished white space. Montorsi felt that curiosity as the twin to his own intuition, a powerful automatic current that led a man in different ways to a distant but seemingly graspable truth. For this reason, he didn't mind Fogliese's insistence. On the contrary, it amused him.

"No. I don't think you know."

"We don't know yet or we'll never know?"

"In a few days. Be patient."

"Let me propose an exchange," Fogliese said.

Even this boldness Montorsi liked. "Let's hear it."

"You tell me what it's about. And I will do the research for you."

Montorsi twisted his mouth into a smile. He had little room to maneuver. He thought of Arle. He thought of the impossibility of asking questions. Of Boldrini, who was watching him closely. Maybe it was worthwhile to pressure Boldrini and those who had taken the case away from him. He could unleash a journalist to ask the questions that he couldn't. "Let me think, Fogliese. Maybe we can do it. Let me think for a minute."

He went back to the paper until he found the news. It was only a short piece. The partisans had been killed. Listed were their names and dates of birth. No motive. No photograph. It was pure news, anonymous with the chill of the final utterance of those names.

He noisily folded the open copy and moved to the other paper. The journalist's green eyes sparkled questioningly.

"Just a moment, Fogliese. Let me check here, too."

He began at the end, backward. The pages of this issue felt newer and crackled under Montorsi's fingers. February 3, 1945. A few days after the first execution, a second. He found the little article about it. Again it was bare, the news of death cold and inert as the conserving dust on the paper. Tiny letters converged to form names and dates. Not a hint of a cause, of the motive that had impelled two firing squads to exterminate some boys. Was it retaliation? Had there been some secret accusation against them? Maybe his research hadn't taken account of that. *There is something behind it, always*. But what?

There was another paper, February 12, 1949. Perhaps the researcher had dug up some reference to the dedication of the plaque. Montorsi was discouraged by now; it was visible in his face. The journalist had observed the tiniest advances of that pallor of discomfort that perhaps, at some time, had invaded him, or would in the future. "It's no good, eh? Useless search?" Fogliese asked.

"If I don't find anything, I won't tell you anything, Fogliese."

February 12, 1949: The portrait of a nation trying to rebuild, after the disaster of defeat. The news was all internal, with strings of numbers indicating an economy in shambles. An ad for a candymaker now out of business, the prices laughable.

Then, in the local news section, he saw the photograph, the headline, and the short article that served as a written basis for the large image.

At the center, the plaque was visible—suffused by a hazy sunlight evident also on the marble in the photograph. People in overcoats and wide-brimmed hats gazed darkly at the lens: three on the left, four on the right, and two emerging, vague but recognizable, behind them.

> Martyrs of Giuriati
> *Plaque placed to the eternal memory*
> *of the sacrifice of the partisans of Milan*
> Milan—Yesterday, at 10:30, the mayor of Milan, Antonio Greppi, uncovered the plaque laid in memory of the Fascist massacre at Giuriati Field, in which fourteen young partisans lost their lives. Present at the civic ceremony, in addition to Mayor Greppi, the vice-secretary of the Communist Party, Luigi Longo, the communist senator Giancarlo Pajetta, secretary of the National Association of Partisans Mario Annone, and the president of AGIP, Enrico Mattei, who during the Nazi-Fascist occupation all fought in the Resistance that restored liberty to the Italian people.

Enrico Mattei. "Huh . . ."

"What is it, Montorsi?"

"No, it's just that, speak of the devil . . ."

"The CIA?"

"No, no. Mattei. Weren't we talking about Enrico Mattei?"

Fogliese, curious, got up, walked around the desk, and leaned over Montorsi's shoulders. "This . . . This is Mattei . . ."

"This on the left?"

"Yes, it's him."

"The others? Do you recognize them?" Montorsi asked.

"Wait . . . Next to Mattei . . . No, this one I don't recognize. Then Pajetta, yes, it's Pajetta, with the pipe. . . . Let's see . . . On the right . . . On the right, next to the plaque, is the president of the partisan association, Annone. I interviewed him a year ago—a formidable man, a cutting sense of humor. And this is Longo, certainly. And the one with the sash over his shoulder must be the mayor. The two in the back I can't make out—I don't know who they are."

They were silent. The paper seemed to crumble in the eye of the lamplight. Fogliese got up. He sat down again. "Satisfied?"

Montorsi was scratching his neck. "I don't know."

"Have you thought enough about my proposal? I do the research. You give me the exclusive."

He had thought enough. "Do you have time?"

"I'm all ears."

"All right. Fogliese, listen, though—not a word goes out of here."

Fogliese tightened his lips.

"Understood?"

"Understood."

Montorsi sighed. "Here's the story."

He explained everything. He explained to Fogliese how the skin of the arm of the child under the plaque at Giuriati, outside the plastic bag, had impressed him by its consistency—plastic, purple, like the limb of a doll. He explained the attempts to identify the connections with the ring of pedophiles—if such a ring existed, in Milan. Did Fogliese know anything about it? No, he knew nothing, but he could find out. Montorsi told him about going to the historical archive of the Resistance. He told him about the missing cards—*no trace of the partisans killed at Giuriati*. He was silent for a moment, while Fogliese continued to observe him, before telling the reporter about the mummy, the woody corpse of the anonymous partisan kept in the glass display case in the last room of the archive. He told Fogliese about the child in the photograph opposite the display case, and about the bug he had found in his office, and about discovering that the case had been taken away from him and given to Vice. He told Fogliese about Forensics, about the dark, heavy atmosphere in the dissection room, about Dr. Arle and his assistants, whom he discovered were visiting Boldrini while he was investigating Giuriati. Dr. Arle and his people at Forensics, who were like a sect . . .

"A sect . . ." Fogliese rubbed his chin, puzzled, pinching a flap of skin on his neck between index finger and thumb, the fingers of the other hand drumming on the desk.

"A sect, yes. But perhaps that's my idiosyncrasy. You see, the fumes of formaldehyde go to my head. Or being around corpses. Why? Does something come to mind?"

"No, it's that . . ." Fogliese inhaled. "You speak of a sect . . . and from information that I have . . ."

"On what?"

"The investigation. The investigation I was telling you about. The one I gave to *Il Giorno*. The report on the Americans, on the CIA here in Italy."

"Yes?"

"This remains confidential, too, right? Between you and me?"

"Of course, Fogliese. I've practically disgraced myself, saying so much. You know what would happen if they knew in Fatebenefratelli that I had spoken to you about something that hasn't been released to the press?"

"Okay. The point is that, from what I can understand, the Americans are arriving in Italy with a sect."

"A sect?" Montorsi asked. "What do you mean? But if they're already coming to set up here, if they're already coordinating with the military bases, as you were telling me, then why—"

"Yes, yes. But those are the official channels."

"Why, are there channels that aren't official?"

"Yes. . . . Precisely."

"A sect?"

"A sect. I have a name."

"The name of the sect?"

"Of the figure at the center of the sect."

They looked at each other in silence. "What's the name?"

Fogliese was silent a little longer. And then he spoke. "Ishmael. His name is Ishmael."

Paris
March 23, 2001
22:40

Ishmael is great. Ishmael was pulling on his threads. In Paris, one had broken. In Milan, perhaps, on Via Padova, another had broken. Guido Lopez was lost in the dimensionless night outside the Quai. Paris was bubbling up, a nocturnal whirlpool, beyond the Seine.

He was driven to his hotel in Montmartre. He would return to Milan the next day. Serrault remained at Headquarters to interrogate Clemenceau's deprogrammer, the man who had got him out of Science Religion. The boy kept a photograph of him in his room—how was it possible that the deprogrammer hadn't realized the threat of Ishmael? Serrault said goodbye to Lopez with a warm, fraternal handshake. There was a feeling of kinship, almost, between the two men. Serrault would deliver the printouts of the files from Clemenceau's computer directly to the hotel the next day; the technical team would work on it overnight.

The hotel was decent, nothing special. Lopez watched the unmarked police car drive off. He went in to the lobby, handed over his documents, asked if a fax had arrived. It hadn't. He didn't feel like staying in his room, and it was suffocating in the hotel lobby. He decided to go out for a short walk. The cold was piercing. The boulevard was crowded with whores, derelicts, fags in leather, pimps, people selling lighters. Two fags were inhaling poppers at the corner of a narrow cross street. Lopez took the joint out of his pocket and lighted it. The air was clear and the red lights of the Moulin irritated his eyes. He crossed the boulevard, to where the porno clubs were, glancing back distractedly at the hotel. Next to it was a gigantic, four-story porn supermarket. Behind the display windows he saw the inert bodies of perfect latex dolls, mannequins that seemed less artificial than dead, their gazes penitent and stupid. Molds of lovelessness, funereal plastics. Lopez felt the weight of them. Their synthetic hair shone like that of an incontinent old woman. The mouths were half-open, the lips set in an expression that mimed an exotic promise like a stay at a vacation resort.

Toward the ascent of Montmartre he saw two clumsy-looking tourists, perhaps father and son, overwhelmed by weariness, the father grizzled and thin, the son plump, both of them with bulging eyes, both looking disappointed, two men alone, keeping each other company. A curly blonde pretending to be a madam approached them; looking at their shoes to deduce what country they were from, she greeted them in Italian and invited them in to a club with red lights. "You like girls, maybe," she said. Lopez observed the older man, who was about sixty, and who clutched his olive-green raincoat, give the whore a smile of fierce yet absent wisdom, of melancholy spent passion. The young man, who had a dark complexion, looked like a moron; Lopez could see he wanted to stop and talk with the whore. The Italian tourists kept going, and before the whore could say a word to him, Lopez crossed the threshold.

He drank a beer while a weary woman of around thirty, smooth and sinuous, practiced a listless lap dance. The floor was stained with beer and receipts and wet cigarette ash. The bartender had overdeveloped membranes between his fingers, as if he were some decadent amphibious being that had evolved there, in the dark, pouring beer and listening to blather, in this place where it seemed to Lopez that you could fuck under the tables and on the couches around the stage, spend all night in a whore's embrace, lose yourself, and fall asleep.

While he was trying to swallow his beer, which was annoyingly fizzy, a whore came up to him. She was pretty, pale, and small; her eyes sparkled in the smoky dissolute shadow. She carried with her an idea of distant purity—the idea of a place, perhaps, a mountain village where she was born. Lopez smiled. The whore smiled, too. Her name was Claudine. She didn't feel like talking about herself. Did he feel like sex?

You can enter her without a condom and stop thinking about losing yourself, feel with all your skin the resistance of her unmoistened walls, and observe at the same time the furrowed face that mimics pleasure. You can push, in spasms, with a sense of how vain all this is, the construction of a false self, the fiction of yourself that starts from the big toes and pushes upward. Her small body stiffened with every pulse; she was like wrapping paper that rustles when you fold it, an undocile docility. She was a small obdurate needle's eye, impossible to get the coarse frayed thread through, coat it with saliva so that it will go in, and it doesn't. You push as far as you can, until, for a moment, you're rubbing the tip against her cervix painfully, and for a second she allows the pain to crease her face with a truth she wasn't capable of before. She murmurs words in a language familiar but unknown to you. And you push, push until in this act of advance and retreat everything is forgotten, because you know the vague scent of tin, at the end, when suddenly you reenter the world and the world reenters you, in its livid presence. You push, push and you come. The dull mechanical pain of it immobilizes you and leaves her exhausted and dry, without color, and the flow of saliva that should fall from your lips to hers doesn't, because for a long time now every form of love has been forbidden to you.

At the end, Claudine the whore, in her Inspector Clouseau Italian, asked what woman he was thinking of when he made love. Lopez didn't answer. He lighted a new joint, and they smoked together in silence on the unmade bed that stank of dust and perhaps the sweat of others, in the room above the ceiling of the night.

When he came out, the wind whipped him. The streetwalker with the blond curls was still there, chattering and strident, encouraging possible customers and haranguing the passersby in various languages. He went back into the hotel. No fax from Calimani. He took the key, said good night to the porter, went up the stairs—his steps muffled by a woolly red carpet that was too thick—opened the door of the room, and sank into the bed.

He woke at quarter to seven. He didn't remember his dreams. He could say only that he had been, in some way, in a warm absence of thought. No nightmare. He was as tired as if he had barely slept an hour. The printout of the files from Clemenceau's hard drive had arrived when he went down to breakfast; a squad car had dropped it off before seven. They brought him the sealed parcel. He sat down in the dining room, apart from a couple who were talking in low voices as they ate. The technicians had worked all night. They reported that the computer had a prehistoric antivirus scan and no passwords or protections. They had had to work to reconstruct the online routes of Clemenceau's Web navigations. Since the e-mail box saved all mail—spam, requests to join Internet clubs, short messages to relatives, all of no interest—the technicians had suspected that Clemenceau's important correspondence was via mail with access through the Web. They had tried to trace it by decoding the cache memory, entering the server of Clemenceau's provider to look for traces of the routes of his IP. They had tried the more well-known Web mail servers—iName, Hotmail, Yahoo. No results. It was a desperate attempt. Clemenceau could have deleted the entire contents of his mailbox. The police would have needed a warrant to search the backups of millions of users. The owners could refuse to open the servers, citing privacy rules.

In the end, the technicians had succeeded. They had looked *outside* his computer, since *inside* there was nothing. They had searched in the most banal way you could search—by asking. They had submitted various queries to the search engines: Clemenceau, Georges; Kissinger; Science Religion. And also Ishmael, obviously. The result had turned up late in the night, in response to the query "I. + Georges." It had been an invaluable guess. The search engine had responded. Lopez had before him the printout of the result. A Web page satisfied the search criteria. It was posted on a Web mail server: Wanadoo.fr. Obviously, the page was no longer there. The search engine had somehow intercepted the text, breaching the server's defensive firewall. From the engine's response, they had figured out the first lines of the e-mail Clemenceau had received. It was in English:

Dear Georges, that's ok for I. in Paris as we've been working for. You just have to provide to the last duties in Hamburg and then . . .

The technicians of the Paris police had entered the servers of Wanadoo.fr. Clemenceau's mail account was "lewis." The password was "jesus." They had been able to recover three e-mails; one was from Bob. The address corresponded; it was the Bob of the e-mail the Americans had given to Santovito, the only bit of evidence of Ishmael that up to now had been available. The technicians couldn't make sense of it.

From: bob@liebernet.de
Date: February 10, 2001
To: lewis@wanadoo.fr
Subject: Hamburg

Georges,

All ok for I. in Paris, following the plans. After your final obligations in Hamburg, go ahead. The boys expect you the 15th. The appointment is in the Bahnhof, in the bar of last week's mail. The arrangements on K. remain unchanged. Rebecka will also be there and another person from the Swedish group. The great American oak will be felled, it's certain now.

Let me know on your return.

Remember that we're working together for the glory of Ishmael. You, too: glory in Ishmael.

Yours
Bob

From: lewis@wanadoo.fr
Date: February 11, 2001
To: bob@liebernet.de
Subject: Re: Hamburg

Bob, the tickets arrived. So, everything ok.
Glory to I.
Georges

From: lewis@wanadoo.fr
Date: February 11, 2001
To: bob@liebernet.de
Subject: All O.K.

Bob, I didn't write you tonight because I was distraught. Thank the whole group for their trust. There was no problem. The documents are perfect. If the will of Ishmael is done, we should see each other in Stockholm 3/25. I will wait there for you. You in the meantime say hello from me to the fine boys in Hamburg, who worked really well.

Glory to I.
Georges
PS Rebecka is perfect for the central role!!! Really beautiful!!!

Lopez was starting to decipher the strategy. Clemenceau had relied on others in the church of Ishmael, people in Hamburg and Stockholm. No name from Italy had yet turned up. Kissinger was supposed to be killed in Paris. The great American oak was to fall and would fall: "It's certain." But why? Who was Ishmael to arrange an attempt on Kissinger? Why, in fact, Kissinger? A man out of power, and not even of the highest rank, not a president but his counselor. Clemenceau really had gone to Hamburg (Lopez reached instinctively for the two plane tickets removed from the apartment in Raspail; they were still there). And in Milan? Would Ishmael try to kill Kissinger in Milan, too? At Cernobbio? There was no trace of a link between Ishmael and the Italian group. But then what group? There wasn't a single fact to start from. There was only one link: the bruises. The bruises on Clemenceau's battered body and the bruises on the corpse of Via Padova. Rites, maybe. In the United States, the raid that had broken up Ishmael's group occurred during a kind of sadomasochistic ceremony. In France, an identical rite had occurred, at its center a child. Kissinger, pedophiles, assassination attempts, churches: it was *too much*; there were too many elements, too many dates, too many crimes, too many perspectives, too many cities, too many mysteries set one inside the other inside the other.

He reread the e-mail. *Rebecka is perfect for the central role.* What role? Lopez whispered, "Fuck." He went up to the room. He had time to smoke a joint, and he did. Two hours later, he was at the airport.

From the plane he observed angelic layers of clouds, and told himself he ought to think something profound, but he couldn't, and he was still bitter as—squashed in his seat, his gaze on the smudged, scratched double plastic of the window—he descended toward Milan Linate.

Milan
October 27, 1962
17:40

Montorsi could hardly believe it. While Fogliese was rattling off names, dates, and places, he felt that he was in the very heart of the complicated mechanism of a chain of intuitions.

The rumor had come from contacts in the Swedish intelligence services. Fogliese had an ex-wife who was Swedish. He had met friends of hers in Stockholm and had remained on good terms with them. Every so often they passed him secret information on persons related to the Italian intelligence services. A journalist has to work that way, Fogliese said—has to have contacts outside Italy to understand what is happening inside Italy. He had recently got new information from his Swedish friends. The international situation was worsening. The Cuban crisis proved it. However, the game with the Soviets was being played, above all, in Europe—also, and above all, in Italy, with the PCI, the Italian Communist Party, which had the largest membership of all the Communist parties in Europe; and with the most powerful man in Italy, Enrico Mattei, who commuted between the interests of the U.S.A. and those of the U.S.S.R. The Americans would not only install an impressive battery of agents in Italy. They would not only set up offices. They would not only establish coordination with the military bases. *They were ready to start developing a form of civil enlistment*. It would be something like a religion, from what Fogliese had gleaned in his research and from further conversation with his Swedish friends. A lay religion. A sect, in short. It would keep files on the Italian members, would draw up reports on their friends and acquaintances. It would gather evidence about every rumor, every action that came to its knowledge. The group would be transplanted completely into Italy, far from Vatican circles. At first it would merely provide information to the

Americans; it would establish a beachhead, operating in the territory, as an organization above every suspicion. In a second phase, this association, having grown larger, could easily become a lobbying group, influencing political processes, exerting pressure at a high level. It had all been worked out. The contacts in Stockholm had revealed to Fogliese that the sect's forms and rituals had been decided, that the Americans were ready to fish in the sea of preachers they had at home. There were substantial funds to devote to the operation. They had chosen the men.

"What men?" Montorsi asked.

"The man, actually."

"The one to be at the center of the group?"

"The cult figure," Fogliese said.

"I suppose I couldn't find out anything about this figure. The name . . ." Montorsi said.

"The name?"

"The name," Montorsi said again.

"Ishmael?"

"Ishmael, exactly."

The Americans. Mattei.

The Americans. Ishmael.

The child under the plaque at Giuriati. Mattei *in front of* the plaque at Giuriati.

"What do you think about this Giuriati business?" Montorsi asked.

The journalist shifted onto his other buttock, recrossed his legs. "There are two elements of interest. I would start with them."

"Which elements do you mean?"

"Well, the first is the plaque, obviously. If someone murders a child—I mean if a person is a maniac, the first thing he does is try to hide the body, right? If you hide the body, you hide the crime, unless the child was kidnapped, or, I don't know, its disappearance has been reported. But there has been no public report of a missing child?"

"No, I've checked," Montorsi said. "Though the man in charge at Vice, who knows more than I do, says that there is a ring of *lovers* of children, probably a high-level ring that the police wouldn't touch."

"There have always been such things. But to leave the body

there, in plain sight, next to a plaque, means taking a risk. You can be seen. For better or worse, it's a public place. And besides, you know it will be found soon. How many hours between the death and the discovery?"

"Not many. Very few."

Fogliese was thoughtful. "Exactly. I see it as a warning. I don't know—a rite, or a signal."

"That's somewhat the idea I have myself. So there must be a connection with the plaque."

"Yes. Otherwise, what meaning would it have? How do you figure out the meaning of a gesture like that?"

Montorsi furrowed his brow. "But it means something to someone who knows, in effect, what link there is between the child and the plaque, right?"

"But whoever put it there knows that first of all the police are going to find it. Either he's giving a sign to someone in the police or he hopes it becomes known—that it gets in the papers, right?"

Again Montorsi was uncomfortable. "We have to work with what we have—the information on the partisans and the plaque, which is practically nothing. The cards on the partisans are missing. Fogliese, you can be really helpful. You can move, whereas I—"

"Look, the second fact that to me seems relevant is this: They took the case away from you. To me it seems that they took it away because you didn't let it go."

"It depends. It's not the first time that they've taken an investigation away from me."

"Yes, but if they took it away, it means that someone understood the warning—or the meaning of the gesture."

"Someone at Headquarters?"

"If my premise is correct and they've taken the case away from you, let's say to bury it—well, it means that someone in the police, above you, understood that certain things shouldn't be touched."

Montorsi was quiet. "We have so little. The names of the partisans. The dates. And, at most, a photograph of when the plaque was dedicated . . ."

"The photograph of Mattei and the others."

"I don't even know that Mattei was a partisan."

"Yes. He was in the leadership of the Corps of the Volunteers of Liberty."

"Which is?"

"The white partisans, the Catholics. There were three groups fighting the Fascists. On one side were the Communists. On the other was the Action Party, the lay people, republicans. On a third side, closing the triangle, were the Catholics. Mattei was among the elite of the white partisans' leadership." Fogliese frowned. "It's strange, though: Pajetta and Longo, who are Communists, and also the president of ANPI, an association of red partisans, together with Enrico Mattei. If it's all right, I'll start my investigation here."

"In the meantime I'm going to talk to Arle at Forensics."

"When?"

"Tomorrow."

"Then I'll try to track down some details on the execution."

"Yes, let's try. Test the ground," Montorsi said.

"It may lead nowhere."

"In that case, we will have tried. Certainly we won't have done any harm." Montorsi shrugged.

Fogliese leaned forward, eager. "Even if we find nothing, you'll give me the news of the child first, right?"

"Meaning?"

"Meaning that if you know they're going to hold a press conference, you'll warn me?"

"So you'll scoop the others? You're a vulture, Fogliese." Montorsi looked him in the eye, but kindly, in spite of the fact that the journalist was several years older than he. Fogliese wasn't a vulture. It was the athletics of indifference called journalism.

Fogliese looked at him intently. "I'll tell you something else, Montorsi. I want to move to *Il Giorno*. Anything that helps to get me out of this ossuary is welcome."

"To *Il Giorno*?"

"To *Il Giorno*."

"To Mattei."

"To Mattei."

Suddenly something changed in the stale air of the vast circular hall. It was a quiver, an increasing vibration. Even the spiraling ramps and the office platforms seemed to shake. The voices lowered. All the faces, surprised, agitated, turned to the center of the great space. In the arena, an immense crowd was filling the ramps. Then Montorsi heard a mute noise, a noise without noise. The air compressed, then expanded, in a warm breath. Something dark and radiant seemed to have exploded in the immense space, seemed to break it into two semicircles. Like a landslide in time, like a dangerous radiation suffusing everything and everyone. Then, slowly, the elevator cage emerged and a figure, stiff and straight inside it, ascended slowly from the depths and came to light at the center of the hall. It was the Editor. He was in a dark suit, his face like wax, his eyes feverish, staring at a point in the direction of Montorsi and Fogliese, but behind them, in an infinite distance beyond the circle of the walls. The door opened. Wavering, like someone dying, the Editor took a few steps amid the dozens of mute white bodies that crowded the room. There was a second landslide in the air, smaller, perceptible around the figure of the Editor. He spoke softly, his mouth trembling, while like a smooth heavy egg the News came from his lips, repeated and echoing out from the center to the walls, getting lost and growing softer, and then intensifying again, first half a syllable, "de-," and then, repeated at different levels, it became distorted, "da-," "d" almost, and finally silence.

He said: "He's dead. He's dead. They have killed Enrico Mattei."

A few minutes afterward, Montorsi and Fogliese had the news wire in their hands.

> Dispatch ANSA. October 27, 1962. 19:10.
> MATTEI PLANE CRASHES
> Milan—After final radio contact with the control tower at Linate at 18:57:10, the executive jet known as I-SNAP, with Enrico Mattei, president of ENI, on board, did not confirm signals to begin landing procedures. From investigations now under way it appears that the plane went down in the hamlet of Albaredo, in the town of Bascape, in the province of Pavia. There are no survivors. On board the flight, along with Mattei, were the pilot, Irnerio Bertuzzi, and an American reporter, William Francis McHale.

They read it. It was already infinitely too late.

Enrico Mattei

Sky above the hamlet of Bascapé (Pavia)
October 27, 1962
18:55

The Master of Italy looked at the Moon. He was the Italian closest to the Moon, at that moment, six thousand feet above Milan the Fastidious, with the swamps and all the rest around it, and crowned by the vaporous plain of the Po. The Moon was as pale as Italy; the clouds were great continents of tar under the plane, which was about to start its descent to Milan the Reticent. Great masses of air, convulsive as powerful ideas, floated under the belly of Enrico Mattei's jet, the volumes of air injured by this white lance that so swiftly left behind the noise and the past, ready to sink into the chest of Milan the Impure.

The impassive Moon grew pale, from mile to mile, observed as from the tip of the pendulum one observes the center. It was a spherical machine moved by obscure forces, by mechanical operations that raised the tides, determined the menstrual cycle, threw the revolving planet off balance. These had always fascinated him, and in them he projected what was impossible to project on the bewildered earth. Here he had to take care of empires. Great powers. He had to cover and probe the entire surface of the earth. From the planet's depressions he had to figure out whether oil was concealed in boiling depths, in whirlpools hidden from sight, in subterranean convulsions. He had to understand, seize, fight. He had to taste the grass, examine the white veins in every stem, in the shadow where the hill spreads into the plain. The earth at times was rich, at other times sandy and immune to suspicion. Nature gave him both obstacles and deliverance.

With his jet he plowed above all the hopes of a people. The nonexistent Italian people waited to give him a mandate to probe, sniffing the mineral waves of the continent to find where the oil was, like a desperate dog with its nose to the ground. And he,

Enrico Mattei, had found it. If he didn't find it, he invented it. First, setting up machinery shiny as black coral, he drilled in the tropical sun far from his people. He had made deals in Africa, Asia, Australia. He had been face to face with the Powerful, without mocking them and without fearing them. His fearlessness was the most hostile of all attitudes—the one that the Powerful do not tolerate.

He smiled at the impoverished yet conquering and archaic aspect of his land.

He moved his back away from the seat. It was sweaty. His sweat was dripping toward Milan the Mysterious. They were almost there.

If he was asked who Kennedy was, he answered: A doll who commands children. If he was asked about Khrushchev, he answered: An eater of onions whom Marx did not foresee. If he was asked who Castro was, he answered: A peasant like me, except for the cigar.

What did he think of Communism? That it was better not to think. What did he think of Europe? That these were decisive times, that for the moment Europe didn't exist. What did he think of Cuba? That it was a pawn ready to redeem the queen.

If he was asked who de Gaulle was, he answered: A friend.

What did he think of America? America was an idea. The Americans do not exist. He had said it and said it again. At one conference, in the sticky heat (in a toilet before speaking he had smelled the sweat through the armpits of his shirt), he had said, "America, I know what it's doing. America doesn't exist. You have understood perfectly. All you journalists, go on, write it down. According to Enrico Mattei, America does not exist. Does not ex-ist. America is an experiment. The experiment of America is to replace man. With what? With the American. The American is not a man; he is an American. He is something more and something less than a man. He is faithful, and in this he is something more than a man. He is faithful because he is in the dark about everything. Tell that fact to the American, and tell it to the bosses of your papers, my dear journalist friends, those of your bosses who are Americans. But the American is something less than a man, in that he is *too* faithful. Being ignorant, he neither acts nor suffers. I know, I know very well what this continental experiment that is America will lead to. It will lead to the replacement of man by the American. Well, this, gentlemen, is called genocide. It may be silent, it may be a mental genocide. I admit that. But it is an infamous plan, one that Enrico Mattei—and that means Italy—will oppose now and forever."

He looked around. They were all stunned. "You see, I'm well acquainted with power. Everyone knows Kwame Nkrumah, the father of Ghana. No one knows, however, the name of the president of Nippon Steel, which produces more steel than Italy and France put together."

He went on, "The value of humor is not familiar to me. Learn to recognize the expression on my face. A man like me who talks at a meeting like this can be involuntarily amusing to you, on the condition that he is also embarrassing. I want to tell you a story, a story that I heard as a child. I was born poor, as you well know." The Americans present at the conference, the journalists and the people from the Seven Sisters of oil, became uncomfortable. "This is the story. There is a knight who takes an oath. His hundred friends have betrayed and abandoned him, and his life is now meaningless. But he takes an oath. He will kill the hundred friends who have betrayed him. This gives him meaning, and he sets off. He kills ninety-nine of his traitorous friends. Then he falls into an ambush and dies. But on his skull, dried out by the sun, a man will stumble. Pay attention—it will be the hundredth traitorous friend who, stumbling, will die. Imagine who could be the knight and who the hundredth traitor.

"I, facing the powerful, am a wetched thing, and with me Italy, too, is a wretched thing. By Italy I mean Europe. Yes, a wretched thing. It is a piece of wood or, if you like, a skull. But I say pay attention to that skull: He who stumbles on it dies.

"I am sure of what I'm saying, since I have no desire to shock you, gentlemen. If someone asked me why I do what I do, I would answer with another story. I'm not getting rich, dear journalists. In spite of the stories that your American bosses make you write, I'm telling you that Enrico Mattei has not put in his pocket a single lira. Here's the story. Ten local wise men have gathered around a table in a village tavern. With them is also a stranger, someone they have never seen, who is wearing a dirty shirt that was once white. The wise men are discussing what they desire most in the world. One says, A good husband for my daughter. Another, A luxurious house. Another, A mountain of gold and lands, vast lands. When each of the ten wise men has expressed a desire, they turn to the stranger, and ask him what he desires most in the world. And he says that he would like to be a powerful, venerated king, whose enemies gather at the borders of his kingdom and invade it, and every resistance to them is vain, and they arrive at the royal palace, and he, the king, is awakened at night and, forced to flee, has just time to grab a white shirt and climb on his horse, spur it on, and get safely out of his kingdom, and he becomes a stranger in an unknown land, and the horse, exhausted, dies, and he takes shelter in a tavern like this one in which people are discussing what they desire most. The wise men, puzzled, ask him what sort of desire this is and what he would get from such a desire. A shirt, is his answer."

The plane flew on, lost in a nocturnal sky. Vigilance is all. Everything dries up, loses sap. Who knows if there is oil on the Moon? If there were oil, he would go and get it even there. He is the Master of Italy. He is because he is the only Italian who exists, this Italian plowing the sky. Man will not live long here on Earth. He will emigrate, but not to the Moon. The Americans have prepared the perfect double of man: a man who is correct, a man who corrects nature, who cures his own illnesses, who is suspended in time. But time doesn't exist. Space and time are threads that get entangled in one another; they are fossils of the mind. Not even the mind exists. Something beyond the mind exists.

Italy is this something beyond the mind. It has a sweet taste; it is a calm and luminous shadow. It is like sleep without dreaming. We know we are there, but we are not there, in any respect. Italy is this something beyond body and mind, and the war Mattei is waging is for the salvation of this shadow, of bodies that believe they are bodies. America is an arid and defeated kingdom, which believes in time and space and doesn't grant itself the least faith and hence will not survive. Burned, deprived of sap, desiccated, it will be dust because it is already dust, and its might will end in an immense, grotesque fall. Man must be saved, for man is ready to become an American and the American is ready to annihilate himself. Italy is the idea of salvation between man and America.

His eyes were shining. In his pupils the silver gray sphere of the Moon was reflected, every single crater and dry depression, every question and every woman, every silvery gray smile of a woman.

A telegram had been sent to the airport in Catania.

Body of child found in Milan. This morning. Giuriati field. Near monument to the Resistance.

Then his information was correct. He would call the chief of police, the next day. He knew that Ishmael would begin to work in Italy, too. He had expected it daily. He knew that Ishmael was ready to conspire against him. He was ready to publish the dossiers.

The pilot radioed Linate. It was 18:57:10. The executive jet was designated I-SNAP. It was a twin-engine jet made in France, Morane-Saulnier MS 760-B, the ninetieth of the series Paris II, property of SNAM. It had been registered after testing on November 10, 1961, with a legend in which "I" stood for Italy, "SNA" for SNAM, and "P" for president. By now it had logged 279 hours of flight and 300 landings. It had had a checkup on June 17, 1962, after 150 hours of flight, and another checkup on September 29, after 229 hours of flight. The meteorological bulletin from Linate at 18:25 indicated calm winds, visibility 1,000 meters, rain 8/8, layers of cloud at 150 meters, temperature 10°C, atmospheric pressure 1015. On board, in addition to Enrico Mattei, were the American reporter for *Time* and *Life*, William Francis McHale, and the pilot, Irnerio Bertuzzi. Bertuzzi had experience in the Royal Air Force, in the air force of the Italian Social Republic, and in private airlines. He had had 11,260 hours of flight, of which 600 were in planes of the same model as I-SNAP. William Francis McHale had three children.

The Moon was reflected in the pupils of the president. If he had been asked who was Enrico Mattei, he would have answered, Italy.

The Moon moved in the pupils as the pupils moved. Then the Moon went out. Flames advanced on the pupils and dissolved them. The explosion had occurred.

* * *

There was a thud, a long sequence of very slow short actions. He smiled as if saying a gentle farewell. He entered the dark, luminous, very sweet substance that he had thought was Italy. His head split, and for an instant he saw flowers blooming, and all was fragrance. The heat died down, a gust billowed, and then came the numinous cold of clouds in tumult, penetrating as an arm was lost, and the hand of the arm, and the trunk burned up as it split. Half of the head was sucked down, and there rose a feeling of regret, that the hundredth traitor would not find the skull whole, and then the serene security of knowing that the traitor would stumble and die anyway, and the other half of the head continued to fall, straight down, and he saw the dark Pavian countryside, soaked in heavy rain, coming close, he saw the flocks of birds and thought *Italy Italy Italy Italy*, until he saw outside himself, and the sky suddenly began to smile as he was smiling, a wide grin that pierced time, emerging from forgotten eras of the past.

3

ITALY, EUROPE

Milan
March 24, 2001
10:20

Lopez had telephoned Calimani from Charles de Gaulle airport. Calimani was waiting for him at Linate. Forensics had quickly taken care of the unusual request—the photograph of a cadaver, with the eyes open, so that it would look like an I.D. photo, as if the man were alive. Calimani had it with him. They drove into the city on Viale Forlanini, and Lopez examined the dead man's myopic gaze, the gray shadow of the hairline, the hair tangled by the cold of preservation. The two full, translucent pupils, inanimate, were ready to dissolve as the body decomposed.

Calimani informed him that the police had no infiltrators in the Church of Science Religion. It was something for the intelligence services, not the police. They sped along the empty avenue, which was curved like a back and bathed in rippled, melting frost. Serrault, too, had said that Ishmael was a matter for the intelligence services. Lopez asked where the main headquarters of Science Religion was. It was right off Forlanini, in Via Abetone. But the Church was about to move to Scalo Garibaldi.

They detoured to the Science Religion building before returning to Headquarters.

It was near the labyrinth of housing projects at Calvairate, their thick walls crumbling, the paint flaking in pieces like enormous eyebrows frowning over the filthy streets. Pitted, broken asphalt. A line of old people huddled in front of the shadowed entrance to a clinic. In the doorway of a café, men in dark jackets drowned their talk in the faded wool of their scarves. A smog-encrusted tram creaked along the Viale Molise service road. Lopez saw Moroccans looking out from behind the steamed-up windows.

Calimani made a U-turn on the broad, desolate avenue. The

surface was icy, and the tires skidded. He turned onto a narrow street. On the right was a squalid neighborhood market, on the left a depot belonging to the Transportation Department, and at the end of the street the slaughterhouse. Calimani stopped the car and they got out, sniffing the ferrous odor of coagulated animal blood in the freezing wet air. There was no traffic. In the distance, the bellows of dying steers came from the slaughterhouse, its smooth brick walls stained with iridescent spray paint in a random design.

Through an unlocked metal door they entered a courtyard. Facing them, a few steps up, was the headquarters of the Church of Science Religion.

It was like entering another era, immune from sorrow, sunk in secrecy. Men and women crossed a large lobby warmed by a soft light that fell onto a lens-shaped counter, where a freckled blond girl sat reading a book. Lopez looked at the church propaganda posters, photographs taken in anonymous places, places that could be Copenhagen or Los Angeles, of events flooded with happy people smiling effortfully. In one gigantic image, a man and woman sat on either side of a small desk, the woman smiling and touching her hair, the man smiling and maneuvering little knobs on a machine. Behind the girl at the counter, an immense poster showed a crowd of people dressed like officers in some military organization, raising their arms on a stage, and you could guess at the heads and hands of spectators below the stage, applauding, in a kaleidoscope of colored lights. In a photograph to the right of the counter was the crumpled, pachydermic face of the Founder; it had been given a sepia tone that obscured the wrinkles.

Calimani did the talking. He introduced himself, he introduced Lopez, he took out his police badge. He asked for the person in charge. The girl was unruffled. In a narrow doorway next to the poster of the people in uniform, a thin man appeared, leaning against the jamb, and stood looking at them while the girl telephoned to find a person in charge.

Beneath the counter was a curved display window exhibiting all the works of the founder, Lewis. Little piles of leaflets on the counter kept visitors from leaning on it. Lopez examined the leaflets, staring at the covers in order to observe the man who was observing them.

After a few minutes the girl said that the director was in the office and would be right down. The thin man went back inside the room, closing the door behind him.

The director was a tall, large man, his massive head embedded in a helmet of dark hair, his gaze oblique and shadowy, his eyebrows too thick. His handshake was overconfident, like a pincer. He greeted them coolly and led them up a service stairway to his office on the second floor.

Again Calimani did the talking. Lopez watched the director's reactions. Calimani told about finding the corpse on Via Padova. He didn't explain why they suspected the victim was a former member of Science Religion. He lingered over the autopsy report's description of the condition of the body. The man behind the desk blinked his eyelids in a calm and calculated rhythm. Lopez remained silent. He met the other man's gaze a couple of times. Then Calimani took out the photograph of the corpse taken by Forensics. The Science Religion man looked at it carefully, then let a few seconds pass before twisting his mouth in a grimace of indifference. He said he had never seen him. Calimani asked him to look more carefully. The man reexamined the picture and shook his head. Calimani asked if there were records of people who had left the Science Religion organization. The man said yes, there was a database, but that because of privacy laws he couldn't show it to them, unless the police had a warrant. Did they have a warrant? Calimani admitted that they didn't.

In a hard, dry voice, Lopez interrupted. "Who is Ishmael?"

The man turned to Lopez. For an instant his gaze penetrated to the depths of Lopez's. There was a ritual pause. "What is the last name of this Ishmael?" he asked.

They sat in silence for a few moments more. Then Lopez got up. Calimani shook hands with the man, and they went out.

They went down the service stairs toward the lobby. "What do you think?" Calimani asked. Lopez said nothing. When they arrived at the counter in the lobby, Lopez whispered to Calimani, "Wait here for me."

He went back up the stairs. The walls of the stairwell were peeling, blue. He opened the door onto the hallway where the director's office was. He looked around, right and left: no one. He stopped in front of the door to the man's office.

He entered without knocking. The man was on the telephone,

dialing a number. His mouth dropped open, and he had barely time to say "What—"

Lopez ran his open hand across the desktop, sending papers, photographs, even the telephone to the floor. The man got up in a rage. He was much taller than Lopez. Lopez shoved the desk against him and, as he doubled over it, pulled the desk forward. Immediately he was behind the man, who was still doubled over, and gave him a kick in the knee joint. The man fell.

Lopez said nothing. The man was on the floor hugging his knee and groaning. The groans became weaker. Lopez leaned over and grabbed him by the hair. "Now give me the file for the man on Via Padova, you piece of shit. If you make any goddam trouble you had better watch out every time you leave here, because I'll be back and I'll kill you, you piece of shit. I'll kill you, get it? I will come myself and kill you. Now get up and give me this shit file. Understand?"

The man groaned and made no sign of moving. Lopez yanked on his hair. "Do you understand or not, shithead?"

The man nodded. Lopez released his grip. A lock of hair was stuck to the sweaty palm of his hand.

When Lopez went down to the lobby, a quarter of an hour later, he had the identification card of the corpse on Via Padova. Calimani watched him leave the Science Religion headquarters and followed him. They came out across from the slaughterhouse, in front of the housing projects of Calvairate.

His name was Michele Terzani, and he was born in 1954. A former member of the New Order, he had been sentenced twice, in the late seventies. Nothing serious—he had only shown hospitality to more important bosses of the movement. In jail he had done little. In the mid-eighties, he had joined Science Religion. The card gave no information about relatives interested in him; no one had complained on his behalf about the money he had wasted supporting the programs of the church. He had traveled to Copenhagen, Paris, and Miami for Science Religion. Ten years after he entered he had left, threatening lawsuits and major revelations to the press. On the card appeared the note "Hostile." Obviously, he had not followed up on the threats. But Science Religion had kept an eye on him. From what Lopez knew, groups of former members seemed *very* aggressive toward the mother church, and Science Religion evidently monitored the activities of those who went against it. Paulette Rowling—the target of Operation Freakout described in the report Santovito had gotten from American intelligence—was "hostile." Staying vigilant against possible scandals, recovering lost sheep, making secret agents of its own apostles—these were the ancient tactics that every church had adopted in its confrontation with the world. The good old imprint of God on the secular earth.

Lopez checked to see if the card made any references to the Ishmael group. None. Then he went to the basic information. Address: Via San Galdino 15. He looked at the map of the city while Calimani started the car. The street was in the neighborhood of the Cimitero Monumentale, off Piazza Diocleziano. They turned on the siren, and Lopez asked for a backup patrol, barely containing his excitement that, within just a day of finding the body, they were about to enter the apartment of the man of Via Padova.

They followed the wide curve of the parabola made by the Cimitero Monumentale's striped marble walls, the tops of grave monuments and the tips of cypresses barely sticking up above the buttresses. It was cold here, the metallic, magnetic cold of the earth that covers the dead. The flower sellers' kiosks were deserted. The cemetery must be nearly empty of visitors. The long smooth wall to the right of the entrance followed the avenue that curved toward Piazza Diocleziano. A tram passed, slow and long, orange, splaying the thick tufts of dry grass growing between the tracks. The sky had expanded; there were no houses to crowd it. The siren cut the silence. Low, uniform purple clouds broke up near the horizon, cut by the profile of buildings that rapidly began to appear as they sped toward Via Cenisio. Calimani blocked the next intersection racing through the red light. The tires squealed as the car took the broad semicircle of Piazza Diocleziano. He turned onto the narrow, dark, tree-lined street that went off at the far right. It was Via San Galdino. At No. 15 a squad car was already waiting.

Michele Terzani's apartment was on the third floor. It took the police officers ten minutes to force the lock. They entered into darkness and an almost total absence of air, a suspension of dust in which they were barely able to breathe. Calimani raised the shutter of the window in the first room and opened it, and the sharp air rushed in. It was a more than decent apartment: two rooms, a lot of books, the bath orderly. In the bedroom, above the headboard, Lopez gazed at a white ribbon fastened with three small nails to the wall. Tiny characters in black ink composed the legend ISHMAEL IS GREAT. It was identical to the one hanging over Clemenceau's bed. He felt a clammy, nervous burst of stale euphoria.

There was no computer in Terzani's apartment, no possibility of tracing mail. The two backup agents from the patrol car were searching the closet, but they didn't know what to look for. The temperature was dropping; from the open window came a rude cold. Lopez opened the kitchen drawers. He looked for photographs and didn't find them. In the bedroom he inspected the dresser. In the bathroom he opened the medicine chest. On a small shelf next to the mirror over the sink he noted an array of antidepressants. Then he went back to the bedroom, ripped off the sheets, pulled off the mattress, and looked under the box spring. Under the bed was a pack of magazines, tied up in a plastic sack. He tore it open. They were porn magazines. Sadomasochistic magazines. Some pages were missing. In others, photographs had been cut out. They were the same magazines Lopez had found with Serrault at Clemenceau's house. The same cutouts, the same missing pages. Lopez thought about what he knew of the rites of Ishmael. Outside Paris and in Detroit, the police had surprised Ishmael's faithful during a sadomasochist rite. At the center, always, there was a child.

He leafed through one of the magazines, passing by the cutout pages indifferently. Two papers fell to the floor. He bent over to pick them up and was startled. They were not markers. They were two airplane tickets. A Milan–Hamburg round trip, leaving February 15 and returning the sixteenth. From his jacket pocket he took out the tickets he had found in Clemenceau's apartment: Paris–Hamburg and return, February 15. The places coincided. The dates coincided. On February 15, Ishmael's faithful had gathered. He compared the magazines' glossy images of sadomasochism: women with breasts reddened by whips, men's testicles gripped by pincers, buttocks marked by bruises, wrists raw with rope, enormous dildos and dilated anuses. The marks were exactly like those on the two bodies of Ishmael's followers, the one in Paris and the one in Milan. He was certain. Ishmael had celebrated one of his rites in Hamburg.

He nodded to Calimani. They left. He gave instructions to the officers to seal Terzani's apartment. Time was rushing forward. Cernobbio was approaching. The Americans were right; Ishmael would strike there. He didn't know how or why. *He didn't understand*—emerging from the background was the ordinary face of Henry Kissinger, and for an instant he saw again the specter of La Défense. He didn't understand. But now he knew where to look and what to look for.

Milan
March 23, 2001
19:10

The hard days of sacrifice were arriving. The American, leaving the Engineer's office, collided with the dense crowd flowing in the direction of Corso Buenos Aires, the street of bright lights, half-price watches, and fast-food restaurants thronged with Africans. He let himself be carried by the stream of people, making their uncertain steps between body and body, toward the main stretch of the street, which was even more crowded, obese with traffic. The bars displayed red lanterns. Window plants assented mutely to the chemical wind of the exhaust fumes. He entered a coffee bar, sniffing the warm sugary air, the odor of boiling chocolate, and the silvery traces of lighted cigarettes. He closed the glass door behind him, watching as the complex of people, cars, and windows on the street went silent, a mechanical centaur that unrolled its powerful tail toward Porta Venezia, and the center.

He ordered a coffee. He reflected.

The Engineer was one of the priests of Ishmael in Milan. He had agreed to every request, noted whatever concerns the American had expressed. He nodded, his face thin and oddly withered around his sparse whiskers, his neck appliquéd with a fuzz of fine hair, his eyes sharp behind clean—unnaturally clean—eyeglasses. He was calm, prepared. The American had been afraid of meeting another novice, like the Pakistani the Old Man had killed. With the Pakistani, the American had almost lost his life. The Engineer calmed him. He was a cold man; in certain circumstances he would be ruthless.

He organized the sadomasochist group. The American knew that Ishmael used that group as a channel; the Engineer sent messages, gave instructions for his rites, and informed members when the meetings were to be held. Ishmael had swooped down on the Engineer like the sun falling on an arid land. For years, the Engineer had done Ishmael's work. He was one of the few, in Milan, who were able to advance to a higher level, to *get close to* Ishmael. Ishmael is great. The American would help him make the sacrifice. The Engineer knew it.

He had asked for a child. The Engineer had said simply, "It can be done." The American had responded, "It *has* to be done." The Engineer had nodded. It was complicated. Times were hard. The child was at the center of a rite. An exclusive rite. A rite *extremely* close to Ishmael. The Engineer had understood.

Ishmael's faithful in Milan were to initiate two new members. They would use a child. They would bless it in the name of Ishmael. The gathering would be held outside Milan in an industrial shed, following Ishmael's precise instructions. The Engineer organized the ceremonies personally, disguising them as gatherings of sadomasochists. Ishmael's orders were to *conceal* the rite. The Engineer would reveal the meeting's time and place at the last minute. The American knew the procedures; he agreed to the Engineer's plans, but asked for the coordinates in advance. He had to be very careful. He had told the Engineer about the Old Man and about the mistake made by the Pakistani. The Engineer shook his head. He gave the American a note in code telling him of the time and place of the meeting the following evening. At the end of the ceremony, he would give the child to the American. He was proud that Ishmael had chosen him for the "first matter" of the rite. There wouldn't be any problems. The police didn't know anything about Ishmael. For years the rites in Milan had been held in secure places and there had never been any trouble. The American said goodbye. The Engineer asked if he had all the equipment that he would need for the rite. He said he had it. It was in a bag that he had left in the baggage claim at the station, but this he did not tell the Engineer.

Couples lingered over coffee, and three old women were deep in conversation at a corner table near walls upholstered in worn red velvet. Behind the bar, silent and efficient, the barman organized his work. Outside the café, the traffic of persons and things continued on Corso Buenos Aires, a mute river that the American watched with absorption, the human water that washes away great opportunities. He was irritated.

He would stop by the Central Station. He would pick up the bag. He had to find somewhere secure to sleep. The Old Man worried him. He had picked up the autopsy report on the body of Via Padova. He knew that he hadn't succeeded in killing the American.

He unfolded the note that the Engineer had left him. He deciphered the code in ten minutes. His coffee was almost cold, and the American tasted it in disgust. An abandoned hangar near Pioltello, just outside Milan. At twenty past midnight. There he would retrieve the child who was needed by Ishmael. Then he would have to deliver it. And then he would return. To Cernobbio. In France they had failed. Kissinger was expecting him.

He paid, went out, crossed the crowded Corso, passing through the absurdly polluted gaps between the cars, which were lined up, infinitely, in both directions, heading away from and into the center of the city. He walked to the station, avoiding the addicts who in a mumbled, fragmentary language asked for incomprehensible things. At the baggage claim he retrieved the bag. He listened to the echo of his footsteps on the marble pavement of the station bounce off the cold walls of the empty space. Outside, the darkness was pierced by the reflection of the building's white marble and by an immense cube of ads illuminated by tiny spotlights.

He headed away from the station, toward Piazza della Repubblica, and the center, in search of a safe place to spend the night; he walked along the deserted street, interrupted only by the scattered figures of the addicts, and was swallowed up by the darkness.

Bascapé (Pavia)
October 27, 1962
19:35

Montorsi hurried back to Headquarters, between two rows of tall dark buildings, his mouth secreting a dense white saliva. The rain was starting. It was a little after seven-thirty, according to an opaque clock he saw, its face clouded by water that had seeped into it.

Enrico Mattei was dead.

Under the furious rain, he ran toward the squad car waiting for him at the end of Via Senato. He had arranged it with Omboni directly, telephoning from the human earthquake of frenzy in the *Corriere* editorial arena and its roar of connections and thoughts, with everyone mechanically in motion while the Editor cut through the mob giving directions and orders: "Telephone ANSA," "Find Montanelli, find Montanelli," "Ten pages on Mattei," "The story, the story of his life," "Call the RAI," "Find his relatives, his wife," "If it's not his wife, it's no good," "Someone on the inside, at Metanopoli—I'll call directly for an interview with one of the No. 2s at ENI."

Montorsi and Fogliese had stood there stunned. Mattei was dead. The Editor had said that "they killed him." Montorsi immediately telephoned Headquarters. He had trouble hearing the ring and pressed his ear to the receiver, which hurt. He had asked for anyone from the Detective Squad. Omboni answered. It was hard to hear him.

"It's a mess, Montorsi. . . . Where are you?"

"At the *Corriere.*"

"What the hell are you doing at the *Corriere*? Get here, fast. We're all meeting. . . . Mattei's plane went down. . . . We have to get there."

Montorsi jumped up, Fogliese behind him. Fogliese walked him out.

"Christ," Montorsi muttered.

"Good God—"

"It's a shock. It's . . ."

"It's the end. The end of Italy, I'm telling you." Fogliese shook his head.

"Killed . . ."

"Yes, but you'll see. They'll haul out the nonsense of an accident."

"Yes, but who will believe—" Montorsi began.

"Exactly. But you'll see, you'll see. If I know this country, someone who believes it will appear. And in the end everyone will believe."

"But think about it. A mere accident that gets rid of the Master of Italy. Someone who's stepped on the toes of half the world."

"The richer half is what he's stepped on." Fogliese paused. "Are you going to the crash site? Will everyone on the squad be there?"

"Everyone. Think of it, an investigation like this. They'll tear each other to pieces for jurisdiction. Especially if there's anything suspicious."

Fogliese shook his head.

"Who do you think it was?" Montorsi's words were nearly drowned by the human roar of the *Corriere*.

Fogliese looked at him, slowly lowering his eyelids. It was a calculated gesture, and he kept walking, jerking along. "Who do *you* think it was?"

"The Americans."

"The United States," Fogliese said. "He was too big a pain in the ass to them. Imagine what would happen if the Seven Sisters tolerated a revolution that starts with an Italian. They would lose fifty percent of their oil revenues in the Middle East. They killed him."

"They killed him. This is a big one."

"It's big, yes. Since Mussolini and the end of the war there hasn't been anything this big."

They had left the editorial offices. The roar of the journalists diminished. They were almost running. Montorsi had to meet

Omboni; he was no longer thinking about anything else. He almost jumped when the reporter asked him, "And us, now?"

"What do you want to do?" Montorsi asked. "They'll put me on Mattei. I'll never be able to go on with the child at Giuriati, with a case like this."

"They'll have to have the intelligence services. It's going to be a big mess," Fogliese said.

"What are you thinking you'll do, Fogliese?"

"If you want, I'll go ahead with the case of the child. Among other things . . ."

"You think it has something to do with it?" Montorsi asked.

"The child? With Mattei?"

"Yes. Weren't you talking about a rite, before?"

"A rite practiced by a sect. Yes. But I didn't mean—"

Montorsi had pressed ahead and was in the lobby. Now he turned and said, "Maybe it's only a coincidence, no?" Then he was outside, already lost in the icy driving rain.

Coincidences are made of the same mental substance as time and ideas.

In the car heading for Pavia, where the Master of Italy's plane had gone down, listening to the tires peeling the skin of water off the asphalt while the rain and wind shook the body of the car, Montorsi, Omboni, Revelli, and Montanari—four inspectors from the Detective Squad—followed with their eyes the red taillights of the police car in front of them. The Chief had left ten minutes earlier, and was probably in Bascapé already. The country on either side of the car was a dark gorge. In the damp silence their breath fogged the windshield. The air was suffused with mold and the leather of the seats; they listened to the rustling and thunder in the distance and the windshield wipers swinging left, right. The car in front, which contained four other inspectors, spewed columns of water to the right and the left. Montorsi's skin was livid, and his coat was damp with rain, the water warmed by contact with his cold body. He distinctly felt the wrinkles that creased his fingertips. He began to sweat. Between his nostrils and upper lip the hairs were growing rapidly, nourished by warmth and sweat. The rear window was pearled with water; the engine buzzed like an eardrum. They were cramped, mute. The news of the death had summoned something of the death itself.

Omboni lighted a cigarette. No one said anything.

The car in front put on its turn signal, slowed down.

They turned onto a muddy unpaved road that threaded between the trees. The headlights cut through the thick foliage and suddenly a baffling cupola of bright light emerged and grew larger, without dimensions, as they approached its center.

They got out into mud. Their shoes sank in, to the tops. The mud licked their pant legs. Montorsi felt the viscous cold at his ankles. Omboni threw away the cigarette. They were shadows silhouetted in the cold shining light of headlights. The rain seemed to evaporate in the light. Ahead of him, Montorsi saw flaming pools and smelled the shocking odor of a human grill. In the trees were shreds of fiery material, burning out. A jacket dangled on a branch. There were men running in every direction, black silhouettes fleeing the central blaze, cars in muddy tangles on the dark trampled grass, bloodstains, noise, sirens.

To the right he saw part of a head lying in a puddle, swollen, tumescent, and shiny. The hair had burned and was stuck to the flaps of skin, a blackish blistered substance like hardened tar. Montorsi thought of the mummy. The light hit them, gusts of distant fire evaporated the rainwater. It created a warm, luminous dome, the mark of a civilization coming to the rescue far too late, verifying the signs of an end, of many ends.

They separated.

Immediately, under an old leafy tree, he saw what looked like melting ice. A large piece of the jet's wing lay there, shiny white, plastered with crushed turf. It had hurtled into a clearing that had been enveloped in pristine dark silence before it was disfigured by relics falling from the sky. The sky was reddish, swelling, turbulent. You didn't notice the rain. The trees were burned black arrows launched straight up from the ground. Obscurely men spoke, shouted, ran, crisscrossing, in disordered, convulsive, exhausted movement.

Two smells, almost a stink. Fuel and burned flesh.

A group of reporters had gathered in a circle with three officials from some agency or another. From a distance, Montorsi could see a man speaking, his umbrella wavering a bit, his green farmer's boots sinking into the ground, face made stupid by the cold. It must be a witness. He talked and talked and talked, mumbling in an irksome cadence: ancient Lombard stupidity. Montorsi got closer, edging past the journalists, close enough to hear scraps of phrases. The officials looked at him, without saying a word.

"The sky . . . was red . . . burning like a big bonfire . . . the flames descending all around. . . . The airplane . . . the airplane was burning and the pieces . . . were falling on the fields, in the rain," he said. The reporters bent over their notebooks in the rain.

Farther on was another group. Two reporters were writing intensely as they listened to an old woman. She nodded and pointed at the sky, at the rain, with a pale wrinkled finger. Her staring eyes shone, feverish, wet with rain or tears. Her voice—the same idiot Lombard mumble as the farmer—was firm and dry. She wore a pale green shawl, now soaked with water. Montorsi could make out words and fragments. "In the sky a blaze . . . a burst . . . stars that came down . . . they were like shooting stars . . . little comets." The officials nodded, the reporters wrote.

Montorsi wandered alone among the dark leafy tangles of trees bent by the rain and by the accident. He examined every branch and every meter of ground; he saw blood, burned, fried, solidified. His colleagues, too, were looking closely, with their flashlights, constructing a diagram of the impact.

The blood had become concentrated and brown from the heat of the explosion. Montorsi touched a large spot. It had the consistency of plasticine. His finger left an imprint. He looked at it. The rain made it liquid again. He watched the lumpy stripe release on his skin. He thought about blood.

He pointed his flashlight up, toward the leaves that rustled at the touch of the water. Now it was very cold. The fog rose from the fields toward that thin forest. It illumined the leaves closest to the bloodstains (he had identified five, quite extensive). *Nothing.* On the underside of the leaves there was no trace of blood. The bright flare of intuition exploded in him; it made him shudder.

The first trunk provided no hold. On a second one, he managed to find a grip with one foot, he hoisted himself up, touching a branch with his free hand. *The upper side of the leaves, the one facing the sky, was scarred by pools of blood coagulated by the heat.* He got down and examined a third tree. Again, blood on the upper side of the leaves. He tested the correspondence of the blood on the leaves with all the stains on the ground. On tree after tree, the brilliant cold light of the flashlight bared the bronze bloodstains that had dried in the conflagration. *The blood had fallen like rain, from above.* The plane had been smashed in the air, not on the ground.

Montorsi was about to call the others when he asked himself another question.

He searched for the parts of the plane, one by one. One wing had remained practically intact, splitting two slender trees as it fell (he saw the green wounds in the trunk, the dripping sap), but the other parts were just small pieces of metal, with the paint on them bubbled. He made out the propeller. He looked back at the jacket he had seen earlier, hanging on a branch. The plane couldn't have crashed. It had exploded before it touched the ground. If it had not exploded before the impact, it would have crushed the trees, mowed them down, flattened them. But the trees were intact. There had been an explosion, at a high altitude.

He had before him, desolate and packed with light and words, the scene of an assassination.

Maura Montorsi

Milan
October 27, 1962
21:10

Maura and Luca arrived separately at the Comollis' party. The Comollis lived on Via Illirico, beyond Viale Argonne, on the outskirts of Milan. An inexplicable scent of jasmine, resistant to the rain, flooded the stairs as Maura ascended. A frosted glass window was open onto the stairwell, and from the courtyard came a rustling sound, the quiver of dark plants dripping, made glassy by the rain. Some dry brown putty between the glass and the black wrought-iron frame. The lights of the façade on the opposite side of the courtyard illuminated the landing on which the window opened, and a cold breath carried essences not of Milan: jasmine, and rabbit. A sauce, stewing. Food of the south, Maura thought. Southerners are good cooks. In the darkness she leaned on the banister; it was iron, and warmer than she had imagined, as if someone had touched it just before her. On the third floor she stopped.

She knocked at the first door. Already she heard music and the chirping of chatter. Inside, her school colleagues were talking, drinking. She thought wearily of David. Maura had heard the news on the radio. The airplane of the Master of Italy had crashed. Enrico Mattei had died outside Milan. She imagined that David was there now.

Intense tremors racked her. The afternoon with Luca had canceled them for a short time. She rang the bell.

Fabri Comolli opened the door. They kissed each other. The usual greetings. Fabri's husband peered out of the living room into the hall, leaning on the doorjamb, one hand in his pocket. He touched his glasses. Maura knew that he liked her. She always counted on the seductiveness that her skin radiated. Also her freckles, her blue eyes wide open in an expression of calculated innocence, her pale lips and almost white hair, her slender hands. "You have the hips of a mother," David had said to her. She knew it and liked it, and liked to flirt with that image of herself, the fragrance of desire suppressed. She could launch that image into the world to quench the vacuous fires of her own insecurity, the anxiety that forever devours the day. It was impressive how she managed to detach herself from herself, as she saw how her ingenuous beauty, her small defenseless figure, stirred tenderness to a paroxysm of desire. Others were vanquished by it—she could trust the electric shock she radiated. And yet when she was alone—and she was always alone, alone with herself—that magnetic beauty didn't count. The inner trembling, the impossibility of knowing where the convulsions of her earthquakes came from, debilitated her.

She didn't know what to do about the child. She had thought about it again. She wouldn't speak to the gynecologist. Should she tell Luca? She was thinking that the child would shake her out of the torpor that terrified her.

Fabri's husband shook her hand. The voices from the living room wished to be heard. They vibrated in the stale air and rose. They were talking about the death of Mattei.

She looked into the room for a moment. Luca was there. She trembled. Luca looked at her. She looked at him.

There was Cri, another colleague, in mathematics, and her husband, Luigi, who was stroking his beard. There was Fabio, in philosophy, alone; he wasn't married. And Luisa, philosophy, with her husband. Nino. Maybe his name was Nino.

She said hello to everyone, turned suddenly, headed toward the bathroom.

The pale light was reflected on the shiny white enameled tiles. She looked at herself in the mirror. She ran the water. The tremors increased; they became an uproar, a sandy grinding in her head.

What should she do about the baby? Why had her husband become, day by day, a memory? Ten years earlier, his hands, his skin, his words, but above all his hands had obsessed her. He had bartered the security his presence gave her for unlimited love. Together they had learned that it was first an indecent contract and then an impossible one. In her was some potent vortex that required meaning. Perhaps the meaning would be the child, a life joined completely to hers. She looked at her profoundly blue eyes in the mirror and saw in the depth of the iris a black hole, beyond which it was impossible for her gaze to go. Then it seemed to her she was suffused with a warm gust of love, as if someone from her past had sent her from the future a consoling thought of purest love. As if her life and that of the unknown who loved her from the past and the future were missing a link. As if she had to be reborn to complete the task of being definitively joined.

In the living room, the conversation was warm and pleasant, if disconnected. Talk of Mattei had abated. Luca kept looking at her. They spoke as if they were simply acquaintances. He seemed amused. Maura felt better. The tremors were diminishing. She tried to relax. The gentle jazz in the background slipped into the clear dreamy tranquillity where Luca's voice led her. He looked at her as if he wanted to make love, right there in the midst of everyone.

Luca drove her home. The windshield wipers intersected the water, giving definition to their way. She thought, I'll tell him about the baby. Now. That I'm pregnant. That I don't know what to do. I'll go with him. Now.

She felt herself melt.

She couldn't speak.

He stopped the car and drew near her. He turned toward her. He put a hand behind her neck. He came close to her. He kissed her. For an instant, and only an instant, her trouble disappeared. They kissed for a long time. Then she slid her tongue over his neck. His thin, tapered fingers touched her face, probed it as if noting every freckle. She detached her tongue from him and kept her eyes closed and her hands clinging to his face, feeling the shadow of his beard. They remained like that, a breath apart, each touching the other's face, as if she were a blind woman trying to read him, while he saw the healing future, the two of them bloodstains lost in the night.

Inspector Guido Lopez

Milan
March 24, 2001
11:40

"What do you intend to do?"

Chief Santovito was lighting his most recent cigarette. The ashtray was overflowing with crushed, flattened butts, their filters tar-yellow. Lopez had already rolled and smoked a joint in his office, so he was calm. He had explained the scenario to Santovito, but Santovito didn't understand. He didn't understand what the meeting of the children of Ishmael in Hamburg had to do with the assassination attempt on Kissinger at the Grande Arche. He didn't understand why it was significant that the body of the French assassin bore the same marks of violence as the body of the dead man in Via Padova. What did the former members of Science Religion have to do with all this? What did this Terzani have to do with it? And why were the intelligence services keeping the Detective Squad going on a case—Ishmael, at this point, was a case—that belonged to them? Perhaps they expected the police investigations to fail and planned to blame Santovito and his men. Santovito pinched the cigarette filter, moving it around inside the ocher paper, so that the saliva-coated nicotine reappeared in the already ruined fibers. Yet as the hours passed and Cernobbio approached, he could see—at the center of a frame whose edges he could not make out—the black hole of an attempt on Kissinger, or someone else at the meeting at Villa d'Este, expanding. On the desk were the creased pages of a fax, its ink emitting a poisonous smell. It provided information about the final guests at the Cernobbio summit. Also present, besides the past government leaders, would be the business giants. Agnelli. Prodi. Romiti. Delors. De Benedetti. The directors of Vodaphone.

Santovito asked Lopez yet again to explain the scenario to him. Lopez was unable to lay out a coherent plot or motive. He proceeded from one gleam of light to another, working by rapid intuitions. It was more a *sensation* he had, complex and fragmented yet close to rational. Something continually seemed to escape him. How could he *translate* an instinct, the experience itself, into an array of comprehensible facts? He started again: Clemenceau bruised and then shot; Terzani's identification card at the office of the Church of Science Religion; the sadomasochists' rites in Paris and Detroit; Bob and the men in Hamburg. And Santovito shook his head. There was a moment when Lopez seemed to himself to be speaking mechanically, the words coming from a distance and ejected into the distance, brushing him by chance, with Santovito in a waking trance.

"What do you intend to do?" Santovito asked, interrupting that automatic loop.

"You have to give me carte blanche."

"Haven't I already done that?"

"Yes. Only I need a couple of okays."

Santovito did nothing but sniff his own danger. "Here we all get fired."

"I need a contact in Hamburg, Giacomo. I want to start with this Rebecka. I have to get the authorities in Hamburg to make the connections for me."

"What connections?"

"Connections with the exiles from Science Religion. If the Hamburg police can find this Rebecka, we're on our way. She saw both Clemenceau and Terzani. Both of them went to Hamburg—at a sign from Bob, the one you read about in the Americans' report. I think Hamburg is where they decided the details of the operation. How and when to strike—in Paris at Kissinger, and here in Cernobbio at we don't know who."

"Yes, but we found this Terzani dead before anything happened at Cernobbio."

"You're right. I know, Giacomo, it doesn't add up. But this is what we have. And we have to work with it, right?"

"And then? All you need is the contact with Hamburg?"

"No. I have another trail in mind."

"And that is?"

"The rites. The sadomasochists' rites."

Santovito smiled, discouraged, then shook his head dully. "I leave it to you. We don't have much time left. Get in touch with whoever you want. Here we're all going to get fired."

Lopez got up. As he went out, he said to himself that it wasn't true: He was the only one who would be fired.

He called the Detective Squad in Hamburg himself, speaking in halting English. It took ten minutes to identify a person in charge of investigations who was interested in contact with the Italians. He couldn't understand his name—Wurz or Wunz or Wunzam. Lopez told him about the Paris attempt, avoiding direct mention of Kissinger's name. He spoke at length about Ishmael. He asked if they knew anything about such an organization in Hamburg. In hard, rasping English, the German inspector told Lopez it seemed more a matter for the intelligence services than for the local authorities. He had never heard of Ishmael. Lopez referred to the meeting that the followers of Ishmael had organized in Hamburg and the Hamburg connection confirmed in the report written by the American NSA. There were the tickets to Hamburg found in the apartment of the Paris assassin and in the apartment of the man who had been murdered on Via Padova. He described minutely what he knew of the rites of Ishmael. He spoke about the former members of Science Religion who had been drafted into the cult of Ishmael. Lopez asked if the German could do a check on the former sect members—in particular, a Swedish woman named Rebecka, who was definitely one of the contacts for Ishmael's group in Hamburg and had met Clemenceau and Terzani shortly before they died. The German said it wouldn't be easy; there was tension between the German authorities and Science Religion; the church had filed lawsuits. Lopez smiled, thinking of the lock of hair that had stuck to the palm of his hand when he hit the director of Science Religion in Milan.

He emphasized to the Hamburg inspector the fact that children were at the center of Ishmael's ceremonies. The German seemed interested. Hamburg, like all ports, had its shady side. Yes, there was traffic in children that went through Hamburg. Lopez asked his colleague for any information he had on pedophilia, child disappearances, anything. The German volunteered to do the investigation himself. They made a telephone appointment for the late afternoon. In Milan time was running out. Cernobbio was just around the corner, and so, perhaps, were its dead.

* * *

He went down to Vice. He had a couple of friends there, one of whom he often worked with, when the names of prostitutes or homosexuals turned up during investigations. The man was in his office. Lopez asked if there was an organized sadomasochistic community in Milan and, if so, did the police have any infiltrators. The man said there were both, a community and an infiltrator. There was no comparison with San Francisco, but there was a publisher who brought out specialized titles, magazines that published announcements, requests for contacts. Vice had on record all the postal codes of the announcements. From the documents, they were able to trace the identity of those who had placed the ads. In fact, of the various sadomasochist circles in Milan, one was centered almost entirely on those magazines. Other circles usually met through the Web. The police kept an eye on all of them. The informer told them about the gatherings. The system worked like a rave; the participants knew neither the place nor the time of a meeting until the last minute, when they were told via a round of cell-phone calls. The sadomasochists' gatherings were called PAVs, an English term that the Milanese had made into an acronym: Pronti, Attenti, Via—Ready, Set, Go. They were orgies. They had never gone too far, according to the informer. No one had ever been brought to a hospital. Vice had never seen the need to intervene. Lopez asked where these PAVs took place. He was startled when the agent from Vice answered that they were often organized in abandoned factories or hangars outside Milan.

As in Detroit. As in Paris. It had to be Ishmael. The man from Vice stared at him, questioning. "Can I meet the contact?" Lopez asked. It was urgent. There was no more time.

The informer was about thirty, a former carabiniere. Unemployed, he scraped by through cooperating with the police and, probably, with the intelligence services. He lived south of Milan, in San Donato. Lopez called him, and the man understood immediately. They made an appointment for two, in San Donato, in the central square. The conversation was brief and decisive. Lopez had to move fast.

In the dark vaulted space of a disused factory set among the evening lights in the outskirts of Milan, he glimpsed the luminous, elusive face of Ishmael.

Bascapé (Pavia)
October 27, 1962
22:25

Stepping through the tall grass and mud as the last fumes from the fuel rose, David Montorsi came closer to the cupola of light that was the wreck of the airplane of Enrico Mattei.

It wasn't an accident. It was an assassination.

If only the sides of the leaves facing the sky were stained with blood, and if the trees were intact, then the blood had come from above, before the plane crashed. It was already in pieces when it fell to the ground. Wet and feverish, hindered by the mud, he searched for the men from Detectives one by one. More cars had arrived, and the farmer and the old woman—*the witnesses*—had disappeared from sight. The Chief was observing the terrain, listening to a man Montorsi had never seen before, probably someone important, since the Chief's head was bent and he was nodding, his lips grimly tight. Neither Omboni nor the others were in sight. Montorsi wanted to show them the area with the burned bloodstains, on the ground, before the rain.

Then two dazzling headlights blinded him, rising up from a dip in the ground to point directly at him. He moved aside and let the long dark car pass by, shielding his eyes. The car stopped ten meters farther on. Three men got out. Two were the assistants at Forensics whom he had seen that morning at Giuriati—and then at Fatebenefratelli. The third was Dr. Arle.

He couldn't find his colleagues. The Chief had been released from the grip of the unknown superior. Montorsi went up to him. The Chief's eyes were sunken and reddened.

"Chief . . ."

"Montorsi, what the hell? It's not the moment—"

"Chief, it's important."

"Go and get in the car. The others are waiting for you."

"What do you mean, the car?"

"The car, Montorsi."

"But . . . the investigation?"

"What investigation? It's no longer an investigation, Montorsi." He walked away. "The judges will get it directly, with the help of the intelligence services. It's not our business anymore." He was shouting in the rain.

"Chief, it's important that you know—"

The Chief turned and looked at him, ghostly, amid the fat drops. The din increased as new sirens pierced the air. The Chief moved toward him. "Don't you understand? It's no longer our business."

"Chief, there are signs. It's . . . unequivocal. . . ."

"What? What, Montorsi?"

"It's an assassination. The plane . . . It exploded in flight."

The Chief gripped his arm, jerked him. "It's an accident, Montorsi. It's an accident. Do you understand?"

"No, Chief. There are traces . . . It's not an accident. . . ."

The Chief let go of his arm. Montorsi felt the warmth of his blood as it flowed again. "It's an accident. It's an accident just the same," the Chief said.

Montorsi went back to the car. The Detective Squad had been dismissed. Orders from high up. Perhaps they would help in the collateral investigations. Perhaps they would make some inquiries at Mattei's company, ENI: unskilled labor. They were out. The stink became moral. The luminous halo was burning up the countryside, chalky and salty in the night.

He saw Dr. Arle standing beside the scorched remains, which seemed to have the same consistency as Arle's body—flesh burned off, plastic on fire, the wreckage tall and thin in the rain. Near Arle were stretcher carriers. And the two assistants. And the officials who had first interrogated the farmer and the old woman.

Montorsi's colleagues, in the car, turned the headlights on him. He raised a hand, clothed in a beam of distant light. Just a moment. He gained another moment.

Arle stood straight, fatigued now more by age than by the chaos around him. He didn't even notice Montorsi. But one of the two assistants saw him—*observed him*—and made no acknowledgment. Arle was talking to the officials, the pitiful half trunk of a corpse at his feet.

"He died on impact with the ground," Arle was saying.

"You exclude explosions? A conflagration in the air?" one of the officials asked.

"I have to see in the lab. But I would bet that we won't find any trace of explosives. The lacerations and the fractures are from a uniform impact. The rib cage is crushed. It must have ricocheted. Let's say twenty meters. And then fell again. But I would have to ascertain it in the lab."

The officials looked at one another. Then they looked questioningly at Arle. Arle nodded. He gave orders to his men, asked for watertight bags, and sent them out to pick up the remains of the bodies.

When he reached the car, Montorsi was breathing hard, a silent fury, like a body within a body, trying to get out through his pores. All that rage was like the labor of birth. He grabbed the cold door handle of the Alfa and got in. The car pulled away. The luminous cupola disappeared behind the hill, a phosphorescent aerial fog where Enrico Mattei had died.

The four inspectors drove in silence toward Milan. The rain had not lifted its siege of the black city in the freezing night. No one felt like talking. Montorsi was feverish. The smell of blood and airplane fuel lingered in his nostrils. It seemed to have settled in his skull, his bones. He felt the odor oozing from his skin.

Omboni spoke, cracking the silence. "What do you think?"

They all had the same thought. And in the silence that thought was a hammer.

"They're shelving it," Montanari said.

"They're making it pass for an accident," Montorsi said. "But it's not an accident."

Revelli, driving, was silent. Omboni said, "I saw the remains. In my view, there was an explosion. In the air."

"Arle said the opposite," Montorsi said.

"Arle says what they tell him to say. And maybe even more."

"Forensics is on the other side. We always have them against us." Montorsi's anger flared.

"It's American territory," Montanari muttered. "It's obvious. We take orders and shut up."

"And the jacket? Did you see the jacket?" Montorsi asked.

"The one on the tree?" Omboni said.

"Who knows how it got there," Montorsi said. "From the sky."

"Exactly," Omboni said.

"Arle says the bodies ricocheted. Something like twenty meters."

"And they took off their jackets, they took them off. While they were ricocheting."

"I saw blood."

"On the ground. It was soaked with blood."

"No, on the leaves."

"On the leaves where?"

"On the leaves of the trees. The part facing the sky."

"And underneath?"

"Nothing."

"No splash from a rebound."

"No. And the trees, did you see them?"

"Untouched. Not a branch broken."

"Only in the area where the wing came down."

"It broke up in the air."

"It exploded. It was sabotaged."

"It's an assassination. They'll make it come out as an accident. I'd like to see the judges' conclusions."

"Yes, the judges. When the judges move, you can be sure that America is behind it."

"Or Mattei."

"Precisely. Now that there's no more Mattei, there's only America."

They were silent until they reached Milan. At the corner of Viale Cirene, Montorsi got out. It was nearly midnight. He felt a fever on him, an unnatural fever, yet he was sharply lucid. He opened the door of the apartment, fell inside like a dead man, got into the bed, and didn't even take off his coat, which was soaked with cold water. Maura was in the bathroom; the light was on.

Milan
March 24, 2001
12:35

The sadomasochists would gather that very evening. What to do, Lopez wondered. Intervene or investigate?

Look for Ishmael, anyway.

The infiltrator into the sadomasochist groups, Marco Calopresti, talked and talked and talked, and Lopez couldn't be certain where he was a police infiltrator into the sadomasochist community and where he became an infiltrator from the sadomasochist community into the police. His eyes alight, he digressed continually, almost automatically, from Lopez's questions to his own opinions, which didn't matter at all to Lopez. He was thinking of Ishmael. He needed quick, concise, straightforward information, and the man was blathering, smoking cigarettes, flicking the butts onto the slab of ice that covered the plaza in front of the modern church of San Donato, where they went on emitting a fine, thin smoke. Lopez let him speak. *If they talk, they unburden themselves and lower their defenses; they become inclined to tell you what you want to know.* He was there to listen.

At the end of the square, a child wrapped in a red scarf, mongoloid, limped slowly, leaning on the hip of a massive old man, who wiped his nose in a handkerchief. Arriving, Lopez had seen the squat, shining black towers of the AGIP complex, with their aquamarine glass, which Enrico Mattei had built outside Milan. They were shining and polished but they were ruins. Modern ruins. Marking the driveway with their complex geometries were rows of stunted climbing vines. Now he saw that the large new wooden doors of the church—a sharp pillar against the flat white sky—were closing, and he couldn't make out the figure of the priest or sacristan who was pulling them inward. Hungry, Lopez yawned.

This Calopresti said he had never heard the name of Ishmael, and Lopez was inclined to believe him. For years the informer had been acquainted with one of the old organizers of the sadomasochists' gatherings, someone known as the Engineer. "He's a smart guy, you know? He wants secure, consensual sadomasochism, and under his leadership the circle has grown, with never an incident, no drugs—everything is under control."

"And you? What do you do for us in that group?"

Calopresti inhaled his cigarette smoke with a gesture of bronchial liberation. "Well . . . I have a good time. . . ." And he laughed.

"They pay you to have a good time?"

"Well, look, there's a lot of pussy. And I'm interested. Sadomasochism interests me, I'm not ashamed to say it. I'm in those circles. That's why they pay me. I investigate. I inform. I deliver a monthly report, the people who participate are all listed. . . ."

The man seemed inexhaustible. "Listen," Lopez said.

"Yeah?"

"I don't give a shit about your circle. Understand?"

Calopresti tossed away the end of the cigarette, the smoke making an uneven parabola in the air. He nodded.

"I don't give a shit how you fuck. I need information."

"All you have to do is ask," Calopresti said. "If you ask me about this Ishmael, I tell you I've never heard of him. They're all Italians in the sadomasochist group. No immigrants. They're clean. They've got money. They're professionals, managers—there are even university professors. It's not a bunch of Moroccans."

"I want to know everything that happens there."

"Well, it depends . . ."

"Depends on what?"

"Depends on who's there. There's a meeting once a month. It's announced in all the magazines. The first Monday of the month."

"Where do they meet?"

"Milan. At the Metropol—a club near Ripamonti. But it's a calm, normal group. I've got information, but it doesn't interest you. The meeting is open to everyone. A recruiting session, in effect."

"And then?"

"There are private parties. Never more than ten people at a time. In private houses. Also in Milan."

Lopez considered this. These were occasions that had nothing to do with Ishmael. "But tonight there's a big gathering, right? In a hangar, here in the outskirts . . ." As in Detroit and Paris. And, maybe, in Hamburg. Ishmael's masses.

"It's a PAV. That's a rave, invitation only. Once, at most twice a year. There might be a hundred people."

"Where are they held?"

"No one knows before it happens. The Engineer organizes the whole thing. I help him, so I know the time and place, and I can tell Vice. It's the routine. Your colleagues want to know in advance, even though they've never interrupted a PAV."

"The place—it's different every time?"

"Yes. The Engineer says that's for security purposes. He wants to protect the participants. I'm telling you, it's people of a certain level. . . ."

Could this be Ishmael's ceremonies? But Calopresti knew nothing about Ishmael. "Listen."

"Eh?"

"Children. Are there ever children?"

The man lowered his eyes. He shook his head. He took his time; he lighted a cigarette. The mongoloid child at the end of the piazza had taken off the red scarf and the old man was trying to wrap it around him, but he was agitated, resisting him. "It's not a group of pedophiles."

"I know. But are there children?"

Calopresti spit. The saliva seemed to fry on the coating of ice. He inhaled smoke, exhaled a gray-blue vapor. He sniffed. He turned to Lopez. "Twice," he said. "At two PAVs there were children."

Bull's-eye. Lopez tried not to alarm the man. He had to squeeze out everything he knew. He had to act paternal. Reassure him. Be his accomplice. Trust is a poison. "You've never told Vice. . . ."

He twisted his nose, then stared up at Lopez. "No." Lopez remained silent. "If I told them, they would raid. But . . ."

"But?"

"But . . . the children are brought by the Engineer without any one of us knowing anything. I didn't ask questions. I was afraid someone might get suspicious. But I swear, nothing happened to them, the children. They were there only twice. They were blindfolded—they didn't see anything, they didn't do anything. They were like . . . a presence . . . scenic. . . . Yes, like a decoration . . ."

"Pieces of shit." Lopez was beginning to understand. The design was coming into focus. The ceremonies of Ishmael were *occult*. They occurred during what was basically an event for sadomasochists, but not all the participants knew. They were concealed rites. They took place secretly while something else was happening. And perhaps Ishmael was present, and only a few knew it. *He had hit the bull's-eye.* Ishmael's contact was the Engineer. The use of children in the rite was one of the signs of Ishmael's occult mass. Exactly as the police had discovered in Detroit and Paris, the child at the center of the scene was the sign. Among those present, anyone who wasn't a follower of Ishmael didn't understand.

He asked Calopresti if the Engineer had contacts with Hamburg. Calopresti didn't know. He had never heard of Terzani, Clemenceau, or Rebecka. Lopez had him examine the postmortem photo of Terzani. Yes, Calopresti had seen him sometimes with the Engineer. But he couldn't say if he had participated in a PAV, because during the gatherings everyone wore a mask, either leather, rubber, or plastic. No one appeared with his face uncovered.

Lopez asked Calopresti where and when the sadomasochists were meeting that night, for their PAV. Calopresti seemed reluctant. Lopez mentioned that Calopresti risked jail if the Vice officers found out that their informer had not told them about the presence of children at group orgies. He extorted from Calopresti the place and time of the gathering: A hangar outside Cernusco, in Limito di Pioltello. At midnight. Calopresti wanted to know if Vice would intervene. Lopez reassured him they wouldn't. He had Calopresti describe the Engineer to him: dark eyes, thin hair, a narrow mustache that would be visible in the opening of his mask. Did it take a password to enter? Or an invitation, or some countersign? Calopresti gave him the password.

It was a matter of hours. Ishmael was near his end.

The square seemed like a pool emptied out for the winter. The mongoloid seemed to be swimming in air and so did Calopresti, who nearly slipped on the icy steps of the church as he went off.

The police would intervene. Lopez would get an arrest warrant for the Engineer and interrogate him personally. "A smart guy," Calopresti had called him. The Engineer was a piece of shit who had involved children in sadomasochistic orgies—as "a decoration." Calopresti would make a deal to avoid criminal charges; he would provide testimony about the children. The Engineer would tell Lopez what he knew—about Ishmael, Hamburg, Paris, the plans for Cernobbio. He would seize Ishmael the next day. Maybe, in fact, he would find him at the PAV, among the representatives of the proper upper classes of Milan. The investigation wouldn't end the way it had in Paris. It wouldn't be buried. Ishmael's days were numbered.

Turning toward Mattei's towers, Lopez yawned. The AGIP building, wrapped in the fumes from an enormous chimney on the roof of a hotel, seemed to be coughing, vibrating in the air, an immense mongoloid child coughing.

Milan
October 27, 1962
23:20

Maura had left the party early. Luca had taken her home. They had sat in the car. They had kissed, touched. They hadn't spoken. She hadn't said anything about the child, about David, about her crises.

She had gone inside trembling.

The apartment was empty. David wasn't home yet.

The trembling had grown more intense. She barely managed to brush her teeth. She couldn't hold the toothbrush.

In bed, in the dark, she seemed to sink into an abyss of fear and terror. Her head was spinning, her heart pounding.

The child. The child would grow in her stomach like an enormous smooth mouse. The child was tenderness in its pure state; she already loved it. The birth would be painful, she would faint, she would die. The birth would be the sweetest moment of her life. The child would come out slippery as an eel. She would hug the child in her arms, she would melt into tranquillity at last. She would be terrified at the idea of hugging him; she was afraid of denting his head. Her veins were pulsing; she was suffocating. The child, too, would be suffocated.

She had turned on the light and sat up. Sitting on the bed she tried to catch her breath. The *crisis*. The seismic force was at its peak.

She had lain down again, with the light on.

As soon as David came home, she would tell him, I don't want it, I don't want to have it, I don't want it. She was crying. She was gasping for breath. Would David help her? She hated David, she loved him. David was nothing, he made love to her as if she were a shapeless pulp. David had never truly made love to her. It wasn't David she wanted in life.

There was no hope. No hope. Anxiety constricted her throat. She wasn't breathing. There, she was dying. She wasn't dying. The future closed around her like a claw.

It was all shadow. She wasn't strong enough to have hope in Luca. She hadn't spoken to him. It wasn't love. Luca didn't love her. Nor did she love Luca. Luca wouldn't protect her. No, Luca did love her, she loved him, their bodies responded, their attraction had been spontaneous, his skin drove her wild. He drove her wild.

She had tried to let go by crying but couldn't. She was crying without crying.

She got up but couldn't stay on her feet.

The door of the bathroom. Get to the door of the bathroom. If I reach the bathroom, I'm safe. David loves me. Luca loves me. The baby will love me. I am nothing, nothing, nothing, nothing.

The bathroom. Maura opened the door. She sank down, tried to lean her back against the wall, her head hanging. The salt of tears and the mucus, sweet, ran into her mouth. Her mouth was a rag. Her wrists hurt, her calves. The blood wasn't getting to her hands. She didn't have the strength to cough.

She saw David's razor, in the medicine chest, open above the sink.

She saw the package of tranquilizers.

She managed to get up and close the bathroom door. David's razor, the pills. She fell to the floor.

Her stomach was a clenched fist. She was shaking.

Her thoughts vanished, to a dark, faraway corner; she tried to lose consciousness and couldn't.

Milan
October 28, 1962
00:40

Maura was in the bathroom; the light was on. Montorsi felt an unnatural fever on him, yet he was sharply lucid. He undressed, found Fogliese's number. He called him.

Fogliese answered immediately. "So?"

"A disaster. Appalling, Fogliese. Appalling."

"I read the article by the reporter we sent there."

"Don't rely on the article, Fogliese. It's a cover-up." Suddenly there was some interference on the line, something scratchy. Maura had not come out of the bathroom, and the fever chills were growing more intense.

"What did you say, Montorsi?"

"A cover-up, Fogliese. There's a cover-up going on."

"But it's too big—"

"They've taken the investigation away from the Detective Squad. It's stuff only for intelligence, for higher authorities and the judges. We were cut out."

"No, come on. It's madness."

"Yes, and you'll see the official version, what it will be."

"An accident. The official version is an accident."

"Fuck that," Montorsi said.

"The evidence doesn't correspond to an accident?"

"Zero. Zero correspondence."

"But how can you say that, Montorsi?"

"It doesn't add up. We all saw it. The others from the squad and I."

"Do you have proof?"

"Look, Fogliese, it's absolutely certain. Irrefutable. But it's not a good idea to talk like this, on the telephone."

"Before the eyes of a nation . . . Madness. They're putting a gag—"

"You haven't had time to check anything, I suppose."

"No, but you can imagine. It's been a mess here. Among other things . . ."

"What?"

"They say that in the editor's office . . . It seems that they made a toast, to the death of Mattei."

Montorsi's head felt intensely hot. "And they won't be the only ones. Listen, Fogliese, I wanted to tell you—that thing that you sent, to that place, you know what I mean? To change your job." *The dossier on Ishmael that Fogliese had sent to* Il Giorno, *Enrico Mattei's paper*. About the Americans in Italy. About the dark religion. "Obviously you gave it to a friend, right?" With Mattei dead, did the report on Ishmael put Fogliese in danger?

"Why?"

"Can you get it back, the copy you sent? It would be better to get it back."

"You're right. I'll see about it tomorrow. You're right. Should we meet tomorrow, Montorsi?"

"Yes, that way I can explain." Montorsi sighed. "Do you have some plan about what to do, tomorrow, on that thing at Giuriati?"

"Yes. I'm working on the identity of the others who are in the photograph. The more I think about it the more it seems to me . . . how to put it . . ."

"Absurd, right?"

"Yes. Because Mattei is in that photograph, too. It's disturbing."

They agreed to meet at the university, around noon. They said goodbye.

Maura was still in the bathroom. He stretched out on the bed. The ache in his shoulders was more a shivering than a stabbing, a pain on the surface of the skin, as though it were wrinkling. He rested his head on the pillow. It was cold, which annoyed him.

He couldn't wait for Maura. He sank into sleep, a dead man ready to touch the luminous dead.

He came out of the black water of dreamless sleep in which he was submerged. The light was on. It was four o'clock. Maura wasn't in bed. He realized the light in the bathroom hadn't been turned off.

His heart pumped fear.

He got up and ran, endlessly, it seemed, over a tiny distance. The bathroom door was closed. He called. No answer. He pushed it open with his shoulder.

Maura was sitting on the floor, leaning with her back against the wall. Her body was gray. Saliva was dripping slowly from the corners of her mouth. Her eyes were wide open. Her breath was shallow, panting. He put his hands under her armpits. It was like picking up a sack. She couldn't stand. She was crying.

It was a crisis. Again.

He asked her "What is it? Mau, what's the matter?" and kept on asking her, five, six times, and she was weeping and seemed to be suffocating. This was an extreme, almost deranged state he didn't recognize. Maura had never had such a violent seizure.

He grabbed her by the head, felt it warm and beating, felt the sweat under her crushed hair. She was gurgling. In the mirror he saw her lean forward toward the sink; he moved her like a broken doll so that she could bend over it. He ran the water cold, then stuck her head under the faucet until she began to cough. She coughed, sobbed, and shook violently. Her upper lip stuck out like the lip of a child. She was red in the face now, and saliva and mucus kept coming out, but she was crying. And she was breathing; her breath was strong now.

He moved her out of the water and lifted her up. He put a towel around her head and carried her in his arms, a tiny thing, to the couch in the living room. He sat down and held her in his lap. Maura began to moan like a small animal.

He had not realized how far away her despair could take her, her cry receding, growing weaker and thus more desperate.

He had constructed his love for her on the great void that she carried within her. Her very gaze radiated the plea *"Protect me!"* and he responded, bringing animal warmth where there was none. Their love was a violent force that tore them away from what they knew and dragged them into the unknown. He had always felt that *in some way* they were equal, mirror images. "If we were to separate, and years later we were to be on the same tram, I would know you by your odor. It's a chemical thing. Magnetic. We belong to each other," she had said to him before they were married. She felt an emptiness that nothing could fill: because what she did could be different. *Life can be different.* Wherever she was, freedom and aspiration were somewhere else. They had tried to have a child. "If I don't have a child, my life will be without meaning," she had whispered one night, in the grip of a crisis.

He rocked her. She was still sobbing, but more weakly. She was worn out. "Go away . . . Go away. . . ." she kept saying to him, her words mechanical and sorrowful. "Go away." He didn't understand. He felt the fever again. He loved her with an indestructible tenderness; he would always love her, even if she left. And that tenderness cured nothing, didn't fill her.

"Go away. . . ." It was the unhappiness talking. It wasn't Maura. She was unhappy even now that he had given her a child, and life was filling her, the tough faith of life in itself. But even when she had the child, nothing would change, he thought, because nature doesn't change, and life is no compensation for suffering. He felt an infinite sense of failure. He rocked her. He tried to calm her, to calm himself.

Two human beings, one beside the other, they slept on the sofa. The gray light of the chemical dawn woke them, the milky early morning light of Milan.

Inspector Guido Lopez

Milan
March 24, 2001
14:50

Lopez sat for an hour in a line of motionless traffic at the Corvetto entrance for Milan.

He would tell Santovito that he wanted to go to the PAV on the outskirts of Milan that the informer had told him about, and that he wanted to stop it at its climax; he was sure that the Engineer had something to do with Ishmael, and he was sure that the event was a rite of Ishmael. An orgy, a rite. He would ask Santovito for men for the operation, and they would make their raid at the climax of the ceremony, but he wanted to be there himself, so he could communicate with the others directly from the inside the moment the raid began. He would ask Vice about the outfit he would need to blend in among the participants. Calopresti had said that during the gatherings everyone wore a mask of leather, rubber, or plastic. There wasn't much time to prepare. The PAV would take place at midnight, in Limito. Ishmael's hours were numbered. Lopez was surprised to notice how hard he was gripping the steering wheel.

On the way to Headquarters he ate a small gummy sandwich. He met Calimani on the stairs, both of them out of breath. He called the inspector in Hamburg. No trace of the phantom Rebecka. As for the ring of pedophiles, an operation was set for the next day, the German said in his guttural monotonous voice. They would intercept a "delivery" to be made at the port in Hamburg. They didn't know the contents of the "delivery," but the Vice Squad was certain it was children, children leaving Hamburg. Maybe Slavs. Or Turks. Packaged for destinations unknown. Was the raid something that might interest Lopez? Yes, it interested him. It was difficult to be active on all fronts of the investigation with so little time, but it was worth trying. He thought of

Bob, of the e-mails, and hoped that Ishmael's followers were meeting in Hamburg to organize the "delivery." He asked his colleague in Hamburg to check on one more thing. He knew that Ishmael's men had met there on February 15 and that Terzani had returned to Milan the following day. Maybe Rebecka had put him up, but Lopez asked his colleague in Hamburg to check hotels, inns, and hostels, to see whether on the night of the fifteenth of February Terzani had reserved a room. Bob, in his e-mail to Clemenceau had said that "the appointment is in the Bahnhof, in the bar of last week's mail." Did that mean something? The man in Hamburg said he would investigate.

He felt a vaguely euphoric certainty: whether in Milan or Hamburg, Ishmael's hours were numbered.

Santovito was puzzled, but he signed the authorization for the operation in Pioltello. The connection between a raid on the sadomasochists' PAV and trouble at Cernobbio was not convincing, and Lopez understood perfectly the reasons for his skepticism. As in Detroit, as in Paris, the police would surprise representatives of the upper middle classes in the middle of an orgy. Diplomacy would be required. Santovito would have to fend off external pressures. They agreed that they would release anyone they considered unlikely to have participated in the Engineer's rite. As Calopresti had confirmed, probably only a few of those attending the orgy would be participating in Ishmael's ceremony in the midst of the others, who would be completely unaware. Lopez's theory was that Ishmael, probably, would be present at the rite. For Santovito it would be enough if Lopez could ensure that the meeting at Cernobbio would take place without incident. Lopez told him that silencing the members of Ishmael's Italian organization would give Santovito's hope its best chance of becoming reality. Santovito grimaced and signed the authorization, the repellent cigarette squeezed between his lips, shifting his body obliquely so that the smoke would not get in his eyes as he signed.

Lopez immediately arranged to intercept the Engineer's cellphone calls. With Calimani he organized the setup for the raid. He asked for twenty plainclothes agents, and distributed to them the maps of the Limito di Pioltello neighborhood. He decided to check out the place, with Calimani. They went in Calimani's own car. They didn't speak. It was already getting dark. They took Forlanini; beyond Linate they turned. They saw in the murky fog the small ferris wheel at the amusement park at Idroscalo. They crossed the bridge at Segrate. The fields were white; mist rose from the damp earth and hovered heavily on the edges of the rough asphalt road. They stopped at the first gas station they saw, its clear smooth cement seeming to glow for a moment more than the sky—an absurd upside-down concavity, dully metallic. They turned left, breaching the intermittent line of swiftly moving headlights, and crossed over a bridge into dense trees. It wasn't easy to make out the curves of the unpaved road in that narrow space. Then they came to a tiny, inhospitable clearing, its pale grass dry and resistant, and descended along a hollow. Now the road was simply mud, no longer dirt. Trees rose, thin and black. Beyond the trees was a new muddy clearing, a gate with narrow rusty bars, then an open space roughly cemented over and the parallelepiped of the hangar where the PAV was to take place. Not a soul was in sight. They left the car among the trees and continued on foot, deciding the position of the plainclothes cops. The only way in was the one that led to the open space in front of the entrance to the hangar. On the sides and in the rear of the hangar, the underbrush was thick, growing on the slopes of the little hollow that surrounded it. Beyond the underbrush, as you came out of the hollow, there were fields and more brush. They would have to be quick, to block the access route. The police would station themselves near the bridge, headlights out, and move at a signal from Lopez, who would call on his cell phone from inside. There would be total darkness, except for the single light at the entrance. It would not be a comfortable operation. But the twenty men would be sufficient.

They tried to make a circuit of the hangar, but it was impossible. The slopes alongside were too steep, a tangle of briars and tree trunks. The ground was mud; it sank under their feet. The light was waning noticeably. The air was so cold it hurt their faces, and their shoes were encrusted with mud. Lopez shook his head. The gust of wind stirring the tiny leaves on the trees seemed to him the frigid breath of the temple of Ishmael, right before their eyes.

Calimani gave him a questioning glance, and for a moment

doubt seized Lopez. He might be entirely mistaken. The connections were plausible but thin. He shrugged. They got back into Calimani's car and returned to Headquarters.

Lopez took out a police cell phone just for the operation, connected it to the radio of an unmarked car, and arranged it so that one of the fixed frequencies would directly intercept calls to and from the Engineer's cell phone. There was no need to tail him beforehand. Lopez knew where he would end up, at midnight.

At the cafeteria, where he met Calimani and the twenty agents, he barely ate. Before the others finished, he left and went to pick up his outfit from Vice. He had asked for a full mask, leather. He went back to the cafeteria and set the time with Calimani, who was peeling a bruised apple. He then returned to the inner courtyard of the building and took the car and drove home to Sabotino. The apartment was cold; he hadn't been there for two days. He stretched out on the couch. He rolled a joint. He smoked it slowly, savoring the slow and crackling progress of the paper ash, in the dark.

He went out. In the car, he set the radio to the frequency of the Engineer's cell phone; it was completely silent. The rain had stopped. Nine. It was cold, but the car wasn't steamed up. It was a black Audi; he wouldn't look out of place. He had changed into a jacket and tie. In the driver's seat, he tried on the leather mask, a light, soft skin with a slightly bitter odor. He pulled tight the fastening, looked at himself in the rearview mirror. He saw two pale crevices, two lively eyes, a specular hallucination that was not what he expected. He was unrecognizable. He took off the mask and put it in the inside pocket of his jacket.

He sat waiting, in the dark, parked, with the engine off, in Viale Sabotino, in front of the luminous noise of the Blockbuster.

Milan
October 28, 1962
08:00

Montorsi stretched as he walked, a cold glow enveloped him. He yawned in the icy air. It was cold, but not raining. It wasn't even eight. He had left Maura on the bed. She had been brought back from unconsciousness to sleep. She had the day off; she didn't have to go to school. So much the better. She would sleep for hours. He saw how the tar between the paving stones shone, even though everything was gray, iridescent with a dusty frost.

Had Italo Fogliese discovered anything about the presence of Mattei at Giuriati? His last image before falling asleep, while he was still rubbing a warm shock of Maura's hair between his fingertips, had been the stiff, frozen arm of the child sticking out of the folds of plastic, in the mist on the field. The mummy at the historical archive of the Resistance had tortured him in a dream that he couldn't remember. But he had waked in the warm, intermittent breath of his wife, sleeping outside the night's pain. They would talk. She would agree to go to a specialist. It had been a devastating attack; it was impossible for her to go on like that.

A black dog with yellow eyes, hairless around the right haunch, came up to him, sniffing the wet air. He was supposed to see Arle. He felt disoriented. The image of Maura subsided, breaking up under his footsteps on the damp asphalt. A fat man went by, maybe the owner of the hairless dog. He shook himself in his overcoat. Italo Fogliese had to retrieve his report on the Americans from *Il Giorno*. Who was Ishmael? What was the sect that Fogliese had referred to at the *Corriere* the night before? What would become of Italy, with the Master of Italy gone? It was the morning after the death of the King.

He went into a café and ordered a coffee. It was hot, burned his tongue. He added sugar, but the coffee was still bitter. The papers on the newsstand reported in giant, full-page headlines the news of Mattei's death. The term "accident" recurred. Spread across the front page were black-and-white photographs of the crash site, much less impressive than the reality he had experienced in the grip of his lucid fever the night before. Khrushchev, Kennedy, and Cuba had disappeared from the front page.

Perhaps Maura really had managed to go to sleep. He felt a sweet, fleeting satisfaction in having led Maura out of her circle of sorrow. It had been tremendous. Tremendous. He saw again the faintly rusty surface of the mirror last night, while the fierce cold water brought Maura back to herself, drove her back into the world of shelters, guilts, compensations. He had to find a specialist. Maura would agree. She was expecting a child; she had to be seen by someone. The fetus had been sleeping in her womb for two months, without dreams or bright lights, before the royal entrance of the spirit into the kingdom of anxieties, among the spirals of self and others.

Once the business of Mattei and the child at Giuriati was over, he would look for a psychologist himself.

From the telephone in the café, he called Headquarters. Only Revelli was on duty. He answered the telephone in a voice thick with sleep. No news. The Chief hadn't even come back. There were no orders to follow. They really were cut out of the investigation. "They've shelved us. It's over. The Chief was right," Revelli said. Montorsi nodded, the receiver in his sweaty hand. The café was oppressively warm. He needed to breathe, outside, mouthfuls of damp heavy air. From the window he saw a taxi slow down on the other side of the street. A prostitute got out, with a client, who paid the taxi driver. The woman and her client went into the doorway across from the bar.

Maybe the Detective Squad would help the judges assemble the facts before they issued a conclusion, Revelli said; it was the only possibility. Mattei was a matter too big for them. Montorsi agreed and hung up. He went out, breathing in the cold as soon as he reached the threshold, to chase out of his lungs the unpleasant warmth of the bar. He thought of Maura. He crossed the street. The taxi that had let out the prostitute and the man was driving off. He was too early for Arle. He would go to Headquarters later, after Fogliese and Forensics. There was time. He decided to occupy it. He went through the doorway the whore and her client had entered.

The concierge looked at him as he climbed the stairs, but he said nothing, and she said nothing, watching him darkly, her face the color of morning in Milan.

He stopped at the second floor. The door was unlocked and the sweet scent of the whore's perfume lingered in the air. *Flesh had passed through here.*

He opened it. An entrance hall. Dim lights. The treacly scent of whore's perfume was more insistent. Something ticked in the next room.

He didn't have time to investigate before the madam came to receive him. She was an old woman collapsing under the weight of cosmetics and abuse. Her eyes protruded slightly from the line of heavy mascara, and an aura of powder preceded her, anesthetizing the nostrils. Her silky black dressing gown allowed a glimpse of a massive withered breast. She was wearing clogs. As soon as she saw him, she smiled. Then she stopped. She looked behind him, for an instant, for the whore who wasn't with him. She understood immediately.

Montorsi—the image of Maura at the center of his mind, like a magnet, invasive—shoved the old whore aside violently, and her flaccid bulk slammed into the doorjamb. He went into her room. Cheap crystal figurines were arranged like little altarpieces on the wooden shelves. A disproportionately large glass chandelier, unlit, hung from the ceiling like a pear bruised on every side. The madam's record book was open on a low table, beside a chair whose upholstery was faded by the rubbing of the buttocks that had sat on it. On the wall opposite the shelves with the crystals, a painting emerged like a piece of darkness, too dim to be deciphered. To the right and the left were two doors, closed. He opened the one on the left.

In the shadowy light that smelled of a baby's skin, a whore was sleeping, squeezing her arms to her chest, her hands gripping the sheet. She didn't even stir when Montorsi closed the creaking door. Then he opened the other door, while the madam, sitting on the floor, her swollen knees cupped by similarly swollen hands, as if vice had been stored in every fiber, leaned forward to spy on him.

In the room, the morning filtered through gauzy blinds gray

with neglect, testimony to a more profound neglect of bodies and words. The man was intent on top of the young prostitute. His bare back was sweaty. His pants, slightly lowered, left the top of his buttocks uncovered, tense and pulsing, and hairy. The whore looked straight at Montorsi as the man pumped; he wasn't aware of anything as he pumped and panted, sweat dripping from his tufted hair.

Montorsi approached and the whore said nothing; she opened her eyes wide but said nothing. *Maura's white face, shaken in the dark by furious tremors.* With one hand, he grabbed the edge of the man's pants, as he kept pumping, and then suddenly he turned and muttered something, and Montorsi pulled and managed to lift the man. Their muscles tensed, and the man was ranting, stammering out indignant grunts, louder and louder, and a thread of spit spurted onto the whore's chest, as she continued to look at Montorsi, who was looking at her, as if the man between them didn't even exist. Then, all of a sudden, the pants ripped as the material gave, and in Montorsi's hand was a torn bit of the white lining. The man straightened up, shaken, turned toward the whore and then toward Montorsi, and grabbed his shoes and ran out, avoiding the enormous body of the policeman standing tall in the middle of the room, while the whore, lying down, kept looking at him.

Then Montorsi went over to her, pulled her toward him by one calf, and landed a punch on her thigh, missing his mark.

He went out in silence, observing the smudged mascara of the mistress of the brothel, after spreading his arm to send all the crystals on the shelf shattering to the floor. The madam said nothing. The concierge, too, watched him leave in silence, a twig broom in her hand, the thick floor wax in an odd, small pail, and he lowered his eyes to the newly washed floor, which smelled of disinfectant.

Inspector Guido Lopez

Milan
March 24, 2001
23:50

And when he went in it was like a dream.

Lopez had reached the neighborhood of Limito di Pioltello a little after eleven. He was raving, literally. He had bombarded Calimani's cell phone with calls, monitoring the preparations. The squad that would search the office and home of the Engineer was in place; they had observed the Engineer leave his house, and go toward Buenos Aires, an avenue deserted at that hour. The Engineer had not used his cell phone. Until eleven-thirty, Lopez had driven aimlessly around Segrate, then toward Cernusco, on streets that were dingy under the white street lights, between flat black fields broken by the silhouettes of industrial plants. At twenty to midnight the Engineer had made a phone call. Lopez identified the number; it was Calopresti's cell phone. The Engineer gave the signal. Calopresti would probably start the telephone chain alerting the participants to the event's location, but Lopez hadn't thought of that possibility; Calopresti's cell frequency couldn't be intercepted.

He drove on, approaching Pioltello. He had seen high-powered sedans and smog-fouled compacts passing, as he looked for the right road to the place he and Calimani had been in the late afternoon. He rolled another joint and smoked it, watching the rear window steam up with the exhaled smoke, a faint white halo that reduced the glass to a finely pearled surface impossible to see through. He turned on the heat. It was a little before midnight. He drove into the open space that led to the hangar. He retraced in the dark the route he had taken that afternoon. He went slowly; it was hard to tell which way the road curved. The darkness was thick.

Some thirty cars were crowded outside the gate. He saw the

entrance to the hangar, illuminated by the small lamp. He saw the outline of a man at the entrance and heard him asking a couple for the password. He felt the tiny chirping of the skin on his back. Ishmael was inside. It was the end. He put on the mask, checked his cell phone, opened the car door, got out.

A loud rumble sounded—a generator. The hangar had no electrical outlets, evidently. Around him was *total* darkness. Even the steep inclines of the hollow were invisible. At the gate, he encountered a couple: a grizzled man, without a mask, a studded collar squeezing the muscles of his throat, was holding up a younger woman, who was bent over, seemingly in the grip of coughing fit. The man looked at Lopez as if for understanding, and said, "It's nerves. . . . It's her first time. . . ." The woman groaned noisily, taking no account of Lopez's presence. When she stood up and her coat parted, he saw she was naked. Lopez left the couple at the gate and walked on, annoyed by the quagmire of mud, the smacking sound it made against the soles of his shoes. The bouncer at the threshold of the little door stared at him. It was Calopresti, but he didn't recognize Lopez. Better that way. He asked for the code word. Lopez said it. Calopresti moved aside, to let him go in.

And when he went in it was like a dream.

The space was not very large, but because of the darkness the back wall was barely visible. The soft vague light of a giant aquarium. The people inside moved slowly, as if overwhelmed by the high vault of the broad roof. Some sixty people. A few lamps broke the semi-darkness, and tall, sinuous women made their way through the space, like long strands of seaweed in a dense, dark, phosphorescent water. He couldn't identify the Engineer. Men and women were scattered between *scene* and *scene*. Everything appeared ridiculous in the vast empty belly of the building. At strange metal structures, small groups moved slowly and rhythmically around persons who were bound and pressed, nearly invisible, against the obscenely cold walls. It was like a theater of living portraits, tableaus separate from one another and unrelated. He saw a rough imitation of a bar near the back and walked toward it, down the center of the space, proceeding as if suspended, in a dream, a confused messiah who doesn't know what world he has descended into. Bound to a metal cross was a woman wearing only a small black mask; he could almost feel the rubbing of the leather thongs on his skin and the cold surface of the red metal. Three men were waving a soft whip over a thin young woman, on all fours. He saw her nervous back and the fish scales of the vertebrae raised along her spine, the dark helmet of smooth hair and the exposed white buttocks. Passing the foursome, he let the scent of them penetrate. Farther on, a man carried astride his bent back a middle-aged woman with wrinkled skin, her face covered by a brightly feathered carnival mask. Two women were fiercely stabbing at a young body; he couldn't tell if it was male or female.

He reached the bar. A young man in a mask nodded at him, Lopez asked for a beer. Beside the young man, a red-haired girl appeared, her face uncovered, and, with the furtive look of one who has nothing to do with what is happening around her, she smiled at him.

"Are you rich?" she asked, suddenly.

Lopez smiled silently, or made an effort to smile.

"If you're rich and you like these games, maybe we can go further. . . . What do you say?"

He swallowed too much beer. He turned to the scenes. He turned back to the girl behind the bar. "I'm not rich," he said. He meant that he didn't like these games, but he didn't say it, and suddenly he recognized the Engineer. He thought, *It's him, he's Ishmael.* The Engineer was standing, thin and somewhat fragile-looking, his arms folded, face uncovered, fine hair, small mustache arced by a smile like a cherry, his lips wet. He went over to him. The Engineer welcomed him, smiling. "What do you think?" he asked.

"Of what?" said Lopez.

"Of the evening."

Lopez nodded.

The Engineer asked if it was his first PAV.

Lopez was about to mention the name of Ishmael but controlled himself. He said yes, that it was his first evening.

The Engineer asked if he didn't want to "play."

Lopez sipped his beer, which was by now disgustingly warm, and said that he preferred to watch.

The Engineer announced that the *sacred tableau* would begin soon.

Lopez nodded again and made a vague gesture.

The Engineer said goodbye, twisting his face into a wrinkled sneer, making a show of courtesy.

Lopez raised his warm little bottle of beer in a farewell salute. He did not let him out of his sight. The Engineer approached a scene. A man was photographing two women wearing underpants with dildos protruding; a boy was on his knees between them, playing one dildo and then the other with his tongue. The Engineer whispered something to the photographer; the flashes, like sudden electric charges, broke up the deep shadow from which the outlines of the players emerged. Lopez touched the inside pocket of his jacket, felt the inert body of his cell phone, went back to the bar, and put down the bottle. The muffled sound of the scenes continued around him, a soft and sonorous carpet spreading everywhere, without a source, *from many sources*, decentralized. Smacking and howling sounds pierced it. Lopez seemed to be sleeping, dreaming. Then, suddenly, a loud screech caused silence to fall.

Drawn by half-naked bodies, a large cart bearing an enormous upright metal wheel advanced, detaching itself from the shadowy background. Attached to the wheel was a woman. Lopez watched as the wheel was dragged noisily to the center. He saw that it was secured by ties at the base, and didn't wobble. The woman on the wheel was spread like Leonardo's man, naked and silent. The wheel was set up in the exact center of the hangar; it was a long, mechanical moment, a suspension of the dream. Lopez stood dazzled and motionless within the image that the wheel radiated.

All those present arranged themselves in a semicircle in front of the wheel, and the woman began to turn with the turning of the wheel.

Lopez thought, Is this the *sacred tableau*? A large man, wearing leather clothing that masked his neck and face, brushed past him. The woman turned and turned.

And they started.

The men and women around the wheel began to whip her. The blows lashed in the air, dry and precise, but the sound on the woman's skin was dull and hammering, almost like a butcher pounding meat on a marble slab. The woman moaned, then started to break down and cry, and the others kept beating her.

Where was the Engineer? *Where is Ishmael*? Lopez searched with his eyes and couldn't find him, and meanwhile the woman was whirling on the wheel, and growing more agitated. With every lash, Lopez heard her deep, violent breathing; her face by now was a mask of mucus, and then she began to sob. The rhythm of the blows grew faster. The woman was fair and innocent; she was like a child. Lopez put his hand on his phone. He would end this torture. Then he stopped.

Behind the people who were whipping the woman, who was now pale and limp, disjointed, Lopez saw the Engineer moving, but couldn't figure out what he was doing. Seven men and women, their faces covered by masks, stood around the Engineer, their arms raised, as in a ritual procession. The woman on the wheel had begun to bleed, and what happened immediately afterward was instantaneous and slow and complicated, like certain dreams that persist, vividly, even after you awake.

They all stood still, hypnotized by the wheel. The woman had stopped moaning. She was a pale curving mass, striped by the marks of the whip. The Engineer disappeared behind the wheel. Lopez followed with his gaze and discerned the oddly bulky outline of the Engineer in the darkness. Then Lopez understood. He was carrying a child. It must have been three or four years old, it was blindfolded, the Engineer seemed to be rocking it, and no one seemed to be paying any attention to him.

Lopez withdrew behind the crowd, slipped the cell phone from his pocket, pressed the code for Calimani, and said "Now!" The wheel was slowing down; those who had been whipping the woman had stopped. The wheel halted. The half-naked men who had dragged the wheel untied the ropes and the woman sank into their arms. One man, dressed as a female, pretended to cry over the whipped woman. Everyone applauded. The Engineer was behind the wheel, unnoticed by all but Lopez. With the blindfolded child in his arms, he went over to the large man in leather who had brushed by Lopez earlier, and handed over the child, who seemed asleep or drugged. Lopez moved, but people were clapping and pressing toward the center of the room, and Lopez lost sight of the man with the child. At that moment Calimani and the others burst in through the door, and Lopez turned toward Calimani, and as he took off the mask he felt the cold, and sweat poured off him.

What happened then was confused, sudden.

One of the agents shouted, "Don't move! It's only a police

check!" but everyone was rushing for the exit. The agents and Calimani blocked the door, but the crowd, in a panic, surged against them, shouting as they tried to get out, and someone broke through the cordon of agents. Lopez looked for the man in leather carrying the child. He saw the Engineer walk with apparent calm toward Calimani, but he couldn't see the child. As he passed by the wheel, he noted the wan, violated beauty of the woman who lay beside it, her eyes half-closed, her cheeks smeared with mucus, and then behind the wheel he saw another exit. He ran out into the cold. Nothing. Only darkness. He groped his way. The land rose sharply; he took a few steps, but the vegetation was too dense. He turned back to the hangar. Outside was a chaos of police cars and headlights. He had a hard time reaching the entrance. He telephoned to ask for reinforcements from Limito di Pioltello. It was urgent, he said—there was a child and it had disappeared. And now it was late, it was too late, and he stood in the night illuminated by headlights, with the hangar behind him, staring into the darkness.

Milan
March 25, 2001
01:40

It had almost failed. Even the Engineer, who had guaranteed him maximum security, was a dilettante. Like the Pakistani the Old Man had killed. Ishmael is great; his men are not.

He was all sensation. He perceived everything. He heard the sleepy breath of the child unconscious on the seat beside him. The strips of turned earth, frozen by the night cold, guided his tires like tracks. The American tried to control the slippery rolling of the steering wheel. The BMW, its headlights off, was furrowing the darkness like the prow of a ship. They really had nearly failed. The pale head of the half-sleeping child rolled from one of its shoulders to the other, following the irregular rhythm of their passage through the plowed field. He, the American, had managed to escape because he had calculated everything beforehand, in spite of the Engineer's assurances. In Italy no one knew anything—except for Ishmael's faithful. The American had calculated the possibility of a police raid. It had happened in Detroit—he had been there! He had been on the squad that raided the warehouse, planted there by Ishmael. It had happened in Paris. Now it had happened in Milan. Ishmael is great. He knows the vast secret movement of those who oppose his slow, unstoppable dominion. He had sent him to Milan because he knew, and the American had acted exactly as Ishmael wished him to act.

He had driven from the south that afternoon, through a dense network of unpaved roads, to inspect the place where the rite was to be held. He had left the other car a short distance away, where it was now waiting for the transfer. He had walked for half an hour in the damp cold exhaled by the deserted fields. He had sighted the crown of trees around the hangar. The Engineer had told him it was an isolated place. The vegetation was thick, bushes, briars, tangled branches, underbrush. It descended, almost impenetrable, toward the bottom of the hollow in a fog that smelled of manure. He had walked along the belt of trees and found a way through. It was unlikely that the police would be stationed in the scrub. He ascertained that the hangar had a back exit. Ishmael had ordered the child to pass through the rites. The ceremony in Milan was only the beginning. The American was to pick up the child and take it to others of Ishmael's faithful, who were closer to Ishmael and more deeply concealed than those in Milan. The child was to end up in Brussels. The American would get him to Hamburg, where others of the faithful would take care of him. The transporting of the child had been organized, as a perfect mechanism that would allow him to return to Italy and perform the second operation—the most important!—that Ishmael had commissioned from him.

Tonight he had parked the BMW in the fields beyond the scrubland. There were no roads or dirt tracks. Perfect. He had come out of the undergrowth, in the dark, and reached the entrance to the hangar on foot. When the police raided, he was ready. He had grabbed the child from the Engineer. He had considered—for a lightning instant—whether or not to kill the Engineer. But the Engineer knew nothing about him. He couldn't harm him. And Ishmael would protect the Engineer. Ishmael was powerful, he was great. The people in the hangar had been shoving toward the main door, in total chaos. The way to the rear exit was free. He had been fast. He knew blindly at what angle to cut into the dry underbrush that made a hedge around the building. The child was unconscious. No problem. Still, he was panting when he reached the BMW.

He couldn't see any lights in the rearview mirror. He had done it.

After more than an hour of slow navigation in the dark, he turned to the left, then again to the right. After a short stretch, the narrow dirt track, between evergreens silver with frost, curved again. He crossed the hollow. Here he had to turn on the headlights for a fraction of a second. He illuminated the dark outline of the Mercedes that he had left there in the late afternoon. He had parked it forty minutes' driving distance from the hangar. He had been prudent. He had rented the Mercedes in Milan, with a French passport. (He spoke French perfectly. He spoke Italian perfectly.) Forty minutes through the dark would be enough, he had calculated, to get beyond the police blockades. After parking the Mercedes, he had gone on foot, crossing a flat clearing, as far as the state road from Melzo. He had waited for the bus to Milan, to the Central Station, where he had parked the BMW, rented with a Spanish passport. He smiled.

The child was semi-conscious. He opened the trunk of the Mercedes, looked in the outer pocket of his bag, and took out the case. He removed the syringe he had prepared that afternoon before returning to Milan. He uncovered the pale arm of the child, who was trying to open his mouth to yawn. He injected the liquid. He waited a few seconds. After the child collapsed, as if dead, he picked up the little body and laid it in the trunk. He didn't even have to bend it. He closed the trunk. In the weak beam of the parking lights, he inspected the BMW a final time. He wiped off the steering wheel again, carefully. He unscrewed the license plates. He got into the Mercedes. He accelerated in the dark.

Half an hour later, before reaching the state road that led to the highway to Germany, he opened the window and threw into the black field the two white, iridescent license plates, watching them land and disappear like bits of burning paper.

Milan
October 28, 1962
08:40

David Montorsi walked slowly across Milan. He was going to see Dr. Arle, and he was early. The sky opened up, split by colossal cracks like an enormous orange peel, a plantlike cupola breaking over the city. The sky above Milan, from which Mattei had fallen, in pieces. Milan was waking up without its Master, without the Master of all Italy.

A man on a bicycle was whistling, and the inner ring road was half-deserted. The dense threadlike plumes of smoke from the chimneys almost gleamed, like mobiles cut out against the sky. The air was bright; it bore the scent of an end or a beginning, the scorched electric odor of mornings. The sharp lines of the corners of the buildings were crushed against the deep celestial cracks of the clouds. One area of the vaulted sky allowed in more light: like a specter dropping from on high, dramatically oblique, the face of Enrico Mattei loomed, immense and transparent, above the city. From this sky Mattei had crashed in pieces, in fragments of bone, down to the salt earth, in the night. . . . Montorsi couldn't think about it. His gaze moved between the dim sparkle of moving vehicles to the stores whose grimy shutters were being raised. He walked without noticing who came toward him and who passed him by, and he shook at the electric rattling of the tram that ran at irregular intervals. At a newsstand, Montorsi bought *Il Giornale*. The headline: MATTEI IS DEAD. Accounts, reactions, commentary. Togliatti with the position of the Communists. The Christian Democrats in mourning. The official version: an accident.

Shit. Shit on shit.

He tried to concentrate on his appointment with Dr. Arle, whose lackeys had drafted the autopsy on the child at Giuriati.

With them, Arle had gone to Headquarters, to see Boldrini. Montorsi had seen him, white and fleshless, order the recovery of Mattei's remains at Bascapé. He didn't know why. Only he felt that Arle was *important*.

Forensics. There was no one in the lobby; the guard booth was deserted. He passed through the entrance and into the corridors of the first building. He met a small group of workers joking in low voices, one slapping another on the back. Montorsi didn't smile at them. He was thinking of Arle's taut face the night before, like clay decomposing under the hard rain, next to the distended half trunk of the corpse on the field where Mattei's plane had gone down. Maybe Fogliese would discover something. Maybe there really was some relation between the child at Giuriati and Mattei, and Fogliese would discover it.

He made his way toward the source of the formaldehyde exhalations, following a corridor illuminated by fluorescent lights in the low ceiling. Something familiar radiated from these walls, something not completely known and yet not unknown, the artificial scent of something similar but not identical to power. The lights were growing weaker. Behind him came a clanging of metal wheels. An empty gurney. He turned left, into a darker, narrower corridor. Turning right, he was in an identical corridor, but brighter, and he came across a secretary. Montorsi asked for Arle.

Arle's office lay behind the office of his two assistants, one sitting opposite the other, the men almost twins in their movements, their resemblance a result of the narrow space their two bodies and two minds had inhabited for years. He asked for Arle, and they told him to wait.

He waited. Perhaps Maura was sleeping; perhaps she recovered from her sorrow by forgetting everything. The partisan mummy the day before had made an impression on him, and he had thought of it, for a second, the night before when he lifted up Maura's unconscious body, with its consistency of an emptied, dry chrysalis. Arle, too, reminded him of the mummy, its insides sucked out. Montorsi still had to see—he would do it that afternoon—if anyone had gone into his office again, at Headquarters. He would settle the score with Boldrini once this business was over. He couldn't help feeling a hidden but *palpable* link between the arm of the little corpse at Giuriati and the lacerated body of Mattei at Bascapé, nude and livid and already distended in the rain.

Then one of Arle's assistants called him. He could go in.

Arle said that he had very little time, to excuse him. He spoke, but it was as if he were not speaking. There was something toneless, mute almost, in Arle's voice. His eyes were glassy but deep. And he waved his hands, too. Yet he was a calm man. On the right corner of the desk sat a small terrarium of dim, dirty glass, full of dry sand, in which a dark little turtle was burrowing, the grains sticking to him.

Without considering whether it was prudent, Montorsi asked Arle about Mattei. After all, Arle had received him in spite of a frantic night, with the intelligence services waiting for the autopsy report. It was a delicate operation, because it had to be swift and at the same time precise, and a myriad variables had to be taken into account. It had been an oppressive night.

"I was there last night, too," Montorsi said.

The turtle seemed on the point of turning over. "It seems to me that it is no longer of interest to you on the Detective Squad," Arle said. He didn't even curl his lip. The sarcasm was totally implicit, effective because it was contained in the words themselves.

This infuriated Montorsi. He carefully concealed his anger and alluded quickly to the case to be archived, the excuse for the appointment. Arle asked questions that Montorsi was unable to answer. Arle persisted. Abruptly, Montorsi steered the conversation to the Giuriati case.

"Yesterday," said Montorsi. "The child found at the Giuriati playing field . . . ?"

No reaction. "Yes."

"I would be interested in an additional investigation, Doctor."

No reaction, again. "Let me call my assistant who is involved in it."

It was a bureaucratic response. It brought Montorsi immediately to the end of the conversation. In the files now in the hands of Forensics, surely, was the trail of the investigation's transfer from Montorsi to Boldrini. Detectives had turned the case over to Vice. Montorsi was no longer authorized to get involved. Arle would soon have the advantage. He had to do something, instantly.

"The signs of sexual violence on the child, Doctor—what do you think of them?"

Arle was motionless, then half closed his eyes. He brought his hands to his chin, as if in a gesture of prayer. "There is always some lunatic around. That's what I think."

"How many children pass through your department every year with similar signs of violence?"

Arle smiled slowly. "What number would you like me to give you? Six? Seven? Twenty? Do you have a theory to present, Inspector Montorsi?" His lips were dry but shiny with saliva toward the inside.

Montorsi didn't answer. He felt frightened. He rose, and as he turned to the door he gave a last discouraged look at the turtle. He went out. He stopped in the doorway; Arle was stone. "Thank you, Doctor," he said to him. "Thank you for everything." And he went out, definitively.

In the corridor he looked behind him and saw a dead man. Four doctors, their shirts splattered with dark stains, came through a swinging door, shook their heads at him, and smiled.

He was seeing himself reflected in a plastic window, as pale as he had ever been.

Arle was covering up the assassination of Mattei. Arle was covering up the ring of "pedophiles." This was the reason that the case had been taken away from him. Between Arle and Boldrini there was *some* agreement.

He quickened his pace. He had to meet Fogliese.

The angle of a wall as it turned a corner seemed to him the prow of a strange small ship. He ran into an empty gurney; the sheet that covered it hung longer on one side than the other. The orderly pushing it was wearing a frayed mask.

Ishmael Ishmael Ishmael Ishmael Ishmael.

Outside. Sun. He passed a group of university students. He had to see Fogliese, had to tell him that now he was in more danger than ever. Arle was covering up those people who were guilty of the death of Mattei. Arle was covering up a ring of pedophiles. The file Fogliese had delivered to *Il Giorno* was a threat to him. He had perhaps touched on the truth without even knowing it. Montorsi had to tell him what he felt, that everything revolved around the dark and secret name of Ishmael.

Milan
March 25, 2001
02:50

At Headquarters things were a mess. The police had brought everyone in; very few had managed to get away during the raid. End of the party. *End of the sadomasochists' party*. But Ishmael had escaped. Lopez had made an enormous blunder. He had been counting on surprise; it wasn't enough. The child had disappeared. The man to whom the Engineer had handed the child had vanished. The men and women who had concealed the exchange, waving their arms around the Engineer as in a procession, were not identifiable now. It had been one mistake after another. First during the reconnaissance, he and Calimani, because of the steep, densely overgrown slope, had failed to notice that door—however small and nearly hidden—at the rear of the hangar. Second, they should have had the place surrounded, with agents positioned even on the wooded sides of the hollow. Lopez should have asked for more men. He hadn't thought of a *military* operation.

He was depressed. *Elementary* mistakes.

The agents came and went on the fourth floor. The benches were crowded with people sitting in subdued embarrassment, still dressed for the PAV, grotesque, pathetic, their stares fixed. The woman on the wheel, who had lost consciousness, had been taken to the hospital. Santovito had appeared only to collect the Engineer and bring him into his office. He had leaned out to growl at Lopez that he had caught nothing, nothing useful for Cernobbio. And now Lopez was forcing him to deal with who knew what pressures. Santovito ordered that there be no interrogations without his permission and went back into his office; Lopez saw the Engineer sitting there.

Lopez didn't have a single card in his hand and he knew it.

There was no trace of the child; the Engineer would conceal everything. It was completely circumstantial. Every five minutes Lopez picked up the telephone to get information on the roadblocks. No trace of the man with the child. As in Paris. As in Detroit. Ishmael couldn't be caught.

Santovito came out. He was in a rage. He gave the order to Calimani that everyone was to go home. "Fuck you, Guido. What the hell did you think you were doing, getting me involved in this, with Cernobbio coming up?" Santovito's relentless diplomatic efforts—an unrefined form of fear—irritated Lopez. Santovito was insuring his jump in rank by solving the problem of Cernobbio and also by *not* solving it; he kept his eyes open, but closed them when it was necessary to close them. Lopez knew that it had all been in vain. Santovito was waving the failure in his face: a page-one operation without concrete results. Organization without precautions. A joke. Lopez observed Santovito, his bluish eyes, his overlapping yellow teeth. Then Lopez shook his head dismissively. Yes, let them all go home. Fuck Santovito.

Santovito wanted to talk to him privately. Calimani took advantage to get rid of the participants in the PAV. The Chief was uncontrollable: "Christ, Guido! What the hell were you trying to accomplish? They called for him, for this goddam Engineer. Jesus Christ, check things out before you make a move! You acted like an amateur. . . . You can't imagine *who* called! You'll screw me, with this bullshit of yours!"

Lopez remained expressionless.

"And do me a favor, Guido, don't touch any one of those who were at this party, this orgy that you ruined. Okay? The informer, the dickheads who were there, this goddam Engineer—leave them alone. Am I clear?"

Now it was Lopez's turn to be furious. "You're releasing him? You're mad, Giacomo. You're mad."

"Yes, I'm releasing him. You're an imbecile. An imbecile. Fuck off, Guido!" He turned around and went back to his office. To let the Engineer go.

Pieces of shit.

Lopez shook his head. He had in hand the woman on the wheel. She was his last hope to get something out of the disaster of the raid. Maybe the woman could speak. Maybe the woman knew.

He had to face Santovito. He would wait for him to calm down.

After a quarter of an hour, he went to see Santovito. He needed authorization for a guard and for the interrogation of the woman in the hospital. Her name was Laura Pensanti. From the file, he saw that she was to be kept there under observation. According to the report of the agent who had followed her in the ambulance from the PAV to the hospital, the woman had regained consciousness but wouldn't talk, confining herself to giving only the basic information. The emergency-room doctors had reported that her bruises and welts were not serious, a slight trauma. They would let her go the next day. She was thirty-seven, divorced, a resident of Milan, Via Friuli 58. No children. Profession: psychotherapist in the public health service, Clinic 24 on Viale Puglie 1. Lopez was puzzled. He saw again the limp body tied to the wheel, and the blood. He saw her eyes, clouded, blue. He read the file again. She was a 1990 graduate in psychology of the University of Padua, a member of the Association of Psychologists since 1992. She was Lopez's last hope. If he came up empty with this woman, the trail in Milan would be cold. There would be nothing to do but wait for Cernobbio. There—he was certain now—Ishmael would strike.

Santovito was still furious, more than before. "What's got into you, Guido? Can you explain that to me?"

"What's got into you, Giacomo? There was a child, do you understand? There was a child in the midst of all those people. . . ."

"I don't care. It's stuff for Vice. You have to bring me results on Cernobbio. Cernobbio blows up? Then we blow up. All of us. I first of all. And then you. Bring me results on Cernobbio. I don't give a damn about the rest. Children or old men or horses or faggots." He lit another cigarette. "Dickhead . . ."

Lopez was trembling; his wrists hurt.

"Fuck off, Guido. All you've done is make trouble for me with this sadomasochist business. Big, stupid trouble." Santovito shook his head. "Get your ass out of here, Guido."

He handed Santovito the request authorizing a police guard for the woman and the interrogation. Santovito began shouting: "Get the hell out of here! You don't seem to understand—get the hell out!"

Lopez didn't move. "Sign, Giacomo." He stood there. "I'm asking you, please. Sign."

Lopez went back to his office. Santovito had signed. He arranged for two shifts of a single agent outside the woman's room.

It was three in the morning, he was destroyed.

He looked in his pockets for a joint; he didn't have one. He would go to sleep. He would think about Laura Pensanti the next morning.

He looked in the drawer. No joints.

He got ready to leave. It was late. The telephone rang.

It was his colleague in Hamburg. They had found Rebecka. They had found Ishmael.

Milan
October 28, 1962
11:30

Fogliese did not show up for the appointment. Montorsi waited for half an hour, at least, in Largo Richini, sitting on a bench amid the trees in front of the university's ancient façade. The journalist was late, but that was typical of journalists. A strong wind shook the leaves and branches, and the building's burnished brick showed through dully, because the air was dark and opaque. A boy with uncombed hair and thick, fogged-up glasses was reading a book on the bench opposite Montorsi's. Students walked slowly, like people who come and go, talking of Michelangelo. Office workers went by, muffled up, and bicycles slowly negotiated the wide curve at the entrance to the little piazza. Summer was far away; Milan had been besieged by the cold for days now.

Arle was covering up everything. The finding of the child. The death of Mattei.

What had actually happened before the discovery of the infant's corpse at Giuriati? Whatever had been decided had begun there. No sign of Fogliese. Montorsi tried to give order to his thoughts and to the facts. Maura ravaged: It made his head spin to think about it. He was certain that the business of the Americans in Italy was fundamental. The Americans were occupying Italy: again, in more subtle ways, following strategies difficult to identify. He had seen it himself first-hand, in the corridors at Headquarters the day before, crowded with Americans in dark suits—the United States decides to establish an intelligence corps to contain the agents of the Soviet bloc in Italy. Probably the Cuban missile crisis was intensifying the secret clash between Americans and Soviets in Europe. According to the information put together by Fogliese, the Americans would install themselves in a military base outside Verona. And then . . .

and then the Americans would subsidize further operations, which would not be immediately classifiable as military or security actions. The sect that Fogliese had mentioned was one of these activities. It had plenty of financing, and lists of names, places, organizations. Had Ishmael been sent to Italy for this purpose? Would he form the first vanguard of the occupation? Would it be cultural, spiritual? Was he really acting apart from the military stratagems of American intelligence? Or was he entangled in its operations? Had the octopus Ishmael already extended and knotted all his tentacles?

Montorsi was inclined to the theory of a cultural and spiritual occupation of Italy. He *felt* it, in the hidden and improbable bond between the finding of the child at Giuriati and Mattei's assassination. It had been an assassination, he was certain. The bloodstains on the leaves, the undamaged trees at Bascapé—he had seen them himself, had touched them with his hand. If he started from there, everything found a place. He could measure every link of the chain. Arle is responsible for the autopsy and the collateral tests. He is in the ideal position; he can cover up the truth, how and when he wants. He is quoted in the newspapers declaring the crash an accident, perhaps due to an error by the pilot, who had been drinking. Meanwhile, every aspect of the investigation is removed from the jurisdiction of the Detective Squad—as a result of pressure from high up. Montorsi is removed from the investigation of the discovery at Giuriati as soon as he hypothesizes a ring of "pedophiles"—also as a result of pressure. Was it the same pressure? What had the investigation of the little body at Giuriati led to? To Mattei. The only factual connection was that photograph he had found in the archive at the *Corriere*: Mattei with other former partisans, *at the exact spot where the body of the child had been found.* Who was that behind Mattei in the photo, that pale face with its unnatural shadows, its eyes sunk in almost artificial obscurity? And the pressures from high up—hadn't Montorsi seen those in the archives, in the missing cards of the partisans who had died in the slaughter at Giuriati, *at the exact spot where the body of the child had been found,* and in the vanished newspaper articles, the ones that he had later discovered at the *Corriere?* But what did it mean?

It was as if something wished to reveal itself, but not completely. So that those who had eyes could see? Who was supposed to have the eyes to understand those signals? Was the finding of the child at Giuriati a signal? For whom? For Mattei? Was it the signal to begin? To begin the dominion of Ishmael? Who was Ishmael? Who was it the Americans were relying on? And why here, in Italy? A few hours after the death of the child, Mattei dies. Undoubtedly the killing of the child had been the signal for this second, secret American occupation. The meridians and parallels were expanding, the longitudes and latitudes lengthening and extending. The White House, Cuba, all Italy, the planet . . . Montorsi sat there in a stupor, unable to draw conclusions or even to formulate doubts, simply stunned at the complexity of a precise, intricate, and perfect design. At the center of this inlaid globe, Montorsi saw, in a luminous silhouette, the sublime name of Ishmael.

At 12:40 Fogliese had still not showed up. Montorsi decided to call him later in the afternoon at the *Corriere*. When you're a journalist time is unpredictable, and you can be sent off wherever from one moment to the next, a little like a policeman. He thought of telephoning Maura. He didn't feel like going to Fatebenefratelli. He could eat lunch with her and confront immediately the curtain of shame that fell between them after a crisis. He saw a phone booth. He went to call her.

Milan
October 28, 1962
00:40

When he was alone, in the living room or the kitchen but especially in the bathroom in front of the mirror, Italo Fogliese made faces. He twisted his mouth, opened it wide, and stuck out his tongue until the pain in the tendons of his neck forced him to stop. Then he retracted his tongue and went back to stretching his head, like a turtle. He did this every morning and every night before going to sleep, to keep the doors of remorse from opening and letting their truths emerge.

It was late, but David Montorsi had telephoned—as soon as he returned from Bascapé. He said that Mattei had been assassinated. Fogliese had put down the telephone calmly.

He had smiled. Ishmael is great.

He had turned on the dim light in the kitchenette, had put some water on to boil. Maybe he would make himself some chamomile. His wife had been gone for a year and a half. He had his faults, like everyone else. There had been the little misunderstandings, the shame and the soothed conflicts, the tireless and banal flow of days. This might be the greater indecency. It was painful to think of his wife.

Ishmael is great.

The water boiled, quietly. He didn't feel like turning around, facing the pale circle of the kitchenette, the gray-green surface of the table, the plastic wood.

He went back to thinking about Montorsi, who looked but didn't see. Ishmael was right before his eyes, without his even suspecting what Fogliese knew: the degree of refined and sophisticated complexity with which the plot had unfolded here in Italy. In Milan. He smiled at the thought of Montorsi's anxiety about his, Fogliese's, personal safety, about getting the dossier back from *Il Giorno*, to avoid risks now that Mattei was dead. Poor fool, this Montorsi. But soon he would understand. One way or another, Ishmael would lead him to understanding.

Ishmael is great.

When Montorsi showed up at the *Corriere*, with all his research on Giuriati, Fogliese had been astonished. It was the same day that Ishmael had placed the symbol of the child at Giuriati. The rites of Ishmael always had a baroque perfection. The symbol announced the advent of the era of Ishmael, which would begin with the death of Enrico Mattei. And just a few hours after the child was found, this Montorsi arrives at the *Corriere*, to do research into the plaque at Giuriati. Montorsi had already made the connection between the plaque and Mattei. Fogliese had had a moment of panic. He had excused himself, leaving Montorsi to wait for the results of the research, and gone down to the telephone booths at the entrance to the *Corriere* and called his contacts with Ishmael. They told him to remain calm. That there was no problem. To direct the young policeman on the right path. To let him guess without revealing anything. Fogliese didn't understand, but he had obeyed. He had spoken to Montorsi of the file that Ishmael had asked him to expand and get to Mattei, providing Mattei with scattered elements that might give an idea of the design.

Ishmael is great.

Joining the band of Ishmael's faithful had given Fogliese a meaning, a purpose. Ishmael was great. Not too long from now, finally, Ishmael would be everywhere and everything. Time was in Ishmael's favor.

He went back to the living room, pausing for a moment at the yellowed cast iron of the radiator beside the window. He pressed his face to the cold glass. It was still raining. Ishmael had begun to operate some hours before. He had just removed from the planet Enrico Mattei, the Master of Italy.

Fogliese turned. The typewriter was at the center of the ellipse of light shed by the table lamp, on the green cloth. He sat down. He began to write. Ishmael's men wanted a report on how the Mattei news had been received in the editorial offices. He would devote the final part of the report to Montorsi. They had asked him to lead Montorsi toward Ishmael. To reveal a little, to let him intuitively grasp, to set him on the right path.

Less than an hour later the report was finished.

Italo Fogliese washed and went to bed; it was late. As he fell asleep, the image of his wife emerged, in a calm without pain, like the bleached-out body of a woman coming to the surface of the dark water.

He woke with a start, the telephone already ringing. Five in the morning. He mumbled into the receiver, in the grip of despair—even though windows and shutters were closed, he had a distinct sensation that it was cold and still raining outside—when they told him they wanted to see him immediately, and where. It was Ishmael's men. That Ishmael needed him again—yet again, after he had fulfilled the request to let the news that Ishmael was now in Italy reach *Il Giorno* and Mattei—gave him a strange, frenetic strength. He dressed quickly and carelessly. A few minutes after the phone call, he was going out into the street.

Now the rain had stopped. When he opened the car door, he noticed the wet grime under his nails, a dark pulp. The windshield immediately fogged up.

He turned into Piazzale Maciachini. He took the new state road to Paderno Dugnano. It was five-thirty. The city was spectral, pierced by the halos of the hemispheres of the hanging lamps. He saw electricity sizzle in contact with the wet cables of the tram. He drove out of Milan, in the dark.

In Paderno Dugnano he saw the central square and turned left, following the directions he had been given. He seemed to smell a sweet burst of grass and mint, inside the car. He could almost feel the beard growing on his thin, lined cheeks. He passed the first of the two squares they had told him about on the telephone. At the second, he stopped. He saw the little street on the left and took it to the end. Here were the gates of the tire factory, as he had been instructed. Ishmael's two men were sheltered under a lamp, skin whitened by the light, like plaster statues, immensely old and vaguely threatening. As Fogliese got out of the car he observed the rust stains on the door under the window. He held the report for Ishmael under his arm.

He approached the two, smiling.

He shook hands with them both and handed over the report with a smile of useless cunning. He mentioned the schedule and decided to ask if there was a new task. They asked him about Montorsi; he told them everything he knew and was astonished when the man on the right fired the first pistol shot. He slipped backward and heard a slight rustling behind him. He was a shape made of curiosity and genuine amazement as he fell. Then came the second shot, a distant echo from a world that he no longer belonged to, and then the third shot, and the shuffle of steps and the wet smell of the asphalt and a new clear whiff of mint and indifference.

Inspector Guido Lopez

Milan
March 25, 2001
08:50

The night had been like a hallucination and the day that followed even more so. When everything was falling apart, a pathway had opened up, and now Lopez could breathe. They had found Rebecka, the Swedish woman who had met with Clemenceau in Hamburg before the attempt on Kissinger, and with Terzani, Ishmael's contact in Milan. She was the woman "perfect for the central role," about whom Clemenceau had written to Bob in the e-mails found in Paris. Lopez had provided the Hamburg police with the information from Clemenceau's e-mail, including the fact that Rebecka had something to do with the neighborhood of the Bahnhof. His colleagues in Hamburg had checked with their contacts in the Bahnhof but got nowhere. Then they had concentrated on the pedophile ring that worked through the port of Hamburg. The vice squad in Hamburg, busy protecting the good burghers of the city, like vice squads everywhere, had put up the usual smokescreen. According to the Department of the Ruhr, the traffic in children was run by organized crime. But, looking for Rebecka on Lopez's tip, they had sifted names, dates, and addresses, to see if a Swedish woman was the connection between the destinations and the criminal organization. They had found her: Rebecka Nörstrom, thirty-four years old, resident of London, financial intermediary. They had obtained a summary of her trips to Germany. All they knew was that she was based in Hamburg. The authorities were violating the implicit pact of "containment" of vice: keeping their hands off the second level, that of good society. The informers inside the crime organizations had been detained at the police stations. It was feared that they would reveal the police operation at the port. The Hamburg inspector confided to Lopez that if such information leaked, the politicians would react. Lopez heard Santovito's voice in the corridor. His rage mounted. In Milan, Lopez said, that was exactly what had happened: the politicians had reacted.

The operation in Hamburg would begin at ten tomorrow night. They would intercept Rebecka at the same time. Would Lopez come to Hamburg? Yes. A car would meet him at the airport. He would follow the operation as it developed. They would put Rebecka at his disposal, immediately, for an interrogation. Again, only a few hours after his failure, Lopez felt the cold breath of Ishmael.

It was three in the morning when he left Fatebenefratelli. His adrenaline had diminished but still he wasn't tired. He drove around the ring road, waiting in vain to feel like sleep. He stopped at the all-night tobacco shop in Via Crema, behind his house, asked for a little coke, and got it. He sniffed it in the men's room. Deep in his nostrils he felt the burning hit, tasting of chalk and disinfectant. His mouth became pleasantly bitter. He had two beers. His anger exploded as the face of the Engineer rose smiling before him. A police patrol came in; they recognized him, greeted him, went off embarrassed. The operation at the hangar in Pioltello had been a disaster, and the humiliation burned, in waves. At five he went home. He couldn't sleep. He thought of Hamburg. Of what he would ask Laura Pensanti in the hospital. Of what a graduate in psychology was doing at the center of a sadomasochist orgy. And what linked her and the Swedish woman to the dark yet dazzling name of Ishmael.

He left the house at eight. He had made himself eat breakfast; the milk made his throat sour. He didn't pack anything for Hamburg; he would return to Milan as soon as he had talked to the Swede. His legs were floppy as he went outside, and he felt incredibly weak. The hospital was a ten-minute walk. He went into a café nearby. At nine he was in front of Laura Pensanti's room, the gaze of the guard on duty fixed on the floor. He roused himself when he noticed Lopez. Lopez nodded to him to stay seated. He went in without knocking.

Laura Pensanti was standing next to the metal closet, wearing a white hospital gown, her eyes dark, her arms bare, and the marks of the whips, coagulated, striping her white, plastic-looking skin, a crust of dried blood on her calf. She regarded Lopez the way a child stares at an unfamiliar toy. She was removing her clothes from the metal hangers. For an instant Lopez saw her revolving on the wheel, abandoned and bleeding.

She placed the clothes on the bed. She turned to look at him. "Are you the person who was supposed to come from the police?"

Lopez grabbed the aluminum chair and dragged it next to the bed. "Inspector Guido Lopez. How are you?"

The woman rubbed her fingertips on the edge of a white shirt lying on the unmade bed. She looked at Lopez with detachment; he felt as if he didn't exist. "Fine. It's nothing, really. I can go. The doctors said that I can go home."

From the window came a milky light. "I have to ask you some questions. It's important."

She nodded. *Flash:* The thread of spittle, the night before at the PAV, fell obliquely from her mouth as the wheel slowed down. "I'd like to ask you about Ishmael," Lopez said.

She opened her eyes wide. She contracted her forehead. The skin was translucent, fine. The blue veins beat imperceptibly. "Who are you talking about?"

"Ishmael."

Silence. She shook her head. "There are no non-Europeans in the group."

Flash: Laura Pensanti is taken off the wheel, like soft marble. Small purple rivulets on her arms fall like tears, a body crying. "What group do you mean?" Lopez asked.

"The group from last night." There was bewilderment in her voice, but also tenderness and eagerness. "Excuse me, but what are you looking for, Inspector?"

"Ishmael. I'm looking for Ishmael."

The woman set aside the shirt. She breathed deeply. To Lopez she seemed a dream called up from far away. It seemed to him that she was speaking from the wheel. "I'm telling you, Inspector, the group is serious. The Engineer is rigorous. Security is important. We know each other. We have desires. Desperations, even. We satisfy them. We are all consenting. And we know each other. There is no one in the group who is called Ishmael."

She's telling the truth, Lopez thought. He tried again: "There was a child, at the end. Just before the raid, your Engineer, who is so careful about security, brought in a child."

"It's impossible." Her body was throbbing weakly, like a vein. His body throbbed too.

"There was a child."

"There have never been children. There never will be children. It's a game for adults. As I told you, we are all consenting."

"You lost consciousness." Another flash, and he saw her shining eyelids lowered, her limbs unbound as she was lowered from the wheel. "Then the child came in."

"Who is the child?"

"We don't know. A man took him away."

"What did the man look like?"

"He wore a mask. Leather."

"Everyone wears a mask in this game." She spoke of the event as if it were an inanimate object, a shell, a fossil. Something remote that could not touch her.

"Do you usually wear a mask, Signorina Pensanti?"

"Usually no."

Flash: She was revolving and revolving, she was beginning to bleed. Enveloped by pain, she felt nothing. Lopez felt a surge of embarrassment. "How many . . . of these 'gatherings' have you been to?"

She didn't smile. "I've been going to the group for a couple of years. This was my first PAV." She raised her head, stared at him in a silent challenge.

Lopez looked at his hands. In his nostrils he smelled the burning of last night's cocaine. The base of his tongue was rough and bitter. "So in two years you have never seen children taking part in one of these gatherings."

"Never. I usually go to gatherings that are more private, as I said to you. We aren't pedophiles. We don't do anything illegal."

Lopez felt the detergent taste of the cocaine. He had an intuition. "Signorina Pensanti, if I ask you about the 'central role,' does that mean anything to you?" He had thought of Rebecka, who according to Bob was "perfect for the central role."

Laura Pensanti shook her head. "It's not part of the vocabulary of sadomasochism."

He would learn nothing from her. She knew nothing. The Engineer kept everyone in the dark. No one knew anything about

Ishmael. Lopez's eyes fell, enchanted, on the luminous folds of the shirt lying in the slight hollow of the pillow. His gaze returned to her. "No. I'm sorry to have disturbed you." He rose, feeling the fatigue suddenly, in his neck.

She watched from the bed while Lopez wearily dragged the aluminum chair to the wall. When he turned, she said to him, "Ask me."

Lopez felt himself grow pale, as if he secretly knew something that he couldn't grasp. "What am I supposed to ask?"

She bent her neck, her gaze slid along the sheets, and she turned again to Lopez's eyes. "Why I do it. Ask me why I do it."

Lopez remained standing. He felt that he felt nothing. And he asked her why, why she did it.

They talked.

Lopez forgot the name of Ishmael.

They talked for an hour.

They shared the darkness.

At noon, in the airport, when he tried to sleep on the hard narrow chair in the departure lounge before the flight for Hamburg was announced, Laura Pensanti's words whirled in him like a luminous wake, and as he traversed the oblique suspended runway toward the plane he felt unbalanced inside, swayed by a sweetness that unbound him; he felt that something had secretly seized him and drawn him far away.

Milan
October 28, 1962
12:45

When David telephoned and asked if she wanted him to come home so they could have something to eat together, Maura could barely contain her hatred. It had assailed her as soon as she awakened, late, weak, and exhausted from the night's crisis.

She no longer understood anything. She was in a daze from the tranquilizers. The child, David, Luca: Everything was rotating slowly inside her. She had tried to create order, but hatred was eating at her heart. Her head was heavy, with powerful blasts of anxiety.

She would talk to Luca.

She would not talk to David.

At one David arrived. They observed each other in silence. He had tried to start a conversation, but she shook her head, she caressed him. She concealed her hatred by showing her pain.

The sun jumped between the iron rods of the balcony railing and was reflected on its stone floor, which was now drying in large patches. The light came slanting through the window, sparkling on the glasses and the water, on the plates, suffusing the emerald green of the salad and the little drops on the surface, striking the glass in the cupboard and the dusty fabric of the couch on which Maura and David had slept that night. They sat facing one another in a daze: Maura between sobs and the throbbing in her head, and her twisted stomach and the gathering salt of tears; and David in pure forgetfulness. The reflection of the sun expanded slowly along the wall into the other room.

He sat her on his knees. He kissed her. She seemed to forget herself. Her saliva still possessed the mucus of tears that makes a woman's mouth viscous and good. She had cried, quietly, without hurry and without anxiety, and closed her eyes, whispered something disjointed. They kissed for a long time. She seemed to be thinking of nothing. They made love, on the sofa. Brief, conclusive, intense love, gentle and sordid. She had come immediately, after not even three thrusts, which in his mind had to do with being grateful and feeling protected, and which for her involved approaching abandonment. She saw in the light the face of Luca, and was silent.

He licked the salt traces of the tears on her cheeks, tasting the skin, feeling the freckles. She thought of the other man and didn't know who she was. David didn't suspect, didn't understand that he was alone in the light above her.

Then they ate, observing one another, like animals who play and yet do not trust. Her gaze passed through states he didn't understand. He got up from the table to kiss her. He caressed her stomach, where the creature was sleeping. They had coffee, barely speaking. David mentioned the possibility that after the birth, in anticipation of the depression that would come with it, Maura should see a psychologist. She thought of how David didn't understand, didn't understand at all, and accepted his words in silence, to make him be quiet.

Going out onto the balcony, David felt the warmth on his gray skin awaken distant urges in him. For an instant, everything was silent. Then a cloud descended toward the sun, and with a shudder he came to himself and the grace faded. Mechanically he looked behind him, saw the sad mesmerized gaze of his wife behind the glass. He turned toward the darkness of the stairs and left.

Maura went to the telephone, stood uncertainly, dialed Luca's number, and asked to see him. There was some interference on the line. They had trouble hearing each other. Luca asked her if she was all right. She said no. She said that she had been sick. She said that she wanted to talk to him. Luca proposed a drive in his car. She accepted. There was even more interference on the line. They made a date to meet at Viale Umbria, at the intersection with the Nuovo Verziere, the vegetable market, at four.

She would tell him everything.

At three-thirty, she got ready.

She went out.

To Viale Umbria.

She felt that she was being followed. Was it David?

She was restless.

4:10. Viale Umbria, at the intersection with Nuovo Verziere.

Luca didn't come.

She felt alone, ready to be extinguished forever, in her pain.

A car. The door opened. It wasn't Luca. It was a colleague of his. He said that Luca was sorry. He said that he was waiting for her at home. The demands of work had intervened. He said that Luca had sent him to pick her up. He said to get in.

And Maura got in.

Inspector David Montorsi

Milan
October 28, 1962
14:20

David Montorsi arrived at Headquarters at almost two-thirty, feeling ill. Maura was ill, he was ill. They had made love in order not to say that they were ill. He went directly to his office, ignoring Omboni, who was trying to speak to him. He opened the door cautiously. The piece of paper that he had left in front of the door had shifted toward the wall. They had gone in. He opened the drawers. He had memorized the position of the papers, and he saw that they had been moved—slightly, but moved. He sat down, sank his head in his hands, and put his elbows on the desk. He sat thinking of nothing. He didn't want to think. It was all so impossible to put together, all so evanescent and yet complicated. Someone knocked. He said come in. The door opened. Omboni stood on the threshold and said only, "Come," and Montorsi followed him silently, amid the rustling of paper and tapping of typewriters in offices, and only in the courtyard, as they got into a police car, did Omboni tell him: "A journalist is dead. From the *Corriere*. Italo Fogliese, I think."

Montorsi tried to think and the news seemed fake to him. He tried to put the elements together and immediately his thoughts slipped toward Maura. He tried to connect the murder of Italo Fogliese and his meeting with Arle, and he couldn't; he felt like thinking of Maura. He shook himself.

Fogliese was *dead*.

Ishmael had struck.

Omboni cursed the Milanese traffic as he drove to Fogliese's apartment in Lambrate.

The house of a single man. Signs of solitude were everywhere: the rancid dirt around the rubber closure of the refrigerator, the scale-encrusted kettle in the middle of the sink, the typewriter on the kitchen table, a dozen books piled on the floor beside the sofa. The clothes rack of polished wood, where the single man places his clothes, providing the appearance of order to lean on and the reassuring feeling of taking care of oneself. In the bathroom, expired medicines on the shelves beside the mirror; rust stains between the bands of the milky green metal shutters; and black dust, coagulated in a thick opaque crust on the tiles of the balcony.

They had found him in Paderno Dugnano. He had been shot three times. The body had been dragged behind a tire factory. The Forensics people put the death at between four and five in the morning. Montorsi thought, Arle. Fogliese's body was soaked with rain, his clothes heavy with water. One shot, probably the third, had gone through his brain, entering from below, where the resistance of the cranial cavity was less, splitting his upper lip in two, and forcing out the incisors, cracking the nasal passage and exiting right in the middle of the neck. Ishmael had moved. Montorsi was afraid.

He said nothing to Omboni about Arle, Boldrini, the child at Giuriati, the photograph in the *Corriere* with Mattei. But he began to search the apartment for a copy of Fogliese's file on Ishmael and the Americans, the one he had sent to Mattei's *Giorno,* or the photograph of Mattei at Giuriati. He went through the drawers (unironed shirts, which still smelled of starch and mothballs). He looked through the books. Even in the kitchen he looked, among the dishes and in the jars. Omboni watched him furtively, without understanding the almost rancorous care he applied to the search. Montorsi searched in the bathroom. He saw tranquilizers, not even opened and already expired. In the living room, Omboni examined the photograph of Fogliese's wife, scratching his head. "She'll have to be told. No one's done it yet." Montorsi nodded. He went back to the books. He opened the dresser in the bedroom again. He looked in the inside pockets of the jackets. There was a ridiculous rust-colored tie. He tried under the bed, between the mattress and the box spring, and Omboni stood in the doorway, more and more perplexed by Montorsi's furious zeal.

Now Montorsi lifted the typewriter off the table, examined the bottom, picked up the green cloth that covered the tabletop. He looked at Omboni. He nodded. Then he said, "Let's go to the paper. Let's go check at the *Corriere*. Maybe something in his desk . . ."

Omboni closed the door. But on the stairs, halfway between the floor below Fogliese's apartment and the next, Montorsi stopped. He asked Omboni for the keys—"Just a minute. I'll be right back"—and went up quickly, opened the door, and in the darkness went right to the typewriter on the table, felt under the cover for the spools, unscrewed them, and took the ribbon. He wound them until he could place the two black metal spools, shiny even in the dark, on top of one another, and put the ribbon in his pocket. He went out. Omboni was on the landing, puzzled. Montorsi shook his head and closed the door, saying: "Nothing . . . Nothing . . . One last little question."

At the *Corriere* they found nothing. The editor welcomed them in person. He was upset. He said that Fogliese was a good fellow, such a good fellow; they had already drafted the little obituary that would be published the next day. Montorsi examined the reporter's desk. Omboni interviewed the editor and the journalist who would follow the investigation of Fogliese's murder for the *Corriere,* and who made it clear how much the paper had been shaken up by the news of Mattei's death, perhaps even more than the other papers. The editor had put five of his people on the story. Fogliese wasn't part of that group. He did local news and crime news. Especially in the outskirts of Milan. He also did features for the national news pages. Not much politics. Anyway, the editor would have his articles collected—those of the past three years—and have them sent to Omboni. Maybe some useful element might emerge from them. Montorsi had found nothing in Fogliese's desk drawers. He had checked in the archives: The photograph of Mattei at Giuriati had been taken by Fogliese himself, and he hadn't had time to bring it back—and this, too, he did not tell Omboni.

They returned to Headquarters. They would wait for the Chief's orders regarding who was to work on the Fogliese case and how. Maybe Montorsi and Omboni would work together, maybe not. The fourth floor of Fatebenefratelli was still in an uproar because of Mattei's death. Omboni stood staring at the floor, disconsolate. "This is turning into one big mess," he said. Montorsi said goodbye, went to his office, and locked the door behind him. He took the ribbon from Fogliese's typewriter out of his pocket. He would need time to examine it, to retrieve the text written by the journalist. He began to unroll it and his fingertips were immediately covered with ink. He could see the line of letters and the first coherent words began to appear.

Hamburg
March 25, 2001
14:50

At the Rathausmarkt, a galleria near Domstrasse, around the corner from the Town Hall, Lopez sat at a table in the Ganzfeldt Cremerie eating an enormous piece of chocolate cake. At the northern end of the galleria he could just make out the driver sitting in the Audi that had picked him up at the airport. He was waiting for two agents from the Hamburg detective squad, Stefan Wunzam and Lucas Hohenfelder. They had told him to meet them here rather than at Headquarters. Lopez had understood immediately that they were trying to avoid having their investigation obstructed the way Lopez's had been by Santovito. The investigation into traffic in children had intruded into the political level. They would attempt to interrupt the exchange planned for Dock 11 at ten that night, and seize Rebecka for their Italian colleague. All without Ishmael's being able to set his connections in motion, as he had done in Milan.

Lopez yawned. The cake was disgusting. A stream of people crossed the Rathausmarkt in both directions. He thought of Laura. She had talked to him for an hour, and he listened, stupefied. She had said that, in the end, he was the morbid one, not her. That he wanted to see the dirt and hadn't the courage to look at it. That his eyes betrayed the dissatisfaction of an unknown desire. That he did not dare to ask her what he really had to ask her, and that what he asked her had nothing to do with the reason that he was there with her. That the child was nothing. That Ishmael was nothing. That the investigation meant nothing. That he thought she was perverted but in fact "you are the pervert." That he wanted to know what that form of pleasure was that he had barely tasted, the night before, when he had seen her "playing." She used that word, "playing." She had said he was a "limp dick." She had smiled, shaking her head. He looked at her in silence. He didn't answer; he let himself be submerged by her. He smelled the last bit of cocaine he had sniffed at dawn. She stared at him, her blue eyes widened. He could leave and didn't. Ishmael seemed a vague memory, a bewildering, shadowy outline behind the answer that Laura had given him when he tried to confront her and asked what *she* was looking for. "You don't understand," she said. "Go back to your case. You can't understand, can you?" and she had begun to undress, so she could put on her clothes and go home, and he, dazed, had left the room and at the last moment had managed only to turn and tell her that probably he would have to talk to her again, and she had smiled scornfully, and said, "You don't even have the courage to ask if you can call me." He had gone away exhausted, stripped bare. Now, too, as he sat waiting for the two policemen at the Rathaus, the thorn of shame pricked him. He could think only of the liquid, foul sweetness that had been released in his body when she had called him a "pervert."

He pretended to eat a mouthful of cake. He could barely swallow. He made an effort and wolfed the cake, almost suffocating in the process. He thought of the hangar, of Laura, unconscious, turning. He thought of the leather masks, the odor of genitals. He thought of the child who had escaped, the man who had carried him off. The man might be the father of the child. He might be someone important. He could be Ishmael.

Two men pulled over some chairs and sat down. It was the German cops. They introduced themselves; they all spoke a hiccuping English. Stefan Wunzam was the more sympathetic. He was blond, with a clear, inoffensive gaze, a little taller than Lopez and the same age, and it was he who, of the three, managed best with English. The other detective, Lucas Hohenfelder, irritated Lopez. He was stocky, younger than Wunzam, taciturn, with a look of near-psychotic belligerence. Lopez spoke only to Wunzam. They had brought the records of calls to and from Rebecka Nörstrom's cell phone during the previous forty-eight hours. They had her under close physical surveillance as well and had a black-and-white photograph of her. Long straight hair, a thin, almost sullen face. Wunzam said they had expected a babe, after reading Rebecka's c.v.: Swedish, thirty-four years old, a habitué of financial circles. He smiled; the other was expressionless and mute. Lopez smiled too, and there came to his mind the pallor and the challenging smile of Laura Pensanti.

It was getting colder; the Rathausmarkt was swelling with tourists and locals. Together they examined the cell-phone calls. There were fifteen, four made by Rebecka, eleven received. Wunzam explained that they had identified all the numbers except for one, which they were working on. Wunzam listed the outgoing calls: Steve Piaczewick, an American, an employee in the embassy in Berlin, to set up a meeting between United States and German financiers involved in new technology; Franziskus Klamm, a cocaine dealer in Hamburg; Steve Piaczewick again, to make sure that a manager from Cisco Systems would be present. The fourth call was the key to the operation at Dock 11: Mario Ljuba, a Slav, an intermediary between the shippers and the customers at the port. With him Rebecka had confirmed the delivery of the "little packages" that evening at ten. Ljuba had asked her, before speaking, if the cell was secure, and she had started laughing.

Rebecka had received eleven calls from six people. Three calls from Franziskus Klamm, the dealer, to confirm that Rebecka would find the coke at Pall, a club a hundred yards from the hotel where she lived (the Vorbach Hotel, Wunzam told Lopez, in the neighborhood of the fairgrounds and quite far from the city center; according to the hotel register she stayed there three weeks out of every month, working from her room). One call was from Klaus Baum, twenty-eight years old, residing in the area south of Hamburg, a male prostitute with a drug record, who, interestingly, had been charged a year earlier by the police in connection with the presence of children in a private sex club for couples swapping. Wunzam didn't think that Rebecka had intervened with the police. Baum had been exonerated thanks to the efforts of a German bureaucrat, Karl M., at the E.U., in Brussels. Lopez read his name lower down on the list of persons who had called Rebecka. In Baum's phone call, he had asked the Swedish woman if she felt like "playing," that night, at his house; there would be a couple of "interesting" woman friends there, he said, who "play the way you like." Lopez thought of Laura talking about the "game." He had an intuition that this was Ishmael's circle. Rebecka had said no, she had engagements that night. Wunzam remarked that the bitch called her "little packages" "engagements"; she was "engaged" with child trafficking, the Swedish shit.

The following phone call was from Piaczewick, to confirm the arrival of the manager from Cisco. Next on the list was Karl M., flunky at the European Parliament. Wunzam said that the police had had to keep the text of the phone call secret. It was explosive. It went beyond the Hamburg politicians directly to Brussels. Wunzam summarized the phone call for Lopez. In effect Karl M. asked how business was going, if Rebecka was occupied with her friends the undersecretaries, if the contacts that he sent her responded positively. Then came the bombshell: Karl M. asked Rebecka when she anticipated those "machines" being delivered to Brussels, and she said within a day or two, that she was preparing everything that very night. The "little packages" had become "the machines." For Wunzam there was no doubt, and Hohenfelder nodded with conviction, not saying a word.

The children were going to Brussels.

Lopez was excited. Wunzam was upset, pale with worry. They went to the end of the list of calls on Rebecka's cell phone. Four were from the Swedish embassy in Berlin, one from an official, Klaas Knudsson, about organizing a party at the embassy, mentioning contacts, telephone numbers, nothing of interest. One call had not been taken by Rebecka, from Baum again; she had not called him back.

The last call was a problem. It had come from an unidentifiable cell phone. Probably foreign. Rebecka didn't know the caller. But the man had told Rebecka that he got her number from Bob. Bob: the former member of Science Religion. Bob: Ishmael's man who appeared in the Americans' report. Bob: the one who had activated Clemenceau and Terzani. It was from Bob's e-mail that they had identified Rebecka. Obviously there was no trace of him in Hamburg. Wunzam and Hohenfelder had tried to track him from the first moment, when Lopez had sent them the Americans' report on Ishmael. When the man who telephoned mentioned Bob, Rebecka's tone of voice had changed. She had asked if the man could follow the instructions and he had said yes, he had the instructions. He had asked for confirmation—were the place and time those of the instructions? Rebecka had said yes. Then she ended the call.

* * *

The plan, according to Lopez and Wunzam, was this: Children were being sent to Brussels, with Ishmael's group in the person of Rebecka as the intermediary. The exchange would take place at Dock 11 at the port of Hamburg. The man who had mentioned Bob would bring the children; Ljuba would load them on some form of transport; the delivery, in Brussels, would take place in two days. It all added up: The rites of Ishmael as they had been described ever since the first report from the American NSA; the participation of Rebecka, who represented Ishmael's interests in Hamburg, as the Engineer represented them in Milan; and a cover-up for these emissaries at the highest political level—a cover-up that would be useful to Ishmael's emissaries if something went wrong and also useful to Ishmael himself, in view of *his* operations, like the attempt on Kissinger in Paris or the one that was being planned for Cernobbio.

The strategy was to have a stakeout at Dock 11, where the "little packages" would be delivered, and arrest the courier, Rebecka, and Ljuba. Lopez was interested in Rebecka and the courier, who might well be the man who had taken the child from the hangar at Pioltello the night before. It would be an operation on a grand scale, Wunzam said. Lopez recounted to Wunzam and Hohenfelder how the small-scale operation in Milan the night before had been a total failure. The humiliation still burned. Wunzam shook his head and said that in Hamburg it would go differently—here, both the men and the means were available. Lopez asked for a security protocol, which he needed to resist the overwhelming pressure that would come from the politicians: he wanted two hours alone with Rebecka, away from police headquarters, to interrogate her about Ishmael and Cernobbio; after the two hours, he would hand her over to Wunzam.

Lopez and Hohenfelder would watch the Vorbach Hotel and follow Rebecka's every movement; Wunzam would coordinate the operation from Headquarters. They would be in continuous contact. Wunzam would open a line in Lopez and Hohenfelder's car so that they could intercept Rebecka's calls. The three of them would meet at Dock 11 once the arrests were made and the children freed.

The Rathausmarkt was filling up with cold-reddened faces. A cold wind swept the broad streets of Hamburg. Hohenfelder drove without speaking, in slow, heavy traffic. Dark evergreens lined the edges of the road in the neighborhood of the canals. They arrived at the Vorbach Hotel in half an hour. Hohenfelder parked opposite the entrance, set the radio to the frequency indicated by Wunzam, and began to smoke. Lopez got out to stretch his legs. Most of the windows of the Vorbach were lighted. He wondered which one was Rebecka's room. He looked in his pocket for a joint, found it, lighted it. He knocked on the car window and asked Hohenfelder for a cell phone. He found the number he wanted in an inside pocket. He telephoned.

Laura Pensanti answered immediately; she laughed on hearing Lopez's voice. Lopez said that he wanted to see her; she laughed again. They were both talking at once. He said he was "outside Milan." She said she was going to work the next day. He asked if he could see her.

When Lopez closed the cell phone, he felt the cold wind of Hamburg on his skin.

It was 17:40. It was all about to end.

Milan
October 28, 1962
16:10

His hands stained with ink from the ribbon—red and black—Montorsi began deciphering the words that Fogliese's typewriter had tapped out.

He had unrolled the whole ribbon and rewound it onto its original spool, as if it were new. The letters were an incoherent strip of Morse code. He had to retrieve their outlines by putting the ribbon against the light; then he was able to identify them, traced in the red of the lamp. The spaces, obviously, were not recorded by the ribbon, so it would be an additional task to separate the words. He had confined himself simply to recording the letters on a sheet of paper. The spaces between the words he would insert later.

He was sweating under the lamp because of the difficulty of the job and the excessive heat from the radiator; all the air was hot. A stupefying proliferation of language unrolling on a single plane, indecipherable. It seemed to him that a dead man was speaking to him from the carbon of the ribbon, spirit-rapping from the hereafter. Montorsi was spellbound. It would never end. The ribbon kept unrolling, it seemed infinite. The end seemed to recede continually.

And now he had got there. He didn't understand what it said as he was separating the letters into words. Then he read.

Bull's-eye.

He had identified pieces of two documents. The first was evidently part of the file on Ishmael that Fogliese had sent to *Il Giorno*. It was incomplete; the journalist had started and then had replaced the ribbon. Montorsi had only the end.

[. . .]hamlet of Nogarole, in the province of Verona. It is anticipated that the headquarters of this intelligence corps will be built at the American base, and furthermore that it will be independent of the organs of the CIA and the NSA, at least as far as concerns the operation of the nucleus. The tasks of this intelligence corps consist essentially of:

-the control of territory in support of groups that already exist, with the purpose of fighting the Soviet intelligence presence in Italy

-drafting a broad archive of names within the groups led by the Italian Communist Party

-infiltration at high institutional levels in order to attain objectives of destabilization of the country, in case of electoral progress by the Communist Party

-not sporadic but regular training of volunteer bodies to use in possible terrorist actions

-the protection of high American personages present in Italy

-throwing off course investigations of the carabinieri and the Italian police

-infiltrating the diplomatic and civil spheres of the Vatican

-installation, protection, and revitalization of an active religious group, anti-Catholic in function, in Italy first and later elsewhere in Europe, which--according to the programs--is to support a vast network of adherents who do not know the real nature of the group, and by means of it to realize a vast network of information and create pressure, in the style of a lobbying group, on the institutional elements. The parareligious group would be centered on the name of Ishmael, of whose personality little is known. The sources consulted (among them eminent and well-informed figures belonging to the intelligence services of the Scandinavian countries cited above) emphasize how it is characteristic of the strategies elaborated within United States intelligence to penetrate culturally the nation in which the U.S. wishes to exercise tighter political control. The arrival of Ishmael in Italy must be "ratified" and made visible through an operation of terrorist stamp and sensational portent, probably included in a standard symbology of the sect that the United States is helping to build in Italy. Occasional and not completely reliable information concerning the identity of Ishmael is not here reported. Here is reported, instead, the "unofficial" voice that Ishmael's headquarters wants, with offices in Milan. The Americans think that, in a decade, Ishmael will be a sufficient threat to be able to attain his goals and those of the intelligence unit stationed in Nogarole: hence, of the Administration in Washington. It is important to emphasize that both establishment figures and non-establishment figures, in Italy, were warned of the arrival and the meaning of the installation of Ishmael in our country.

Remaining imprecise, in this picture, is the degree of fusion that will be effectuated between the two structures: intelligence and the parareligious. It isn't possible, in effect, on the basis of the information gathered, to know if and how much Ishmael will be independent from the intelligence nucleus. The sources mentioned above emphasize that the two structures could be fused and indistinguishable from one another.

This, then, was the story of Ishmael. Montorsi was stunned by the coherence of the plan, by the dry, precise exposition that poor Fogliese had given of the American strategy. Yet everything still escaped him about Ishmael. There was no certainty about anything. Who was Ishmael? What were the symbols connected to Fogliese's file? What "sensational" operation was it referring to? The death of Mattei?

He tried to think. He couldn't. He called Maura. He sat listening to the phone ring and ring. He decided to decipher the second bit, the one corresponding to the first letters he had deciphered, at the end of the ribbon, the last words written by poor Fogliese.

He did it. And was stunned, like a man just before dying. *He was completely mistaken.* Everything was the opposite of what he had imagined.

No one—no one was safe anymore.

October 28, 1962
From: Italo Fogliese
To: Continental Church Milan/Italy
Subject: Information on Ishmael and Mattei accident; *Corriere della Sera* and other papers; Detective Squad of Milan

Following the Enrico Mattei operation, the initial act of the manifestation of the Sublime Ishmael in Italy, I report on the state of journalistic investigations, with an appendix regarding possible disruptions.

As far as I know, the death of Enrico Mattei will be interpreted immediately as an accident. At least as far as regards the major national newspaper, the version of an accident will be the official interpretation. The same situation goes for the other editorial offices. It seems that in the Communist sphere there is reluctance to assert the hypothesis of an assassination, also having to do with embarrassing episodes that link the leaders of the Party to the figure of Enrico Mattei.

In short, everything that was predicted by the Sublime Ishmael is taking its course according to the expected modalities. It should be emphasized that all the papers--without exception--will report without undue emphasis the news that the Detective Squad of Milan has been excluded from the investigations; as is well known, some figures on the Squad maintained close ties with Mattei. It seemed completely natural that the judiciary should take over the investigation, with the obvious support of the secret services, where our covers are highly efficient.

Yesterday, at the *Corriere*, the young inspector David Montorsi showed up. He was working on an investigation concerning the Symbol of the Child, in spite of the fact that our internal covers succeeded in muzzling the case and handing it over to controllable elements.

Despite the fact that the case was taken away from him, Inspector Montorsi is investigating illegally on his own. He does not in the least have a clear idea of the meaning of the discovery and, above all, he is unable to connect it to the death of Enrico Mattei. The Symbol of the Child, for the moment, is considered a case on its own. Yet Montorsi was able to find, in the archives of the *Corriere*, an image from right after the war, taken at the partisan monument at Giuriati playing field, exactly in the spot where the Symbol of the Child was placed. Montorsi was unable to identify the presence of one of our covers among the persons who appear in the photograph. I received instructions to communicate to Inspector Montorsi the existence of Ishmael. I carried out these orders, assuring Montorsi that I would cooperate with him, to track down possible further elements.

This is what I have learned about him. David Montorsi, 26, is married to Maura Paolis. He has been on the police force for seven years, at various levels. Two years ago he was made inspector on the Detective Squad. He has no ties to his colleagues. His pay is slightly lower than that usually given in the post of inspector. It is not certain that he is corruptible, although he is ambitious, and other elements in his private life might be useful for the purpose of eventually turning him.

I remain in expectation of instructions.

Before the eternal greatness of the Sublime Ishmael his faithful disciple bows

(Italo Fogliese)

Montorsi could hardly breathe. His heart beat irregularly, sending bursts of blood through him. He was gray. He rubbed his cheeks, feeling his unshaved beard. He got up and went to the window. He breathed hard, on the glass, to chase away the shadow of danger behind him.

Between his dry tongue and his sticky palate, he seemed to have a presentiment of a taste of tin and blood. He seemed to perceive in things an imminent end. He lowered his shoulders and his stomach began to tremble. So Fogliese was a "faithful disciple of Ishmael." So in the photograph of Mattei at Giuriati appeared the face of one of Ishmael's many powerful covers. Who had killed Fogliese? And why? Did he know too much? Had Ishmael got rid of him?

Ishmael knew about Montorsi. Fogliese had asked for and obtained instructions on how to behave toward him. Ishmael had ordered him to communicate the existence of the sect.

Fogliese had written: "*It is not certain that he is corruptible, although he is ambitious, and other elements in his private life might be useful for the purpose of eventually turning him.*" What did it mean? Did Ishmael want to approach him?

He thought of Maura.
A whirl of names and voices swirled around him.
Then, loudly, the telephone rang.
It was Dr. Giandomenico Arle.

Hamburg
March 25, 2001
20:20

Sitting for hours, in the car, in front of the Vorbach Hotel, Lopez and Hohenfelder had exchanged few words. It was a long stakeout in the company of an asshole, and Lopez had got out a couple of times to smoke away his weariness with a joint. On the telephone, Laura Pensanti had laughed. They hadn't talked about Ishmael. They hadn't talked about the sadomasochist group. He hadn't told her he was in Hamburg. He had asked if he could see her. She had made him repeat what he said. She told him to repeat it slowly. He had repeated the question slowly, smiling. She had asked if he was smiling, and he was silent. She had said to him: "Now say it slowly. And without smiling." He had obeyed. She had started laughing. She would think about it, she said. They had talked a little more, general information about their jobs. Then she had said goodbye, reminding him of what he wanted to be reminded of: "You want to ask me about it, right? You want to ask me to talk to you again about last night, right?"

Then Hohenfelder had stuck his head out the window, had nodded to him, and he had quickly said goodbye to Laura. Wunzam was calling on the radio; everything was ready. Since 20:00, two squads of plainclothes agents had been watching the entire area around Dock 11, checking the cargoes. Two more agents, also in plainclothes, were following Ljuba. Rebecka was at the Vorbach Hotel. She had made no phone calls. Maybe she was sleeping. Maybe she was working. As soon as they saw the Swede, Lopez and Hohenfelder would call Wunzam.

20:40. Nothing.

20:50. Movement in the lobby of the Vorbach.

20:55. Rebecka.

She walked quickly out of the hotel. She didn't take her car.

Hohenfelder got out and Lopez stayed in the car. They were thinking of the cocaine that Klamm, the pusher, had left for her at the Pall, the piano bar on the corner, a hundred yards from the Vorbach. When they arrived that afternoon, they had driven slowly past the wide windows of the Pall. Sitting at the piano was a character with absurdly curly hair, wearing a blue smoking jacket that was too big for him. Otherwise, it had seemed an anonymous sort of pub, quite spacious. From the car, Lopez had sighted every entrance and exit. Now he watched Rebecka disappear inside. Hohenfelder went into the Pall a couple of minutes afterward. He came out first, though, and walked to the corner. Rebecka came out, without a bag or package. If she had picked up something, it was in her purse. She returned to the Vorbach. Hohenfelder stood still at the corner. Rebecka went into the hotel. The whole excursion had taken ten minutes. When he got back in the car, Hohenfelder told him they had been correct; she had gone to get the cocaine. No problem.

21:10. The radio crackled: Rebecka was telephoning. A man answered, and they spoke in German. Hohenfelder attentively took notes. Rebecka and the man said goodbye. It was Klamm, the German policeman said. Rebecka sounded enthusiastic about the delivery she had received from him. She had already sniffed it.

21:20. Rebecka appeared again. This time she had car keys in her hand. She opened the door of a BMW. Hohenfelder called Wunzam on the radio to say they were moving. He started the car and stayed no more than thirty meters behind her.

The traffic was thinning. Rebecka drove nervously. Hohenfelder had trouble staying behind her without being noticeable. They had only half an hour before the "delivery" at Dock 11. Lopez made radio contact with Wunzam, who told him they were all in position. The agents who were following Ljuba had joined up with the others, at the port; Ljuba had gone into a bateau-bar, near Dock 13. Of the man who was to deliver the children there was not a sign.

Rebecka accelerated. Lopez didn't take his eyes off the BMW. Rotherbaum. She accelerated again, in Mittelweg. She turned onto Kennedybrucke. On the right were the lights of shop windows, no pedestrians, and few cars. On the left lay black water, perhaps the enormous bend in the river, a broad elbow that reflected nothing. Adenauerallee. Then a turn. Another turn, to the right. She got tangled in traffic in Spaldingstrasse. Hohenfelder said he didn't understand; Rebecka was pointlessly making the route to Dock 11 longer. Lopez asked if he should tell Wunzam. Hohenfelder said to wait—maybe Rebecka was trying to be careful, driving a confusing route as a precaution. Oberhafen. Suddenly before them was a huge bridge over a strait. The irritating lights of the cars came toward them in a slow line. From the bridge, the water was black and practically invisible. Then they were again in the city, the southern part. Moldhaufen. Kleiner Grasbrook. A new turn. A labyrinth of streets. Aslastrasse. Hohenfelder shook his head. He opened radio communication and spoke rapidly in German; Lopez understood nothing. When he was finished, he said he had told Wunzam that Rebecka was still driving around the neighborhood of Amingstrasse. They were far from Dock 11.

21:53. On the right was the black river. The streets to the left were dark. They went beyond the Farkanal. Left, away from the river. Steinwerder. A sudden left turn. Nehlstrasse. Rebecka stopped the car. She got out. She stood there, in the cold, smoking under the street light next to the BMW. Lopez and Hohenfelder had stopped forty or fifty meters away. Hohenfelder called Wunzam. Ljuba, they were told, had moved. He had met a group of sailors, probably Middle Eastern; they had left the bateau-bar and were heading for Dock 11. The police were waiting there. Ljuba and the sailors looked nervous and continually checked the time.

21:58. A blue Mercedes sped past Lopez and Hohenfelder and braked with a skid at the streetlight. Rebecka threw away her cigarette. She went up to the driver's window. The door opened. A man got out. Then Lopez saw him. He turned pale. He was stunned.

The man getting out of the Mercedes was the man who had been killed on Via Padova.

It was him. It was *almost* him. Lopez had seen him dead, lying purple and white on the table in the morgue at Forensics. He was astounded. Hohenfelder stared at him, then at the man as he shook Rebecka's hand and spoke. The double of the dead man on Via Padova stood out in the beam of light from the street lamp and looked around. Rebecka followed him as he walked to the trunk and opened it. The man and Rebecka looked inside, their backs to Lopez and Hohenfelder. The man closed the trunk. Rebecka spoke. Then they moved quickly.

The man got in the driver's seat of the Mercedes; Rebecka got in beside him. The car accelerated impressively. Hohenfelder had trouble getting out into the roadway; they had lost at least a hundred meters. Hohenfelder pushed the accelerator to the floor. Lopez called Wunzam. It was 22:07. Wunzam said that Ljuba and the others were still waiting, more and more anxiously, at Dock 11. Maybe there was a delay. Lopez told Wunzam he had seen the double of the man who had been killed on Via Padova. Wunzam reported that the "little packages" had not been delivered. Maybe the Swedish woman and the courier were heading for Dock 11.

But no.

They went toward Travehafen, amid rusted freighters, phosphorescent in the night, like ancient archeological finds. On Lopez's side of the car rose a salty dampness that fogged the windows. Hohenfelder shook his head. He said they were heading out of Hamburg. Lopez called Wunzam. Rebecka and the unknown man were not going toward Dock 11, he said. Wunzam, furious, said that they had been screwed. Lopez passed the phone to Hohenfelder. They mustn't lose the Mercedes, Wunzam insisted; he would order roadblocks on the ring roads. He asked where they were. The Mercedes was a hundred meters ahead, Hohenfelder said; they would overtake it at the next traffic light or stop sign. Wunzam told them there wasn't time. He said he was going to have Ljuba and the others arrested. He cut off the call. The Mercedes had halted at a stop sign. They were gaining on it.

Then the unknown man went into reverse.

Hohenfelder didn't have time to brake; he swerved, and the right side of the car slammed against a row of parked cars. Lopez's knees were jammed into the dashboard and Hohenfelder hit his left temple on the window. For a drawn-out, painful moment, Lopez saw Rebecka look across at him through the window of the Mercedes. He drew his gun. The Mercedes suddenly accelerated forward, and Lopez wasn't in time to shoot. Hohenfelder was shifting slowly on the seat, losing blood. Now Lopez aimed at the tires. Then he realized what Rebecka and the man had looked at in the trunk, and held his fire.

He had understood. In the trunk of the Mercedes they had

hidden the child he had seen at the orgy in Milan. The man he had seen tonight was the same one he had met at the sadomasochists' gathering.

Everything was slow and fast at the same time. The radio wasn't working. Hohenfelder was unconscious and bleeding. The window on Lopez's side was blocked by the cars they had run into. Lopez had to climb over Hohenfelder. People were looking at them from their balconies in the cold. Some came out to help. Lopez found the cell phone, looked for the number, and called Wunzam. He had arrested Ljuba and the others, and he was arranging the roadblocks. Lopez asked for an ambulance. Wunzam cursed, or something like that. Lopez knew it was too late.

At 23:40, a little outside Hamburg, they found the Mercedes. Next to the driver's seat was the body of Rebecka, her face crushed.

INSPECTOR DAVID MONTORSI

Milan
October 28, 1962
17:10

"Inspector Montorsi?" said the voice on the telephone.

He knew that voice, a pitch without passion. It was Arle. "Yes, Montorsi speaking."

"It's Arle. Dr. Arle."

"Yes."

"Excuse me . . ." There was a protracted, unnatural silence.

"Yes?"

"Excuse me, I wanted to ask you if . . ." Interference on the line: was it random? ". . . if it would be possible to meet."

Montorsi felt a chirring of the senses, the purest fibrillation of the nerves in the face of danger. "About what, Doctor?"

"What we talked about earlier today, Inspector . . ."

"What we talked about earlier today?"

There was a metallic silence between the fragments of carbon in the magnetic field of the line. "Yes. What we talked about today. The child. The child at Giuriati. I've thought about what you asked me, Montorsi. About how many children in that condition we've seen at Forensics in recent years."

Bull's-eye. Montorsi decided to hide his euphoria: *show confusion. Wait.* "Yes?"

"Is it possible, Inspector?"

"I think so."

Now there was a hissing at the other end of the telephone. "Good. Very good."

"When can we meet, Doctor?" Montorsi asked.

"Can we make it tonight? There may be some urgency . . ."

This time Montorsi paused. "All right. Tonight." Then another sentence from Fogliese's report to Ishmael came into his mind. *The Detective Squad of Milan has been excluded from the investigations;*

as is well known, some figures on the Squad maintained close ties with Mattei. Who maintained close ties to Mattei? In a flash, he saw the face of the Chief, and he let his words become vague. "Yes, okay, tonight. But after dinner. I have a meeting, here, at Headquarters."

"Yes, of course . . . Shall we make it nine? Is that all right, Inspector?"

"Yes. Perfect." He allowed a moment of calculated silence. "I am very interested. Where shall we meet? Shall I come to your office, Doctor?"

"No, no. Not at Forensics." There was a crinkle of worry in Arle's hurried answer. "I'm leaving Forensics to go to the directorship of another institute. I am devoting myself . . . to something else."

To what? "Is it a private institute, Doctor?"

"Yes, it's private. Let's meet there. It's on Viale Argonne. Thirteen Viale Argonne. Go in and ask for me. I will expect you in the office at nine."

He didn't know of any hospitals or medical institutes on Viale Argonne. His senses whirred like insects. "All right, good. At nine. You said 13 Viale Argonne?"

"Yes, yes. You'll come then? I'll be expecting you . . . Until then, Inspector."

Everything was moving. Ishmael had begun by eliminating Mattei; and now Arle was moving, after Montorsi had hypothesized to him the existence of a ring of pedophiles. Maybe Arle was calling him so that he could continue to cover up the ring? Something escaped him.

It was a weak but plausible link, the child and Mattei. The Symbol of Ishmael, which Fogliese's report mentioned—the violated, murdered child, put in position under the partisan plaque at Giuriati—announces the Event, anticipates it. The Event is the assassination of Enrico Mattei, the man who was Italy. Ishmael was an occult, tentacular power. A predator who remains in the shadows. Many know about Ishmael; many are already his "faithful disciples." But each one knows only what pertains to him. The Child and the Father of Italy were joined in death, under the golden, silent name of Ishmael. Ishmael had proclaimed his coming with the assassination of Enrico Mattei. From Washington to Rome and outposts throughout Europe, to Moscow, was Ishmael announcing a new war, frighteningly silent?

Fogliese, from the start a "faithful disciple" of Ishmael, had betrayed him. In a whirling ashen wind, Fogliese's words rose in him—National Security Agency, Central Intelligence Agency, "stationed at," "Nogarole." The name of Ishmael rotated in his mind, and Maura's face, Fogliese's torn lip, the bullet that had pierced the reporter's skull, the soapy-white arm of the child under the stone, the mummy of the anonymous partisan . . .

They had killed him—why? Was it Ishmael's men? Did Fogliese know too much? Had he seen Ishmael face to face? Montorsi felt himself reduced to nothing before the broad prospect of Ishmael's world.

And who was he in all this arcane movement of men? Why was Ishmael preoccupied with him? In the report to Ishmael's lieutenants Fogliese had cited him. Would they threaten Montorsi himself? They would corrupt him, turn him, pervert him. They would expose the mummy in him. In his mind, Fogliese's frank smile revolved around the golden letters of the name of Ishmael.

Anxiety shortened his breath, already raspy from the warm air of the radiator. He telephoned Maura. She didn't answer. Everything seemed to him too enormous to be true. Maybe Maura wanted to sleep, had unplugged the telephone. He ran a hand through his hair; it felt greasy. Weariness is usually converted into dirt, sewage, foul humors. He saw Maura's white face beyond a zone of darkness. Who at Headquarters could have close ties to Mattei?

He got up, left his office, left his thoughts, his shreds of thoughts, and went directly to the Chief's office. He had decided to speak to him about Ishmael.

Inspector Guido Lopez

Hamburg
March 26, 2001
01:50

Lopez had been at Headquarters with Wunzam when the call came that in the parking area behind a highway rest stop on the Autobahn to the west, the Mercedes had been found with the body of Rebecka in it. The police had responded to a call from the Autogrill reporting the theft of an Espace owned by two French tourists. The squad car had been delayed in getting there, and then the cops had had a hard time with the car's owners; they didn't speak German or even English, and the cops barely understood French. They had talked at length. Just to be certain the car had been stolen, the police had searched the entire rest stop, the parking lot car by car, then the gas station, and finally the cars parked near the exit to the highway. There they had found the Mercedes. They had thought that someone was sleeping inside; they had seen Rebecka's body recumbent in the darkness, and had knocked on the window. When Rebecka didn't stir, they had broken open the door. She was bent over, facedown on the seat, with her face against the fabric. Two bullets had smashed her forehead, the roof of the car stained by two precise splatters of blood and gray matter. The police had called Headquarters.

Now, in the middle of the night, Lopez and Wunzam were staring at each other in silence.

Hohenfelder was in the hospital with head trauma. Lopez couldn't stand for long; the blow to his knees had caused two large painful bruises, and the left knee was swelling. Wunzam ordered a search for the Espace at the roadblocks, even at the border. The man who had killed Rebecka, the carrier of the "little package," the double of the dead man on Via Padova, had disappeared. Lopez and Wunzam imagined that he would steal another car, maybe in a crowded city center; it would be impossible in a short time to establish what he would be driving when he tried to cross the border. It wasn't even certain that he would try to cross the border. He might try to deliver his package in person to Brussels, if indeed Brussels was the destination of the "machines."

The transfer at Dock 11 had been a diversion. Ljuba had been interrogated for hours. Lopez had caught a glimpse of him, passing in the corridor outside Wunzam's office, his right eye a swollen sac, dripping blood, his hair encrusted with sweat, his shoulders bent. Wunzam had come back to the office. He shook his head, and told Lopez that Ljuba knew nothing about either the children or Brussels.

They had searched Rebecka's two rooms at the Vorbach. The hard drive of her PC had offered no resistance, but on it they had found only work documents, financial plans, unsuspicious e-mails. They had checked her electronic diary: no trace of Bob, Clemenceau, or Terzani. But on the headboard of the bed, woven and knotted, Lopez found the same white ribbon inscribed in black ink he had seen in the rooms of Clemenceau and Terzani: ISHMAEL IS GREAT. Lopez had the ribbon brought to Headquarters. He had stared at it until Wunzam came back from the interrogation of Ljuba, and then the call had arrived from the highway rest stop.

They didn't know what to do. The politicians would not intervene. There would be no outside pressure. The death of Rebecka removed any necessity for caution. Wunzam and Lopez kept open the trail of Karl M., the flunky of an E.U. deputy in Brussels. But they couldn't take any official steps. There was no trace of the children. The intermediary had been eliminated. They had available a telephone trail that was not at all persuasive. The links with Paris and Milan were an interpretation, nothing more. The dead wouldn't speak and the living either knew nothing or had escaped. Wunzam had Rebecka's pusher, Franziskus Klamm, and Klaus Baum, the one who had proposed a "game" to her on the telephone, brought to Headquarters and interrogated. They didn't know anything. He had them arrested, but it served no purpose.

They talked for several hours. Lopez's theory: a group of Ishmael's adherents, with deep access to the political world, acted in Europe undisturbed; the group gathered to celebrate rites, which involved children it procured from pedophiles in Europe; it carried out Ishmael's programs, which included sensational actions—like the attempt on Kissinger in Paris—and more or less secret ones. In the second case, Ishmael's adherents on the political level suppressed intervention by the forces of order. The death of the man on Via Padova, who resembled Rebecka's courier, had to be connected to the events in Hamburg. Days earlier, representatives of Ishmael's group had visited Hamburg; shortly afterward, one of them had made an attempt on Kissinger's life. Within a few days, according to the American intelligence report, Ishmael would attempt an operation at the meeting in Cernobbio, where Kissinger would be among the participants.

Wunzam nodded, persuaded, while Lopez laid out the design. In Wunzam's view, all they could do was wait for Cernobbio, try to protect the leaders, and hope that, as in Paris, Ishmael's operation would fail. Wunzam was right, Lopez said, but he at least had to try to rescue the child he had seen disappear in Milan. There were two alternatives: screw the political pressure on Santovito and squeeze the Engineer, who, he was sure, knew something about Ishmael; or try the Brussels trail, continuing to believe what, up until an hour before, they had believed about Rebecka and the exchange at Dock 11. Wunzam was puzzled. Could the child in Milan be the child of one of the participants in the orgy? It was clear that the rites of Ishmael took place during the PAVs, unbeknown to the majority of the participants. The man who had taken the child from inside the warehouse might be someone who had nothing to do with Ishmael.

Maybe Wunzam was right. Lopez had to decide whether to return empty-handed to Santovito or take a chance on Brussels. He would sleep at Headquarters and catch a mid-morning flight to Brussels. He smoked a joint and tried to calm down, but couldn't get out of his mind Rebecka, the man in the Mercedes *identical* to Terzani, the child, the Engineer, Laura.

Laura. The thought of Laura hammered at him. Again Laura! He thought of Ishmael, of the Engineer. The Engineer had silenced everyone. The pressures on Santovito had to be coming from high up. The Engineer had contacts at the top levels of intelligence. Lopez had no doubt that Laura knew nothing of Ishmael. But she was part of the group around the Engineer. He was afraid that the Engineer or whoever was above him would move against

Laura. Rebecka had been eliminated because she knew. Lopez didn't know what Laura knew. He was afraid.

He went back to Wunzam's office, but Wunzam had gone home. He called the Pruna brothers.

The Pruna brothers lived in Via Tommei, in Calvairate. There were three of them. Usually, however, there were only two; one, in rotation, was always in jail. They lived on small-time pushing and department money that Lopez paid them for tailing, surveillance, and other dirty work. He thought they would be perfect.

When the Prunas finally answered, they told him to fuck off. But they needed money. Lopez gave them the addresses of Laura Pensanti and of the Engineer. He wanted both of them watched. He would communicate with them by cell phone for reports. He explained the situation briefly: The Engineer was a pervert and in the middle was a child; Laura was a victim, she was to be protected. The Prunas understood perfectly. They agreed on a price and on favorable treatment for the third brother, who was in prison in San Vittore. Lopez insisted that surveillance had to begin immediately. Again the Prunas told Lopez to fuck off, and then they gave in.

"And what do we do with her man? If she has a man how the hell do we carry on, Lopez?"

"She doesn't have a man."

Silence. They had understood. "And at work?"

"I'm paying you. You figure out how to keep an eye on her at work."

"And how long will it last?"

He was bewildered. How long would it last? "A couple of days." If it wasn't enough, he would extend it.

"And the other guy?"

"The Engineer? Just follow him. We've been in his office. We have the taps. The cell is under control. Just don't let him near Pensanti."

"But should we hurt him?"

He thought about it. "No. No, don't do anything. Just don't let him near the girl."

The Germans gave him some pajamas; he had brought nothing. He didn't brush his teeth, and his mouth was dry and disgusting from the joints and the tension. He got undressed. His knee was no longer swollen, but the bruises throbbed with pain. He thought of Laura. Of Brussels. He thought of the trunk of the Mercedes. He was sure that the child was lying there, pale and quiet. Perhaps it was already dead by now, somewhere. Maybe the man had got rid of it, as he had got rid of Rebecka.

He smiled only a moment before falling asleep, thinking of Laura who had called him a limp dick.

He woke at seven. His mouth was a sewer: he washed it out with soap and a bitter layer remained on his tongue. The bruises were better, but his legs were shaky.

At eight-thirty, Wunzam arrived. Together they read the transcription of the phone call to the bureaucrat Karl M., and Wunzam gave him a file on the man and a photograph. Lopez photocopied everything. The file was thin. Karl M. had tried his political luck with the Greens, running in local elections four years earlier, in a constituency outside his home in Munich. He hadn't made it. He worked for the party organization as an intermediary in various areas of coordination. A flunky, in short. Until he had been called to Brussels as assistant to two Green deputies in the European Parliament. He had contacts with everyone, including people from all the German political parties, and not only with the Germans. He spoke English and French perfectly and understood Italian. He had no police record. A bachelor, he was forty-three years old. The deputies he worked for had not been protagonists in any battle that signified anything to Lopez—nothing on pedophilia or drug trafficking, no particular enemy. They were signatories of certain proposed laws, one of which did interest Lopez: a request for a system of tax exemptions for churches and sects. He thought of Ishmael, but the sect of Ishmael had nothing to do with a system of tax exemption. Practically speaking, the police had nothing on Karl M., except the interception on Rebecka's cell phone. Lopez didn't know what to do. He would land in Brussels and would think of something. He weighed the possibility of talking to Santovito, to get some entrée among the Euro parliamentarians, but rejected it.

He called Calimani and told him he would be gone one more day. Calimani didn't ask how it had gone in Hamburg, since it was clear that it had gone badly in Hamburg. It had gone as badly as it had in Milan and Paris. Calimani did say that Santovito was on the verge of collapse over the business at Cernobbio. In Fatebenefratelli, the night before, there had been a lot of activity among the American intelligence agents and security people. They had drawn up a plan. Santovito had given Calimani the orders: American services, Italian services, carabinieri, and police, with the Detective Squad acting as a kind of roving team. The plan was supposed to make everything seem secure. In fact nothing was secure.

Lopez waited until ten to call the cell phone of the Pruna brother who was following Laura. He was sleeping and he told Lopez to fuck off—it was a shit job. Then he made his report: after a peaceful night, at eight-fifteen Laura, who corresponded perfectly to Lopez's description, had left the house, walked to the Metro station at Porta Romana, taken the Metro to Corvetto, where she had got on the 93 and got off in Viale Puglie, at the clinic where she worked; Pruna had gone to the waiting room and pretended to ask for an appointment; he went back into the clinic, which was crowded, at intervals of twenty minutes; he had seen her once, and she seemed calm. Lopez called the other Pruna, the one who was on the Engineer. The other Pruna told him the Engineer was still at home.

He telephoned Laura. She told him she was with a patient. She had told him that psychotherapy in a public institution was in effect social work. Her voice seemed softer; she asked if he would call in the afternoon. He said he would be away from Milan in the afternoon, but that he would call her. She said goodbye without calling him a limp dick. The patient was there; she couldn't.

Wunzam went with him to the airport. He said that Hohenfelder would be released from the hospital that afternoon: they had given him a CAT scan, and there was no evidence of brain damage. Lopez said he was glad, but that Hohenfelder irritated him. Wunzam smiled, nodded, and said that Hohenfelder drove him crazy, too.

They embraced as they said goodbye.

At one o'clock, Guido Lopez landed in Brussels.

Unknown locality
March 26, 2001
03:40

Rebecka's blood had spurted on the sleeve of his jacket and dried into a narrow brown stripe that annoyed him as he drove. The American yawned, to release the tension. For days he had slept little. And he slept badly. His hands were about to start shaking; he could feel the tremors announcing themselves. He dug out a Valium from his pocket and swallowed it. He would get sleepy, and he had to keep driving, but he would be calmer. He looked in the rearview mirror. A face of fear. In Brussels, he would hand over the child and would be able to rest for a few hours, before picking up the little corpse and returning to Milan. Ishmael had called him; he had responded.

He sped at 210 kilometers an hour, toward Brussels. Earlier, he had left the highway because he knew that the Espace he had stolen at the rest stop might be noticed at the border, and also the highway police might have been informed of it. Better to change. On the outskirts of some nameless town deep in the black countryside, he had spotted an Audi in a fairly isolated parking lot. There were other cars there too, most of them without much power; they were no use to him. He needed to run. He needed a capacious trunk. There were only three phials of injections for the child. He had to get to Brussels before afternoon. It had been simple to disengage the Audi's anti-theft alarm, open the trunk, put the child inside, and take off. The police would discover the theft the next morning, and it was unlikely that they would find the Espace at the same time. He would have no problems until the border.

Rebecka was an imbecile and not even a good-looking one. The instructions he had been given had from the start made reference to the fact that Rebecka's cell phone was safe. An error. A serious one. Ishmael is great but his men are dilettantes. They were supposed to meet to exchange the child in Nehlsstrasse, and then she was to take care of the rest: get the child to Brussels and return it to Milan, directly to the American himself, for the burial. Those were Ishmael's orders: to bury it before Cernobbio. Ishmael could count on him. At Cernobbio they wouldn't fail as they had failed in Paris. It was a complex but perfect mechanism. Ishmael is great.

He suspected that Rebecka had been intercepted. The instructions had included the address of the Swedish woman, "to contact only in case of serious emergency." The American smiled. He had positioned himself at the Vorbach Hotel, to see if they were watching her. They were watching her. The American had seen the Italian inspector smoking and talking on his cell phone, on the opposite side of the street, in front of the Vorbach. The American had not got out of the driver's seat. He had earlier injected more of the drug in the child: It would sleep for hours and then it would be Rebecka's concern. He didn't understand how the Italian cop had got to Hamburg, to Rebecka. He thought of the Old Man. Probably the Old Man had tipped off the Italian. He had expected to find the Old Man in Hamburg, but not the Italian. He was ready to eliminate the Old Man there, on the spot, to get rid of him, given the impending action at Cernobbio. But the Old Man was a professional. The American had to be extremely careful. The Old Man could ruin everything. He was angry at not having killed him in Milan. Professionals don't make mistakes. Fucking old man.

He had waited for hours in the Mercedes, keeping an eye on the Vorbach and the police car. At a certain point Rebecka had left the hotel; he had started the engine and was about to leave his spot when, from the unmarked car, one of the cops—not the Italian—got out and started following Rebecka. The policemen's car stayed there. The American didn't know what to do. He thought they would arrest her and she would be his ruin. He didn't trust cunts. Rebecka would talk. If they arrested her, he would have to leave for Brussels immediately, hoping that the intelligence services and the authorities would not move before he had got the child back from Ishmael's people in Brussels, to be buried in Milan. But no. Rebecka had gone into a pub on the corner; five minutes later she returned, and so did the cop who had followed her.

He had waited until nine-twenty. Rebecka had gone out and left in her car with plenty of time. The Italian policeman's car was behind her. She was taking a roundabout route. He had hoped that she realized she was being tailed. But it was difficult. The traffic jerked along. The two cops had no idea they were being followed. Finally Rebecka had turned onto the bridge, going toward Nehlsstrasse. He had decided to leave Rebecka and the cops' car and had detoured to get ahead of her, two streets before Nehlsstrasse. With just two cops, there could be no stakeout. He and Rebecka had not mentioned Nehlsstrasse. He was in time to make sure. There were no police. There were no plainclothes agents. No video camera. He had only to avoid giving the child to Rebecka. He had to get her in his car. Then he would take care of her. He would fix the two police officers; that was no problem.

He left, tires burning, went two blocks at top speed, then came to a stop. Nehlsstrasse. The cops' car was in position. Parked under the street light, according to instructions, was Rebecka. She got out. He told her to act relaxed; they were being followed. He told her to behave normally. Rebecka had no confidence. He had her look at the child, asleep in the trunk, a whiff of shit and pee. Rebecka looked at him and, panicking, asked what they should do. He told her to get in the Mercedes. They got in. He left, tires screeching.

They had to get rid of the police. They had to change cars.

When he came to the stop sign and saw the car with the Italian cop trying to catch up, accelerating rapidly, he went into reverse. The cop who was driving was a dolt. He was pressing the accelerator too hard—was no longer in control. The police car slammed against the row of parked cars. He waited to make sure that the driver had lost consciousness.

There was plenty of time to change cars.

At the rest stop, he had checked out the Espace. He broke the main lock. Before transferring the child, he shot. Twice. Rebecka had barely realized what was happening. She knew too much and yet she was an imbecile. She had panicked. He would deliver the child in person to Brussels. And in person he would take it back to Milan.

He had turned Rebecka's head, positioned it as if she were sleeping.

He had cleaned off the window, keeping an eye on the Espace beside him.

The blood had spurted and stained the sleeve of his jacket.

Milan
October 28, 1962
17:20

David Montorsi sat across from the Chief, on the other side of the desk. The older man's face was drawn, the skin milky and gray in the fluorescent light. He was nodding silently, finishing Fogliese's report for *Il Giorno*. Montorsi hadn't even mentioned Fogliese's report to Ishmael, the one that referred to him, that threatened him personally. It was evident that the file for *Il Giorno* was a report—a report from Ishmael intended for Mattei. Perhaps Mattei himself had received it. The Chief twisted his mouth, touched his nose with closed fingers. He gave Montorsi a long look.

Then he spoke. "All this was clear to us, David. It was very clear. It has been for a long time. But this . . . Ishmael . . . this strategy of the sect . . . we weren't aware of that . . ."

Montorsi, his arms crossed, slid his gaze beyond that of the Chief. "I think . . . Well, it's significant that we weren't aware of it."

The Chief nodded. "We had instructions regarding the installation, here, in the north of Italy, of an agency of American intelligence. The men yesterday, the ones in the dark suits . . . We at Headquarters are supposed to be hosting their team. At least until they have duplicated our records."

"After which, I suppose, they'll move outside Verona, right? To the American base. That's what Fogliese's report says."

"As far as we know, yes."

They were silent again. Then Montorsi spoke. "I think the sensational operation he refers to in the report, the one that's supposed to signal the existence of Ishmael—well, I think that operation consisted of sabotaging Mattei's plane."

The Chief allowed himself a long sigh. "You're convinced that the plane was sabotaged?" The Chief gave him a tired smile, bending his head to one side.

"Chief, there must be a reason that they took the investigation away from us."

"What did you see, David? How did you come to be so certain?" The Chief tried to concentrate. "Last night you wanted to speak to me. What did you see, exactly?"

"The blood, Chief. The others saw it, too. Burned blood on the tops of the leaves. Blood that fell from the sky. The plane exploded in the air. And the trees. Undamaged. If the plane had crashed, it would have broken the branches."

The Chief nodded. "And what do you want now? What do you want me to tell you, David? We're out of it. The death of Mattei, in the space of a day, has changed things. Many things. Yesterday might as well have been an epoch ago. Everything is changing."

Montorsi sniffed. "I'll make you a proposal, Chief. It depends on you. You see from the report that we at the Detective Squad are one of the targets. But we can go back into the case of Mattei. We can search his office."

The Chief's gaze grew empty. His eyes were like abraded iron valves. "We're out of it, David. Don't you understand? We're out. How do you think we can get back in?"

"With the murder of Fogliese."

Silence. "So. You want a warrant to search Mattei's office for this file? Fogliese's file?"

"One team goes to *Giorno*. One team goes to ENI, in Metanopoli, to Mattei's office. Then there's Mattei's house, his study. It's a collateral case, Chief. But we stay with the central body of the Mattei investigation."

"It's a twist, anyway. A surprise attack. But you think they can't take that sort of murder investigation away from us."

"Exactly."

They were silent, again. The Chief scratched his forehead. It was getting dark outside. "It's risky, David. It's risky."

A helpless silence fell between them. "It's all risky. For me it's also a risk to stand still."

"But like this we expose ourselves. It's going against . . . Against how they were arranging things."

"At most all they do is take the investigation away from us."

"It may be that you'll lose your job. And that I will too. And others in the department."

"You might lose it just the same. Even if you do nothing, Chief. You might lose it."

"It's true. I might lose it just the same."

"We could at least search Mattei's house and office. We could manage it. Before they take away the investigation, I mean."

"It's a question of three hours at most. It's enough for someone at ENI to call the judge and have it taken away. No more than three hours. And if they don't take it away, we'll go ahead."

"Will you let me do it, Chief?"

The Chief sighed again, a kind of anticipatory, liberating sorrow. "No. I'm exposing you too much. You're the youngest here. Officially I'll give it to Omboni. But you do what you want. Report to me, not to Omboni."

Leaving the Chief's office, Montorsi turned around to look again at the man's soft, suffering body, calm with the calm that yields to an imminent end that it sees in advance. He had clear, bovine eyes. His skin seemed even grayer. He was lighting a cigarette. He seemed to find no comfort in it. The Chief looked at him. "I knew Mattei well."

So it was him. The Chief was the official who, according to Fogliese's file and his report, had "close ties" with the Master of Italy.

Montorsi sat down. The Chief talked, unburdening himself. Once Mattei had invited him to go fishing. He had him picked up by a chauffeur sometime before dawn one foggy morning, driven to Linate, and catapulted, in a private jet belonging to ENI, to the rocky coast of Iceland, raked by the glacial sea. The Chief had seen Mattei, amid patches of dry snow and hollow rocky outcroppings, bending over as he toyed with the hooks, showing a meditative, almost ancestral patience. He had turned suddenly to greet him, with a clear smile. They had embraced. The two men had known each other a long time. Mattei had made him sit beside him. He had told him about what he called the "second wave," in which the Americans would try to occupy Europe. An American Europe. He was trying to resist the pressures. He said that the Americans had infiltrated everywhere. The political parties were the least of it; they were out of the great game. The Americans were in ENI, the intelligence service, everywhere. He said that the pressures were enormous. Mattei told the Chief that sometimes he counted on the Vatican for help. Then there was a tug on the fishing line, powerful jerks in the rough silvery water. The sky broke open, a jagged crack of northern lights and irregular, shining clouds. The fish was pulling from below. The titanium rod, which Mattei had had made in a laboratory at Metanopoli, was bent. It arced; it seemed to break. His face, the Chief said, was as if wounded by concentration. Finally, with a sharp tug, Mattei had brought the rod up, and for a second the salmon could be seen sparkling in the air, above the foamy spray, a fluid body suspended in the air, yet as if disjointed, shaking its tail. But then the line broke—it was all very quick, a breath, a moment—and with an exasperated plunge the salmon dropped back into the luminous whirlpools of icy water. Mattei had exploded into a noisy laugh. The Chief had smiled too. He had been afraid that Mattei was annoyed, standing there like an idiot, stunned by the recoil and the broken line, and nothing in his hand except the empty rod. Mattei had turned, winked, and said, "That salmon . . . That salmon, you see, is me."

Three hours. Montorsi would have three hours to pretend to search for Fogliese's report in Mattei's office. He would have three hours to find the fingerprints of Ishmael and the Americans among Mattei's papers.

He would have to be quick. He spoke to Omboni. They decided on a plan.

Before leaving for Metanopoli, he tried to telephone his house. Maura didn't answer. Maybe she didn't want to talk to anyone. Montorsi stood there, staring at the telephone and thinking of Maura, without love and without anxiety.

Hamburg/Brussels
March 26, 2001
13:20

The trip on the airplane was revolting. The rows of seats were pressed tight, one against the other, and Lopez was forced to stick his bruised knees into the seat back in front of him, and the pain as the plane took off was piercing.

He tried to sleep and couldn't. He listened with his eyes closed to the agitated beating of his heart. The uncertainty of what he would do in Brussels was eating away at him. He had given up the idea of getting help from Santovito, who, instead of providing contacts, would recall him to Milan to coordinate the plan for security at Cernobbio.

Midway through the flight, he began shaking with anxiety. The man in the Mercedes could have got rid of the child and be far from Brussels. Lopez couldn't inform the Belgian authorities about the investigation. Better to draw no attention at all. He was about to step onto a political level higher than the ones that had exerted their influence on Santovito or on Serrault in Paris. And he didn't know what he was going to do or how he would do it.

He ate at the airport McDonald's. The meat was disgusting—it tasted of pee. The rice in the cold salad, in a round, steamed-up plastic package, tasted like soap. He spent fifteen minutes in line. In the restroom the urinals were filthy; he waited until a stall was free. The air in the terminal was stale, and through the vast glass wall looking onto the runways he saw a white cargo plane struggle to lift off; to him and to the others who were watching the runway it appeared to bank perilously. There was an outcry of surprise.

He looked at the faces, nervously, attentive as one is attentive in a hallucination. Was he hoping to make out the face of the man in the Mercedes? He couldn't even smile at himself. He went to the currency-exchange window and changed some money. Outside he couldn't breathe deeply; the air was heavy, saturated with exhaust from the planes.

He took a taxi. Address: the European Parliament.

The taxi driver spoke French and fortunately wasn't in the mood to ask questions. Lopez didn't like Brussels: low houses, dark Gothic churches, abstract modern sculptures, yellow canals, crowded squares. At one point, the taxi driver pointed out a complex of giant, glazed metal spheres, held up and connected by rods made of the same alloy, and said, "This is the Atomium, Monsieur." The Atomium, a monument that had seen better days. Lopez passed the back of his hand over his dry lips, and the taxi driver said nothing more.

He got out in Rue Belliard. The stocky glass buildings of the European Parliament stuck up among the trees. The street was deserted, apart from the tour buses parked at the entrance to the complex. Overgrown flowerbeds ran along the sides of the street. He found a spot next to two empty buses and knelt among the bushes. He took out his gun. He folded the pages of Wunzam's report on Karl M. around the gun. He looked for a hollow at the base of a bush and placed the packet there. Still squatting, he tore some branches from the bushes around it and laid them on top. No one went by. There were no video cameras around the enclosure of the Euro parliament on the opposite side of the street. Anyway, the buses concealed the scene.

Having hidden the gun that the metal detector at the entrance would have revealed, he got up. He walked toward the visitors' entrance.

To the left was an oval building, topped by a tall, oblong arcade. He read the sign: Batiment Spaak. On the right was a wider, more articulated building, connected to the Batiment Spaak by a bridge. Batiment Spinelli.

He chose the Italian name. He went to the reception desk.

He asked for Karl M. and was told to wait—did he have an appointment? He said he was there to make an appointment. Huge concentric steps went upward in a spiral at the center of the lobby, clinging to a thin, tentacular body, in a fantastic sculpture that ascended like an alien excrescence. From the outside, the glass walls had seemed to him a million windows, from which it would be possible to lean out and cast a million different glances on the city. From the inside, it seemed like a single, gigantic window, homogeneous and vaguely tyrannical. Through the glass, the trees were accretions of dust, filtered by the smoky glass. Anonymous bodies were in motion, going up and down in elevators that unloaded men who were alone and shabby; silent, elegant women; and, intermittently, groups of visitors whose gazes were lost in the enormous spiral of the stairway.

Karl M., the receptionist informed him, was in his office. She asked for additional identification. He had left his passport at the entrance, so he searched for his European driver's license; he did not want to leave his identity card, which gave his profession. Karl M.'s office was on the third floor. Lopez joined a group of Spanish tourists and went slowly up the stairs; he had to move aside to let officials and secretaries go by, who seemed to know by heart the routes within that vast, airy space.

He had no trouble finding Karl M. A long corridor followed the semicircular shape of the façade. He read the names on the nameplates. Karl M. was fifty yards from the stairway. He knocked.

He was told to come in.

Shorter than Lopez had expected. Energetic. Nervous. Brusque. He asked why Lopez wanted to see him. Karl M. understood Italian, but he responded in English. Lopez said he needed to find out about the developments in the legal plan for exempting religious associations from taxes. He introduced himself as a representative of the Italian CICAP, the agency that oversaw groups involved in the paranormal and the status of sects. Karl M. listened, nodding, blandly wary of his visitor's motives. Lopez said that CICAP would like to set itself up eventually as a clearinghouse for religious associations in Italy seeking tax exemption. Karl M. nodded, convinced. He had been hoping for just that sort of help from the agencies. He said that the proposal for the law was still a matter of discussion, and he got up and opened a closet, talking and talking in a rapid English that annoyed Lopez, and took out a bundle of documents. He asked if Lopez wanted to photocopy the plan drafted by the two German parliamentarians, which was going to be added to the proposal for the law. Lopez let out a "Fantastic!" and Karl M. called a secretary and asked her in French to make photocopies. Within two minutes the secretary had knocked and had taken the file, leaving the two men alone. Karl M. opened his Palm and, his stylus poised, asked Lopez for the appropriate phone numbers, e-mail, and addresses. Lopez improvised, staring at the Palm. The secretary returned with the photocopies. Karl M. studied the file, removed some pages, then handed it to Lopez. They said goodbye with a handshake, and Lopez promised to get in touch in the next few days.

After the German closed the door, Lopez inspected the corridor. It was empty. Many of the nameplates were blank; Lopez deduced that the offices were empty or perhaps incorporated into the offices next door. He kept going, to see if the secretaries had work stations that looked onto the corridor. He came to the door of the restroom. He went in.

He went into the middle stall. He found that if he climbed up with his feet on the seat he could see the sinks and the urinals. He managed to verify that from above he could see the stalls next to his. Only the toilet stall farthest away was outside his range. He got down and went over and broke the lock of the farthest stall so that it remained open. He prepared to wait, hoping for a stroke of luck.

For at least ten minutes, the restroom remained deserted. Then the door opened. Lopez heard the rush of water in the sink. He got up on tiptoe; it wasn't his man. He had to wait a few more minutes. Others entered. He heard a fuss around the door of the stall whose lock he had broken. He stayed attentive to the sound. He saw the grizzled neck of someone he didn't know.

Suddenly he saw Karl M. Lopez had time to squat down after catching sight of the German's profile. He heard the faucet go on. He didn't know what to do. If they had been alone, he could have emerged and surprised the man. He waited. Karl M. went into the stall to the right of Lopez. Lopez flushed the toilet, opened the door, and left the men's room. Two officials were talking in low voices to his right, paying no attention to him. He went back toward Karl M.'s office.

He knocked as a precaution. If the secretary who had made the photocopies or someone else was there, he would say he had forgotten some notes. The office was empty. He went in.

Quickly, he opened the drawer from which the German had taken the Palm. He found it immediately. He put it in his pocket, closed the drawer, and went out. No one was in the corridor. He joined a group of visitors. He looked behind him. He searched for the face of Karl M., who could not, however, have realized the theft yet. He was sweating.

He went through the reception area. No one recognized him. At the visitors' exit he wasn't stopped. He was outside, but it wasn't over.

Tourists were being loaded onto the buses in front of the bushes where he had hidden his gun. Lopez made a wide circle. He managed to get to the bushes. No one looked in his direction. The gun was still where he had left it; he retrieved it.

He walked quickly. He turned to the left onto Rue Van Maerland, went straight. Left, right, again right. He looked for a square. He went into a dark basement bar and ordered a Guinness. In poor English, he asked where one could rent a car. They gave him the directions.

A quarter of an hour later, he was at the wheel of a BMW 520. He struggled to decipher the names of the *rues*, the *straats*. He had taken a risk. As soon as Karl M. reported the theft, the police would probably have Lopez's name and check it against the database of car rentals, according to procedures, and would also find out that he was an Italian police detective. Still, he should have a good five hours of anonymity.

He parked at the Gare Léopold, at the corner of Rue Belliard, where he could watch the Parliament entrance reserved for employees. He would wait for Karl M. to leave and in the meantime he would examine the Palm.

He opened Karl M.'s Palm and began to manipulate the screen, glancing from the Palm to the Parliament and back to the Palm.

There was no sign of Karl M. Officials, secretaries came and went. On the benches near the entrance a big old man sat, feeding the pigeons, and mothers talked as they watched their children play.

His fingers searched nervously. Address book. Appointments. Mail. Telephone numbers.

A group of Parliament employees were chatting. A woman stretched, as if just waking up. The old man continued to crumble bread for the pigeons. The mothers said goodbye and went off with their children.

In the Palm were notes, a calendar, and more notes. He opened the record for notes.

Bull's-eye.

A note on Rebecka, in German, with two telephone numbers: Rebecka's cell phone and the Vorbach. Nothing else. He looked for Bob. Nothing. He tried Ishmael. *Nothing*. Otherwise there were just cell numbers of deputies and their staff people, all useless to him.

He found Karl M.'s address and looked on the map. It was about a kilometer from the Parliament. Perhaps waiting for his car was pointless.

He thought of telephoning Wunzam and having him translate the note on Rebecka. There were three scant lines. Better to continue watching. He felt a wave of discomfort.

The old man finished the bread, crumpled the paper, threw it in a basket, and went back and sat down. The bureaucrats were still in front of the entrance.

Lopez yawned.

He sharpened his gaze.

Karl M. was coming out.

Milan/Metanopoli
October 28, 1962
17:50

Montorsi and Omboni were in the first of three squad cars heading to Metanopoli, the headquarters of Mattei's ENI, the little city built just outside Milan, big glass buildings rising in the plain, with canals all around. Two cars were going to *Il Giorno*. The Chief would undertake in person, as delicately as possible, the investigation of Mattei's house. He had decided to warn the widow, saying that he was coming and not to worry. Montorsi would join him later, coming directly from Metanopoli, to look for traces of Ishmael.

Not even six and it was dark. The Alfa 2600s had their headlights on, and their monotone sirens announced them from afar. In a square, a woman was chasing a dog that had burst out in the direction of Corvetto. Fantini Cosmi, an immense factory in Piazza Bologna, spewed thick smoke from rusting chimneys. A weed-choked drainage canal cut across Viale Lucania, where the tall new houses made a barrier against the winds from the periphery. As they accelerated toward the smoky outskirts, the street lamps beamed on the smog crusting the dull cars, and already the smoke from Fantini Cosmi, rising at a slight angle, grew distant. Near Viale Omero, cans with brightly painted sides were stacked in the street beside the broken curb; ten meters ahead was a truck, and some men were packing the cans under the truck's heavy gray tarpaulin. Next door, the custodian had come out to watch them, and from the other direction two women approached, loaded down with bulging canvas shopping bags. The pale grass, pushing up through the sidewalk, shone in the evening light, and straight ahead the sky opened up, in the direction of Chiaravalle, with the usual orange cracks.

Then they turned onto Via Emilia, curving upward onto the overpass, while Milan stood out below, strange fumes rising amid a swarm of cold lights, the straight course of perpendicular streets interrupted by the nuclei of the squares. Then they descended again, passing the canal as they headed for San Donato, on the direct road to Metanopoli, to the entrance gate of the center built by Mattei. Through the bars of the gate Montorsi could see the iridescent glass of the main building, emitting an ambiguous light, like the reflection of a sunset close up, and on high the distinctive flag was visible, its form distorted by the wind, until it unfurled, miraculously taut, and they all saw the black dog with six paws, on a yellow background, breathing out fire from his jaws—the symbol chosen by Mattei for AGIP.

The ENI building was like a tooth rotted out by decay. Already the death of Mattei had sucked it up from inside, like an instantaneous cancer. The polished lobby was overflowing with flowers that gave off an unnatural odor of sweetish death, a scent of licorice, a warm sticky odor that seemed to soak into clothing and skin. All the policemen looked pale there, including Montorsi. Omboni was greeted by the ENI vice president, an obsequious little man, who spoke of the misfortune, as he called it: "the misfortune," "the misfortune," "the misfortune."

He accompanied them to Mattei's office. Forty minutes had passed since the start of the operation.

The office was spacious, empty. The furniture had been polished with a zeal that left halos on the smooth wood. There were few books. The vice president of ENI followed them as they examined the room, showed them papers. They photographed everything.

Montorsi found what he was looking for immediately. The file on Ishmael, signed by Fogliese, was in the second drawer from the top in Mattei's desk. Mattei had underlined everything, practically every word.

He had known that he was to be Ishmael's first victim.

The others remained to take more photographs, to confiscate what could be confiscated. Montorsi left, to return to the center of Milan. He drove fast, through streets that now were empty. Kids were playing ball on the asphalt near Via Toffetti.

Half an hour later he was in Via della Moscova, at the house of Enrico Mattei.

There were three cars outside the entrance. Montorsi went in with long strides, devoured the steps (of thin, almost translucent marble, a scent of sweet wax) to the open door, guarded by an agent who recognized and greeted him, but he was already in the front hall, a dark space invaded by the same flowers as the lobby at Metanopoli, and he saw hanging on the wall, beige in the shadow and framed under glass, the figure of the dog with six paws. It was probably the original drawing—a dog breathing fire in a corridor, amid blasts of incense from dead flowers.

In a room at the end of the hall they were speaking in low voices. The Chief was sitting in an armchair, leaning forward toward the woman, his hands between his knees. They looked up as Montorsi entered. Mattei's widow was a pale reed, obviously marked by a grief without limits, and yet with a presence in her puffy dark-circled eyes, a presence of pride. She was facing the end of the world. Of her world. Her husband had exploded, above clouds bursting with rain, plunging from a flight that had lasted a lifetime, and now she, too, was dead, had died an evil death. And yet pride already seemed to grab her, with its mechanical bite. As if in a short time she would be able to become another woman. As if soon she would be able, in spite of everything, to sink her nails into other flesh.

The discernible power of a woman. Mattei's death appeared to reconstruct her from within, harden within her a new skeleton that was shiny, solid, supple.

They shook hands, the widow and Montorsi, in a pact of mutual, sudden antipathy.

The Chief spoke first. "Signora Mattei has assured me, Inspector, that you may look for whatever you like. It is a tragic moment for her, but she assures us that you have her cooperation."

Montorsi didn't know what he was looking for. He handed the Ishmael report to the Chief. He said, almost in a whisper, "It was in his office. He read it. He underlined it. He knew. He understood."

The Chief glanced at it and assented silently.

Montorsi sat down beside the widow Mattei, who drew in her

legs, crossing them modestly. There was fear and assurance in this woman.

"Signora Mattei . . . I will disturb you only for a short time. I have only one question . . ."

"Please." She nodded with an extreme and false sort of modesty—a noticeable defensiveness, a silent yet clear, legible warning.

"Signora . . . Your husband . . ."

"Yes."

"Did your husband ever mention the name Ishmael?"

"Ishmael . . ." Was she thinking? Or was it a pose? Her skin was snow. She seemed young if you looked at her wrists. "Ishmael, yes . . . Perhaps something to do with the Americans . . . the Americans in Italy . . ." She broke into a contained smile, bringing one hand to her forehead. "God. It was his obsession. My husband's obsession . . . the Americans . . ." How old was she? "He spoke always and only about the Americans. . . . To me, however, he said little. He cursed, sometimes, here, at home, after a phone call. He cursed the Americans. . . ." The Chief nodded along with her.

"Who telephoned most often? I mean, here at home."

"He was always away. Those who called knew how to find him. They knew his movements. Above all Giorgio . . . Giorgio La Pira . . ."

"Ishmael doesn't mean anything to you, then?"

She lowered her gaze, as if concentrating. "Just what I've told you, Inspector. I'm thinking of the new oil platforms, in the Middle East. . . . Ishmael is a Middle Eastern name, isn't it?"

Montorsi looked at the Chief. He shook his head in silence. It was over. "Yes. Perhaps something to do with the Middle East." He got up. "Before I go, Signora . . ."

The Chief's eyes widened in embarrassment. He had been hoping to end the matter. To leave the widow Mattei alone.

She raised her eyes, dark and cutting, keen. "Yes?"

"One last thing, Signora . . . Did your husband keep a photograph album?"

In the study, a dozen boxes were packed in a big closet whose walls were covered with a smooth dark-green velvet. They were improbably full of photographs. Fortunately, Mattei had marked them, tracing the year in tiny figures, one for each box of pictures. The widow left Montorsi alone in the study, which was illuminated by two dim table lamps. The telephone rang continuously; she answered all the calls. He could hear her whispering in the shifting shadows of the hall. The Chief had stayed in the living room, keeping the widow Mattei company, between one phone call and the next.

Montorsi took out one, two boxes. There were hundreds of photographs. Mattei with a smiling man in suspenders. Mattei and his wife at a table, the Master of Italy with his mouth half open, a grimace between a laugh and an announcement. Mattei and the workers on a sunny oil rig, the light powerful, implacable. Montorsi felt a seeping despair. He would never find the picture he was looking for, the one taken at Giuriati. There were hundreds of images. Mattei had annotated them all, with the date, the year, the people next to him, the places, the occasion on which the photograph had been taken. The man in suspenders, appearing in various images far apart in time and space, was Giorgio La Pira.

He concentrated and tried to remember—as Italo Fogliese's smile, the day before, at the *Corriere* came into his mind—at least the year of the article in the *Corriere*, with the photograph in which Mattei stood beside Longo and Pajetta. He recalled the sentence in Fogliese's report to Ishmael: *Montorsi was unable to identify the presence of one of our covers among the persons who appear in the photograph*. The telephone kept ringing, and the widow's whisper crept into the room like the smell of mothballs from the closet. What year was it? Then he heard the mumbling of the Chief into the telephone, and as he listened the memory struck him, a flash. 1949. February 12, 1949.

He found the box on which Mattei had inscribed in his even handwriting "1949–1950." He went rapidly through the photographs. Their serrated edges irritated his fingertips. The Chief's voice was becoming more resonant on the telephone in the hall.

The photograph was buried midway through the box. At first it didn't seem to him the same image that had been published in the *Corriere*, the picture he and Fogliese had discussed the evening before in the editorial office. It was larger. There was more to see. But the people were the same as those who had appeared—identified and unidentified—in the picture in the paper. He quickly turned over the photograph. He saw Mattei's pointed, even script. *"Milan—February 11, 1949—at the commemoration of the partisan martyrdom at Giuriati field—With me: Longo, Pajetta, Annone, Mayor Greppi. Behind: Recalcati and Arle, former comrades in the Volunteer Corps."*

He inhaled the sharp smell of naphthalene, and the light seemed to go out. *Behind Mattei was Arle.* A former comrade in the partisan struggle. Ishmael's cover, whom Fogliese had alluded to in his report—it was Arle. He was the missing link. Montorsi had found it. Before Ishmael captured him, David Montorsi had captured Ishmael.

At that moment, the Chief, his face ashen, his cheeks striped by an unhealthy redness, appeared in the doorway. Montorsi, kneeling before the box, held up the black-and-white image between thumb and index finger and showed it to him in the half light. He smiled and said, "It's done, Chief. We've got him in our hands. It's done."

The Chief was silent, then suddenly seemed to collapse in on himself. His shoulders sank and he could barely hold up his head. "It's not done at all, David. It's over. They've called from Rome direct to me here. They've taken responsibility for the investigation away from us. I have to go to Rome. They're getting rid of me. Completely." And he turned and walked away before Montorsi could even try to summon a response.

Montorsi remained on his knees. His smile vanished. He stayed there for minutes, without thinking of anything in particular, emptied of will and astonishment. He rested his gaze on Arle's unrecognizable face in the photograph, standing behind the dead gray-black icon of a smiling Mattei. New masters had eliminated the Master. This was the essence of the story, the story of the story. Everything was crumbling. Everything was changing. He put the photograph in his inside pocket, replaced the boxes of photographs in their precise stacks, and shut them up in their cemetery of mothballs.

Brussels
March 26, 2001
16:00

Karl M. had forty meters' advantage. Lopez turned off the BMW's engine and tried to hurry. One of the bureaucrats standing in front of the entrance crossed the street in his direction. Lopez pretended to be doing nothing. He moved forward. Karl M. walked quickly, nervously. Lopez observed the old man on the bench, who was observing him. He passed the Parliament entrance.

Karl M. turned right. Lopez noted his course. Karl M. stopped, twenty meters ahead, his cell phone to his ear. Lopez turned toward a shop window. The sidewalk was crowded and the traffic increasing. Karl M. nodded. He spread his arms. He stood silently, listening to his cell phone. Lopez looked into a window. The German turned around, concentrated on his call. He looked at his watch. He spoke for a few more minutes. He closed his cell phone. He resumed his course. Lopez was behind him, thirty meters, no more. Karl M. should have turned left; Lopez knew his house was in a parallel *rue*. But instead he turned right. He wasn't going home.

Before them was a police station. Lopez thought Karl M. was going to go in and report the theft of the Palm. He didn't. He continued along a gentle downward slope, a tiny street closed to cars. Lopez gave him forty meters' advantage.

Right. Straight.

Karl M. didn't realize he was being followed. He came out onto an enormous square. Buses. A flower market. A horrendous sculpture in the center. On the left a *grotesque* church. The German went into a pub. Lopez stayed behind a flower stall amid throngs of people. Confusion. A sharp sound. Pigeons rose. Karl M. came out of the pub. He walked to the right down a narrow, damp street. Odor of brass. Sparks from a blow torch in a store. He went left, into an enclosed arcade, then straight, to the start of a wide *straat*. Hotel Des Colonies. Karl M. stopped and stood in front of the hotel entrance. Outside were two doormen in livery, English style. A bus trundled by without stopping; Lopez was on the other side of the street, thirty meters from the German. Karl M. looked at his watch three times in five minutes.

A Renault slowed down. The doormen hurried to open the doors, and a couple got out. Karl M. didn't even look at them. The doormen unloaded the trunk, and one of them got in the Renault, driving it into the underground parking lot to the right of the hotel entrance. The tourist couple and the other porter, carrying the bags, went into the lobby. Karl M. looked nervously at his watch.

An Audi pulled up. Karl M. leaned forward to see the driver.

All hell broke loose.

It was instantaneous and very clear. Behind Karl M. appeared the big old man who had been crumbling bread in front of the Parliament. In the milling crowd, no one was paying attention to anyone else, but Lopez saw it all. The old man arrived quickly and decisively, wearing a raincoat, and stretched out his arm. Lopez didn't hear the report; the old man shot with a silencer. Karl M. crumpled. Lopez couldn't see him; he was hidden by the Audi. The old man was aiming at the windows. It happened in an instant. Two shots fired, the windows shattered, the tires of the Audi smoking, a loud screeching sound. The old man took a few steps and shot three more times, piercing the car body. The Audi accelerated without stopping, people were uncomprehending, someone looked at Karl M., on the ground. The Audi's tires squealed, it skidded, and there was a sudden crash, as the driver lost control, regained it, accelerated again up the hill, crested. The old man was already fifty meters from the hotel entrance; Lopez saw that no one was following him. A knot of people had gathered around the body of Karl M., and it disappeared amid the bodies leaning over it. Lopez took off.

He ran. The old man had turned right onto a downward sloping street. Lopez turned the corner. The street was deserted. Twenty meters from the corner some men were unloading pressurized barrels of beer from a truck. Lopez ran toward them.

Breathlessly, in English, he asked the men if they had seen an old man running. They looked at him as if he were mad. Lopez dashed into first one bar and then the next, searching the toilets, and then he searched all the shops on the street. He looked through into courtyards, to see if there was a rear exit.

The old man had vanished.

He heard sirens around the corner.

He returned to the Hotel Des Colonies. Two police cars had arrived, their lights flashing. From the middle of the square an ambulance shrieked. Lopez went up to the officers and said he was an inspector from the Detective Squad of Milan and that he had seen everything.

For a moment he turned from the policemen toward the body of Karl M. People were moving away from it, pushed along by the cops. The stretcher was unloaded from the ambulance. One shot, in the back of the neck.

The noise was deafening. The ambulance siren was still going. More police cars were arriving. A mess.

A policeman was pulling on his sleeve, telling him in English to follow.

In the car on the way to police headquarters, Lopez told the officer about the Audi, and the policeman communicated the information via radio. His face, reflected in the window, was tense. He tried to calm himself. He thought of the Audi. The driver must be Rebecka's courier. There was a connection. Who was the old man? Was he the same old man who had stolen Terzani's autopsy report in Milan? Everything came back and everything got lost again. And at headquarters he would have a hard time; he would have to call Santovito.

At headquarters it was very hard, in fact. They made him wait half an hour, in an interrogation room. Two inspectors whose names he didn't understand introduced themselves. He told them everything. He handed over Karl M.'s Palm and explained how he had taken it and why. It turned out that Karl M. had made the police report from his office. Lopez brought up the joint investigation with the police in Hamburg, and one of the inspectors went out of the room to get in touch with Wunzam. The other reprimanded him, unbearably: Lopez should have notified the authorities, Lopez should have waited for permission, Lopez had committed crimes in Belgian territory in the course of the investigation, Lopez . . .

The other inspector returned. He had talked to Wunzam, who confirmed everything and took as much responsibility as he could for the investigation that had brought Lopez to Brussels. Lopez asked if he could call Santovito. The inspectors discussed it for a few minutes, in a corner. They had the telephone brought in, but one of the two went out and said he would call Santovito himself and then turn the call over to Lopez.

Silent minutes passed. The inspector with Lopez looked at him without speaking. Finally, the telephone rang.

Lopez waited for him to hand over the line.

"Hello? Guido?"

"It's me, Giacomo."

Silence. "You're a dickhead. A dickhead."

"Giacomo . . ."

"Giacomo nothing. Be quiet and listen to me. You are an idiot, Guido. As if I didn't have enough problems, here. What lunacy has got into you? You make a huge mess in Pioltello—you bring into headquarters someone who has a very influential protector. You get me fucked by his protector. You disappear, you don't call, no one knows where you are. They tell me you're in Hamburg. And now they call me from Brussels because you didn't ask for authorization and there have been some deaths . . ."

"One death, Giacomo."

"Two dead. One in Hamburg and one where you are. And you are in the middle of both of them. What the hell's got into you? Do you understand that you're in big trouble now?"

Lopez was silent, ready to explode.

Santovito wasn't finished: "Here we are, we've got Americans up to our ears, and you are going off on your own fucking track. Cernobbio is in danger of disaster, and you are off on your own track . . ."

"I'm on the track that I'm on, Giacomo. And if I don't follow it, you can be sure that something really will happen at Cernobbio. Fuck you, Giacomo. Fuck you."

"Fuck you. Now, you come back to Milan or the proceedings they're starting against you in Brussels will be your problem. Don't come asking me for anything. Understand?"

"You're the one who doesn't understand. You're damn well

not going to leave Detectives, your little political games damn well won't work, if something happens at Cernobbio. I'm here trying to protect your ass and you make me listen to a sermon."

"You can afford to eat because you listen to my sermons. Do you understand? Your job is at stake. You're going to sit and listen to my sermons. Fuck you, Guido."

Lopez was boiling. "So now?"

"I'm talking to the person in charge of the Detective Squad in Brussels. If there are problems, I'll have him telephone the Americans. Do me a favor and shut up and write me a report on what you have done and what you have not done in the past two days. And come back to Milan. Then after Cernobbio we'll settle this business."

"A report. I'm supposed to write you a report."

"A report, exactly. And take the first flight to Milan. Do me a favor. Call when you arrive. We'll talk tomorrow."

The Belgian police gave him permission to leave in half an hour, along with a written warning against staying in Belgian territory. Lopez had time to write the report for Santovito and sign a witness statement. He called Wunzam and explained everything, thanking him. Wunzam was discouraged. They had lost all along the line.

There was a flight to Milan at seven-twenty-five. He was put in a police car for the trip to the airport. Ten minutes after they left headquarters, Lopez heard the call come in on the police radio. They had found the Audi, in the parking lot of a discount store outside Brussels.

In the airport, from a public telephone, he called the Prunas. He couldn't get his ideas in order. Was the man in the Mercedes in Hamburg the same person as the man in the Audi in Brussels? The old man was a nightmare. He saw again the clean hole in the back of Karl M.'s neck. The child, by now, was lost.

The Pruna who was watching Laura answered, saying everything was peaceful. Nothing had happened. She had worked all day and then come home; now she was in her apartment. Lopez called the other Pruna, who had nothing to report. The Engineer had stayed home until late morning, when he had lunch with a couple of druggies ("The girl was a whore, Lopez. A rich fellow with a whore.") and then had returned home. He asked both Prunas to continue until midnight.

He called Laura. Two rings. Three rings. Four. Then "Hello?"

"Hi, it's Guido."

"You sound like a voice from the dead . . ."

"I am dead, more or less."

"Where are you?"

Now he could tell her. "In Brussels. I'm coming back to Milan."

"Um . . . And with that voice from the dead, does Inspector Lopez have a question?"

Silence. "Yes. Do you feel like seeing me?"

Pause. "Yes."

They would meet at a pizzeria near Laura's house, in Via Friuli. Lopez would take a taxi there. He would ring her bell between nine-thirty and ten.

The joints were gone. It was hot in the airport. He saw again the glass walls that looked out at the runways, their tiny brilliant lights in confused motion. He reread the report for Santovito.

There was nothing to do. Wunzam was right. They would have to wait for Cernobbio, try to avoid disaster. They had to play defense.

He saw an old man; he started. But it wasn't the same old man.

He read the warning given to him by the two Belgian inspectors; he didn't understand a word.

Then the flight was announced.

At 9:05 he landed in Milan.

Brussels
March 26, 2001
19:40

Fuck. Fuck fuck fuck.

Fuck the Old Man. Fuck the German bureaucrat, the child, the Swedish woman, the Engineer, the Pakistani, the Italian cop. Ishmael is great. He is great.

The American was lying on the bed in a room in the annex of the Villa. He had done it. He had taken huge risks, and he had done it. He had arrived at the Villa in time. He had done it. He was hoping to sleep and he couldn't. The adrenaline in his body was making him jittery. Ishmael is great. Ishmael is great. Ishmael is great.

He had called the contact in Brussels, in late morning, directly on his cell phone, according to the instructions. The delivery had not yet failed, even if this Karl M. had heard about what happened in Hamburg. The contact had seemed nervous. The American had advised him to pay attention. He was a boy, another boy. They would speak on the phone again in the afternoon to decide where to meet, in some public place. Karl M. would get in the Audi and the American would drive him to the Villa. The American had not followed him, as he had the Swedish woman; Brussels had an absurd traffic system, and many streets were closed to cars; it was better to organize everything on the spur of the moment.

He had called Karl M. a quarter of an hour before the appointment. The bureaucrat was furious because his Palm had been stolen. The American thought this was suspicious and reassuring, at the same time. If they had taken the Palm, they were not intercepting him. The American had him describe the person he suspected—an Italian who had come to his office. It was the Italian cop. The American had advised prudence. He had set the meeting in front of the Hotel Des Colonies. It would be twenty seconds, Karl M. would get into the Audi. Then they would go to the Villa.

Instead the Old Man had turned up. The American had been expecting trouble from the Italian cop, and instead the Old Man showed up. Fuck the Old Man. He was a bastard; he was a professional. Just as the American was about to open the door for Karl M., he had collapsed, and behind him was the Old Man, pointing his gun. A silencer: an extremely clean job. The American had accelerated, the four side windows had shattered, the windshield remained intact, the Old Man hadn't hit him, and he accelerated and felt the body of the Audi buckle three times as the old man fired. He had lost control for an instant, but only an instant.

He had barely had time to get out of Brussels before the roadblocks went up around the city. He had pulled into the vast parking lot of a discount store. He had consulted the instructions. The Villa was outside Brussels, but in the opposite direction. He would circle around the ring road, on the network of state roads. He had sat there waiting until darkness fell. He had waited for someone to park next to him. A Pajero. He had waited for the two guys in the Pajero to get out and walk into the store. There was no one in the two rows in front of and behind him. He worked rapidly. The stink in the trunk of the Audi was intolerable: shit and pee in a closed space. The child was still unconscious. He had covered him with a blanket that was on the back seat of the Audi. He had started the Pajero.

At seven he had rung the intercom of the Villa.

The dogs had commenced a furious barking. It was cold. When the intercom crackled, he had answered according to his instructions. The gates had opened. He had gone in with the Pajero. It took at least five minutes to cross the park, in the darkness, amid black foliage. Then he saw the white gravel of the parking area. Faint lights came from inside the Villa. Two men were expecting him. They spoke in English. They were English. They knew what had happened. They knew they could count on the American. Ishmael is great. They had taken the child, still unconscious, from the trunk. The American was overwhelmed. It wasn't possible for him to stay in the Villa. They were to perform the Rite. He tried to look in through a high window, where the heart of Ishmael was beating. Ishmael is great.

One of the two Englishmen took the child in his arms into the Villa, and the other led him to the annex.

In an hour it would all be over. He didn't even have time to sleep. He thought of the return. The child's body. The burial. Cernobbio. Ishmael required faith, self-denial, a form of love beyond love. He was afraid of the Old Man. If only he had eliminated him in Milan . . . Now he was worried about the burial. He was worried about Cernobbio. He would have to keep his eyes open. He didn't give a damn about the Italian cop. He got up, got the things he needed from his bag, and went into the bathroom to disguise himself.

The hair dye smelled like rotting grass and turned his stomach. He went into the small kitchen and looked in the refrigerator for something to eat. He had a little brie, some red wine. The tension was diminishing. He opened, yet again, the report on Cernobbio. With an almost maniacal scrupulousness, he knew by heart the maps, the plans, the schedules. He read again the list of names of the participants. He stared at the name of the one who was to be killed. He checked his documents. Everything was in order. He opened the map of Milan. He looked at the red cross on Via Padova, the apartment burned by the Old Man. He went over the way into Milan, the ring road, the Lambrate exit, fixing the route in his mind.

To the Giuriati field, where he was to bury the child.

He read again the instructions for the burial. At the plaque for the war dead, raise the stone. Underneath, there is some space. Put the body there. Replace the stone, but in such a way that it is clear it has been shifted. These were Ishmael's precise instructions. Ishmael is great. His men had failed in Paris, in Milan, in Hamburg, and also in Brussels. But Ishmael had not failed; his instructions were perfect, his will had been done.

Just before eight, they knocked on the door.

The two Englishmen said that it was over, that the American could leave. He followed them to the entrance of the Villa, where he had parked the Pajero. He said that the Pajero was stolen, that it was a hot car. He needed another car, one that was legal and clean. And fast. The Englishmen nodded. They left him at the Pajero. One went back into the Villa and the other headed for a low, broad garage. The American saw him reflect, open one of the garage doors, and back out in a BMW. Perfect.

The other Englishman arrived soon afterward, carrying a large metal valise. The American opened the trunk of the BMW and helped the Englishman lift the suitcase, feeling the dead weight roll around inside. He closed the trunk. He asked the Englishman if the suitcase was in order. There had to be a repellent layer inside, in addition to the wrapping, so the dogs at the border would not smell anything suspicious. The Englishman smiled. Perfect.

It was 8:20 when he turned out of the gate of the Villa.

Midway in the journey, he wondered if he shouldn't stop. No. He couldn't risk arriving in Milan after five. He accelerated.

He didn't think about the dead child in the trunk. He was thinking about the Old Man and when he would see him again. Apprehension seized him like a wave of radiation.

He would have to pay careful attention at Giuriati field. He would make no errors. He would inspect the neighborhood. He would take every precaution.

Two hundred twenty kilometers an hour.

He saw on the dashboard the pillbox with the Valium tablets that he had taken out of his pocket hours earlier. He slowed down, opened the window, and threw it out of the car.

Milan
October 28, 1962
20:20

Montorsi went alone, in a taxi, to his appointment with Arle, the Evil One. He had decided to leave out the Chief and the others; he didn't want Headquarters to be able to trace him to Arle and his institute in Viale Argonne, the place the doctor was preparing for himself after his departure from Forensics.

He had found the Giuriati photograph at Mattei's house, and behind the Master of Italy was the grim Arle. *Was Arle Ishmael?*

There wasn't much traffic. It would freeze tonight. The taxi left the city center, heading south. Spirals of white smoke from the chimneys of the housing projects rose heavily, called back chemically by the granular wet sleep of asphalt; the mysteries of earth persisted in their unequaled magnetism even here, in the heart of the city. The fake leather of the taxi seat released a gentle warmth, a sweet sweat of comfort. The air seemed to exhale itself. He settled back and felt his neck stick to the curve of the seat.

The stars, too, were visible. A star itself might no longer exist, yet the light that it projected pierced space, persisting white and frozen. The force that saddened his wife's face, the mechanism that triggered Maura's body to sobs—had they in other times shaken celestial bodies? And now the luminous convoy launched by the star, like a long thin cry of animal despair, was arriving here, beyond its own death; the heavenly mouth that had emitted that cry no longer existed.

And so it seemed to him that he was himself and yet, already, was himself no longer. He was falling asleep. He shook his head, the conditioned reflex of a child between two light states of sleep. It was almost a dream: the cars, the streets, Milan, the so-called Boom flooding the city with money. He saw Milan liquefy in vast washes of money, he saw men in the driver's seats of cars become as shiny and opaque as money, he saw money flowing, catapulting onto itself, devouring itself in a strange, sparkling circle . . . What is the rate of exchange between sorrow and gold? He thought, he dreamed. The elastic consistency of need . . . Need makes the stagnant air glow: It's like an ingot of incalculable value, crystallized coal, shiny and black, from which limitless amounts of money can be made, bills engraved with the profiles of great administrators . . . Needs . . . he saw, for a second, Maura shitting . . . and fell like a dead man, forgetting himself, on the seat of the taxi. He had a dream.

The dream: Enrico Mattei was sitting on the shore, leaning over a rocky bank, his fishing rod tensed and slightly curved, the sparkling line sinking down to the distant crashing surge, a broad expanse of roiling water, a gray-blue vastness that mingled in the distance with the sky. It must be Iceland. Mattei was bending forward. David could see the nape of his neck as he let himself rock in the wind. And he was approaching Mattei; he heard his labored breathing. The figure of Mattei rocked gently, like a mother rocking a hypothetical child. A very pale child . . . He saw his arm reach out toward Mattei, he saw the checks in the pattern of Mattei's shirt and his curved, supple back, rocking. Then he touched him and he seemed to touch a dead man. The horror devoured him instantly; he felt he was trying to cry out and couldn't. And then he saw . . . It wasn't Mattei, it was Maura. It seemed to be Mattei and it was Maura. She was like a doll, made of wax, and she was smiling. Her eyes were so prominent that they seemed painted, livid. She was smiling at him. She was smaller, even smaller than she was in reality. A child, in fact, a very pale child. In her arms she was gently rocking a little livid fetus, lifeless, also of wax, with two livid lidless eyes, as if painted, shining and black. Maura was smiling at it. Then she began to cough, first lightly, then more strongly, the coughs shaking her from the inside—or was she not coughing but speaking? He was motionless. She coughed and began to spit. She spit earth, dry rocky earth. And teeth, fragments of teeth. She had stopped rocking and was coughing hard, and she was spitting out earth and teeth. . . . Then Montorsi woke up.

* * *

He was a bath of cold sweat.

The damp sticky warmth of the seat annoyed him. The nightmare disturbed him. The image of Maura seemed to have stamped itself on his cornea. Reflected in the window were those fixed, livid eyes.

Piazzale Susa rolled by, green and dusty. The dark neck of the taxi driver followed the curve of the piazza.

They had arrived. On the nameplate beside the entrance were etched the initials *ISGM*. And below, "Institute for the Study of Genetic Malformations." What did it mean? He stared at the nameplate. What was Arle going to do here? Was this an outpost of Ishmael's?

David Montorsi touched one of the round nails set into the burnished door, an ornament with a fake and vaguely medieval flavor. It seemed to him that he hadn't completely awakened from the nightmare. He turned to look across the street. One, two cars. A few hundred meters farther on, beyond the bridge, you left the city and were outside Milan. A street perpendicular to Viale Argonne, on the other side of the wide roadway, maybe Via Illyrico, gave off an unnatural glow, and what seemed the smell of jasmine. He thought of the recent years of his life as sand without scent. He thought of solitude and of Maura. It was all a mistake; it wasn't supposed to end here. Behind this door Ishmael breathed. Who was Ishmael the Mysterious, Ishmael the Bearer of Death, Ishmael the Occupier, Ishmael Without Time? Who was that golden, shapeless name in the darkness. Was it Arle?

There was a single bell. He rang.

A small door carved into the entrance opened suddenly, automatically. He went through it. Inside he was met by the porter, a short, stocky fellow in a dusty black shirt, with a broad nose, his hair combed in large, strangely stiff waves, as if it had been dipped in lacquer. He said he was Inspector Montorsi, from the Detective Squad, and asked for Arle. The porter said Arle was expecting him. The man spoke in a hoarse voice, with a remote but evident inflection of dialect, of the Po valley, perhaps Emilian. He told Montorsi to follow him, that Dr. Arle had left instructions. They crossed a narrow courtyard. Montorsi asked if Arle had been the director of the institute for long, and the man stumbled over an answer, then said fleetingly that it had been six months, maybe seven. Were there many patients in the institute? Around two hundred and fifty. It's not clear what sort of patients they are, Montorsi remarked. The man said it was better that way, better to know nothing of those creatures. They die, often before the age of seven.

"Before the age of seven?" Montorsi asked.

"Yes. The children. Children with birth defects. They don't live long. Seven years, no more. They don't survive. Better for them. Better."

Suddenly Montorsi understood. He understood where the dead child at Giuriati came from. He would ask for a further inquest when he returned to Headquarters. He would ask for another autopsy, this time not performed by Arle or his men. He was certain they would discover some physical malformation in the delicate little corpse from Giuriati. The child came from Arle's institute.

They were crossing a second courtyard, bigger than the first. The porter was mumbling about how people can't even imagine the misfortunes that can happen. Did he, Montorsi, have children? Montorsi said that his wife was expecting their first, and the porter said nothing as he shuffled the soles of his clogs across the courtyard. The shoes must be too big.

There was a third courtyard, farther inside, shadowy and narrow, like the first. The porter stopped beside him. With his chin and a half-gesture of his arm, he indicated a glass door, illuminated from within. He told Montorsi to go through it. Arle's office was at the end of the corridor, after it turned, on the right.

Then he told Montorsi not to look to either side but to stare straight ahead. If you were impressionable it was better not to look.

The corridor was long and narrow. About three feet from the floor, at regular intervals, were wide windows. Looking at them, Montorsi had the sensation that the glass on the windows was thick, perhaps double-paned, and perhaps wasn't even glass but a plastic material or something similar. They were window walls. There might have been as many as a dozen before the corridor turned.

He began to walk down the corridor, slowly and steadily. *He thought of the mummy*. He was all nerves.

He felt as if he were crossing a magnetic field and that the facing windows, one on the right, one on the left, were poles of attraction. His gaze slid toward them and he tried to contain it, but it no longer seemed to be under his control.

The first two windows were dark. Montorsi could make out nothing beyond the thick glass. He observed, on the right window, only a strip of dried spittle, as if the mucus had stuck as it slid slowly down, like a suction cup that doesn't hold.

Then came a patch of wall. Then another pair of windows.

From the window on the right came a thud that startled him. A body had flung itself against the glass. He tried to turn his gaze to the opposite window, on the left, which was dark. He heard the thud repeated, continuously, frenetically now, and still he tried to keep his eyes straight ahead. The thuds followed him, rhythmically. In a fleeting nervous impulse he turned suddenly, in time to see the wide pupils of a child, the deformed neck, a large bubble of flesh that ended in a bony callus, and the hands stuck to the glass, its enormous dilated pupils leaving no space for the whites of its eyes, and it was smiling, smiling with an idiotic smile, or perhaps it wasn't even a smile, and it drooled on the glass, beat its hands, and he couldn't tell if it was blind or if it could see him as it dived with both hands against the window, as if it did not feel pain, and he saw the disproportionate membranes between the fingers, and he closed his eyes, and when he reopened them, two steps farther on, the window had given way to a white wall.

Now he counted. There were eight windows before the turn.

And he looked. He looked in them all.

They were gurgling. There was a trunk with a head lying on the edge of a bed. The lights behind the windows were faint. Probably they were all blind. There was no one around. He leaned against the wall, between two windows. He caught his breath.

Arle was at the end. He reached the place where the corridor turned.

Here there were no windows. The corridor seemed blind. The place itself seemed a tubular appendage of Arle. Montorsi felt as if he were walking in the ducts of an intestine.

He saw the white door. He knocked.

He heard Arle's voice. The voice of Evil. Arle said come in, yes, come in.

Milan
March 26, 2001
21:40

Lopez got off the airplane like a walking corpse. The fluorescent light of the arrivals hall irritated him. He flopped on the back seat of a taxi, a sack of emptied flesh.

He got out in Via Friuli. Opposite Laura's house, he saw the Prunas' car parked. He went over, saw the older brother, smoking, and told him everything was all right, that the money would arrive in a few days. The Pruna brother drove off.

Lopez spoke into the intercom. He hoped that Laura would let him come up. She didn't ask him. She came down.

She looked beautiful. Still damaged, but beautiful. Her blue eyes radiated light; her pale hair and the freckles intensified their luminosity.

She began teasing Lopez immediately.

They ate in a pizza restaurant near Via Friuli, around the corner from her house. They talked continuously; there was not a moment of silence.

He told her everything.

He talked to her about Ishmael. About Paris. About the secret rite at the PAV outside Milan. About the child. About Hamburg, Rebecka, Wunzam, the car accident on Nehlsstrasse, Hohenfelder in the hospital, Rebecka's death, Brussels and Karl M., the old man, Santovito's fury. She narrowed her gaze, smiled a little, shook her head.

"But why do you do it?" she asked him.

He didn't know what to say.

"Is it only a job, Lopez?" She called him Lopez, which he liked, because the informers, the small-timers, like the Pruna brothers, called him Lopez. It amused him.

"What do you think?" he asked her.

Laura put out her cigarette and tried the wine. "I think it's conscientiousness. I think it's a strange form of conscientiousness. From the outside, you don't look like a conscientious person. But you are. More than you think."

Lopez, too, tried the wine. "It's been a while since I've even known what I think."

She smiled. "The impression I get is this: That you are impelled by a scrupulousness. By a need to get to the bottom of something. That it has more to do with you than with the job."

"Yes, I really am going to the bottom."

She smiled again. "Ask yourself this, Lopez: Does Ishmael matter to you?"

He was silent. Really: Did he care anything about Ishmael?

"It's what I was saying to you in the hospital, Lopez. It's that you're morbid."

"Morbid."

"Morbid. There's something black, dark, in this affair. And, I imagine, in the other things you get involved in, in your job."

For years he had been disgusted by the blackness, by the dark. For years he had been unable to do without it. He went ahead mechanically, trying not to feel. But always he went ahead. He knew that Laura was right.

"To do the job you do requires a sort of vocation, right? Justice and peace for people . . . At least, maybe it's that way in the beginning. Then it gets obscured."

"There's a film, I don't know if you've seen it, *Bullitt*," Lopez said. "With Steve McQueen. Do you remember?"

"I love Steve McQueen. What's *Bullitt*?"

"It's the one where he's a cop in San Francisco. They made a car ad from it recently, changing some of the scenes. Do you remember?"

"The ad, yes. The film—I must have seen it, but I don't remember."

"O.K., there's this Bullitt, Steve McQueen. He's a police detective. He's drawn into a complicated case. There are politicians in the middle of it, who are his superiors—and he goes ahead and investigates, *against* them. He lives alone. There's a woman who stays with him every so often. I think it's Faye Dunaway. I think . . ."

"Go on, Lopez."

"A woman is found with her throat cut. Bullitt has no car, because he went on some wild chase and wrecked it. His superiors, who are boycotting him, won't give him a replacement car. So he goes with Faye Dunaway, in her car, to the place where the woman was killed. Faye Dunaway waits in the parking lot. But she can't wait and she goes in. Bullitt is with the other cops, talking on the telephone, and on the floor there's this woman with her throat cut. Bullitt sees Dunaway, puts down the telephone, and shields her. She is overcome by the sight of blood, and she runs away, back to the car. Bullitt follows her and together they go off. Halfway back to San Francisco, she stops the car. She gets out without saying anything. She walks into a field beside the road, and she seems to be sick. Bullitt follows her. The sea is visible from the cliff. She tells him that he is infected."

"By what?"

"By death. By the shit he's seen. That for years he's been feeding on it. Bullitt doesn't say anything. She asks him how he can live like that. He answers that half the world lives like that. She says she realizes that, finally, she doesn't know who Bullitt is. Then she asks him, What do we do now? What does the future hold for us? And he says—it's a historic, crazy remark. He says, 'The future is now—we've already lived it.'"

Laura was silent. "But I know you."

"We've known each other for two days."

"Yes, but I know you."

She talked about herself. The usual shitty childhood. Study at the university in Padua. A specialty in psychology, so she could read herself and read others, and learn to love. Classic female neuroses, but true. A terrible marriage. Dissatisfaction, silence. Then adultery. The skin of the other who revolts you. No children, luckily. After the divorce, the discovery.

She had slept around and tried to clear herself out, forget herself. She had given up the idea of private practice and had won a job in the public health service. She fucked and she fucked. While she was saying it, Lopez felt something deep inside him crumble. She fucked and, in fucking, had discovered that she *liked* pain. It aroused her. She said that at first she analyzed it. She had speculated that the pleasure arose from guilt, a hatred of men that began with hatred of her father, repressed rage, low self-esteem, narcissism. All nonsense. She liked pain. Memories emerged from childhood and puberty, when she had played little sadomasochistic games without realizing it. Now it was like being in a dream: She gave and received pain. She had asked the men she was sleeping with, and then she began to search the Net. There she found sadomasochist communities, groups of people like her who had felt sick and psychopathic but now discovered that they could speak to others who felt the same impulses and desires. She had gone from having conversations in the chat rooms to having dinner with people she met in them. There had been a circle, for years, tied to the Engineer. It was widening. He organized dinners, get-togethers in bars. He looked you over. If he liked you and if you showed you could be trusted, he let you enter the more discreet circles. They "played." She had become obsessed with pain. She thought about it from morning until night. She had lied to Lopez in the hospital: She had taken part in two PAVs. Of Ishmael, truly, she had never heard anything. There had never been a sign of children. Lovers of sadomasochism were in the eye of the cyclone; it would take almost nothing for them to be considered maniacs, and they insisted that everything be "healthy, consensual, and safe." You played if you wished to play, and if someone went beyond your limits there was a key word you uttered and the game stopped instantly. No one had ever uttered the key word. It wasn't necessary to fuck. It wasn't fucking: It was *more* than fucking.

"And when you were on the wheel . . ." Lopez said.

"It's a game. It's only a game. The wheel was a game."

"What did you feel, on the wheel? Pleasure? Pain? At the end you fainted . . ."

"It's beyond that. Neither pain nor pleasure. I didn't feel anything."

"Nothing?"

"I'm looking for that, Lopez. I'm looking to feel nothing."

He asked her if she saw in him the same impulse—if she said she knew him because she recognized in him the same black hole.

"Not in you. In everyone. Everyone has a black hole, in my opinion."

"And what reins them in?"

"Fear. Fear of being nothing. And meanwhile they delude

themselves that they are something, and already they are nothing.''

They drank the last of the wine and asked for the bill.

He walked her home. He wanted to kiss her. She didn't ask him to come up. He drew close to her. She stepped back. They looked at each other.

She shook her head and said, ''Not now, Lopez.'' She turned and closed the door.

Lopez walked home to Viale Sabotino, rolled a joint, and collapsed.

At seven in the morning, he was in a deep sleep when the telephone rang. Cursing under his breath, he struggled to answer.

A child. A dead child had been found at the Giuriati playing field.

Milan
October 28, 1962
21:00

Arle said come in, and Montorsi went in. The office was dark, suffocating. The doctor was sitting behind a worn wood desk, too big for the narrow room. The desktop was piled with papers, the shelves overflowing with books. A lamp on the desk was the only light in the narrow space.

Their greetings were brief and cold. Arle kept his hands clasped as if he were praying: a malevolent secular prayer. His pallor stood out in the half-light; thin bluish veins flashed under his eyes, following the beat of his eyelids. Such fine eyelids. The styes were compressed in tiny sacs of browner excrescences, highlighting the blue, almost white pupils, the same evanescent, impure white as his hair. He appeared to be concentrating on some interior vision that revealed itself only between his words.

"I was at Enrico Mattei's house, Doctor," Montorsi stated.

"I know about the investigation, Montorsi," Arle said. "I have been informed despite the fact that, as I told you, I am progressively extricating myself from the directorship of Forensics . . ."

"Informed of what, Doctor?" Montorsi asked.

"That another investigation has been taken away from you."

His eyes were lost in the icy light. "It's odd, Doctor," Montorsi said. "The decision to take away the investigation was made just an hour ago, maybe not even that. It's odd that you already know about it."

Arle smiled. He unclasped his hands. He began to run his right index finger along a metal paper clip. It was like a scene from a black-and-white film, overexposed, too bright. "Yes. But what is truly odd is the fact that in a mere two days two investigations have been withdrawn from your department. And not investigations of little . . . How shall I put it? " He smiled. He continued to smile but he remained focused elsewhere. "Two investigations that are, I would say, fundamental to you."

"Fundamental."

"Fundamental. Yes. Perhaps that word seems excessive."

"Rather, I am passionate about them." Montorsi almost felt like laughing.

"Passionate. Interesting. What do you see, Inspector, that could stir passion in such matters? Poor Enrico Mattei. Poor Italo Fogliese. They are different dead men, you know. I am speaking as an anatomical pathologist. The rigor mortis is different, the aspect of the body. I have had—if I can put it this way—the good fortune to view both bodies. I can say that I was one of the last to touch them. One must remain interested in the particular type of rigidity, in the gray of certain limbs. But one must remain detached. And pious. One must have a great deal of piety, even toward oneself, to undertake such a delicate task. Such a dirty task, in the end. What do you see that is passionate in this?"

Montorsi scratched his neck. He felt he had grown noticeably older. Days are sometimes epochs, the Chief had said to him. "Doctor, your attitude seems curious to me. You give the impression of being impervious to passions. But you speak of piety. You, too, have been in the grip of a passion. Or am I mistaken?" Montorsi prepared himself for an eruption of uncontainable violence, fueled by the false calm between them.

Arle had clasped his hands again, and rested his chin on them. "You seem to lack the word, Inspector. The word that closes the circle."

He paused in order to say it. "Ishmael. Is that the word, Doctor?"

Arle half-closed his eyes and inclined his head slightly toward the wall behind him, as if he were listening to music. "Perfect. Perfect." He reopened his eyes and stared at Montorsi, his stare an icy dagger that would pulverize any word. "Perfect, Inspector. Can you imagine why I summoned you here, to this place?"

Montorsi remained silent. It all seemed to him improbable, incomplete. Arle could not know about the photograph Montorsi had discovered at Mattei's house.

"No. You can't imagine."

Montorsi would have liked to draw his .45 and shove the dark barrel into Arle's mouth, smash his teeth, shoot, shoot again. His nostrils widened. He could almost smell the cordite, the iron in the blood. "Why the children, Doctor? Didn't Ishmael promise you something better?"

Arle's gaze barely faltered. "Better? You don't understand. . . ."

"No. I don't understand."

"No. You can't. You can't imagine how *fundamental* are the studies that are performed here in this institute. We are involved with tissues, with cells, but also with causes. Malformations. We cross-breed malformations. We identify deep processes. Here and elsewhere. Don't you understand? Genetics. You cannot imagine how vital genetics will be to our future. The world will be devoted to the hidden codes in genes—to the wealth that we are exploring now. We are working on a prophecy. When Ishmael's time has come, what we are working on will have the characteristics of a law. We are composing the alphabet of a new law. We are working on a new law."

"A new law . . ."

"A new law. But this is not what we are here to discuss, right, Inspector Montorsi? David Montorsi. You must have Jewish origins. . . . Are you practicing, Inspector?" Arle's smile folded his thin dry cheeks into two narrow channels of flesh, symmetrical bands of elastic wrinkles.

Montorsi ignored his question. "When will Ishmael's time come, Doctor? Today? Tomorrow? Will there be other deaths before the time of Ishmael is accomplished? How many dead? Ten? A hundred? How many?"

Arle's face became grave. "Yes. There will be many deaths. A new law is not imposed without a tribute of blood. All that is necessary."

"Then it's you, Doctor," Montorsi said suddenly. "Ishmael is you."

Arle's cheeks contracted again into a dense net of wrinkles. An unnatural smile wounded his face. "No, Inspector. No. You don't understand. I am not Ishmael." He kept smiling.

Montorsi was silent for a moment. Then he said, "I would like to see Ishmael, Doctor."

Arle began to laugh; the wound of the smile broadened to reveal small yellow teeth. "But . . . it's impossible. You don't understand . . . you can't understand . . . Consider . . . Consider that you are seeing him." He kept laughing.

"But you just said . . . Are you Ishmael, then?"

"Yes. In a certain sense. But not the way you mean, Inspector. No. You cannot see Ishmael. It is impossible. It has been decided."

"What has been decided?"

"That you cannot see him. You will not be among the Children of Ishmael. You cannot see him." Arle's voice grew low and ponderous. "In a certain sense, you are fortunate. You were chosen. This is the reason I summoned you here." He paused, theatrically, drew closer, and then sat back, his thin shoulders pressed against the studded leather chair. "I have a message for you from Ishmael."

David Montorsi was astonished. The words seemed to echo in the void. Arle's pronouncement had something hypnotic about it, a cold center that radiated a dangerous warmth.

The Doctor began speaking again. "Ishmael wishes to communicate with you. Do not consider yourself *too* fortunate. It is a practical necessity more frequent than you imagine. Unfortunately, Ishmael must foster the very obstacles that stand in his way."

"The obstacles that stand in his way . . ."

"Yes, yes. You can't understand. No one can understand, unless Ishmael has appeared to him. He is of a radiant size, you see? Ishmael reveals himself to you in ways that you don't understand."

"With symbols, right? With slaughtered babies? That's how he reveals himself."

"That, too. The Symbol was necessary I see that poor Italo Fogliese did not take precautions . . ." He was referring to Fogliese's report. The one that Montorsi had reconstructed from the used typewriter ribbon. The Symbol. The body of the child at Giuriati. Maybe that child had come from the cells of Arle's institute.

"Very imprudent of him," Montorsi said. "His mistake will let us throw you in jail—you, Ishmael, and your whole sect."

"Sect? In jail? You really don't understand. You are so far from comprehending the greatness of Ishmael. You think a jail exists that can contain Ishmael and his greatness? You think that a sect would be sufficient to propagate his light? You don't have even a hint of the forces in play. The forces in play are immense. Immense. You are nothing. As I am. It's an old law fighting a new law, the law of Ishmael. Now that he is here, Ishmael is rolling out his power . . ." Arle wasn't simply a man possessed. To Montorsi he seemed a *dangerous* man possessed. Some psychotics don't lose their relation with the world. Arle went on and on like the outbreak of a fever. "Also, what we do here, and not only here, is nothing. It is nothing compared with the power of Ishmael. Ishmael, from now on, is everywhere. This is the message of Ishmael."

"The message of Ishmael?"

"The message he has for you. For you, Montorsi. You understand?" Arle leaned forward a little toward Montorsi. Montorsi was petrified.

"I report it to you not fully understanding its significance. It is a warning. When you understand it, don't try to strike me. You cannot get at Ishmael through me. I don't know the channels of Ishmael's power. Ishmael has arranged my departure. I have stayed here long enough to deliver this message to you, according to the will of Ishmael."

Montorsi looked at him. He wished that the whole Detective Squad were outside the institute waiting for him and Arle. But what could he accuse him of?

"Here is the message, Inspector. Ishmael sends word that you are one of those chosen by lot. The wound that is inflicted will not fail to infect you. You will be forever an instrument of Ishmael. The more that hatred and disillusion grow in you, the more you will serve him. Ishmael will observe you forever, from a distance. You will never succeed in capturing him."

Montorsi was dazed; they were both dazed. Between the two pale faces in the half light a bubble of nothing seemed to open. Arle seemed to grow progressively younger while Montorsi seemed to grow old, until they were without differences, two men as simple as the notion of "man."

It was Arle who broke the silence. "Go. I, too, have to go now." He smiled one last time. "We won't see each other again."

I'll kill him, Montorsi thought. He clutched the .45.

Arle sensed it. He stood up. "It's of no use, Montorsi. It would be of no use."

Montorsi observed Arle's hand, resting on the edge of the desk, holding a small revolver.

Montorsi walked slowly down the corridor in the thin light. The lights in the rooms were out now, and the windows were big dark pits, their depths concealing malformations, rejects, distorted flesh. Genetics. The new law. The law of Ishmael. The glass was smeared, and traces of dry saliva were visible along the angle of reflection.

As he crossed the courtyards, he thought. It would be difficult to get a mandate against Ishmael from the new leadership of the Detective Squad. The investigation was already handicapped, since it could not deal with Ishmael's first two crimes. The headquarters of the sect had to be tracked down, some idea of the connections between Ishmael and American intelligence was needed, and this would require delicate diplomacy and political maneuvers. And with the Chief sent to Rome and his lieutenants dismissed, perhaps the very survival of the department was at stake.

And the message? Ishmael's message for him? Just for him? Fogliese's report, recovered from the typewriter ribbon, had been precious, but it had pointed out the risk: Ishmael knew him. And, in spite of how Arle in his madness had babbled on, he knew quite a bit about Ishmael. In normal conditions—without the destruction of the Detective Squad, without the act of destabilization that had been accomplished by the assassination of Mattei—Montorsi was certain, he would get Ishmael. He was certain, even if it took him weeks or months.

"*The wound that is inflicted will not fail to infect you.*" What did that mean? Who was wounding whom? What infection was Arle talking about? Ishmael's threat made him shudder. He clenched his hands in his pockets. Sweat oozed from his palms. He felt the wads of wool, the worn flannel inside the pockets. "*The wound that is inflicted will not fail to infect you.*" He felt his head trembling up to the bony crown. Fogliese had been instructed to let Montorsi know of Ishmael's existence. Ishmael had chosen him—what did it mean? He was afraid.

He tried to breathe.

* * *

The porter's face was pasty with sleep as he let Montorsi out the front door. The thick band of his stomach was now more visible, disproportionate, under the black shirt.

At the curb was a luxury car, maybe a diplomatic vehicle, its license plate not Italian but unidentifiable. Was this the car that would take Arle away?

Seen in the mirrors of that car as he walked away, Montorsi was a tall silhouette, his arms drawn down into his pockets, that grew distant in the ozone night of Milan.

Inspector Guido Lopez

Milan
March 27, 2001
07:40

A day of shit.

A day of shit after a night of shit. A squad car came to pick him up. He drank a quick coffee at the bar on the corner. Everything was strange. He wanted Laura. She didn't want him to stay. He was tired. The black hole that Laura had talked about called him from within.

A dead child at Giuriati. Why Giuriati? It was a playing field that was practically abandoned. The university students went there to run. Once it had been a rugby stadium, with a grandstand, goalposts, a running track of dark pounded earth. He remembered it. He had followed rugby when he was younger. Then the teams had moved to a new stadium, with three stands, near the railroad tracks; you could see the trains slowly moving past during the matches. And Giuriati had gone to ruin. Why a child? Why at Giuriati? For a second the suspicion arose that Ishmael had something to do with Giuriati too. Fuck Ishmael. He was a voracious dark mouth that swallowed everything.

Ishmael.

At four o'clock, the big shots would start arriving for the international conference. First, there was a meeting at ISPES, the Institute for Political, Economic, and Social Studies, opposite the Mediobanca headquarters, in Via Filodrammatici, and from there they would go to Cernobbio. They would spend the night at Villa d'Este and begin the official forum the next day. According to Santovito, the event required four different security protocols: the arrival and departure at Via Filodrammatici; the journey from Milan to Cernobbio; the actual meetings at Villa d'Este; and the return trip to Milan. If Ishmael's people wanted to set off a bomb, the most vulnerable point was the second. Santovito had coordinated with Calimani inspections and patrols along the Milan–

Cernobbio route, which would be augmented by the carabinieri and the Italian secret services. At three today, Santovito's men had to be at ISPES; agents were to be posted everywhere. Ishmael would strike, Lopez was certain. And now this snag of the child at Giuriati.

The place was *much* worse than he remembered. The field looked like the Roman countryside, full of ruins and tall grass. The gatehouse was closed. The locker rooms—to the right and the left immediately beyond the entrance—were falling down, their floors littered with dirt. The track was deserted, its surface pitted and stained. Lopez could make out the stumps of the goalposts among the clumps of uncut grass. He glanced at the grandstand; flaking plaster was everywhere. The support bars of the pillars holding up the steep roof were frighteningly corroded by rust. Near the playing field, he could see the police at work, gathered around a white cloth lying distended on the ground. The familiar scene. He was facing Evil.

The call had come in at 6:28 that morning to the central switchboard at Fatebenefratelli. A male voice. No accent. He had not let the operator speak. "Giuriati playing field, under the plaque for the war dead, there's the body of a child." The call was untraceable. The police had rushed to Giuriati. They had cut the locks on the gates with wire cutters. The stone beneath the plaque had been shifted. An arm was visible. They had lifted up the stone. The child was there. They had called Headquarters, which had contacted Lopez. Forensics had come out right away. The body of the child now lay under the cloth.

Lopez, sweating, his hands in his pockets, took a few steps toward the cloth. He nodded at them to raise it.

It was the child he had seen at Pioltello.

Back at Headquarters, he tried to figure out why.

Why bring the child back to Milan? Why all those useless risks? Did the child in Milan mean that the courier—the man who resembled Terzani, the man who had killed Rebecka, the man who had escaped the old man in Brussels—had also returned to Milan? Was he preparing Ishmael's operation at Cernobbio? He didn't understand.

Everything was suspicious. No one was safe.

* * *

Santovito looked gray and thin. "The child now, too," he said, a cigarette in his mouth.

Lopez had waited for him on the fourth floor. Before he could lay into him about Brussels, Lopez had told him everything. The child in Hamburg. Wunzam. The ambush at the port. Rebecka. The interceptions. The man in the Mercedes. The accident in the car. Hohenfelder in the hospital. Brussels. The European Parliament. Karl M.'s Palm. The tail. The Old Man. The shooting. Karl M. dead.

He finished by telling him about the corpse at Giuriati. It was the child that he had seen at the PAV, in Pioltello. That was the reason the Engineer had asked for protection from the political level—everything was connected, and it was bigger than one dead child.

Pick up the Engineer, Lopez urged Santovito. Squeeze him. *Really* squeeze him.

Santovito looked at him. "Don't talk about it. Not now." He took two drags on the cigarette. "Afterward, maybe. After Cernobbio. Now it's too late. Today's emergency is the forum at Villa d'Este. And in six hours the meeting at ISPES starts."

He was afraid of whoever had exerted pressure on behalf of the Engineer. "Giacomo, it's important," Lopez said. "If they do something at Cernobbio, they'll do it starting from here. It begins with the child. I don't know why, but that's how it is."

Santovito crushed the cigarette in the clean ashtray. The first corpse of the working day. "No. You will now do me the favor of letting go of the child. Wait for the autopsy, and then read the report when Cernobbio is over. Right now, you are to meet with Calimani and go over the whole thing: programs, schedules, plans, routes. Read the reports on the participants at the meeting. You will make the necessary follow-up phone calls to the others: the Americans, first of all, and the intelligence services and then—do me this favor—even the carabinieri."

Lopez shook his head. "It's a mistake, Giacomo. We have to consider the child. Leave me out of Cernobbio. You have enough men. Leave me with the child."

Another cigarette. "No. And besides I'm up to here with your nonsense. It's a bullshit trail, if you want my opinion. It's improbable and absurd and has led to nothing. What's the point of someone running around half of Europe with a child to bring it back where you started? Why? Can you explain it to me?"

Lopez stared at the floor. "I don't know."

Calimani, uselessly verbose, was eager to make Lopez see that in his absence he had done a good job of covering for him, that the security plan was airtight. Lopez heard him but wasn't listening. He was thinking about the child. The child. The child. The child.

He made the round of phone calls that Santovito demanded. The Americans: the man in charge spoke a lame, comical Italian. He knew who Lopez was. He said that they had coordinated with Calimani. From the Mediobanca headquarters, they could keep ISPES under control. Inside, everything was monitored. Outside, the roadblocks would start at one o'clock. Among the participants were George Bush, the former American president; Pérez de Cuéllar; Kissinger; Carlsson; Gorbachev; Solana. Each of them had four bodyguards who would not let their man breathe out of their sight. What about Kissinger? The American was convinced that they would not try again. According to him, the probable target was Bush. Or else Ishmael would try to massacre them all. Lopez and the American agreed to talk again about the trip from Milan to Cernobbio; they would see each other at ISPES in a few hours.

On the phone with the secret service, Lopez went through the official nonsense of coordination. With the carabinieri, he didn't even have to do that; the national police didn't care what the local forces were doing.

Lopez called Forensics. The autopsy was scheduled for the late afternoon.

He was tempted to arrange the arrest of the Engineer in spite of Santovito. He abandoned the idea. Santovito would be so angry he would probably throw Lopez out of the building and maybe get him fired. He thought of going in person to the Engineer. He looked at the time. Too late. He thought of sending the Pruna brothers. Too late.

The telephone rang.

Static. Through the interference on the line, Lopez said, "Hello?" It was as though the line were about to be cut off. "Hello?"

"Lopez?" said a warm, hoarse voice. The static increased.

"Yes, Lopez speaking. Who is it?"

Silence. Static. Then: "October 27, 1962."

What was he saying? "Hello? Who is it?"

Static. "October 27, 1962."

"But who is it?"

Click.

Lopez sat with the receiver in his hand, dismayed.

He called the switchboard immediately and asked for a trace on the call, the number and place of the call.

October 27, 1962.

Who was it? What did it mean? He didn't understand. Did it have to do with Ishmael? The voice had no inflection. Was it the same voice that had alerted the police to the child at Giuriati? He called the switchboard again and told them he was coming down to check two records.

In the basement, with its low lights and its crowd of computers, he spoke directly to the supervisor. He asked to listen to the most recent call to his telephone and to the record of the call at six-thirty that morning, the one that reported the body of the child at Giuriati.

The man in charge of the telephone center sat at an incomprehensible bluish screen, with a clerk pushing buttons beside him. They had the sound files ready.

First telephone call. The line: clear.

"Police."
"Giuriati playing field, under the plaque for the war dead, there's the body of a child."
"Can you repeat that?"
Click.

Second telephone call. His voice, in the rustle of static.

Static.
"Hello?"
Static.
"Lopez?"
"Yes, Lopez speaking. Who is it?"
"October 27, 1962."
"Hello? Who is it?"
"October 27, 1962."
"But who is it?"
Click.

To the ear, it didn't sound like the same voice. The diagrams confirmed it. He asked about the second call. The number was Italian but otherwise untraceable. The phone calls had been made by two different voices, both were from screened cell phones. Lopez asked what "screened cell phone" meant. The man in charge of the telephone headquarters said that not even the cell-phone numbers given to the police were screened. A screened cell phone was impossible to trace. "It's the intelligence services, maybe," the man said. "Or someone very clever."

Lopez went back to the fourth floor.

It was Ishmael. It was Ishmael again.

Milan
October 28, 1962
22:20

Home, to Maura. He was shivering. Montorsi looked for a taxi in Piazzale Susa. There were none. Arle's words bruised and chilled him. He saw in the distance, beyond the black trees, a noisy band of drunks. They walked off toward Corso Plebisciti.

He decided to wait for the tram. He sat on the curved aluminum bench under the platform roof. Cars sped by. The drivers on the ring road were wax dolls, one identical to the other, motionless, delicately bent over their wheels.

Now anxiety was an abyss centered in his chest.

He thought of Arle. He thought of Ishmael. *"The wound that is inflicted will not fail to infect you."*

He was shaking. The evergreens, thin dark gaping silhouettes in the night, rose all around, fingers pointing toward the sky, toward dark windows protected by shutters and imperfectly closed blinds. Everything was covered and defended, but light would filter in everywhere. Ishmael's time. The fulfillment of Ishmael's time, when everywhere will be like everywhere else. What did it mean to work on a prophecy? Genetics, malformations. A people of membranes, dilated eyes, a people that oozes and drools. Their limbs useless, reduced to stumps.

The wound was supposed to infect him.

The tram arrived. Its round dusty headlights flickered as it jolted and jerked. The electrical cables shook the car. Inside, workers were sitting in a row, sleeping on the inflated fake-leather seats, leaning inanimate against the car's warm opaque aluminum pipes. They wore similar blue overalls, some streaked with grease. The tram was full. He leaned his back against a wall, at the only place in the tram where there were no windows—which were as opaque as the aluminum, coated with a crust of stubborn smog, the violent form of attachment of this black city. The floor beneath him rolled unevenly on the broad curves, as the body of the tram uncoiled.

Fear kept him from breathing.

Ishmael's threat began to solidify. What did Arle mean, that Ishmael would touch him? Would he transmit through his touch his disembodied evil? And he, Montorsi, was nothing. Nothing.

Montorsi got out at his stop. He clenched his hands in his pockets. In contact with the cold night, they had begun to sweat again. A few hundred meters and he would be home, beside Maura.

There was a light over the door of the building. He thought of the embrace of Maura's body, the scent of her skin. He would caress her stomach. They would have a long and ridiculous conversation about the baby. The crisis had passed; they would talk about it. A car was double parked in front of the door. The headlights were on, the engine off.

He began searching for his keys. He heard the metal clicks, almost simultaneous, of the two doors of the car as they opened. Fear seized his body. He thought, Ishmael has come to get me. Danger jolted him, an electric shower from head to foot. He thought of being dead. *That the wound had infected him.*

He turned calmly, resigned. He waited for the shot. He thought of Maura and he thought of the body of Fogliese. He cursed the name of Ishmael. He barely saw the two dark profiles approach him. He tensed inside his skin, a final shudder.

It was as if he felt the shot. As if he felt the shift of air from the silencer.

Instead, nothing happened.

He opened his eyes again. He was still trembling, his shoulders raised stiffly toward his head, waiting. Ready to die. The two figures entered the light, a step away from him. He tried to stretch his muscles. He tried to make the tension flow out in the coursing of his blood. The man on the left was dark, tall, muscular, the features of his face decisive. He wore a hat and had his hands in the pockets of a heavy black overcoat. The man on the right was older. Grizzled hair. A straight nose. For a second the thought came to Montorsi that he was a handsome man. His blue eyes were cracks in his face. He wore a shabby raincoat. They stopped a step away from him.

"David Montorsi?" asked the man on the right, the older man. Could he be sixty? Older? Could he be called an old man?

"Yes, I'm David Montorsi," he stammered. He was still shaking with fear.

The grizzled man put his hand under his raincoat and searched briefly in his jacket. Montorsi watched, resignation settling into him. He thought again, *It's now. Now he'll shoot me.* The man took out a black leather wallet and opened it to display a license in front of Montorsi's white face. He couldn't read it. The man seemed to understand. He said: "My name is Giuseppe Creti. I'm from the Service."

For an instant all instants converged on the same teeming point. He intuited everything and knew nothing.

"My name is Giuseppe Creti, Inspector. Please come with us."

"With you?"

"Yes, it's essential that you come with us."

"M-m . . . may I tell my wife? A moment. On the intercom . . ."

"Please, Inspector. Come. It's of the utmost importance."

"But . . ."

Giuseppe Creti was already opening the back door of the car. "Come along, Inspector."

Montorsi turned and heard the low electric hum of the intercom. His eyes sought the window of their bedroom and didn't find it. He found himself getting in the car. They left, accelerating rapidly.

In the night, the speeding lights of Milan asleep striped the dark windows.

Montorsi said, "You said your name is . . ."

"Creti. Giuseppe Creti."

Montorsi was shaken, stunned. Knowledge was growing inside him. "May I know the reason? What is this about?"

"I can't tell you anything, Inspector. Please. Don't ask questions."

Was he Ishmael? Again there was silence. Montorsi had given up trying to identify the streets, the squares that intersected miraculously outside the windows, and he didn't even try to gaze through the thick glass of the windshield. He let himself be transported like an object.

Awareness was growing in him. The wound was about to infect him.

They drove around a traffic circle. He didn't know where they were. They were leaving Milan.

They passed deserted hangars, enormous caves of opalescent corrugated aluminum, and immense warehouses, a landscape of narrow pipes corroded by damp and rust, metal containers, big steel drums filled with dirty water, mirrors of soft mud that reflected the beams of the side lights.

They took a dirt road.

He saw the white arch of a bridge, the pale belly of a concrete reptile that hugged the city behind it. They skirted the carcass of a burned-out car. The headlights illuminated tire tracks stamped into the thick mud, almost petrified, like an ancestral land already known. The bushes were stripped of foliage, and shreds of old dirty plastic vibrated spectrally among the dry branches. They passed a tall mound of trash, soaked paper and grease—a dump. They turned left. The tires slipped in the mud, and the car slid, almost skidded; Creti worked against the steering wheel. They entered a dark field.

On the right, Montorsi saw what looked like regular rows of trees. They passed a strip of gardens, jammed next to one another, tiny enclosures from which shone cabbages, slithering vines, wooden huts and twisted implements, grates and corroded pipes. Creti accelerated. He turned again, cut through the black geometric rows, and for a moment the luminous woof of the air was lost, and they were in pure darkness. They reached the edge of a canal. The air inside the car grew colder. The two men didn't speak. Montorsi was still trembling.

He was approaching the final revelation.

The canal flowed straight, rustling, and after a few minutes its oppressive sewer smell penetrated the car, a stench of sulfur, manure, and wet paper in a bubble of warmer air. The car rounded a curve and Montorsi saw a halo silhouetting a dark, cubelike shape.

It was a building like the ones they had passed earlier. Its shape had the density of cardboard, but it was much taller and wider than the others, and it expanded as they approached. A geometric swelling in the heart of the untidy Milanese countryside. He saw a road unwind, smooth and even, like a runway, leading from the building in the direction opposite to the one they were arriving from. Creti accelerated suddenly, a last jerk, then turned abruptly. Again he seemed to lose control of the car but wrenched the steering wheel and braked. There were other cars parked there, with figures standing beside them. They were not the cars of the police or the carabinieri. Probably they were from the intelligence services, Montorsi thought, and these were colleagues of Creti and the taciturn younger man. The two agents carefully opened their doors. Montorsi did the same. They got out.

He felt smaller and slight once he was standing in the vast smooth dirt space in front of the enormous shed. He saw a yellow vehicle, a sort of tractor with complicated mechanical limbs like a forklift. The cars had their headlights on, sending thick rays of dim light against the outer walls of the structure.

Creti spoke. "It's an abandoned hangar. This was an airport for a club. They kept the planes inside. It hasn't been used for years." There was something Anglo-Saxon in his face. "Follow me, please," he said to Montorsi. He nodded to the taciturn man in the black overcoat, who locked his jaw perceptibly and stood still. Creti moved off, and Montorsi followed him.

Leaning on the half-open doors of their cars, Creti's colleagues watched them. As Montorsi advanced toward the open door of the building, he saw the carcass of a plane inside, a white-painted biplane. Half of a propeller remained hanging miraculously on a dismantled engine; the windows had been removed.

The other men were watching, following the creaking of their footsteps in the gravelly sand.

From the open entrance—two huge shutters that seemed as though a gust of air could shift them—a light filtered, more powerful than that radiated by the many headlights of the many cars pointed toward the building. Montorsi's face was a question.

Before they went in, Giuseppe Creti turned to him and watched him standing there. Then he began walking again.

Montorsi thought, Now they're going to murder me. They'll interrogate me and murder me. They'll do to me what they did to the child. Again he trembled.

Inside were broken pieces of airplane bodies and, intact in all of its parts, a glider, in sections of pale wood. Perhaps they had been assembling it. The place seemed to have been deserted suddenly, as if catastrophe had been imminent. Montorsi could smell the scorched, chemical odor of catastrophe.

Tattered old rags were hanging on a dusty wood-and-metal hook, attached precariously to the wall. A uniform hung there, too, soiled with dried grease. Curtains with rigid, chiseled folds, like plaster cloaks, fell from a height, ending in a knot of ropes of different thicknesses; they had been parachutes. Clear, intensely white beams of light converged behind the skeleton of a small pleasure plane. Montorsi tried to make out the final point illuminated by the headlights. It was the same light that, on the field in Bascapé the night before, had penetrated the naked, burned trunk that had been Enrico Mattei. Yet the point was hidden. They had to walk around—Creti preceded him—a tall rotor, segmented into fixed metal elements, like a star-shaped map of bronzes, complex and consistent, illegible.

Then they collided with the specter, the specter of light.

He thought, Here. They're going to murder me here.

The light show was violent. It took a few seconds to get the eyes, bleary with exhaustion, used to it. He felt the wound penetrate his flesh. According to the prophecy, the sign of Ishmael was about to be impressed on his forehead bleached by the light.

The body was huddled on the ground. Other men were observing him, like the men who were watching outside the hangar, but blacker against the harsh light. They had landed on a distant planet, a celestial body out of time, with the future collapsed into the present, and both of them into the past.

Fear. Fright. *Certainty of the end*. The pain was spreading.

He was ready for the transformation.

The body was curled up like that of an infant, a child grown.

He saw the wound, stripped of flesh, at the center of the neck. He felt precisely the pain it had felt. He saw the splinter of bone and heard the scream that had torn it. He saw the darkness under the skull. Only a little of the cerebral matter had escaped. The hair was clotted with blood.

He walked like a dead man as he came near.

It was a small pale body. He sniffed the odor of dust, which did not completely cover the scent of a child that came from the sweater. His forehead wrinkled, his face contracted, and he folded over on himself into a line of eyeless flesh. Sucking him up was not grief but something more intense and primal, as if his very being had been torn from him. He saw the pale yellowish face, the bruises under the eyes. He saw the blood. He stroked the hair, felt other clots of blood. He caressed the skin; it was wet coagulated cotton. He felt the freckles under his fingertips. The corpse was nearly pulsing with his grief and solitude. Guilt seized him.

The wound had infected him.

He threw up, soiled his pants.

She was dead. It was Maura.

Milan
March 27, 2001
11:30

Not even four hours until the beginning of the end. Lopez tried to think about the meeting at the Institute, the arrival of the Powerful, and he couldn't.

He could think only of the voice on the telephone amid the static. October 27, 1962. What did it mean? What had happened on October 27, 1962?

Disconnected images came to him in a torrent. The corpse on Via Padova. Hohenfelder with his head bent over the wheel and, through the window, to the left, Rebecka. The man in the leather mask in the hangar. The child. The child at Giuriati. Karl M. falling to the ground. Laura calling him a limp dick. Wunzam embracing him. Santovito putting out a cigarette. "You're morbid." The child at Giuriati. Almost suffocating at the Rathausmarkt as he swallowed the cake. The child at Giuriati. October 27, 1962. October 27, 1962.

October 27, 1962.

He left his office and went along the corridor and down the stairs. The ISPES operation had left. Santovito was already in Via Filodrammatici. On the first floor, at the end of a wide corridor, he saw clerks behind a counter. Fast. He jumped the line, three agents from Vice who were waiting for records. It was the police archive.

He asked for all the files for October 27, 1962.

A quarter of an hour later, in a small, airless room, he began to go through them.

Three cardboard folders overflowing, misshapen, faded. He opened them. He understood. One and a half folders were devoted to reports on the death of Enrico Mattei. Why was someone telling him the date of Mattei's death? What did it have to do with Ishmael? He searched the reports feverishly. *October 27, 1962*: Enrico Mattei dies. Maybe he was assassinated, maybe not. It remained an open case forty years after the events. Mattei had been a politician, a government manager. Maybe the Americans killed him. *Today*, Ishmael threatens the powerful at Cernobbio. They are politicians. People who have in their hands the fate of the world economy and the politics of nations. The Americans were warning of an assassination attempt. Maybe a bomb. There were analogies. But there were huge differences too. What did it mean? He was dizzy. He couldn't think.

He scanned the reports, filed by inspectors from the early years of the Milan Detective Squad: Omboni. Revelli. Montorsi. Montanari. The files were full of omissions. They had gone to Bascapé shortly after the crash of Mattei's plane. Their reports had been confiscated by the judiciary. What had they seen? He read what he could read. Generic descriptions. The usual ritual phraseology of men who could only set down the most obvious facts with fruitless zeal.

He went to the desk and asked for the records for every date having to do with a single subject: the Mattei case. Almost immediately the material arrived. A thin package. He asked the clerk if that was all. That was all. He understood. That was it. On October 28, 1962, the Detective Squad had been taken off the case. On October 29, the Chief of Detectives, Remo Nardella, had been transferred to another position, a rather vague bureaucratic job, in Rome.

He couldn't understand what relation all this had to Ishmael.

He asked for additional reports, for October 28, 29, and 30, 1962.

These folders were thick. On the twenty-eighth, a murder on the outskirts of the city: a reporter for the *Corriere della Sera*, Italo Fogliese. He opened the file. The investigation had been charged to Inspector Guido Mario Omboni, assisted by Inspector David Montorsi. The reporter had been killed in Paderno. Three shots. Authorization by Chief Nardella had been given for searches at *Il Giorno*, Mattei's office at ENI, and Mattei's home. The results of those searches? Missing. He looked in the file for October 29, the following day; the investigation had been abruptly suspended. The Fogliese investigation must have been an offshoot of the inquiry into Mattei's death; the Detective Squad had tried to get back into the Mattei case and had been screwed.

He went back to October 28. There were reports from Vice.

Then he understood. *A dead child had been found at Giuriati.*

The report was a nightmare. He felt a grim fever rise in him. Lieutenant Gianni Boldrini had undertaken what seemed a routine investigation. There was no report on the finding. The autopsy from Forensics made him shudder. Internal trauma. Bruises. Lopez understood: It was as if he had read the autopsy report on his child, the one he had seen, lifeless under the plaque at Giuriati that morning. Still, he could not understand. The voice on the telephone had said October 27, 1962. He reread Boldrini's report. The call had been made to the police that morning; the child had been found on the twenty-seventh, the case was taken by Detectives and handed over to Vice. Inspector David Montorsi had been in charge. Lopez went back to the file for October 27. *After* the Mattei documents came Montorsi's report on the case of the child at Giuriati. Lopez turned pale: the same scene, under the partisans' plaque.

One-thirty. It was late, too late.

Maybe the Detective Squad had handed the Giuriati case over to Vice because it was overloaded by the Mattei investigation. And Fogliese? What did Fogliese have to do with it?

He opened the file for October 29. Nunzia Rinaldi, a prostitute who had been slashed; Antonio Sorace, her pimp, found dead in Lambrate; Luca Formenti, a Bank of Italy employee, dead. There was an appendix on the Luca Formenti file; he lived in Via San Marco, right in the center of Milan. He was young but *important;* several inspectors had been put on the case. The body had been found in a field, outside Pellegrino Rossi, to the north, mutilated. His teeth had been smashed. There was no record of the course of the investigation.

Then he felt as if the breath had been knocked out of him.

October 29, 1962, the third report of the day: at 9:30 in the morning, on an anonymous tip, the body of a woman had been found inside an airplane hangar in the hamlet of Rescaldina. The identification had been made in the afternoon. It was Maura Montorsi, the wife of the inspector. She had been murdered. She was pregnant.

He rushed to the archive desk. He asked to see all of Inspector David Montorsi's cases after October 29, 1962.

He waited ten minutes.

The clerk returned empty-handed.

From October 29, 1962, there was no trace of David Montorsi.

Milan
October 29, 1962
00:10

It was Maura. She was dead. David Montorsi tried to get up and couldn't; he limped stumbling to his knees, his hands became calluses, his whole body became a callus. Then he screamed. As a man naked in the desert screams, he screamed. He seemed to be revolving around a nucleus made of emptiness. He screamed, he felt sand in his throat, and he screamed. He didn't hear himself screaming. He saw the small luminous bundle of his child melt in the great light. He smelled Maura's perfumes, the rancid sweetness of a rotting magnolia. He screamed for a long time.

He fell on all fours, on his knees, his hands on the ground. He had no breath and yet he continued to scream, in silence. He didn't see, he saw darkness, and then he saw again Maura's small body torn and twisted, her freckles darker on the blue skin.

He saw Maura's eyes emptied of sight. One wide open, the other half closed. Her foot was twisted, turned into an unnatural position, like a caricature. They had smashed her mouth. The broken teeth were on the ground, they had been smashed with a hammer, and he saw the hammer on the ground, a few feet away.

White lips, ivory ink, that poured into me the honey of words and of promise, you exist no more. You were beside me, pale grieving shadow. You nourished me with light; you were the flesh of all my sweet tomorrows. And you no longer exist, you no longer exist.

Now his screaming had become a feeble and plaintive cry. He picked up from the ground between thumb and index finger a tooth that was almost intact, blackened. He was lost in the veins of its ivory. It was an incisor. And she was rigid in death.

Cold hand, come back to lift me up. If you are not, I am not. You fall in the rain; you become salt for me. I pick you up if I pick up a handful of earth. He had become a pinch of earth and zinc, that tooth.

He was emptied out. The cry ended in a lament and silence.

She was dead. Maura was dead. And with her, inside her, they had murdered his child, his child, his child, his child, his child.

They had murdered his child.

He couldn't scream. He fell on his elbows. He saw the men around him, he saw their white expressionless faces. He could almost see the space between the threads of the black fabric of their suits. He saw Creti and didn't recognize him. He saw the milky hangings that had been parachutes, he saw the bubble of the sky outside glowing indigo, he saw himself growing distant from all things, he saw the bodies erased, he saw his own body abandoned, lying heavily on the dirty floor, he saw from a new height Maura's small body, from a corner of the ceiling of the hangar.

He collapsed. He withdrew. He felt his flesh throbbing. He assumed the death into himself. It entered into him, a vertical black structure residing in his spine.

It wasn't pain. It was beyond pain.

Afterward, after many hours, he would begin to feel pain, the torturing pain.

The man from the Service, Giuseppe Creti, came over to him. Montorsi seemed to be humming. He was crying. He was emitting a silent, feminine cry. He was stretched out, as if clinging to the ground. He was the same color as his wife. He was gasping. Creti waited until the intensity of the humming diminished. He put his arms under Montorsi's armpits, struggling to lift the big man up, keeping the other men away with a fierce, unanswerable look. Montorsi was an enormous doll, disjointed in many places, like the corpse of his wife. Creti supported him on one side, felt the pressing weight, the bitter sweat. Almost limping, he dragged Montorsi with uncertain steps out of the hangar. Montorsi staggered backward. He began to breathe hard. He dissolved in weeping as he tried to breathe.

Creti dragged him to the car and sat him in the driver's seat, with his legs and head outside, to make him breathe. The man in the dark overcoat was still standing silently beside the car. Then he asked Creti, "Worse than you expected?"

Creti nodded.

He left the man beside the sack of a man that was Montorsi.

He went off, back to the entrance of the hangar, and, turning before he went in, saw that Montorsi had started vomiting again. The other man, hands in the pockets of his black coat, watched him in silence.

Creti began giving orders to the men around the woman's body. He had them take photographs, hundreds of them. The hammer with which her mouth had been smashed was a few feet from the body, near the hangar's windowless wall. Some of the men went with powerful flashlights into the dark corners. One photographed the footprints in areas of the floor where the dirt was thick. The flashes were constant. Creti looked around. When they had finished, he gave the order to evacuate. They would report the body to the police as soon as they had finished their own examination. He recommended an anonymous phone call to police headquarters.

Creti returned to the car. Montorsi was covered with the other man's coat, rocking himself, his gaze livid, lost in the trampled grass.

"Do you have somewhere to sleep?"

Montorsi looked at him in bewilderment, as if he had never before seen the man speaking to him. Then he seemed to return from wherever he was. "At home," he stammered. ". . . Our house . . ." He hung his head, a dead weight.

"No, not at your house, Inspector. It's not safe."

He raised his head heavily. "No? . . . It's not safe?"

"No."

The telephone call had arrived at the Service, directly, at an unlisted number that was used occasionally in Milan. The two agents who took the call were astonished. It wasn't possible that someone outside Intelligence knew the number. Creti had listened patiently, many times, to the tape. The voice was without inflection, and in the crackle of the recording was a magnetic disturbance. "Ishmael has revealed a new symbol. You can find it in the hamlet of Rescaldina. There is a small abandoned heliport. Inside the hangar. It's a woman. Ishmael is alive, until the fulfillment of his time."

The Service had received signs from Ishmael. They knew about Montorsi's investigation at Giuriati. They had pressured the Chief of Detectives to let him continue with it. The inspector had been digging in the right spot. He was heading, like a dog, nostrils to the bare earth, directly to the heart of the being whose existence they had long known of but whose name was new to them: Ishmael. For more than a year they had been alert to the arrival of such a force. Already it was fragmenting the security forces. Few divisions had resisted the power of Ishmael. Giuseppe Creti was the head of the Service, a division safe from that power.

His name wasn't Giuseppe Creti. It was a false name, assigned to him at the moment when it had been decided that a division of the Italian intelligence services would try—as far as possible—to oppose the expansion of the forces of Ishmael. Of Ishmael, however, he knew little. He knew much less than Montorsi knew. When they had gone to remove the ribbons from the typewriter of the *Corriere* reporter, the ribbons were no longer there. Creti suspected that it had been Montorsi. They were keeping an eye on him. Creti had seen him wandering among the fuel-soaked tree trunks in the field, the night before, in Bascapé. He had seen him annoy his Chief. Giuseppe Creti had known about Ishmael's plan to convert institutions to his cause, starting with the intelligence services and the agencies of law enforcement. With the death of Mattei, another era was beginning. Ishmael was taking life. He had chosen Italy as the bridge to Europe. American intelligence nourished him, supported the start of his burgeoning efforts. Soon he would take over everything.

Ishmael was about to wrap all Europe in his tentacles.

Dryly, Creti said, "We'll put an apartment at your disposal. I'll leave my deputy with you for a few nights. Now I'll call a doctor. You need some tranquilizers. You'll have to stay secluded for a while, Montorsi. Tomorrow I'll come have a talk with you." He moved toward his deputy. His name was Andrea Malgioglio. They had worked together for a year and some months, setting up the organization that Creti was supposed to coordinate. Ishmael seemed a black cloud, threatening but ungraspable. They had torn from it only insignificant shreds. They knew about the journalist, Fogliese. They knew about the infiltrators in Vice and in Forensics. The Detective Squad in Milan was clean; it would be the last to fall. The Chief had close ties with Mattei. The rot was in Rome. It was beginning the slow and certain work of penetration at the political level. Then Italy would be Ishmael's. Creti had not understood perfectly the meaning of the work of his division. It seemed to him a lifeboat, far from the cancerous body of the ship, and now it felt prey to new and more ferocious organisms.

He had the general picture. The details escaped him. He would talk about it with the young Montorsi, as soon as possible.

He and Malgioglio decided to return to Milan, to the apartment they used occasionally on Via Podgora, in the center of the city, between the Rotonda della Besana and the Justice Department. Malgioglio would stay with Montorsi for a week, with others relieving him as necessary. Creti told Malgioglio he would come by in the late morning. He turned and waved over one of his men, a medical officer, and asked him to follow Malgioglio and Montorsi in his car. "Be sparing with the tranquilizers," Creti told him. He was afraid that Montorsi would carry out a desperate act. But a smile opened up in him; he didn't really believe that Montorsi would harm himself.

He would make a proposal to Montorsi.

He knew that Montorsi would harden himself. He knew that he would accept.

Milan
March 27, 2001
13:40

It was too late.

Lopez had little more than an hour until the start of Cernobbio. Where would they strike? At ISPES, opposite the Mediobanca building? Or directly at Cernobbio? Who would strike?

What he had found in the files was of no use. October 27, 1962, was, perhaps, the start of everything. Enrico Mattei was, perhaps, Ishmael's first victim. Inspector David Montorsi was, perhaps, his second.

But there had been a child at Giuriati. And now, too, there was a child at Giuriati.

It was useless. It was all useless. Ishmael is great.

He found an official document noting the departure of David Montorsi, six months after the death of his wife: "State of service: Suspended." Nothing else. No other records. No motive. No hint of his next destination.

Two o'clock. He had to move.

In the squad car he drove at top speed to the discreet, funereal headquarters of Mediobanca on Via Filodrammatici. In front of the entrance to ISPES, he saw Santovito in conversation with an American and Calimani talking to a group of officers. The building was blocked off. Lopez glanced at the roof of the Mediobanca building, where men in dark outfits and helmets, with guns, scanned the street below. A group of Americans came out of Mediobanca. The bomb squad had been everywhere.

He went into Piazza della Scala, where there were a lot of carabinieri, who, excluded from the big game, were guarding the periphery. There were few passersby, few tourists. In the direction of Palazzo Marino, from which the cars of the Powerful would arrive, Lopez saw a jagged line of police officers. He recognized some friends from the intelligence services and stopped to speak to them. They knew everything about Ishmael. They knew about Paris, Hamburg, Brussels. They were optimistic. After all, in Paris Ishmael had failed. Lopez thought of Giuriati. Of Mattei. Of Montorsi.

He went into a bar at the start of Via Manzoni, near the bookstore, and had a disgusting coffee. He telephoned Laura; her line was busy. He went back to ISPES.

Santovito, Calimani, and Lopez had a quick meeting. They would be free agents there and at Villa d'Este, at Cernobbio. The police and security forces had intensified the patrols on the route between Milan and Cernobbio; so far, there had been nothing suspicious. The Americans had searched inside ISPES with bomb detectors: The place was clean, no explosives. Calimani, with his men, would watch the ground floor. Lopez, with his, would take the meeting room on the second floor.

They had twenty minutes until the arrival of the participants.

On the second floor, with its marble pavement and dirty white walls, the vibes were bad. American intelligence agents went in and out of the rooms. Lopez had six men; he had them search the toilets, closets, and all sixteen offices, and a corridor that ran along the four sides of the building. All were empty. On the floor above were the institute's archives, transformed into an operations room for the joint forces of the Americans, the intelligence services, police, and carabinieri. Almost every corner of the second floor, including the meeting room at the center, was monitored. Not monitored were the offices, the closets, and the toilets. Lopez arranged a chain with his men, one on each side of the building, checking everything. The two remaining agents were stationed inside the meeting room. He himself would move around.

In the meeting room, the audiovisual technicians were working around the screen, surrounded by Secret Service agents checking the furniture chair by chair. Americans were everywhere, with walkie-talkies and headphones.

Lopez got the signal. On the ground floor, the doors were about to open to the participants.

* * *

Lopez went down to the entrance. Calimani was frantic. Santovito was in the archives, the operations room on the third floor. The participants were supposed to show their credentials at three points. The Americans and the intelligence people were following them, checking even between one barrier and the next. There were three metal detectors to pass through and a couple of Americans with a hand detector. More than sufficient.

The list of participants totaled 572 people. A huge job. It would take half an hour. Then the Powerful would arrive.

The participants were a *Who's Who* of economics in Milan; politicians from Rome; journalists from all the papers. They filed in slowly; the security checks were complex. Lopez saw agents emptying the purse of a woman reporter, who was furious.

Calimani appeared, agitated. "Giacomo says the Americans have given orders not to let a certain reporter enter."

"Who is it?"

"An American. I don't understand. His name is Lyndon Galludet. If he resists, we intervene. The Americans are taking care of stopping him."

They found his name on the list: "Lyndon Gallaudet, *International Intelligence Review*." They had no idea who he was.

Suddenly there was confusion and the sound of raised voices. Lopez and Calimani jumped. Four agents from Intelligence had converged on one man. It was Gallaudet. They had stopped him.

Lopez took charge. The journalist, a young man, was shouting, demanding to enter, calling them all bastards. Lopez ordered him driven away in a squad car. He would remain in detention at Headquarters, to be questioned that evening, once the journey to Cernobbio was over.

No one paid any attention to him. There were good-looking women, as at a fashion show, and wrinkled old men, one muffled in a white scarf and wearing an overcoat that must have cost a couple of Lopez's paychecks. The journalists were a mob. Outside the entrance was a wall of photographers.

Calimani was experiencing *total paranoia*. Santovito was not to be seen—who could say how he was enjoying it, up in the archives, among Those Who Count. Santovito had started his waltz. After Cernobbio, he would dance out of Detectives to a job in Rome. Piece of shit. Lopez thought of the Chief of Detectives in

1962, who had been exiled, eliminated. Sooner or later, they would eliminate Santovito as well.

Politicians arrived, on a grand scale. The Mayor of Milan shook hands with everyone, smiling broadly, his bald head shining. The Catholic president of the region entered, and then parliamentary deputies, a few at a time, all smiling blockheads. Middle-aged women, their faces parchment painted with mascara. Shit. Shit everywhere. Lopez remembered what Laura had asked him the night before: "Why do you do it?"

Out of desperation. He did it out of desperation.

No sign of Ishmael. The last of the ordinary participants, panting to enter.

Then an uproar.

The cars of the Powerful were arriving.

Milan
October 29, 1962
02:40

The apartment on Via Podgora had three rooms and a bathroom. Montorsi drank a cup of hot water. He swallowed the pills Creti's deputy gave him. There were two beds. The silent man stretched out on the one closer to the window. Montorsi didn't even undress. He lay down, pulled up the blanket, brown with café-au-lait stripes, and tried to sleep. His bones felt as if they had been broken. The drugs took effect; he felt a stupid, nocturnal bubble open in his mind. A weight lay on his tongue, a warm round rock that kept him from speaking. But he didn't want to speak. He saw Maura's teeth; he was touching her thin fingers, the beautiful freckles. He couldn't cry.

His mind shook, shuddered. It began to come alive, to ramify: his reliquary.

Maura gets off the train from Como at the Central Station, in a crowd of people, coming back from Montebarro; her blue eyes look for him in the crowd. They are dancing on a beach, at night; Maura is amazed, because usually he hates to dance. Maura is running, and he is running after her, at Castelrotto, at night, the air sparkling with new snow. In the countryside outside Milan he lashes her legs with a dry branch, and she closes her eyes, bites her lips in pleasure. Maura . . .

He would move through his life touching the white bones of these memories. He was beginning an eternal solitude. He was beginning to die.

He slept until midmorning.

He saw Maura; he saw worms.

He woke with an infinite weariness. The man beside him was up and had made coffee. He went back to sleep. He woke to some noise in the next room. The curtains were drawn; they were thick and almost no light filtered through. He was a single bruise. He got up, went into the bathroom and didn't close the door, ran the cold water, and tried to cry. Not a tear came.

He went back to bed. His skin was swept by cold shudders. He felt a fever on him. He couldn't stay lying down. His back hurt. His stomach was shaking. A bitter brown plaque thickened his tongue. He drank two mouthfuls of water, swallowing the pills. His hair had become curly and pasty with sweat. He sat on the bed for a long time. He struggled to stand. He staggered. He felt he was two bodies, his own and that of the illness.

Then guilt began, a knurled animal biting him in the spinal column, just below his neck. She was dead, and it was his fault. He was bombarded by images of Maura. Inserted between them were scenes: her corpse, her broken tooth.

He lost hours and hours in a murky sleep. Volleys of images, surges of images. It was always Maura. *Maura, I still love you.*

He woke and went into the next room. Giuseppe Creti was sitting beside his deputy. Montorsi collapsed on the chair. He laid his head in his folded arms on the table. They sat in silence for a while.

Then he raised his head. The two men said nothing.

He said, "I want to go home."

Creti spoke. "No. It's dangerous. And you are too valuable."

"Valuable."

"To us. You are valuable." He took out a cigarette, lighted it, and drew on it deeply: a yellow *papier mais* that perfumed the room. He passed around the pack. Distantly Montorsi observed the stumpy, straw-colored cigarettes. He took one, let himself yield to the inner spiral of warm pleasure that it gave him, and immediately felt a sense of guilt for that pleasure, an insult hurled at Maura just a few hours after her death.

"Valuable . . ."

"You know a lot about Ishmael, Inspector. You are valuable to us."

He had not had time to think about Ishmael. Now he recognized in himself the tender kernel of hatred that would grow forever inside him. He would learn to balance against it anxiety, guilt, and pain. Hatred saves; it isn't the contrary of love. It is the primal matter, the basic passion, the constant current: time does not exist. *Oh Maura, time does not exist . . .*

He looked at Creti. He said only, "Yes, Ishmael . . ."

In the following days they talked about Ishmael. Montorsi was persuaded to stay in the apartment on Via Podgora. Men were on duty in shifts, playing cards. Creti appeared around midday, often with Malgioglio, and they ate together. Montorsi picked at the plain food on the plate, cooked by whoever was on duty, often from a can. He couldn't keep food down. He was growing visibly thinner. His worst hours were in the morning, when he woke up, when the specter of the dead woman re-entered the black waters of the unconscious, yet a trace of her followed him as he went back and forth between the bed and the bathroom and the pills and bitter water, and he was assaulted by memories of Maura. The doctor came almost every day. A week after Maura's death, the doctor was worried and spoke of the possibility of putting Montorsi in the hospital. Creti was puzzled.

The hours spent talking about Ishmael—feverishly evaluating hypotheses on who he was, how it might be possible to stop his work, while smoking endless *papier mais* that ended up as butts in the heavy glass ashtray—distracted Montorsi. Talking about Ishmael gave him the comfort of hatred. The morbid fruit of hatred within him was growing woody, hardening into its natural saline, mineral state. They talked, and talked, and talked. They reexamined word for word Fogliese's report on the "Continental Church of Milan." They tried to identify the church's center, putting together separate facts that came from the riverlike sources of information available to the team that Creti coordinated.

But he was sick. He continued to be sick. He grew thin, eaten by a fever that exploded at night. He had nightmares. Sometimes he felt betrayed, as if Maura had flown off to another life she shared with other people, with an alien but real man.

Every morning he swallowed the bitter white pills. His tongue was pasty. Together with Creti, he untangled the knots of information, computed with him long tabulations, taken from earlier archives; they identified, one by one, the American intelligence agents in Verona. Creti himself had signed a sick leave for him. He had also spoken with the Chief of Detectives. The Chief had been removed the day after Maura's death and sent to Rome. The resulting vacuum of power would permit Intelligence to dominate the north of Italy, and Ishmael to settle in.

At the end of the second week on Via Podgora, Creti arrived with a dark look. Montorsi was pale as paper. Creti waited more than an hour before he told him about it. Ishmael had released a new Symbol.

It was a child again. Two years old, a little more. It had been discovered outside Courmayeur, in Val d'Aosta. Ishmael's men had again communicated with the Italian intelligence services. The child had been found it, half buried, in a town park, white and covered with dirt, the chest cut open. The telephone message was identical to the one that had communicated the location of Maura's body.

According to Fogliese's report, an Event would follow this new Symbol. Ishmael would eliminate a new obstacle.

The news came the next day, while Creti and Montorsi were working on a series of addresses, trying to match them with internal information that the services had drawn from registries about properties that had been passed from hand to hand and acquired, in recent months, by Americans or by United States fiduciaries. The telephone rang, the man who was on duty answered, and the person on the phone asked for Creti. Montorsi saw his gaze narrow, his jaw lock. He passed one hand through his short gray hair. Montorsi lighted a *papier mais*, and handed it to him while he was still on the telephone; he nodded gently. He had to leave right away. There had been an assassination. The vice-president of the Bank of France had been murdered. He had been vacationing on Mont Blanc.

During the third week, Montorsi began to recover. As soon as he woke, he went into the bathroom and spit out a foamy thick saliva. He had lost more than twenty pounds. He had not been out in the sunlight for twenty days and his skin was greenish yellow. He hadn't shaved, his muscles were soft, and his back was bony. It hurt to move. Ceaselessly he explored his *reliquary*. The images of Maura struck him with concentrated frequency, even when he was working with Creti. After the assassination, there had been a revolution at the top levels of French finance. The Service had been contacted by the intelligence services across the

Alps. Ishmael was settling in France. There was a tremendous flow of information between Paris and Milan. The name of Ishmael continued to emerge, in fragments that couldn't be fit together.

After Montorsi had spent a month in seclusion on Via Podgora, while the activities of Ishmael were at their height in France, Creti decided to take Montorsi out of the apartment. They went down to have a coffee. Montorsi was weak; his knees shook. The feeble sun of Milan—a diffuse gray late autumn light that reflected off the white glow of the vast walls of the Palace of Justice—bothered him as he made the uncertain steps to the bar across the street. They sat down. He bought his first pack of *papier mais*, after having taken hundreds from Creti.

Maura was present, silent and diffuse like the outside light, breathing faintly but tirelessly in him. He and Creti smoked. Creti had a beer. He said his name was Masciopinto. Giuseppe Creti was a cover name. For thirty years he had worked for Intelligence. He had killed many men. He had lost many men. He was a widower. As a special agent he was much in demand, even for killings not linked to the Service. He was a dangerous, yet trustworthy, animal, he had an acute predatory instinct and operated without remorse.

Creti seemed to intercept Montorsi's thoughts. "We are animals on the way to extinction," he said. And took a long swallow of beer.

The next day, Creti made his proposal to Montorsi.

The proposal was a contract written on thin, light paper, with carbons. The typewriter had not done a good job of imprinting the letters. The secondary clauses were in tiny type. It took Montorsi an afternoon to finish reading it. It was a dangerous contract. His missions would constantly change; he would function amid mystery. Creti would be the only constant. And there were no safeguards or supports. In a foreign country, if you are captured or wounded, you're on your own. There is no recourse if you are sentenced by a foreign court; if you are imprisoned, the Service does not intervene. Death hovered in the background, present between the syllables.

Death. Maura. Guilt still devoured him. He wept, often at night. He saw Maura everywhere; the memories multiplied. He wanted to talked to her. Ten years seemed to have passed since he had lost her, snatched away to become Ishmael's message to him. Yet it seemed she was just provisionally distant, temporarily away. For the remaining years of his life, his most intense sensation would be that he was about to meet her, that they were destined to meet, soon, in reality.

He signed the contract with the Service. He decided not to go to Headquarters to say goodbye.

The first operation began a month later. They brought him, in the dark, to a training camp.

Milan
March 27, 2001
15:50

The Powerful, their limousines accompanied by motorcycles, muted sirens, and the flashing lights of squad cars, arrived to a frenzy of photographers. Lopez watched from outside the entrance to ISPES. The tension was extreme. He counted the limousines as they accumulated. Four. Five. Six. That was all.

They began to open the doors.

Solana, the former head of NATO in Europe, got out first. Uneven beard, gray hair, glasses. A fastidious face. Beside him were three bodyguards; the driver of his limousine advanced slowly through the flood of flashbulbs, to leave room for the limousines behind him. Solana walked quickly, without smiling. The security chiefs had come down from the operations room and stood just inside the entrance. Lopez saw Santovito bow slightly toward the Spaniard and shake his hand. Solana was safely inside the building. Lopez could barely make out the sharpshooters on the roof of the Mediobanca building.

The second limo.

George Bush, the former American president, emerged. *Much* taller than Lopez would have imagined. Unlike Solana, Bush was smiling. "Mr. Bush! Mr. Bush!" the photographers called to him, and he turned toward them, a hand extended to wave, in purest presidential style. A single flash from the photographers. Two meters of cordiality. Santovito and the other chiefs had returned to the threshold as if waiting for their meal. Around Bush was a mess of bodyguards, American agents, and, on the outside, security from the Italian services. Was Bush the object of Ishmael? The Americans were betting on him. Lopez understood. Anything could happen. Ishmael could strike. The important thing was to bring home Papa Bush. He was swallowed up by the Chiefs and their handshakes. He struggled to cut through the throng. Then he too was inside, safe.

The third and fourth limousines. Carlsson and Pérez de Cuéllar got out together. Carlsson, the former Swedish prime minister, had taken Olof Palme's place after the assassination. Blond, tall, lean, he could only be a Swede. He was the least important among the elite guests; in fact, no one gave a damn about him. After formal courtesies from the Chiefs, he was inside. Pérez de Cuéllar, who for years had led the United Nations, was now a childlike old man, weakened by cancer; he walked with difficulty, leaning on a cane. Two of his bodyguards supported him under the armpits. The chiefs were respectful, greeting him with a shared, cold emotion. This might be his last public appearance.

Fifth limousine. Henry Kissinger got out. *Unrecognizable.* He was a massive old man, white, his hair snowy. Lopez would never have recognized him if he hadn't known beforehand this was Kissinger. He had nothing to do with the man who had monopolized the news thirty years earlier. Having escaped assassination in Paris, he now displayed a natural assurance. He wasn't smiling. There were three bodyguards for him, too. Again, flash bulbs. The chiefs were unrestrained in their urgency to greet him. Lopez saw Santovito almost jumping in his effort to get close to Kissinger. Yet the man was old, and he seemed to Lopez somehow outside the *circles of power*. Evidently not, because the chiefs were killing themselves to speak to him and hustle him inside.

Sixth limousine, the last. The Mikhail Gorbachev Show. The photographers went wild, roaring, "Gorby! Gorby!" The Gorba-Show. He, too, had grown old. Raisa was dead. Gorbachev had come to Milan a number of times; Lopez had had to get involved in the security arrangements for those visits. He had seen him up close before. Now he was grayer, thinner, paler—old. An emptied wineskin. He was smiling a false smile. Like Bush, he extended his hand to the photographers in a wave to nothing. Bush and Gorbachev: the heroes of the thaw. What had happened in the world in the past ten years had depended on *them*. The Berlin wall falling, the collapse of the Soviet Union, reform of the world economy. It had been *them*.

After them would come the evil empire: the empire of Ishmael.

Amid a delirium of hands and quick smiles, Gorbachev went

through the doorway of ISPES, the chiefs clustered around him. Lopez felt the regurgitation of the bad coffee from Via Manzoni.

Lopez went inside. Pérez de Cuéllar was still only halfway up the stairs. Kissinger and Gorby had reached him; the procession was slow. Lopez passed the chiefs, a few feet from Gorbachev, and saw Pérez's stained withered skin. Carlsson was at the top of the stairs. The meeting room was to the left.

He checked his men on all four sides of the corridor. Everything was in place.

Inside the hall, he saw Bush and Solana smiling at each other, already seated on the stage.

Rome
February 9, 1966
15:20

Rome, Piazza del Parlamento. After four years of training and apprenticeship, this was to be his first solo operation. The objective was to get possession of certain documents that Ishmael's men were about to steal from the office of the parliamentary deputy M.R., a Socialist and an obscure personality of the new center-left, and counsel to Nenni on American questions. Montorsi saw him leave through the rear door of Montecitorio, tall, gray-haired, and imposing, surrounded by his aides, and cross the broad space besieged by the cars of the staff of the Chamber of Deputies, heading toward the trattoria near Piazza di Spagna. All according to routine. He would not return before four-thirty.

Montorsi was at the corner of Via del Corso as the deputy and his people passed by, but he paid no attention. He was watching the Alfa parked at the far right of the parking area, which had an unobstructed exit from the right side of Piazza del Parlamento. A man got out of the Alfa. Montorsi shifted position. From his jacket the man extracted a card giving him unlimited access to the Chamber and went quickly up the wide steps. Montorsi moved forward among the parked cars, on the left side. He saw the man go in, showing the card.

Move according to your senses; at the next-to-last instinct, perform the opposite movement. The lessons of the theory course vibrated behind Montorsi's open eyes in the square lighted by the winter sun. A stale smell of warm exhaust came from the hoods of the cars. Myriad hours of study: theories of perception, of caution and action—the tempest of instructions vibrated in the wind.

If the objective is to kill, kill an instant after thinking it. Think.

Behave like a vegetable, react like an animal. Think.

Montorsi zigzagged among the cars, toward the Alfa. He saw

the driver at the wheel. Ishmael's men were working in a pair this time. The one who had gone into Montecitorio would take no more than a quarter of an hour to steal the documents from the office of M.R. and return to the Alfa. The driver was staring in a daze at the windshield, not paying attention.

Punish inattention inflexibly. Breathe in the mistakes of others and use them. When the target deviates, enter the angle of deviation. Act like a machine. Don't think.

The images of Maura did not fade. She returned even when he wasn't asleep. Maura watched over him. He watched over Maura. They smelled each other, sometimes without even realizing it, from distant interpolated dimensions.

A door slammed noisily, behind Montorsi. Someone was coming. Human acts are never without cause. He prepared to calculate; it could be Ishmael's *third* man.

Distinguish among motivations. To reveal a motivation is a lapse on the part of the other. You fail, often, to throw them off the trail of your motivations, which follow you like a creeping wake of animal odor. Smell the odor of the others.

If you are in a crowded square, look in the windows of buildings to study the eyes around you. The one who is not looking at you is following you. If there are no windows, find a fountain and lean over it to drink with irregular gulps, observing the corner opposite the one you're bent toward. Change sidewalks.

A man was approaching. His hand in his pocket, Montorsi clutched the pistol with its silencer. The man was behind him. Montorsi turned suddenly. The man detoured toward the steps and the Chamber entrance. Montorsi looked back at the Alfa. It was empty, the driver had vanished.

When using the telephone, if you hear two clicks very close together, they are intercepting you. If the voice of your caller remains identical in tone after the double click, they are recording you with a magnetophone. Communications should last less than two minutes, if you do not want to have your telephone identified. If the voice of your caller resonates, as if from the echo in an empty room, they are listening directly. Identify the wormholes in the furniture of the rooms you stay in. Insert the oil, silently. The bug will crackle slightly. Pay attention. Pay attention.

The driver had got out to smoke a cigarette. Montorsi calculated. He needed him in his car. He was to kill him in the car. If he stayed outside the Alfa, the operation would be suspended, and he would have to change plans. Instinctively he turned toward his own Alfa, parked in the left-hand corner of the lot. If the operation was not completed in Piazza del Parlamento, he would follow Ishmael's two men; he would improvise. The driver smoked, staring at the ground.

Your muscles will be hard and tense. Your shoulder will hurt. Nourish yourself on whatever substance you need, but not on dreams. Do not dream. Do suspect, which is different. If the operation is complex and you foresee a possible failure, take a 10 mg. dose of the antipsychotic, to confuse the truth serum.

Act by listening to the flow of your adrenaline. Eyeglasses are dangerous. Sometimes a fancy outfit can confuse you. Call up in yourself like Biblical psalms the basic principles of camouflage. Foresee everything.

The driver crushed the cigarette with his heel. He got back in the Alfa. Montorsi moved.

Four years of training. A year of night flights, of landing in phantom airports, hooded heads swaying on military convoys over rough unpaved roads. *Connect with the anonymous voices of the walkie-talkies. Do not think they are friendly to you. Do not think even that they are deceiving you. Do not think.*

Montorsi was two meters from the Alfa. Ishmael's man had not yet come out of Montecitorio. Montorsi could now see the set, expressionless face of the man at the wheel of the Alfa. He knocked on the car's fender, pointing to the car to the left of the Alfa, and said he had to get out. Ishmael's man lowered the window. It all happened rapidly. The gun fired a silent shot at the left temple. There was not much blood. The man collapsed over the wheel. Montorsi arranged him against the seat back as if he were sleeping. He opened the door and closed the window. Yes, he appeared to be asleep.

Camouflage yourself. Don't be yourself. Hide your most intimate thoughts. In conversations, even casual ones, do not express desires. Make no reference to yourself. Speak always of the other person or persons. Make him speak. If the pupil of the left eye contracts or flashes, he is lying. Tighten your mouth. Adopt a seemingly unconscious tic, forgetting it as soon as you execute it.

Ishmael's man came out of the doorway, walking rapidly, a thin folder in his hand, descended the low steps directly toward the Alfa, crossed the parking lot, and approached the car to open the door on the right.

Learn. Learn. Memorize in order to forget. Take into yourself the most elementary and reactive levels of personality.

Ishmael's man opened the door, saw his companion asleep on the seat, touched him, understood everything, turned suddenly. He was too late.

Eat slowly. Sleep little. Control yourself. You're a homosexual? You're a Communist? You're a Fascist? You're a Catholic? Practicing? Yours is a god of shit. Maura blows the dead. Maura stinks—the worms have eaten her. Maura isn't dead and is screwing someone else, she likes it while he buggers her, he opens her ass like this. . . . Maura is a whore, Maura never existed, you'd had it with Maura, they did a good thing by killing her. Fuck off, Montorsi. You are nothing. You are nothing. A nullity. Swallow. Swallow the spoonfuls of shit.

Montorsi drove the Alfa to a dump beyond the ring road. The two corpses on the backseat seemed to be asleep. He had forced Ishmael's man to get in the back, then aimed at his forehead, the muffled shot of the silenced pistol like a breath of hazy air. Then he had taken the driver out of the car and put him in the backseat. They were embracing, as if one of the two were ill. No one had seen anything. The keys were in the ignition. The folder with the documents stolen from M.R. was sitting on the seat beside Montorsi. It was only a short way to the dump.

He unloaded the bodies into two half-rusted oil drums that they had told him about. He took the gloves out of his left-hand pocket. They had told him the acid might spray. Behind the drums he found the other containers of acid, according to the instructions. Each held three liters and was easy to handle. He filled the drums almost to the brim. He sealed them.

He returned to the Alfa, walking up the muddy slope from the dump toward the dirt road. There was a fire, a pile of wooden fruit and vegetables boxes burning. He took off the gloves and threw them on the flames.

He went up to the dirt road. Far away, a dog on a chain barked.

Milan
March 27, 2001
16:20

Kissinger was silent. George Bush the Elder was having a duet with Gorbachev. The conference was nothing more than six old-timers talking about the good old days. Lebanon. The international crisis. The thaw. Berlin. Other crap. They were speaking of other things, which Lopez didn't pick up. They spoke of new equilibriums. In the audience were the powers of Italian finance and politics, new orders to obey.

The men onstage were relaxed, the audience attentive, the security people—the Americans and the intelligence services—in a high fever. There was a constant coming and going of plain-clothes agents. At the sides of the stage stood the bodyguards of the Powerful.

Lopez's gaze moved back and forth among the stage, the audience, and the agents. He wasn't still for a second. He kept going in and out to survey the four parts of the corridor. Everything was calm. In front of the toilets stood a couple of American agents, one young, the other less, both huge. They were talking to each other. The Americans were easily recognizable: Even inside they wore sunglasses. Lopez knew those sunglasses: spectroscopic vision, with UV protection, in order to see *everything*. The two Americans in front of the toilet watched him hurry back to the main door of the hall.

Inside George Bush was talking about his son. He made a joke with Gorbachev, and apart from those in the first row, got laughs from Gorby and the audience, who were attached to headphones, for simultaneous translation.

Pérez de Cuéllar was as if devoured by illness before one's eyes.

Carlsson was a mannequin from the David Letterman show.

Solana was the only serious one.

Kissinger the most intent, the most bored.

An old man in the audience sneezed. All eyes turned on him. False alarm. The Americans smiled. The members of the Italian Service grew more relaxed.

Lopez scanned the sides of the stage where, against the wall, the bodyguards stood in their iron-gray suits, sporting the usual sunglasses. Twenty men.

He was about to go out again into the corridor when a weird sensation ripped him. He returned to the position from which he could observe the bodyguards to the left of the stage. There were a dozen of them, wearing earphones, their faces flat. One of them was tall and the face reminded him of someone. Yet he couldn't know them. None were Italian. Gorby's bodyguards were Americans, like those of Kissinger, Bush, and Pérez. Carlsson had brought his own men from Sweden. Solana had NATO agents.

It was the third man from the left. He was watching the opposite wall. It was impossible to intersect his gaze, shut in behind the UV sunglasses. He had a broad jaw. He breathed rhythmically. Maybe there was a vague resemblance to someone he knew. Maybe Wunzam. But Wunzam was blond, and this man was dark. The weird sensation persisted. A false suspicion, evidently.

He went out into the corridor.

His men had no problems. He spoke to Santovito and Calimani; everything was calm. He eyed the two Americans in front of the toilet. The younger one smiled. The older one, too. He must be over fifty. What was someone like that doing guarding a toilet? He decided to call them the Blues Brothers. The Jake and Elwood of the toilet patrol.

Again he went into the meeting room.

He couldn't take his eyes off that bodyguard. An American face. Lopez could see him eating a Big Mac. His face was impenetrable behind the dark glasses. Lopez felt the man's cold gaze. Where had he seen him? He thought of going out and asking Santovito the names of the bodyguards. But maybe it was only a mistaken impression, the tension playing nasty games.

Then, on the stage, Henry Kissinger rose.

* * *

Maybe he had to pee. The bodyguards arranged themselves. Lopez did not take his eyes off *his* bodyguard. Who seemed to be staring straight at him.

Henry Kissinger started down the steps from the stage.

The man was part of Kissinger's entourage. He moved with the two others to follow Kissinger. They would exit by the door next to the stage.

That face. That walk . . .

Kissinger's bodyguard turned. His gaze met Lopez's. He approached one of the other guards. Two words. The second bodyguard turned; he looked straight at Lopez.

Lopez moved closer. Tension. The second bodyguard stood still. He looked at Lopez. Kissinger was moving with the two other guards. Lopez proceeded along the sides of the hall.

Kissinger was going out the door, his back to the room. One of the three men escorting him leaped ahead of him to the left, to check the corridor, and gave Kissinger the go-ahead. The familiar-looking bodyguard stayed on the threshold for a moment, covering Kissinger's back, then turned and looked at Lopez.

Then Lopez recognized him.

He was the man in the Mercedes, the one who had killed Rebecka. He was the one who resembled Terzani. He was disguised, but it was him.

It was Ishmael's man.

Quickly, silently, Lopez moved into the corridor, twenty seconds after Kissinger. He saw Kissinger from behind, between one of the bodyguards and Ishmael's man. Who turned, saw him. Between him and Lopez stood the third bodyguard, the one with whom Ishmael's man had spoken. The one who had looked at him.

The third bodyguard planted himself in front of Lopez. Stopped him.

Escorted by the other bodyguard and Ishmael's man, Kissinger was turning the corner toward the men's room.

It was an instant. Behind Lopez was one of his own agents, and at the end of the corridor was another. Lopez showed his identification to Kissinger's bodyguard, who had his hand on his chest and would not let him pass. Lopez turned to his man and shouted, "Handcuff this shit! Get him out of here!" Lopez's man obeyed, and the other agent arrived.

"Get him out of the way!" Lopez's men from the auditorium, the Americans, and men from the Italian services converged on the corridor and surrounded Kissinger's bodyguard.

Lopez freed himself.

He sped to the corner. To the bathrooms.

He ran into one of the two bathroom guards, the younger, charging toward the uproar behind Lopez. The bathroom.

In front of the bathrooms: *no one*.

He shoved the door with his shoulder, went in. One room. Dim light. Two wide doors. Men. Women.

He hurled himself toward the men's room.

He went in. And he saw.

Milan
March 27, 2001
16:50

The Italian cop had recognized him.

Fuck.

It had all gone well. At Giuriati, everything had been perfect. There had been no problem with the call to Headquarters, to report the body of the child. The Symbol of Ishmael was in place.

He had joined the other bodyguards at one in the afternoon. Ishmael is great. Among other things, the escort was incomplete: in Paris, during the attempt, a man had been lost. Perfect.

Kissinger. This man had nothing to do with the Kissinger everyone remembered. The wavy hair held in place with mousse had gone from gray to white, almost blue. Kissinger had got old and misshapen; he looked like an old owl.

He would be dead by tomorrow. The American had planned his move for either Milan or Villa d'Este. It would not end as it had in Paris. *He* would succeed. He would kill Kissinger. He would fulfill the desire of Ishmael.

Ishmael is great.

In the security cordon at the ISPES entrance, he had noted the Italian policeman, the one he had seen in the hangar in Pioltello, the one he had seen following Rebecka in Hamburg.

They had gone in.

No sign of the Old Man. Maybe they had stopped him in Brussels; maybe they had managed it. He had widened his nostrils at the thought. He wanted the Old Man. Sooner or later he would get him. It wasn't the moment. This was Kissinger's moment.

The report had told him that Kissinger had prostate trouble. So, the toilet. The American had calculated everything. He was ready. The plan was clear. He had gone over it many times in his mind, most recently while Kissinger and the other jerks were speaking to the audience, a mob of old men and whores. Italian shit.

Then he had seen the Italian cop. He was staring at him. He had pretended not to notice. The dye and the injections in his jaw were sufficient to insure that the cop wouldn't recognize him. At Pioltello, he had worn a leather mask; the cop might remember the look of his eyes, but here he wore dark glasses. In Hamburg, under the street light, the cop might have been able to memorize his features, but that was improbable. Then he realized: It was the man in Via Padova, whom the Old Man had taken for him. The double had saved him from the Old Man. Now the double was ruining him with the Italian cop.

Shit.

Kissinger had moved. The prostate. A stroke of luck. He thought, Now. Now or never. The Italian cop was moving toward him.

Kissinger had descended the steps. The American turned to the bodyguard beside him and told him about the Italian cop. The American told him to stop the policeman—there was no need for Kissinger to be annoyed. The bodyguard had nodded.

The younger bodyguard was outside the door, checking the corridor. The way was clear.

Kissinger was moving down the corridor. The American glanced back at the Italian, who, now outside the meeting room, was approaching.

Turning the corner toward the bathrooms, he had heard the uproar behind him. An Italian was coming around the corner to see what was going on. In front of the bathrooms were two enormous men from American intelligence, maybe they would be useful, he thought. From behind him, where he had left his colleague to stop the Italian cop, there was even more noise. Perfect. One of the two American guards at the toilet ran past him, to see what was happening. Perfect.

Kissinger went into the bathroom. The American's younger colleague was behind him, and then the American behind them both.

Inside the men's room.

Kissinger went immediately into the last stall at the back. He closed the door. The young bodyguard stood in front of the bathroom door. The plan was clear. The American had fifteen seconds. A shot in the forehead of the other bodyguard. Three for Kissinger. One shot at the wall, to fake a gunfight. One shot in his own thigh. His gun in the hand of the other bodyguard. Two shots at the wall with the other man's gun. He would say that the other bodyguard had shot Kissinger, that he had shot the bodyguard and that, before he got him, the man had hit his leg. Perfect.

Kissinger started to pee.

Now.

A silent shot. The bodyguard fell.

Three seconds.

Four.

He was in front of the stall where Kissinger was. He stretched out his arm.

Five seconds.

The door of the men's room opened. The American turned automatically. He aimed his gun. A gun was aimed at him.

It was the man from outside the bathrooms.

He hadn't recognized him.

Incredible. It was *another* person.

It was the Old Man.

They began to circle slowly. Their guns were pointed at each other.

They heard the door slam and didn't turn, guns pointed.

The door of the men's room opened. Out of the corner of his eye the American saw that it was the Italian cop. It wasn't over yet. He could still get out.

Milan
March 27, 2001
16:57

In the men's room.

He saw them.

They were circling, cautiously, their guns aimed at each other.

Ishmael's man.

And the Old Man.

He drew his gun. He didn't know which man to aim at. Which of the two was closer to Ishmael? *Was* the Old Man Ishmael?

On the floor lay Kissinger's third bodyguard. Lopez kept his eyes on the two men. He shouted the name *Kissinger*. A voice rose feebly from the last stall. Lopez shouted at him to stay where he was.

He aimed at Ishmael's man. He aimed at the Old Man.

Ishmael's man did not look like the man he had seen with Rebecka in Hamburg. Maybe he was disguised. The Old Man was not the old man of Brussels. He certainly was disguised. He was more than disguised. He was *younger*. Barely recognizable.

They were no longer circling. They held each other in their sights. It couldn't last.

The Old Man said, in a calm voice, "October 27, 1962."

Then Lopez fired two shots.

He exploded the head of Rebecka's man. He aimed the gun at the Old Man.

The Old Man lowered his gun to the floor. He said only, "Lopez?"

Lopez shouted to Kissinger not to move.

"Lopez," the Old Man said.

Lopez aimed at the Old Man's forehead: "Who the hell are you?"

The Old Man held out his hands and began to lower them, to place the gun on the tiles.

Lopez glared at him over the pointed gun. "Don't move, dickhead. Don't move." The image of Karl M. in Brussels, the Old Man who shoots him in the neck. "Who the hell are you? Who the hell are you, anyway?"

The Old Man gazed at him. "Calm down, Lopez."

Voices. Noise. They were coming. They were at the door. "Who the hell are you?"

They were about to enter.

The Old Man smiled.

"My name is David Montorsi."

Inspector Guido Lopez and Special Agent David Montorsi

Milan
March 27, 2001
17:02

It was David Montorsi. He was the inspector from the Detective Squad. October 27, 1962. He had found the *first* child at Giuriati. His wife, pregnant, had been murdered the day afterward. Then he had disappeared into a void.

David Montorsi.

Then he had reappeared. He had intercepted Ishmael's man. He had understood Ishmael's plans, that he would bring the *second* child to the plaque at Giuriati.

David Montorsi.

It was him.

In the restroom, tremendous confusion. Lopez lowered his gun as the Americans and the security agents surrounded him and Montorsi with their guns. On the floor lay Kissinger's bodyguards. One of the two corpses was Ishmael's man. The resemblance to the corpse of Via Padova, now, was impressive.

The agents shouted Kissinger's name. Lopez and Montorsi looked at each other. Kissinger opened the door of the stall and appeared, drawn, pale, stained with pee.

For a second Lopez felt like smiling. The agents took everyone away—Kissinger first of all, then Lopez and Montorsi.

In the operations room, bluish from the screens of the laptop computers, the walkie-talkie switchboard humming, the men from the CIA and the NSA seemed to want to grab Montorsi and interrogate him alone. But Montorsi resisted. He was released immediately. He was a special agent of the European Services, an agency Lopez had never heard of.

As Lopez listened intently, Montorsi told the chiefs that the man who had tried to assassinate Kissinger was John Calder, who also used the names Michael Rutherford, Sean Deavey, Arthur Lomas, and Edward Greene. And Slobo Jankovic, Jonas Nordhal, Ferdinando Serpieri, François Sedille, Juan Arturo Rodriguez, and Hans Wolmann. Incredibly, Montorsi rattled off dates, names, times, and places of the operations in which Calder had participated—in Panama, Honduras, South Africa, Spain. Bonn. Moscow. Tel Aviv. Turin. Istanbul. Calder was a former CIA agent and for a short time had been affiliated with the National Security Agency. Then the official records had lost track of him.

Montorsi told the chiefs that responsibility for the attempts on Kissinger in Paris and Milan lay with Calder. He did not mention the name Ishmael. Nor did he talk about Brussels, the child, or his own past. Lopez understood and did not understand these omissions. He realized that the game was *much* bigger than he had imagined. While Montorsi was speaking, he kept quiet.

His interrogation completed, Montorsi rose from the table in the operations room and looked at Lopez meaningfully. Lopez lowered his eyelids. He had understood. He was to play defense and protect Montorsi.

Lopez was interrogated for more than two hours. After the attempt on Kissinger, the meeting had been aborted and the Powerful taken to Cernobbio. Montorsi had given his opinion that nothing else would happen. When the American and Italian intelligence services went on to Cernobbio; Santovito and several of the chiefs stayed behind with Lopez.

It fell to Lopez to describe the scene in the ISPES bathroom. He began with the NSA report on Ishmael. Terzani's seemingly random death on Via Padova. The failed assassination in Paris. The investigation of Clemenceau. The rites of Ishmael, the elusive Ishmael. The sadomasochists' PAV in Milan. The child. When he talked about the political pressure from the elite after the PAV raid, Santovito was *green*; he was shitting in his pants at Lopez's implicit accusation that he had yielded to the pressures. Then he talked about Hamburg. The evidence of trafficking in children, with Rebecka the intermediary. Wunzam's operation and its failure. The death of Rebecka. The man Lopez had killed in the bathroom, he told them, was the same man who had taken the child from the PAV and murdered Rebecka. He talked about interceptions of Karl M., bureaucrat at the European Parliament; Santovito went even greener. How Lopez had gambled by going to Brussels, to find out if the child's journey ended there. He told them his hypothesis that the child had to do with a rite of Ishmael. He described the death of Karl M., killed by an unknown old man. He looked at the faces of the chiefs. None of them seemed to connect the old man to Montorsi.

Montorsi had presented a scenario that went from Paris to Milan. Lopez drew a broader, parallel scenario. Both ended up in the men's room at ISPES.

He deliberately skipped the discovery of the dead child that morning. Santovito didn't bat an eye. Lopez didn't mention Montorsi's telephone call. He didn't mention the scenario of 1962: the death of Mattei, the discovery of the child at Giuriati, the death of Montorsi's wife. The secret work of Ishmael.

He told them that in the meeting hall he had identified one of Kissinger's bodyguards as the man who had shot Rebecka in Hamburg; he was disguised, and his features were slightly different. The chiefs looked at one another. Lopez said that he had tried to stop Kissinger and wanted to restrain the bodyguard. He had managed to jump the blockade of the third bodyguard. He had rushed to the men's room. When he entered, Agent Montorsi and Ishmael's man had their guns trained on each other. Lopez lied again: he omitted Montorsi's remark.

He had reacted instinctively. He had done well. He had blown out the brains of the American agent.

After two hours he was free to go. Santovito gave him a day off and escorted him to the now deserted lobby of ISPES. He said they would speak after Cernobbio. Lopez wasn't paying attention. He was thinking of Montorsi, of the two children found at Giuriati, of Ishmael.

Ishmael.

Who is Ishmael?

Lopez asked if the bodies of the two men from Kissinger's escort were under police jurisdiction. Santovito answered that the Americans were taking care of them—they had already requisitioned the bodies.

It meant that the Detective Squad would not take another step in the direction of Ishmael.

That the case was not closed but was as if closed.

He said goodbye to Santovito and saw him go back up the stairs to join the chiefs in the operations room; they were going to Cernobbio. That piece of shit was going to salvage what could be salvaged. He would continue seeking his promotion at any cost. His *rise in rank*.

Lopez thrust his hands in his pockets. He nodded at the men guarding the door. He turned toward the Duomo.

On the other side of the street he saw Montorsi.

They went into a bar in the labyrinth of Brera, between ISPES and Police Headquarters. Montorsi remained impassive as Lopez continued to replay the scene in the men's room, the blood spurting from the head of the American onto the wall. Montorsi let him calm down. Then he began to speak.

"All told, you saw correctly, Lopez. I want to compliment you. You don't even work for intelligence and you saw much sooner than the intelligence services."

"You weren't in intelligence, either, in 1962. And, from what I understand, you saw long before the intelligence services."

Montorsi sipped his beer. "It begins that way. Surprise me, Lopez. What do you understand of what happened in 1962?"

"I think I understood about 1962 after what I saw today. The story, I think, is this. Ishmael has been in Italy for a long time. Before today, I'd thought it was a terrorist group or a sect, a relatively new organization. But in '62 you came up against an operation conceived and carried out by Ishmael's men. Let's say that it functions like this. There is a ritual component—the sacrifice of a child, both in '62 and today; after that there's an execution. Mattei in '62 and Kissinger today. Am I wrong?"

"Go on, Lopez. You continue to surprise me."

"In 1962, Inspector David Montorsi is investigating the discovery of a dead child at the Giuriati playing field. The same day, Enrico Mattei dies. Both investigations are taken away from the Detective Squad. David Montorsi continues to investigate; he has discovered that a link exists between the body of the child and the death of Mattei. I don't know how he managed to discover this link. I haven't even studied the case. It's certain, however, that a reporter for the *Corriere*, Italo Fogliese, who is found dead in the outskirts, has something to do with it. Ishmael's operation succeeded perfectly. The only hitch is this inspector from Detectives, Montorsi, who is a real pain in the ass. And now here is what I don't understand. They should have eliminated you, Montorsi. Instead they murder your wife. What sense does that make? Something isn't right." Lopez looked at him with firm sympathy.

Maura. White fire in the memory. Montorsi ran his finger around the edge of his glass. "It worked perfectly, Lopez." He looked up. "Let's forget the inconsistencies and uncertainties. I'll tell you what I can tell you afterward. Let's move to today. How do you see what happened? Surprise me again."

Lopez took a swig of beer against the paste of dry saliva in his mouth. "It starts before Cernobbio. It starts in Paris. There is this sect, Science Religion, which is somehow connected with Ishmael. The sect is mentioned in a report by the National Security Agency, the American agency for global control that is now above the CIA. There is an assassination attempt on Henry Kissinger in Paris, but it fails. The assassin is this poor guy Clemenceau, a former member of Science Religion. In his apartment, we find evidence of contact with Ishmael's group. In Milan, in the meantime, there's a man dead on Via Padova. It seems a case utterly unrelated to Ishmael's game. That's not true. I manage to link the dead man of Via Padova with Clemenceau in Paris. I identify the dead man, Terzani. He, too, is a former member of Science Religion. At this point, I identify some definite signs of Ishmael's activity. I understand that it's a kind of church with particular rituals, tied in some way to erotic practices. The corpses of Clemenceau and Terzani show traces of violence: bruises, whip marks, anal dilation. I manage to connect the rites of Ishmael to the activities of a group that centers on a circle of sadomasochists. I infiltrate a gathering. A child appears. I initiate a raid by my men."

Montorsi put his Gitane in his mouth and blew out smoke that stung Lopez's eyes. "Here you disappointed me, Lopez. Here you showed yourself careless."

"Yes, I made a mistake. How do you know?"

More harsh smoke from the Gitane. "I know all the steps you took, Lopez. Either because I was there or because we were informed."

"Yes. It's the usual story of the intelligence services—"

"The services share one quality with God and differ in

another: Like God, they know everything; unlike God, they have created nothing. But the European Agency is more than the Services. Just as the NSA is more than the CIA. Let's get back to your mistake, Lopez. At the sadomasochists' event."

"Yes. There I made a mistake, through carelessness. I lose the child. I fail to intercept the man taking it away—he escapes through a rear exit. The Chief is subjected to important pressures from the political level. I can't distinguish between the intelligence service, the political level, and Ishmael. The Engineer, the man who organizes the gatherings, is cooperating in the investigation, but I am ready to bet that he is a crucial contact for Ishmael. Ishmael's rites unfold at gatherings like this, without the majority of the participants knowing it. It happened that way in the United States and Paris. It also happens in Milan. But what is certain is that Ishmael gave the order to sacrifice a child, because he is preparing the second phase of an operation—which is an assassination. Now we know that the victim is Kissinger. Here, too, I don't understand: if Kissinger was supposed to die in Paris and if Ishmael acts after he has made a sacrifice, where is the sacrifice for the attempt in Paris?"

Montorsi put out his cigarette and smiled. "Perhaps Kissinger wasn't supposed to die in Paris. You are still not used to Ishmael's methods of action. He uses a grammar that is apparently . . . how to put it . . . contradictory. You will learn in due course, Lopez. Again, forget the inconsistencies. Go on."

"Okay, from Milan we go to Hamburg. The day after the kidnapping of the child, it emerges that pedophiles in Hamburg plan an exchange of goods for money. The goods are children. The intermediary is a Swedish woman who, we know from the investigations, is linked to Ishmael. I go to Hamburg. The exchange is a decoy. Nothing happens. The police prepare an operation and come up empty-handed. The exchange happens elsewhere. Ishmael's Swedish woman meets the man who took the child from Milan."

Montorsi widened his nostrils and shook his head. "Here we were the ones who made the mistake."

"What mistake?"

"The delivery of children. We also fell for that. The direct link between the Swedish woman and Ishmael escaped us; we thought she was a supporting player of little importance and that the Slav was the linchpin. We thought that Ishmael was working with organized crime. The Slav had contacts with Ishmael and with organized crime. I stationed my men at the port, with the Slav who was to take care of the exchange."

So the men Ljuba had met at Dock 11 were Montorsi's agents. He said, "All of us were wrong in this business. You, me, even Ishmael."

Montorsi looked at him mockingly, a wrinkling of his mouth and eyes. "Ishmael is never wrong, Lopez. Over the long run, he is never wrong. All we've been able to do is delay the results he seeks. Continue the story. Up to here it's all exactly right."

Lopez took another swallow of beer, his mouth more bitter than before. "I'm lucky in Hamburg, because I'm tailing Rebecka—Ishmael's Swedish woman. Rebecka meets the man with the child. I *think* I recognize the man: he is practically identical to Terzani, the man who was killed on Via Padova."

Montorsi looked at him. "I was the one who killed the man on Via Padova. And you're right. The American was disguised to resemble him. We both fell for it. I recognized Terzani as if he were the American; you recognized the American as if he were Terzani."

Lopez was dumbfounded: "You killed Terzani thinking he was the American."

Montorsi sighed. "Yes, it's an old trick, the double. We were acting in a hurry, practically groping in the dark. We identified the American's safe house and as soon as he came out on the street I killed him. But it wasn't the American, it was Terzani."

"So it was you at Forensics. The fake cop who took the autopsy report. You were there to see if you had in fact got the right man."

Montorsi nodded. "Go on, Lopez. I know from reports what happened to you in Hamburg. We checked with Wunzam's team."

"Yes. We made a mistake at that point also. The American escaped us. You know from the reports that the German inspector who was tailing Rebecka with me was injured. Then the body of Rebecka was found. At that point I bet everything on our man, the American—that he was going to get the child to its destination."

"And how did you know the destination, Lopez?"

"An interception on Rebecka's telephone. You didn't know about it?"

"What interception?"

Lopez smiled for the first time since the blood had spurted on the walls at ISPES. "He fooled you. Wunzam fooled you. He encoded the interception. You're a little less than God, you in the European Agency . . ."

Montorsi smiled too. "Who was on the phone with Rebecka? Karl M.?"

"Exactly. Wunzam was paranoid. In Paris and Milan, the politicians had been unleashed, to bring pressure to stop us. Imagine Brussels. All hell would break loose there. I decided to go to Brussels alone and without cover. I improvised."

"You improvised very well, Lopez."

"But the scheme became confused, in Brussels. You intervened, Montorsi. I could no longer understand who was on Ishmael's side. I wasn't even sure that the American with the child was in the car you shot at. I didn't understand why someone not on Ishmael's side would murder Karl M.—he was the only way to get to the people receiving the child. In Brussels, I was screwed. Then you vanished."

"Tricks of the trade." Montorsi lighted another Gitane.

"One thing I don't understand. If you killed Karl M., it means that he was not as indispensable to you as he was to me. It means that you knew the destination of the child. Why didn't you intervene directly there?"

Montorsi showed a hint of a smile and nodded thoughtfully. "That's another difference between the services and God, Lopez. We are not God. You probably don't realize *who* the recipients were."

People even more important than he had ever suspected. "Can I ask the names?"

Montorsi: "No."

Lopez lowered his eyes.

"Go on," Montorsi said.

"So now, this morning—the discovery of the child at Giuriati. The same child I had seen carried off at the sadomasochistic meeting in Milan. The connection with Ishmael was obvious. Then your phone call, Montorsi. The *obvious* connections with 1962. At ISPES I didn't recognize you standing guard in front of the toilet, but I recognized Ishmael's man, the American. If I had recognized you, I would have stopped you. I recognized the American and I tried to stop him."

Montorsi gave him a little smile. "It's one of the reasons that I made the phone call to you, Lopez. At the Agency we were surprised. A mere policeman who manages to find his way out of the labyrinth. Impressive."

"That was one of the reasons you called me. What were the others?"

He stubbed out his Gitane and lit another. "I've said that we in the Agency admired you. Now I want to make you a proposal."

"To join the Agency."

"Precisely, Lopez."

"No. First I have to ask you some questions."

Montorsi smiled.

The question, *now*: "Who is Ishmael?"

Montorsi smiled again. He shook the ash off his Gitane. "No one. Ishmael is no one, Inspector Lopez. You are making the same mistake that drew me into the arms of the Services. You imagine that Ishmael is someone."

Lopez went white. He was speechless.

"Ishmael is not a person. Let's go back to 1962, to *my* affair," Montorsi said. "The journalist, Fogliese, was the author of a report on the installation of the Americans in Italy—a report that ended up directly in the hands of Mattei. Fogliese's thesis was that the Americans were preparing to strengthen their intelligence presence in Europe and were starting in Italy. With this strategy, Fogliese asserted, the Americans were working toward the creation of a more concealed structure, if necessary as a counterweight to the Vatican's dominion in Southern Europe—a structure not based on opposing the Soviet services. This would be called Ishmael.

"The report to Mattei had been commissioned from Fogliese by Ishmael. It was a warning to Mattei. Ishmael acts in that way—covertly but in the open. *He who has eyes to see will see.* The words of the Gospel are Ishmael's motto. Originally, I thought that Ishmael was a sort of obscure priest of this secret and *religious* structure. And I was wrong. Ishmael is a plan. Ishmael is a broad elite. It is a power. I didn't see that it would soon be set free by its creators, the American services. Ishmael was announcing that it would, in time, triumph."

Lopez was puzzled. "I don't understand. How could Ishmael know then that it would triumph, with all that has happened since 1962? I mean, there's no more Berlin Wall, there's no more Soviet Union—"

"Exactly. This is the time of Ishmael. When the Americans created Ishmael, they were building an intelligence structure with a *long life*. The CIA was occupied with espionage, with opposition to the Soviets in Europe. What need did it have to create a sort of *secret* Freemasonry? Ishmael's meaning becomes clear when Communism is no longer a problem. Now the problem for the Americans becomes this: without the Soviet Union, what is Europe going to do? The Americans had solved this problem far in advance. Ishmael keeps Europe from becoming detached from American interests."

Lopez shook his head. "It's not possible. There are the rites . . . Ishmael's men were marked with blood, in fact. . . . Children are sacrificed . . . Ishmael acts like the supreme priest of a religion. . . ."

"A religion that counts its faithful at *the highest levels*."

"In Brussels, you mean?"

"In Brussels. In Rome, even though Italy no longer really counts in Ishmael's grand plans. It counted in '62, however. For the Americans we count now only because there is the Vatican. And even there Ishmael has its connections and controls."

"But it was the Americans who brought us the report on Ishmael and the planned attempt on Kissinger," Lopez protested. "It's as if they were informing on themselves. I don't understand. . . ."

Montorsi shook his head. "Ishmael isn't the NSA. Sometimes their interests are opposed. Sometimes they coincide." He put out his cigarette. "A father and son continue to be in contact, but the father doesn't know what his son is doing when he isn't watching. I think that for many of the members of the NSA Ishmael is a mystery; they don't even know of its existence. The logic of the services isn't linear, Lopez." He put out his Gitane. "You have to get used to it. You have to get used to it."

Lopez was stunned. "But it's all so incoherent. . . . Why eliminate Kissinger, for example? Who could be more in America's interest than Kissinger?"

Montorsi was smiling. He lighted another Gitane. "Excuse me for smiling, Lopez. You are making the exact same mistakes I did when I started out. I confess that you remind me quite a bit of the young David Montorsi."

"But I don't see—"

"You believe everything is black or white. It's not. At any moment the horizon can shift. It's like life on our planet. To you it seems that the earth is stable, whereas seismologists know that the continents move apart and then draw closer. We are seismologists."

He knocked off the yellow ash of the cigarette. "From the United States came approval for the indictment of Kissinger at an international tribunal. Kissinger controls interests higher than you imagine. It's not just that he won the Nobel Peace Prize. It's not just the knighthood he got from the Queen of England—"

Montorsi went on, "Let's put it this way. For years, Kissinger was Ishmael. Now, as with all kings, his subjects are getting ready to devour him. Ishmael is ready to expel him from the body of his faithful."

"Kissinger?"

"Kissinger. For years some persons close to him worked with us at the European Agency. When Ishmael abandoned Kissinger, Kissinger abandoned Ishmael. Thanks to these persons, we have elaborated entire structures of Ishmael's presence in European territory. Kissinger is crafty and determined, like anyone who has been master of the world. I spent years fighting Kissinger's men. Now I have had to work for his survival. It would be ironic if it were not tragic."

Lopez looked at Montorsi. An impenetrable, impregnable old man. A disillusioned man who for years had been nourished by his own pain. "How old are you, Montorsi?"

"I'm over sixty. Why do you ask?"

"For two reasons. First: you don't look over fifty—today. In Brussels, you seemed closer to seventy."

Montorsi laughed frankly. "It's injections, Lopez. It's games—the oldest tricks in the book. But they work. The trick of the double tricked me in Via Padova. The injections of allergens worked with the American at ISPES."

"There's another reason I asked you your age," Lopez said. "You have lived two lives."

A precise, irrevocable sadness, a repressed despair: "I could say to you that I have lived many more lives than two. But I understand what you mean."

"I mean your wife. Why did Ishmael kill your wife, Montorsi? You were the problem. It would have been sufficient to get rid of you. . . ."

Montorsi shifted uneasily in his chair. "Lopez . . . I've told you that the Services are like God. I'll say it again. Events happen that seem to have no explanation. For years I asked myself the same question you just did. For years." He would not cry. It was as if he were crying. "It happened that Ishmael's connection in Milan, the one who coordinated the operation of the child at Giuriati and the Mattei action, was an important institutional figure. His name was Arle. Giandomenico Arle. He was the head of Forensics in Milan. We met, Arle and I, and he told me that Ishmael would infect me, that he had chosen me as his enemy. I thought I was dead. I could not comprehend what Arle was truly saying. He was telling me that they had murdered Maura. I understood only later. In effect I became one of Ishmael's enemies. I was *infected by the wound.* Then I was contacted by the Services. The European Agency didn't exist yet. It wasn't created until '92: and it's still not an institutionalized center. I have lived many lives, all of them devoted to destroying Ishmael, who destroyed me. When Maura died, I died."

He talked for a long time about Maura. Lopez listened. Then Montorsi told him about Creti, about entering the Services, and about his training. He told him about the investigations into Maura's death—the evidence that had been removed, tapes that disappeared. He had never succeeded in reconstructing Maura's last hours. He had given himself body and soul to the Services. He had tried to forget. He had not forgotten.

"But *why* Giuriati?" Lopez asked.

"It's just a symbolic place," Montorsi said. "Ishmael uses various symbols. He uses children to announce an important homicide. Giuriati was symbolic in '62 in relation to Mattei and his past as a partisan. And it's symbolic today in relation to the *first* child found at Giuriati, which was Ishmael's initial act. Probably it meant that the operation to be undertaken at Cernobbio was *equivalent* to the one that led to the death of Mattei. But these are hypotheses. With Ishmael, meaning becomes clear only at a distance of years. Ishmael may be returning to Italy in a significant way. Maybe not. We have to wait."

Lopez thought. Nothing of the scheme outlined by Montorsi made sense to him. "But why the children?" he asked. "Why cover intelligence operations with a religious structure?"

"Because you think the political level is the highest level. And that's not true. There are other realities that are higher than the political. They are spiritual realities; these realities guide the political level, secretly. One of the ritual mechanisms of Ishmael is clear: shortly before every important assassination, a child is sacrificed. To you it seems ancillary, maybe even superstitious, because you think the fundamental event is the assassination. It's not like that. The rite of sacrificing the child is, on the spiritual plane, much more important than the assassination, which is by nature mechanical. It may succeed or not. If it fails, they can always try again."

"It's still not clear to me. What is Ishmael's game? It's really a religion?"

Montorsi played with his beer glass. "It is also a spiritual operation, yes. The victims of Ishmael are all high-level political or economic representatives: people who work for a united Europe that is definitively detached from the influence of the United States. Ishmael's network provides for eliminating those who try to bring about this detachment. And the detachment between two continents is not a matter of geopolitical power. It is a spiritual matter. And spiritual matters require rites."

"And during these rites children are sacrificed."

"It's one rite among many, Lopez. At the Agency, we have commissioned some anthropological religious research. Sacrificing a child is a sign of death and rebirth. In the case of Ishmael's sacrifices, we propose as a hypothesis that the murdered child, *discovered on the occasion of an assassination*, symbolizes the death of Europe that is trying to be reborn."

"But, Montorsi, that doesn't explain everything. Take the case of the child that Ishmael's American agent carried around all over Europe—what did that mean? Why not kill it immediately and bury it at Giuriati?"

"Because Ishmael's rite is performed at the supreme hierarchies of Ishmael." Montorsi sipped his beer. "Which for the moment are in Brussels."

"But why not get a child in Brussels?"

"Because the children have to belong to the nation where Ishmael's operation is being carried out: the assassination. Don't ask me why. At the Agency we're reconstructing Ishmael's rites step by step."

"But why involve a child in a gathering of sadomasochists?"

"Because it's part of the rite. I wasn't present at the PAV, Lopez. But let me ask you this: didn't you notice *a strange movement* around the child?"

Lopez remembered. There had been six or seven men and women around the Engineer, their arms raised; they were not interested in the wheel that Laura was bound to. "Yes, you're right. A kind of circling procession. People with their arms raised. As if they were dancing around the man who was carrying the child."

"That was the heart of the initiation," Montorsi said. "It's required by the protocols of Ishmael. Not all those who were at the sadomasochists' meeting knew that Ishmael was acting secretly among them. You thought the rite was the PAV itself? The rite was hidden *within* the sadomasochists' meeting. Imagine: a secret baptism of the child intended for sacrifice."

"Why didn't you intervene at the PAV, Montorsi?"

Montorsi arched his eyebrows. "I was convinced that your action would be sufficient. Our job was to delay Ishmael's rite. If you intercepted the child at the PAV, as we expected, we would have achieved our objective. Without the rite, the attempt on Kissinger was off. To take up your previous question: Kissinger was supposed to die in Paris. The body of a child was found at the entrance to the catacombs in the south, at the edge of the Luxembourg Gardens, the day of Clemenceau's attempt." He took a long swallow. "It has happened many other times. Ishmael seems to fail, we manage to thwart the rite or the attempt, and sooner or later Ishmael's network achieves its result."

"Many other times?"

"Many. It's as if the Cold War were continuing, more secretly, but with Ishmael—that is, America—and Europe. The murder of Aldo Moro. Olof Palme. The faked accident in which Princess

Diana and Dodi Al Fayed were killed. It's Ishmael. It's always Ishmael. It's his plan."

Lopez was silent. He was impressed. He felt the mechanisms of Ishmael's plan pressing on his temples. It was incredible. "Help me understand, Montorsi. The American had to deliver the child in person to Brussels and bring it back in person to Milan?"

"I think you disrupted Ishmael's plans, Lopez. I think the American was in Italy to pick up the child and Rebecka was supposed to take care of getting it to Brussels and making sure the little body was redelivered to Milan. Ishmael's agent had to do it all himself, because you intervened at the PAV, and in Hamburg. And if I had not stepped in at the hotel in Brussels you would have disrupted him there as well. But I couldn't count on it. You knew nothing of Ishmael. And we in the Agency had our plans. Brussels was the last chance to intervene. If I had succeeded in getting him, along with Karl M., in Brussels, the rite would not have been performed and Ishmael would not have struck in Milan. However, thanks to you today, Lopez, Ishmael's goal was not achieved."

"But the child is dead," Lopez said bitterly. "Do you know who it was?"

"No. Sometimes we can discover the identity of the children. Sometimes no. They are infants, usually a year old. The oldest are around six. There is a real international pedophile ring in Europe. You remember that Belgian, Dutroux?"

"Yes, the pedophile, near Brussels, who murdered all the young girls . . ."

"He was Ishmael's man. He provided human flesh for Ishmael's rites. But he was obviously a pedophile. Everything is confused. It's Ishmael's strategy: confuse and strike."

"How many sacrifices of children have you discovered?"

"Many. Too many." Lopez half closed his eyes, inhaled the cigarette smoke deeply. They were silent, drinking. Montorsi smoked. Lopez was forgetting the blood spurting in the men's room at ISPES. A feverish weariness possessed him.

Montorsi spoke. "What I'm proposing to you is this: an investigative role at the European Agency. It's a lot of money. A lot of work. Don't answer immediately—neither accept nor refuse. Just think about it." He got up, heavily. He was huge. "Oh, I forgot," Montorsi said. "Stefan Wunzam, your colleague in Hamburg, has already accepted." He handed Lopez a card. It had no name on it, only a number. "If you accept, telephone this number. A cover office will answer. Say that you want to speak to the marketing office. I'll wait two weeks, Lopez. After that the offer no longer holds."

Lopez sat there, stunned, the card in his hand. He managed to say, "I won't accept."

Montorsi shook his hand and went out, a giant shadow moving into the distance.

4

EPILOGUES

Henry Kissinger and President John F. Kennedy

Washington, D. C.
October 16, 1962
16:30

The young Henry Kissinger, man of a thousand faces, was appearing on the face of the world: the white walls of the White House. He was young and not handsome, but he was as lethal with women as he would be with his enemies—or with his friends. Kissinger hated President Kennedy. He knew that Kennedy had done his friend Nelson Rockefeller a favor: John, Rocky had said, I've got this young friend, he's a fox from the university world—he's smart, give him something to do. And JFK had said, Okay, he can give me some lessons in foreign policy.

Kissinger was perfect for Kennedy. He was German. He even spoke German. He spoke American like a German. The President was highly entertained.

He asked him where Mecklenburg was. How's the beer in Bavaria? What can you tell me about Hitler? Is Marlene Dietrich really a great lay?

Humiliating. Kissinger delivered a monologue. He was pedantic, refined, baroque, prophetic. And the President asked him, Who does Adenauer fuck? Kissinger, glowing, acute, outlined the shape of the planet to come. And the President said, I can't believe that God speaks *even* German.

Kissinger was seething with silent rage. The President had underestimated him. Hours and hours at the White House, sitting useless in the small office reserved for him, had taught Kissinger the patience of the weak. He sharpened pencils. He chewed German chewing gum. He waited for the President to be free. He waited. He dreamed.

Henry Kissinger liked the dark ladies of American film noir.

He dreamed of Barbara Stanwyck: the soft face dazzling in the white light, bent back, the lips thin and cajoling, painted red, the soft wrist that twined around his shoulder—and he was kissing her (he had taken off his glasses, before he began kissing her).

He dreamed. He created impenetrable and insidious connections, his personal map of a world dense with networks and secret powers, the ultimate planetary profile and the most beautiful game in the world. The king's singer is always more powerful than the king: He is the hidden king, sheltered from assassination attempts and conspiracies, free to act the fool for the palace court and perform his machinations in the shadows.

To sing. To sing not only for the king. To sing like Frank Sinatra, to be him, to be the Chairman of the Board. To come out of the shadows and be bathed in the light of power; to be the evening's main event, the key singer, the one who makes the audience explode, the one who croons the dreams of the species; to be desired; to go onstage with the Rat Pack; to be immersed in the electric amnion of applause and bathe in the great American freedom—the freedom not to do a damn thing.

He would fight for this freedom. To fight meant to think *more* profoundly, to dream the world that would be. It would be the world of Henry Kissinger. It would be necessary for him to intervene and perform plastic surgery on the planet. It would be necessary to be diplomatic, to function in secrecy, to be obscure, to inflate power in the form of fear. We'll have to make this planet tremble and remember, he said to himself. We'll have to plot, betray, irritate, soothe.

We'll have to incite peoples from whom we are thousands of miles and civilizations apart.

We'll have to make war. Naturally. *Qui sans guerre?*

In the meantime he had President Johnny, this Catholic boor brought to us as a gift from Ireland. He had to give him lessons. Teach him the manners of today and those of tomorrow. This man who believes in God the Father, the flag, and the cunt. This man who hasn't yet understood how he will end up. This man who wants to pass into History and will do so in a way that no one imagines. This thug with the shock of hair and the piglike face, whom women adore. This spoiled young daddy's boy who thinks he's Christ because his father's name is Joseph. This man with the virtuous brother and the Mafioso father. This Gaelic Oedipus. This shit.

Kissinger thought, He has everything I don't have. For the moment.

He dreams as he waits for the President to be free for half an hour to ask, Is the Black Forest a vaginal metaphor?

To dream. To understand America. To understand the planet. To become the genius of conspiracy.

The President was late in getting free. There was a crisis going on, and no one had told the young Kissinger what it was about. Let them fuck themselves. They didn't tell him anything. The President underestimated him. Was that big peasant Khrushchev having a tantrum? Let them ask Kissinger; Kissinger was capable of agrarian reform that would turn the peasant into an entrepreneur.

He would overthrow the Soviet Union. Worse, he would be able to turn the comrades into American patriots. American freedom *sticks*.

He already had a plan. He already had those people behind him supporting the plan. Behind the king were his unknown superiors. The unknown superiors had approved the plan. The unknown superiors had said to him, Henry Kissinger, you're our man. And he had worked hard to put the plan in place, to spread the spider's fingers everywhere. Intelligence is intelligence. Metaphysics is conspiracy. He had realized that. He was just waiting for his opportunity.

Kennedy had said, Henry Kissinger, give me a lesson on Italy. I want to know all about Italy. We went there to free Italy. I want to know my vassal states. I want to eat spaghetti. I want to have fun. Talk to me about Italy. And Kissinger, the king's singer, set out to be the singer of Italy. He had known *zero* about Italy. But he had studied it. And he had learned that from the time of Caesar and Augustus, Italy had been the country of conspiracy. The United States of Advertising are dilettantes when it comes to conspiracy. The Italians have a *history*. To have a history means to have conspiracies. Look at the French Revolution. Look at the October Revolution.

Talk to me about Italy, Henry.

In Italy there are so many spies they could populate all of West Berlin.

In Italy there are Communists.

There are Fascists.

There are Catholics.

In Italy there is the Pope. The Irish President said, Then Italy and I have something in common.

In Italy there is *pussy,* Mr. President. You and Italy, Mr. President, have several things in common.

Henry Kissinger looked at the clock. It was late. He almost left. Then he thought, No, let's imagine kissing Barbara Stanwyck again. Let's imagine again that we're the Voice that Danny Ocean makes in *Ocean's Eleven.* Let's imagine that the Rat Pack comes out of the sewers of Moscow and swindles Khrushchev.

No. Let's read. Let's understand America. Let's learn what it is.

We're not doing shit. We're in America; we're free not to do a damn thing. The planet works for us.

And he began to read *Moby Dick.*

President John F. Kennedy was exhausted: and still he had to start dancing with the Soviets. It was a maximum crisis, Cuba. It was the apex of terror, the first and last chapter, prologue and epilogue.

The situation: Any day now, the Russians will have at their disposal more missiles with which to threaten American cities instantly. Millions dead. The nuclear catastrophe direct from its own hemisphere. The missiles would be covered by vegetation on a base disguised as a plantation. He was already tired; the basic gravitational force that makes the planet revolve around a central luminous star was pointless idiocy, and he, the President, was the legal guardian of the idiocy. The situation was growing more complex from minute to minute. He had to choose among many options, including the final one in which the missile, gray metal with the red star impressed on its nose, would begin its parabola, rising in the sultry blue air, furrowing the sky above the tepid, scented Caribbean sea, arcing over the fierce émigrés landing in Miami, swift, knowing, precise. It would travel along its trajectory, a noisy messianic object carrying the message of the approximation of zero.

The Russian carrier pigeon would carry its message: millions dead. The pierced city would buckle in a soundless instant, vibrating like a pudding, shaking in the thermonuclear silence, and then the conflagration would make the sky fall; men and women and children and dogs and gas pumps and supermarkets and the stadium would be reduced to human outlines stamped in black shadows on the walls. The thirst-ridden survivors would wander the ruins, drinking from cholera-infected, radioactive wells. The next day would arrive with a red, incandescent dawn. The President knew it. We the Americans have already done it. *We* vaporized the Japanese cities. *We* tested inoculations against carcinomas and plague on American soldiers on Bikini Atoll. *We* keep the world divided in two with the paternalistic threat of a final contamination.

We hold the species in our hands.

We will conquer the moon.

We are the final race, the horsemen of the Wasp apocalypse. We are the manna of uranium that will fall from the sky.

He called a meeting of the National Security Council, the guests at the last supper, brainstorming. His brother Bobby the Good was leaning against the wall, arms crossed, dark pouches under his eyes, his hair disheveled, with the face of an Irish and Latin angel. The faithful counselors of the king didn't know what to do. Would they take a soft line or a hard line? Enforce an embargo or force a military engagement? It was essential to talk to the Russians. It was impossible. They suspected that Khrushchev was the hostage of the Politburo, that the hawks of the Kremlin had revoked the peasant Khrushchev's powers. The world was about to end.

Secretary of State Dean Rusk massacred a pencil. Bobby the Good was silent and pensive. National Security Advisor McGeorge Bundy played the pragmatist. Robert McNamara was the tough guy who kept his cool. George Ball was an idiot. Roswell Gilpatrick adjusted his tie. Llewellyn Thompson talked and talked. Theodore Sorensen thought he was writing History.

JFK was weary. A bottle of Coca-Cola fell to the floor and broke. The President asked for another. They brought him one. He took a swallow of Coke directly from the woman-shaped bottle. The woman of glass contained the promise of a light, fizzy liquor with a sweet, zinc-like taste that goes to the head. Real women were not like that. Jackie was not like that. The glass woman who contained the Coke was the intensification of the female offering, perfection in packaged form. The President caressed the glass bottle as if it were a male appendage. He moved his delicate, feminine fingers over the pearled and sweating surface. He sniffed the glass.

The missiles would bring an end to the Presidency and the planet.

Suddenly the door of the Oval Office opened. Cablegram. Top secret. The Russians' demands. The counselors to the king twisted their fingers, one by one, sweated.

Russia was counterattacking, having been the first to attack.

Russia was saying, If you touch Cuba, we start again in Italy and Turkey.

President Kennedy stuck his practical, luminous forehead out over the table. That forehead would break like the branch of a beech tree in a year, and he didn't know it. His personal Cuba.

He stuck out his practical forehead and read the report on Italy and Turkey.

McNamara said, Italy and Turkey are at present the *axis mundi*. All geopolitics revolves around two axes: Italy and Turkey. McGeorge Bundy said, I know Turkey, I'll take care of it.

Sorensen said, Italy is giving us problems; we're losing it. There's a shithead in Italy, a guy who's got the idea of breaking our balls.

We're losing Italy.

This shithead is remaking the world politics of oil.

This shithead isn't keeping us informed about what he's doing.

He deals with the Russians.

He's a threat.

He deals with the Italian Fascists. He deals with the Communists. He's a false Catholic, Mr. President.

His name is Enrico Mattei. He's a peasant who rose to power.

The President felt the idiot gust of weariness. He said, Okay, Bundy's taking care of Turkey—who's going to take care of Italy?

No one answered.

Italy was the most pressing problem of the Cuban crisis. We defuse Italy and we're halfway there. We neutralize Italy. We take it away from the Russians. We negotiate on Turkey but if we lose Italy we lose Europe.

President John F. Kennedy sipped his Coke. He got up from his chair. He said, I have the man who will take care of Italy. He's young, ambitious, cynical, efficient. Let's trust him.

It was Henry Kissinger.

Henry Kissinger was exalted, excited, irritated. The President had included him, raised him from the dust to the stars.

The President had opened the door of Henry Kissinger's office, very nervous, a file folder in his hand. He had said, Henry, things are like this. With this missile crisis in Cuba, the Russians are threatening they'll take Turkey and Italy. The President had said, McGeorge Bundy will resolve the Turkey problem—you'll solve the Italian problem for me. Study the report. There's a big shit in Italy and his name is Enrico Mattei—study him. Get rid of him. Get him off my back. Neutralize Italy for me.

He had left, slamming the door.

Kissinger knew that during the televised presidential debate his friend Dick the Unlucky Nixon had put JFK on the spot only once, and it was on the subject of Cuba. Cuba was Kennedy's Achilles heel, his ruin.

Henry Kissinger smiled as he opened the Italy file. He read. He studied. He drew cautious conclusions. He formulated complex plans. He pored over the report on Enrico Mattei.

Enrico Mattei was practically the king of Italy. A hidden king. He had minimal public responsibilities, yet all the power in Italy revolved around him. He had fought in the Second World War as the head of an important partisan faction of anti-Fascists, scattered and poorly armed. The Allies had encouraged them, providing guns and logistics. The partisans had been the Trojan horse for entering Italy and crushing the Fascist dominion in the north. They had been an army without uniforms, guided by leaders who suppressed personal and ideological antipathies. Rebels, anarchists, Communists, Catholics, liberals—all the partisans had been crowded together, hidden in the mountains in the north, ready for disruptive operations, for disinformation, for the replacement of the Fascist regime by one controlled by the Allies. Enrico Mattei was one of the leaders of the Catholic partisans. He organized the resisters, distributed funds, made sure that the arms provided by the Allies reached their destinations.

The partisans, Kissinger said to himself. We fostered them, we made them grow, we trained them, and we put them in power. Now the Communist partisans hate us. The Catholic partisans love us. Except this Enrico Mattei.

At the end of the war, Enrico Mattei had taken over the management of the Italian state oil company, ENI. It was an absolute zero. Italy has no oil. Mattei had made agreements with the countries of the Third World, revolutionized the tariffs, and subverted the market. The Italian oil authority had become the center of Italian power—and threatened to become the center of European power. Serious. Risky. Why hadn't they got rid of him before?

Enrico Mattei was deciding who would be the Italian prime minister.

He founded newspapers; he caused public opinion to change.

He gave secret funds to the right and the left.

He controlled the center. He subjugated the Catholics. He molded Italian ideas. He was admired all over Europe. He was a de Gaulle more anti-American than de Gaulle.

Henry Kissinger thought, We are losing Europe.

The unknown superiors are wise; they see far ahead.

We're going to take back Europe.

We'll take back a continent of shitheads who are still quoting Dante and Goethe.

We'll hurl the European stone against the giant Russia.

We start with Enrico Mattei.

Getting rid of Enrico Mattei means saying to the Russians: On the issue of Cuba, we do what we want. Hey, Soviet Union, fuck you.

The unknown superiors had foreseen everything.

He, Henry Kissinger, was the chosen one, the superiors' singer. Following their directives, he had already put everyone and everything in place. He would make the Soviet Union collapse. He would fuck Europe—already he was kissing her.

Henry Kissinger knew whom to call.

The President was in a hurry. The Cuban missile crisis was threatening his Presidency. Kissinger would do this favor for him.

He thought, The plan of the unknown superiors is *perfect*. We begin now, immediately. We begin with Italy.

He made a phone call.

The harsh voice answered at the other end. "Yes?"

Kissinger opened the book he had been reading when the President had burst into his office. "It's Henry Kissinger."

"Yes?"

"I'm ready. The plan is perfect. We can begin immediately."

Silence. Hesitation. "Where do you intend to start?"

"In Italy."

"Italy? Are you thinking of the Pope? Italy is where the Pope is . . ."

"I'm thinking of someone who is close to the Pope."

"You decide, if you think it's opportune. There's one last thing . . ."

"What?"

"The name. Its name. You know that's important, Henry."

"I know. Names are everything."

"Names are everything, Henry. Have you chosen the name?"

Henry Kissinger looked at the book on the desk, *Moby Dick*, next to the report on Mattei's Italy, and he said, "Call it Ishmael."

Volterra
September 21, 1971
15:40

The marl gleamed like selenium between the furrows of turned earth. A shovel had been stuck in the soil, among the rows and rows of vines that swayed in the slow wind. The road to Volterra curved gently, climbing the hill and descending to the next mile-post.

The slippery asphalt squeaked under the cars' tires. The black car and the white car proceeded at the same speed, the latter a long distance behind the first. The black car flashed past a crumbling farmhouse, ocher in the afternoon light, and then sank into a new horizon.

In the white car, David Montorsi had to nearly close his eyes in order to see in the sunlight that was wearing out the afternoon. Reaching the crest of the hill, he watched the steady speed of the dark car.

The information had been very costly. He had had to pledge a significant part of the stipend deposited regularly under an anonymous name by the Services. The rumor had started in Ireland and moved to Frankfurt. One of the handful of Italian agents stationed in Berlin had contacted him directly. Montorsi had been told by telegram the news that, nine years after his departure, Dr. Giandomenico Arle was making a trip to Italy.

Montorsi had been waiting all that time. He hadn't managed to glean much about Arle from Ishmael's network. He knew that Arle worked in a genetics laboratory in Rosslyn, that he traveled frequently, often in the United States, and often under a false name. As time passed, the hatred hardened. Now he was eating up road and air in the puddles of light in the valleys of Chianti, rising and then descending toward dark damp foliage and furrows, pockets of deep cold, before climbing again into the sun and ripening vines.

The information had been precise and was worth its price. Arle had been gone since the night Montorsi had had to bend over the body of Maura. He went back to exploring his reliquary. A storm of images arose. Maura was everywhere. He passed his hand over his eyes. He was tired. He felt the familiar annoying knot in his throat. At first he had thought it was a varix. A painful gastroscopy had found nothing. It was the pulsing thought of Maura that clutched him. A "psychosomatic symptom," he was told; they had prescribed tranquilizers that, as usual, had not had any effect.

He saw the black car turn toward Poggibonsi. He accelerated.

Montorsi had seen Arle the night before, fleetingly, leaving his hotel with an escort of three men, English bodyguards provided by Ishmael. He had paid to check the bodyguards' passports, which were false. He had paid, not too much, to find out their room numbers. It had cost him much more to learn Arle's itinerary. Today Arle would go to Volterra. First he would visit the Etruscan museum. Then he would go to the *balze*, the underground tombs. Montorsi would kill him in the Etruscan museum.

Ishmael was growing from moment to moment. There were eight continental churches now. More than three thousand adherents provided Ishmael with information. It was impossible to calculate the number of intelligence agents who supported Ishmael. After Italy came France. Ishmael's most recent attempt to take root had been in Germany, especially in Berlin. According to Ishmael's prophecies, a little before the fulfillment of his time this false, silent, cold war whose center was Berlin would end. The United States and the Soviet Union would cast off their own skins. That was the leap of history toward the reign of Ishmael.

Montorsi had come to understand Dr. Arle's shadowy words during their conversation at the institute, a few hours before the threat took shape. *Little Maura, innocent, and I, alone forever* . . . The devouring and simple force of guilt was only an external sheath of the pain that consumed him. Guilt and harsh absence.

He accelerated toward Colle Val d'Elsa.

The dark car was no longer in sight. He knew that Arle was going to Volterra. Montorsi had to get to the Etruscan museum before Arle arrived.

The land sloped downward, a spill of blood. Big gourd shapes, enormous convex vegetables of earth and clay, collided one against the other, like the necks of Titans buried for millennia. The chalk earth struggled to breathe. The hills became long, one valley folded into the next, and the clay kept spilling in gentle slopes that masked the corrugated foolishness of the earth. He saw bones, or maybe they were not bones. No farmhouse broke the lines of that curved geometry, that mineral tongue, between sky and ground. Heavy blue clouds descended steplike toward the line of the concave horizon.

Before a wide curve near Castel San Gimignano, he passed the black car driven by Arle's bodyguard. He saw the professor, a thin white mummy in the dark light between window and window, straight and silent. After the curve he stepped on the gas and saw the black car disappearing in the rearview mirror, a stain on the horizon.

Near Volterra he began to ascend. He detoured onto a dirt road and circled the broad hill. As he drove, he raised a honeylike ocher dust. He returned to the asphalt. It was the main road, the one from the south.

He stopped the car a few meters from the city's ancient Etruscan gate. He got out. He stepped through the arch, its immense blocks of dry reddish stone laid two and a half millennia earlier, from which protruded three enormous stumps that had been heads, statues in the form of heads, the two on the sides of the arch inclined as if in a gesture of reluctant modesty, the one at the summit central, like an idea, and he inhaled the dense humid air inside the portal, the permanent, millennial odor of the remains of the bodies that had grazed those walls in long-forgotten times. He sensed the fall of footsteps, phosphorescent, on the platform of bare stone. Then he reached Volterra's citadel.

He knew where to go. He had studied the maps at night. He slept very little now. He was afraid—it was an infantile fear—of that specter which embraced him in dreams.

Oh Maura.

He reached the entrance to the Etruscan museum and went into the galleries. He remained in the shadows, between two walls studded with huge cinerary urns and their sketched outlines of journeys in the world of the dead. The urns held the ashes of the dead. The bodies of the urns were slightly curved parallelepipeds, the corners eaten away by the damp of two millennia. He saw the sacred representations engraved on the sides of the urns: Great journeys to the realm of the dead, in chariots, on foot, the pitiful consort silently preceding the dead wife to the inhuman edge of that desolate kingdom, and a judge approaching, dead, drawn by four disproportionately enormous horses toward the river of the silent. A horseman of alabaster with bandaged mouth. A gnome. A Titan.

Arle entered.

The three bodyguards preceded him. They looked around. Arle was looking at the sinopias. He knitted his brow, bent his arms, leaned one hand on his chin. He had aged. He was thinner. He had the thin neck of a human turtle. He stood staring at the sacred scenes. The Etruscan funeral rites. Montorsi suddenly guessed that they were the rites of Ishmael. The Symbols of Ishmael. The cold breath that led to a flat white artificial death was Ishmael himself. Maura had been transformed into a Symbol of Ishmael, she seemed to be marble, to be lying on the cover of an alabaster urn.

Arle decided to go upstairs. Montorsi went ahead of him.

Again the bodyguards preceded Arle, climbing up the marble steps. He examined labels and Latin inscriptions, made an indifferent turn around the statue of the Founder, an eighteenth-century Monsignor who had accumulated the materials of the museum.

Among the cases Montorsi saw the refracted face of Dr. Arle break down into an elastic shape.

He entered the Room of the Utensils. There were hundreds of tools used by the artisans of alabaster, arranged together with imperfect regularity and packed into a large dark case of glass and wood, like teeth of an aggressive fish dug out after a death struggle, curved and straight, hooks and needles, decayed or healthy, brought to a black and perfect shine. He looked into an eighteenth-century display case of anatomical pathology equipment, the instruments like the fossils of reptiles inside the flaming glow of worn wood, behind the perfectly transparent delicate glass.

Arle approached the case. He gazed at the utensils. He stood there, in contemplation.

David Montorsi sensed the last place Arle would go.

The final point.

* * *

He shouldered past the bodyguards, excusing himself. They watched him go down the stairs. On the ground floor he turned to the left. He opened the glass door that led to the garden.

Among the oaks and tamarisks and pines he saw tombs. Saxifrage grew from a dark façade hidden in a seam between arches of white metal, near smooth oozing basalts, at the base of a dry well.

He positioned himself against the railing near the wooded ravine outside the museum, observing without feeling the blue evening smoke that rose from the chalky fields outside Volterra, beyond the ancient city walls. He took out the pack of *papier mais*. He lighted one. He inhaled.

He was ready.

The door opened, but it wasn't Arle. It was a group of four English tourists. They reached the green wooden benches in the middle of the garden on the opposite side. They paid no attention to Montorsi.

Then came two of Arle's bodyguards. They looked around. They walked through the garden toward Montorsi. They settled beside him. One lighted a cigarette. Montorsi finished his cigarette and lighted another. He offered the pack to the two men. They declined without smiling. For them he was only a big man in a white suit. They got up and walked away. They stopped a little behind the four elderly English tourists. One of the two men exchanged a bare few words with them. They went back to the door. They nodded: Arle could come out.

Arle walked slowly, wearily. Montorsi was still, leaning out over the railing. He watched the blue spirals of smoke from the cigarette disappear in the air. He inhaled the smoke, felt it pierce his nostrils. He wasn't thinking of anything. He couldn't think of anything.

He had waited nine years. He was getting close to Ishmael. He was going to get him. He was going to get Ishmael.

Arle advanced with short, slow steps. The three guards were talking among themselves on the steps outside the glass door. Arle looked at the stone votive pine cones, the rapid contraction of the crocuses, the unlikely pulses of the four o'clocks, which opened with light vegetal tears. He seemed almost delighted. Far from any thought. And yet he still seemed concentrated on an inner point that could not be seen.

Montorsi was ready.

Nine years had gone by. The luminous figure of Maura would never abandon him. He remembered the broken teeth.

He turned slowly, keeping his head bent.

Arle was a few meters away.

The bodyguards were speaking in low voices. One glanced at Arle's bent back. He saw the big man in white straighten up from the railing. He wasn't in time to spread his arms. He wasn't in time to shout.

Montorsi drew his gun. He felt the transient weight, near the end of the barrel, of the silencer that he had screwed on the night before. Arle recognized him. The stupefied bewilderment that precedes mourning. It was an instant. Montorsi saw the bodyguard swerving his body, trying to shout, spreading his arms.

He shot three times. Three shots up close, powerful. He had chosen bullets that exploded on contact with the soft material of flesh. The explosions ripped Arle from inside. He had aimed at the stomach. He would die suffering. He had given him no way out.

Turning around, he jumped, over the railing. He had studied the maps, the plans. Two of the bodyguards were on Arle's body. A third leaned over the railing. He began shooting randomly. Six shots, random, into the thick foliage of the ravine.

David Montorsi was already running along the main street. He turned into two adjacent streets, two damp alleys. He saw laundry hanging from the height of the cornices. He reached the road that went south, near the gate opposite the one where Arle had come in and where his men had parked the car.

He started the engine. He turned on the headlights. A blue fog was rising from the warm chalk landscape. The light was falling, noticeably, from minute to minute. He looked in the rearview mirror. He saw the features of the three cut-off heads on the arch of the Etruscan gate vanishing in the blue twilight, and he sped off, in the advancing darkness.

The next day he sat for hours beneath a gnarled tree without leaves, in a dry field of red earth, bent, dressed in white.

Milan
April 9, 2001
18:20

He and Laura made love for a long time. She scratched him till he bled, and he liked it; it seemed to bring him back to life. Maybe Laura was right. In the way they made love a dark truth was concealed. A black hole that silently drew him.

He kissed the faded traces of the wounds on her arms, on her side. He licked all the wounds.

Get up. Go. Lick one another.

They stayed in bed.

She fell asleep.

He thought about Montorsi.

The death of the Engineer had been reported the previous day. The body had been found in the hamlet of Rescaldina. An anonymous phone call had alerted the police. It was the same place where they had found the body of Montorsi's wife in 1962.

At Cernobbio there had been no problem, except for Santovito. Calimani had called Lopez at home to tell him that Santovito had missed the road to Rome. He had not got the promotion and was staying with the Detective Squad in Milan. Santovito would return from Cernobbio in a fury.

No trace of Bob. No trace of Ishmael. Over and over again he repeated to himself Montorsi's words, "Ishmael does not exist. He doesn't exist."

He saw in the bathroom at ISPES the extended arm and the head of the American bursting. Lopez thought: What was he doing? Where was he going? He watched Laura sleep, her mouth half-open, so sweetly.

He thought of Montorsi's wife. He thought of Montorsi.

He had got in touch with Wunzam. They understood each other, without saying anything explicit; Wunzam had said he had resigned, and Lopez had not commented. He already knew Wunzam's next employer: the European Agency.

Outside, in the courtyard, a crazy person was shouting. It was raining to make you sick. Milan was sickening.

Again Montorsi's words: America *against* Europe. What the hell was Europe?

He thought of the name of Ishmael.

He saw again the bruised face of the child at Giuriati, its half-open mouth. He was shaken, spellbound by Laura's half-open mouth.

He lifted her forearm. He saw the scratches, the wounds. He put his lips against a deep scratch. The metal taste of blood made other images flow. The bursts of blood on the pale tiles in the bathroom; the shattered head of the American. The bruises on the body of the man in Via Padova. The Frenchman, riddled with bullet holes.

He counted the dead: Clemenceau, Terzani, Rebecka, Karl M., the American. The child. And before? The American's dead. Kissinger's dead. Montorsi's dead.

He got up, drank from the faucet, looked in his wallet, and took out the card. He telephoned Montorsi.

He left two days later. Montorsi would take care of his departure from the force. He had told Laura only that he was leaving. She had said that theirs was not even a story. He endured a heavy silence. She left.

He did not go to Headquarters. He did not say goodbye to Santovito, Calimani, and the others.

He was about to go into the airport when he saw rising from the runway a huge white airplane, like a continent without a name.

CHRONOLOGY

European Security Agency
Section: A/15
Security: maximum

Chronology of operations of the Ishmael Network
Assassinations related to the finding of sacrificed children

October 27, 1962—Airplane of Enrico Mattei crashes in Bascapé, near Pavia.
October 27, 1962—Body of a year-old child found at the Giuriati playing field.

November 13, 1962—Jean Rochefort, vice-president of the Bank of France, murdered while vacationing in Lesouche, near Champoluc.
November 12, 1962—Body of a child of around two found in the woods just outside Courmayeur, on a tip an anonymous telephone call.

January 2, 1963—Failed assassination attempt on Konrad Adenauer, German Chancellor, in Gottingen [CENSORED].
January 1, 1963—Body of a child of around two found in a carton on Grönerstrasse, in Gottingen, on a tip from anonymous telephone call.

May 13, 1965—Failed attempt on the presidential automobile of Charles de Gaulle, in the area of Nantes [CENSORED].
May 13, 1965—Body of a child found in the woods on the right bank of the Erdre, outside Nantes, on a tip from an anonymous telephone call.

December 20, 1973—Prime Minister Luis Carrero Blanco murdered in Madrid.
December 20, 1973—Body of a child of about four found in a bag across from the Monastery of the Incarnation, in Madrid, on a tip from an anonymous phone call.

April 7, 1977—Attorney General Siegfried Buback, of the GDR, murdered in Karlsruhe.
April 8, 1977—Body of a five- or six-year-old child found in a container in the Karlsruhe Zoo, on a tip from an anonymous phone call.

May 9, 1978—Body of the Christian Democratic leader Aldo Moro, kidnapped by terrorists of the Red Brigades for 55 days, found in Rome.
April 18, 1978—Body of a child of around four found on the banks of the Lake of Duchessa, in Cartore di Rieti, during the search for the body of Aldo Moro, on instructions from a communiqué from the kidnappers [CENSORED].

September 28/29, 1978—Murder of His Holiness Pope John Paul I in his apartments.
September 27, 1978—Body of a year-old child found in a container placed in a deserted area of the Cassia Nuova, in Rome, on a tip from an anonymous phone call.

May 13, 1981—Failed assassination attempt on His Holiness Pope John Paul II, in St. Peter's Square.
May 10, 1981—Body of a two-year-old child found in a box behind the church of St. Thomas Aquinas in Rome, on a tip from an anonymous phone call [CENSORED].

June 18, 1982—Murder of the banker Roberto Calvi in London, under the Blackfriars Bridge.
June 17, 1982—Body of a year-old child found in a box at No. 15 Austin Friars Street, in London, on a tip from an anonymous telephone call [SUPPRESSED].

February 28, 1986—Murder of the Swedish Prime Minister Olof Palme in Stockholm.
February 28, 1986—Body of a five-year-old child found on the edge of the bay in Djurgarden, in Stockholm, on a tip from an anonymous telephone call.

November 30, 1989—Alfred Herrhausen, chairman of the Deutsche Bank, is the victim of an assassination attempt in Bad Homborg, near Frankfurt.
November 30, 1989—Body of a four-year-old child found near Kurpark, in Bad Homburg, on a tip from an anonymous telephone call.

May 21, 1991—Ioan P. Couliano, expert in esotericism and sects, murdered in a bathroom at the University of Chicago.
May 20, 1991—Body of a year-old child found among garbage bags in an alley behind the Drake Hotel in Chicago, on a tip from an anonymous telephone call.

July 20, 1993—Gabriele Cagliari, government official and head of ENI, close to Bettino Craxi, who had been detained in the San Vittore prison in Milan, murdered.
July 20, 1993—Body of a three-year-old child found in Via Foppa, in Milan, in a container across the street from the residence of the Hon. Craxi, on a tip from an anonymous telephone call.

May 1, 1993—Pierre Bérégovoy, minister in the Mitterrand government, murdered on the Loire.
May 2, 1993—Body of a year-old child found in a bag hidden in the bushes across from the Élysée Palace, on a tip from an anonymous telephone call [CENSORED].

August 31, 1997—Fatal accident in Paris causing the death of Princess Diana and Dodi Al Fayed, son of Mohammed Al Fayed.
July 2, 1997—Body of a six-year-old child found in a bag outside the fences around the runways at Heathrow Airport, in London, on a tip from an anonymous telephone call.

May 4, 1998—Murder-suicide by a Papal Guard, Cédric Tornay, in Vatican City. The victims are Alois Estermann (named nine hours earlier as head of the Papal Guard) and his wife.
May 3, 1998—Body of a year-old child found in the countryside near Castel Gandolfo, on a tip from an anonymous phone call [CENSORED].

December 14, 1999—Failed assassination attempt on George Soros in the neighborhood of the University of Utrecht [CENSORED].
December 15, 1999—Body of a year-old child found in a suitcase in the lobby of the Hotel Mitland.

March 13, 2001—Failed assassination attempt on Henry Kissinger in Paris [CENSORED].

March 23, 2001—Body of a six-year-old child found near the entrance to the catacombs at the Luxembourg Gardens, in Paris, on a tip from an anonymous telephone call.[CENSORED]

March 27, 2001—Failed attempt on Henry Kissinger in Milan [CENSORED].
March 27, 2001—Body of a six-year-old child found at the Giuriati playing field in Milan, on a tip from an anonymous telephone call [CENSORED].